NTH

This book should be returned to any branch of the

SKELMERSDALE

FICTION RESERVE STOCK LL60

HIDE
AND
SEEK

Eric Clark

Weidenfeld & Nicolson
London

First published in Great Britain in 1994 by
Weidenfeld & Nicolson

The Orion Publishing Group Ltd
Orion House,
5 Upper Saint Martin's Lane,
London, WC2H 9EA

A catalogue reference is available from the British Library

ISBN 0 297 81465 6

Typeset by Deltatype Ltd, Ellesmere Port, Cheshire
Printed in Great Britain by Clays Ltd, St Ives plc

For May and Bill Edwards
With Love

ACKNOWLEDGEMENTS

I owe thanks to many people. In particular I am grateful to: Susyn Andrews, Royal Botantic Gardens, Kew; Tony Bambridge, the *Sunday Times*; Maggie Barnes; Geoff Beldon; Professor David Canter, Department of Psychology, University of Surrey; Charli Clark; Rachael Clark; Martin Compart; Major Alun Davies; Dr Richard Emmerson; Bob Freeman, Foster and Freeman; Dr Steve Gull, Department of Physics, Cavendish Laboratory, University of Cambridge; Ian Hamilton, International Casino Club; Harold Harris; Raymond Hawkey; Brian Hilliard, editor, *Police Review*; Dr W. J. Hossack, Department of Physics, University of Edinburgh; Peter Jones; Michael Kerekes; John Legge, Whitehall Security Services; Dr Alf Linney, Department of Medical Physics and Bio-Engineering, University College, London; Ian McConachie, Thomas Locksmiths; Christian Mititelu; John F. Nasmyth-Miller; Richard Neave, School of Biological Sciences, University of Manchester; P.N.; Frank R. Pegg, Volumatic; Arthur Phillips; James Roads; John Rodway; Ward Rutherford; Gordon Stephenson; Ray Tibbles, Victoria Sporting Club; Tom Walker; Andrew Young, Rapid Results College; Martha-Ellen Zenfell – and, as always, Marcelle.

'Among the dead there are those
who still have to be killed'

Fernand Desnoyers

PROLOGUE

There was a view he would miss. On the day he was to disappear he drove there – a hundred and five miles through empty blackness on a 2 a.m. impulse.

There were a few other vehicles on the first short stretch of new motorway out of London, but then, after the airport turnoff, nothing. There was just him and the steady, hypnotic drizzle of rain. Periodically he switched off the windscreen wipers to allow the water to accumulate. After a while, he began to lengthen the gaps, until he was driving totally blind for seconds at a time. Although the car was travelling at ninety m.p.h., he was just playing at danger. The road was too straight, too quiet, too evenly surfaced for there to be any real threat, but it suited his mood.

After a while the game palled, and he concentrated on driving to the car's limit. Less than a quarter of the journey was fast road. What was to be the London–South Wales M4 motorway was still only a twenty-four-and-a-half-mile stretch to Maidenhead. The last ten miles of his drive were through winding, narrow country lanes. Nevertheless, he covered the miles in as many minutes. He knew where to pull off the road; he had done it the first time he and Pamela had crested the hill two and a half years before. Held by the beauty of the scene, they had stopped to look down on the ribbon of blossom-heavy lane as it curved over the hillside. In the distance they had taken in the hamlet and they had even – once their eyes had become accustomed – made out the exact house in which they would settle to be happy ever after.

The rain had stopped, but the grassland on to which Kenyon eased the car was soft mud underfoot. The moon was obscured, there were few stars. He stood outside, breathing deeply, savouring the difference between this and the London he had left less than two hours before. Waiting for dawn, still a half-hour

1

away, he felt calm yet strangely keyed – the way he had felt as a small boy in the moments of empty time before the cinema lights dimmed and the movie began.

He reached inside the car for the bottle and the metal travelling cup. The bottle was new, the cap unbroken. He couldn't remember finishing the previous one, and for a few seconds that worried him. He poured out about two inches and drank it in one swallow. It carried him back to the right plane. Next, he filled the cup to near its brim, and began to sip as, at last, the sky started to lighten.

Although he was not drunk – these days it seemed no amount of alcohol could more than blunt the edges of his mind – the liquor brought an odd, detached feeling, as first the far side of the valley and then the hamlet were revealed. The house was last to come into view as the darkness peeled itself away like an uncoiling layer of grey celluloid. Even then it was hard to make out much of the building because of the trees and high hedges that surrounded it. The house stood alone, one hundred and fifty yards from the edge of the hamlet; solid, red farmhouse brick, looking precisely what it was meant to be – timeless, a haven against the world and the elements. 'A real *family* home,' the agent who had sold it to them had said.

Kenyon drank slowly and steadily, drip-feeding his mood. Instinctively, with the nervous movement that he no longer even noticed, he touched the side of his head. His fingertips were gentle though the bullet wound had long since healed.

Dawn light reflected on a strip of red metal and he made out a car, a Jaguar, he thought, but he was too far away to be certain. Not her car. A visitor's. An overnight visitor's. But that was not new, and the time and the drink and what was about to happen in his life made that seem less important than the fact that now he had seen the view again and had imprinted it on his memory like a photograph.

Satisfied, he climbed back into the car, finishing the whisky as he restarted the engine to return to London. Back in town, the others would only just be leaving the gaming club. It was 4.45 a.m. on Monday, 31 May 1966.

He stopped at the airport, tucked away the car in a corner of the long-term car park and removed a hand grip from the boot. In an

2

airport washroom, he carried out the small changes that made him look so different – it took surprisingly little time. Spectacles fitted with fake lenses. Shoes with one heel built higher than the other that would change the way he walked. A black, raglan-style raincoat over a slightly too-tight chainstore suit. Hair re-combed with the aid of a fixative so that it was swept back and without his normal parting.

An airport bus, taxis and two underground trains took him to Euston station via two diversions: the first to a deserted stretch of the Thames, where he dumped the weighted grip packed with his old clothes; the second to make a stomach-churning pick-up from a safety-deposit box. He bought a round ticket to Birmingham. A poster urged him to join 'a new age' – Barclaycard, the country's first bank credit card, was about to be launched.

He tried to read on the train. A columnist was decrying the country's 'decadence' – drugs, pop and long-haired boys 'that you can't tell from girls'. He likened it to the last days of the Roman Empire. A backlash from the previous month's *Time* magazine article that had labelled London 'the swinging city', the place of the decade. The latest article did not prevent the newspaper running a page of photographs of the newly fashionable miniskirt. Elsewhere, a doctor defended the one-thousand-pound rise to GPs, taking their salaries to four thousand pounds a year. The Moors Murders still filled several columns even though it was now three weeks since Ian Brady and Myra Hindley had been jailed for life.

The train was three minutes early arriving, and Kenyon made the Dublin flight with almost an hour to spare.

The stewardess thought it a pity that such a handsome man should have such a pronounced facial blemish. Kenyon had added it just before leaving the train – the final touch. Careful use of an artist's brush and a tiny jar of non-flexible collodion – a clear liquid plastic which contracted as it dried, thus puckering the skin – had produced a realistic scar that ran jaggedly for two inches from the corner of his mouth.

Because of the nature of Kenyon's life, it was another ten hours before anyone began to wonder where he was, a further day before anyone tried to reach him, twenty-four hours more before the realisation that he was missing.

By then he had changed his name and moved on twice more.

Exactly as he had been planning for five months, Michael Kenyon had vanished from the face of the earth.

PART ONE

HIDE. THEN.

CHAPTER ONE

It took less than a half of one second to change Michael Kenyon's life for ever.

The time it takes to clap hands. Or for an insect to flicker its wings. Or for a bullet .63 inches long and .359 inches across to leave a twenty-four-year-old World War II British Army-issue Smith and Wesson .38 at 745 feet per second, ricochet off a fake marble pillar and come to rest inside him.

He did not lose consciousness immediately. Looking back, he knew there should have been no time to absorb images, let alone to separate sensations. Yet feeling, sound and smell divided as clearly as sequences in a movie replayed in single frames. First, the pain, tearing and buring. And *then* the sound. And, finally – and quite divorced – the acrid but sickly smell of gun powder.

Others around him were blurs and shadows. There must have been struggling and screaming. But all he could hear was his own voice, shrill, angry, surprised, rising over everything: 'You shot me. You cunt, you shot me.'

Then, still distanced from what was happening, he felt the cold and the fear and the trembling, and the edges of his vision darkened and began to contract until there was no more.

They carried him out of the club, drove him across London, stretched over the back seat of a car, his head cradled by George, Barton's bodyguard. It was a little after 4.30 a.m., that quiet time when the last late-nighters have gone home and the early starters have yet to venture out. The streets were deserted; in any event, from outside Kenyon looked like a sleeping drunk.

The three other men in the car had all seen gunshot wounds before, though not here in swinging sixties London. A glance had shown them that there was no exit wound: the bullet was still in

Kenyon's head. Each one of them would have dumped him. That they did not was one of three miracles that night.

The first was that the bullet, already losing momentum when it entered the side of Kenyon's head, missed his brain by a fraction of an inch.

The second was that Barton, forced to make a split-second decision, decided that getting rid of a dead Englishman with Kenyon's background was something to try to avoid at this, sensitive, time.

And the third was that Poulton was home and sober when Barton telephoned him.

It was Poulton who operated. Alone and under duress in the clinic near Harley Street where he normally carried out expensive (and sometimes secret) plastic surgery.

He took his own X-ray. The bullet, a tiny comma of light on the plate, showed just above Kenyon's right ear.

'I can't remove it,' he said. 'He needs a proper hospital.'

But no one said anything. They knew he would do as he had been told.

And afterwards, when he said, 'I've done all I can,' only George spoke, and that was to say, 'Now let's get him out of here.'

They moved him to a nursing home somewhere in the Home Counties. It had started life in the 1930s as the residence of the chairman of one of the country's major companies. During the war it had been taken over by the military for some, still secret, intelligence function and, after they left, became a boarding school. Now, as somewhere for the sick rich (and sometimes famous or notorious) to dry out, be weaned off drugs, or hidden from public gaze by their families or management companies, it could not have been bettered: its natural isolation, three miles from the nearest public road, had been reinforced by the high, broken-glass- studded perimeter wall left by the military.

Kenyon remained there for two weeks, confined at first to one room on the first floor. He saw cars come and go, and knew from curtains that opened and closed and from steps that echoed in the distance that the rest of the house was occupied, but the only people he saw were a middle-aged nurse and Poulton.

Poulton showed him the bullet. No more than a flattened, distorted piece of lead the size of a very small coin. Its edges were ragged. Until the day he vanished eight months after the shooting, Kenyon carried it with him, and at bad times would go to sleep with it clenched tight in his fist.

'You're healing well,' said Poulton in the middle of the second week. Early resentment had been replaced by something nearer to a bedside *bonhomie* – helped, Kenyon had no doubt, by the relief that he was not involved in hiding a murder. 'You've been lucky – the luck of the drunk,' he said without rancour, and from his tone Kenyon suddenly knew that the doctor had been there himself.

'I'd had a few,' he admitted, probing for information because, although he had tried, he could remember nothing of the minutes before the bullet had hit him.

'A few! I'm surprised you were still standing!'

Kenyon started to speak, but Poulton raised a hand. 'Don't tell me *anything*, I don't want to know *anything*. I already know too much.'

Kenyon watched from the window as Poulton climbed into his white Bentley. He wondered what hold Barton had over the man, that he would rush to his consulting rooms at four in the morning, carry out emergency surgery on a stranger who could have been involved in anything from a bank raid to a gangland massacre. Money? (Kenyon remembered Barton saying soon after he had first gone to work for him at the gaming club, 'So, say a hundred thousand won't buy somebody. What about two hundred thousand, five hundred? You just keep goin', that's all.' He had said it conversationally, a statement of a fact of life that he had tested and proved a hundred times.) Or was it fear? Blackmail? A favour returned?

It was that day Kenyon came across the woman. There was a small lake, hidden within a circle of trees, about a half-mile from the house. It had an ageless, fairy-tale quality. The woman was in a clearing on the far side of the water. She wore a long, loose, multi-coloured, peasant-style cotton dress, and her black hair was long and untied. She sat on the ground, her back against a tree, a basket containing wild flowers beside her. Her eyes were closed. She opened them when she heard Kenyon and smiled briefly but did not speak. He passed by her without saying anything, tongue-tied. She was a stranger; he knew nothing of her; he never saw her again. But she triggered primitive emotions. That night he

9

dreamed of her, and when he woke his crutch was wet and sticky and there was a smell of wet flour. A wet dream – God, how old was he when he'd last had one of those!

It proved to be a terrible harbinger. It heralded the opening of suppressed floodgates of emotion. The nightmares began the next night; he woke screaming and shivering, whimpering for help. They gave him sedatives. Those helped in the night, but in the day the slightest noises brought sweats and a pounding heart. Away from the house, he screamed and kicked at tree-trunks.

It was not the shooting alone, but the months that had preceded it.

Almost from his arrival at the nursing home, papers for signature had been sent from the club. Now Barton's bodyguard, George, began delivering them personally, waiting while Kenyon made the pretence of reading them (for that was all it was – putting his signature on pieces of paper was part of his role as a front man for the real owners of the club).

Kenyon knew that George's visits were significant. Normally, the man rarely left Barton's side. He even occupied adjoining rooms in the block of service apartments in which Barton lived.

George spoke little, and then it always took Kenyon several sentences to tune in. He broke sentences into senseless blocks of words: 'Guess he tried to . . . pulla out the side . . . street fasta . . .' He looked like a light heavyweight who had constantly been matched outside his class. But he carried with him the aura of being untouched by normal human fear, and you knew instinctively that there was no limit to the punishment he would endure or give without any emotion.

One drink could make him seem drunk, slurring his words, making what he said almost impossible to understand. Kenyon had only seen him take a drink twice, on both occasions Barton had been away – back in Philadelphia with men who knew *his* price and paid it. On one occasion, after hours, one of the half-dozen Americans around the club had made a bell sound behind George's back. It had taken ten minutes to bring George back down, but by then four of the men present, including Kenyon, were bleeding or hurt in some way. The rest were laughing, and Kenyon realised it was a joke that had been played many times before. George himself had two more drinks, passed out, and seemed to remember nothing at all the following day.

George's role, on his visits to Kenyon, was obvious: to provide a mute audience to whom Kenyon could unload himself. Probably Poulton's idea, though Barton was doubtless concerned about how Kenyon would behave once back in circulation – a thought that produced fear and a reminder of the need for constant caution. Kenyon had no doubt that Barton would make his disappearance permanent if he feared the shooting had turned him into a danger. Kenyon's wife and the porter of his apartment block had both been told he was away abroad 'on business'. They could always receive a further message saying that his remains had been found in a burned-out car or that he had been swept out to sea. For Pamela, life would hardly change – their marriage was all but dead; they had separate homes; they rarely met. She would sell the flat, collect the insurance. Certainly no one would make waves.

So although he talked (and in truth he welcomed and needed it) he was careful to say nothing that would alarm Barton when it was repeated (or replayed if George was wired). And at the same time he tried to learn how he came to be shot. Crazy really – he could have asked, blaming the shooting for his memory loss. But he knew it was an alcohol black-out, and he remained quiet.

He pieced it together slowly, sometimes taking wrong alleyways and having to return to pick up another path. It was only confirmed when George was replaced one day by the man they all called 'the Count'.

Raoul Hunter, real name Albert Leoni, had been given the nickname by a reporter in the late thirties. It was inspired by the way he appeared offstage – urbane, cultured, impeccably dressed – in contrast to the villains he played on screen. He portrayed them well because he was a gangster *manqué*. Many of his boyhood friends in America had become genuine criminals and, cocooned from their dangers, he envied them. Having neither the patience, the caution, the unthinking callousness, nor the particular limited but nevertheless real gut intelligence of the true, successful hood, he contented himself with playing them in the movies. Real gangsters, in turn, admired and envied him because his portrayals mirrored the way they saw themselves: not mean or grubby, but noble and grand in their villainy. The men Hunter played did what they did because lesser, more hypocritical men had given them no other real option if they were to remain truly *men*.

11

A thousand criminals, from Mafia dons to numbers runners, felt the tears rise as they watched his movies, for they too had faced such choices and they too had taken the strong way. As years passed, it developed beyond that: real gangsters found they liked to have Hunter near. And, not being fools, they saw too that his presence attracted those they wished to use or exploit. Hunter, in turn, found it more lucrative and less hard work than acting. The gangster *manqué* thus became honorary gangster himself.

Kenyon both liked and, in a perverse way, admired him. Until he was drawn into the club, he had seen the Count only on screen and as a much younger man – shouting defiantly as he went down under a hail of bullets, or walking away from the heroine to violin music because, rat though he was, he wasn't going to ruin her life too.

Hunter was around sixty by this time and he walked so erectly that Kenyon suspected he wore a corset under his double-breasted charcoal pin-striped suit. There was always a button-hole, and in the street he wore grey gloves, tight as a surgeon's, and a grey trilby hat. His voice, though harshened by chain-smoking (Camels placed incongruously in a holder), was soft and inclined to mimicry. His manners, embracing even the smallest gestures, were the most impeccable Kenyon had ever encountered. His greatest asset was his ability to focus totally on one individual, convincing him or her they were the only person he wished to be with in the whole room. But more, he could then move on effortlessly to the next person or group at precisely the right moment, leaving behind a feeling of completeness and pleasure.

Watching him operate at the club, greeting high-rollers who had been flown over to gamble from New York or Boston or Baltimore or a dozen other places, Kenyon had never failed to be impressed: the gentle touch on the shoulder, the continued clasp at the end of a handshake, the carefully tailored stories ranging all the way from racist belly-laugh raisers to gentle ribbing. Hunter made people feel *special*. Depending on how much the club wanted to keep people as customers, Hunter smiled and halloed them, told them a story over drinks, or hosted them meals. If they were big winners, he kept them at the tables – ensuring that they helped bring to pass the first law of gaming: that, in the end, the house must always get its money back and more. And, if they were big

12

losers, he suffered their childish whines, encouraged them to refocus their anger so that it lay on anything but the club itself ('You're right, Joe, a guy like that shouldn't be allowed at the same table – I'm gonna tell them at the door, "From now on, no admission for Mr Big Mouth." OK?'), and saw that they (and their guests) got the best of everything – girls, the Rolls to drive them home, a day at the races, whatever it took to make them happy to come back for more.

He and Kenyon had been easy with each other from their very first meeting. Once, playing amateur psychologist, Kenyon had decided it was because – for all their central roles in the club – neither were complete insiders. Whatever the reason, Hunter was the only one he felt close to – or as close as you could feel in the club setting.

'You know,' Hunter had once confided to Kenyon, 'there're just two kinds of people in this world. Those who make you feel like shit, and those who make you feel Liz Taylor just asked you to fuck her. I'm that second kind even when I'm feeling like shit myself.'

Today he had brought a bottle of Wild Turkey, and he broke the seal and poured two glasses to the rim. 'To you, fella,' he said, and drained one. Kenyon had seen him play the same scene in a Western. It gave him a weird feeling of unreality. He contemplated his drink – the first offered since the shooting – and then followed Hunter's example.

'I gotta say this first,' said Hunter, refilling the glasses. 'You saved my life, and there's nothing a man can say except, I owe you and I'm not gonna forget it.'

They walked in the grounds, and the whole story came together.

It had happened at the end of a busy three days; that Kenyon remembered. There had been a junket out of Newark, New Jersey – seventy-three people ranging from store-owners to obstetricians, their only link that they were all big gamblers. The American end had brought them together, advised how much each was good for after the cash they brought ran out (if someone didn't pay when he got back home that was their end too). Barton arranged the London end: the accommodation, the entertainment, the chauffeured cars (you didn't want anyone getting lost or being diverted to other clubs on the way from the hotel) and, of course, the action itself.

It had been a good junket. Some had gambled for eighteen hours a day. A few had gone back good winners (good, because it showed the action was honest and it was useful publicity – gamblers talked about wins, not losses). But, overall, the club had raked in the kind of cash it takes four men half a night to stack and count.

The return charter jet left at 5 a.m. from a minor airport sixty miles from London. Some of the junketers had played right up until 3 a.m. when two luxury buses (drinks and food on board) had collected them for the airport.

At 4 a.m. only a handful of people remained in the club – Barton and the rest of the Americans, including the Count, a couple of the French floor-managers, and Kenyon himself. They had all been reluctant to leave, letting the tension of the previous seventy hours drain away. They were cynical men whose practised *bonhomie* hid a contempt for their customers, but at times like this they talked of them with something almost like affection. As businessmen, they knew the casino was a set devised so that men could enter a timeless world (no clocks), contained totally within itself (no windows, no signs or sounds of an outside world), and act parts they had given themselves. But now, with the money in the vault, the adrenalin still flowing, the memories of every important dice throw, every crucial wheel spin, still clear, the tawdry glamour was real.

Normally at four the club was still open though winding down; tonight, it was closed, the doors locked.

The night bell clanged as Kenyon was beginning to head for the lavatory. 'I'll check it out,' he said. His voice had the careful precision it took on when he had drunk at least three-quarters of a bottle of Scotch.

Hunter had just finished imitating one of the high-rollers throwing craps. At Kenyon's words, he checked his watch and said, 'It'll be my car. I'll go tell him, wait.' Although Hunter lived no more than fifteen minutes away, a car delivered him every afternoon and collected him at exactly four every morning.

The bar led into a long, wide lobby – plush red silk walls decorated with photographs of big-name members in ornate gilt frames. Some stood in small groups, with Hunter and celebrity entertainers centre. The room was lit by chandeliers. It opened into a small circular lobby, now empty. At one side, there were

14

steps down to cloakrooms. Kenyon started down them just as Hunter checked the peep-hole to the street and then began to unlock the doors. The uniformed driver was new to Hunter, but that did not worry him: the hire company had rotated three or four men up to now and this, after all, was not New York or Chicago or Vegas, but London 1965 – land of garden parties at Buckingham Palace, teas at Fortnum & Mason, and people who said 'Sorry' when you banged into them.

Hunter told the driver to dowse the car lights and come into the club. He was still standing in the foyer waiting when, moments later, Kenyon returned from the cloakroom. Kenyon's steps were careful, deliberate. He had learned to gauge the amount of liquor he could absorb with great accuracy. Tonight, because of the celebration, he had miscalculated. The booze was hitting him now, and he knew he had to go home. He saw the open front door and, thinking Hunter had just left, he staggered towards it, hoping to catch a lift.

Hunter, nonplussed, called out to him. Kenyon spun back into the lobby, and then turned again as he heard a new noise. He took in the driver's face – a jagged scar ran the length of his left cheek. Whether it was that or something in the man's eyes, Kenyon did not know. But in his drunkenness, he swung one arm instinctively. The bony edge of his forearm caught the man across the side of the nose. Kenyon stumbled and fell back, off balance, and that was when he felt the terrible pain.

'The bastard was after me,' said Hunter, 'and but for you he'd have got me.' They were standing beside the lake. Hunter lit a cigarette and tossed away the match, which hissed as it hit the water.

He reached an arm around Kenyon's shoulder and turned him back towards the house.

'Come on,' he said, 'it's getting kinda cold, we've gotta take good care of you.'

CHAPTER TWO

Kenyon did not sleep that night. Hunter had left the bottle, but it remained untouched. For once, thoughts alone were enough.

The terrible irony of it! To be shot for someone else. And by stupid, fucking accident because he was drunk. Hunter might smile and say, 'Thanks – you saved my life.' But he, Kenyon, had almost lost his. What had the doctor said? Another quarter inch, that's all . . . It needn't have killed him to destroy him – he could have ended up paralysed, a fucking living cabbage, maybe able to swivel his eyes and make understandable noises, that's all.

Could he be sure he was OK now? The doctor said he was, said the headaches were normal and that they would go. But the doctor was Barton's man, a minion who did, and said, what he was told. What if he was lying to keep Kenyon from going to another doctor when he was free? What if one day, 'Boom!' a sudden thud of pain and dead?

He had not asked Hunter who had tried to shoot him. You did not ask such questions. He had accepted that when he joined the club as its 'finance director' a year and a half before. Since then he had averted his eyes, pretended things did not happen, could not be true. The original fucking three wise monkeys! Every week there had been more and more need to close his eyes – but, as the list had grown, so too had the rewards. That had been his only concern: money to save his dying marriage, though it had not.

Anyway, he did not need to ask. He knew. Not precisely who had pulled the trigger, but who would have sent him and why. There were few gangland bosses with the courage and muscle. Only two who had not done a deal with the Americans or been persuaded to keep well away. All he had to do to produce the names and the reasons for the attack was reach inside himself and retrieve jumbles of words overheard, bits of paper seen, faces observed, cautiously worded newspaper articles read, and fit them together.

Yet, to reach down, to unlock this cellar, to claw back details from limbo would be a step of great decisiveness. It would be an end to the great pretend game which had enabled him to take the Americans' money and still, after a fashion, to continue to live with himself.

Sweat was pouring off him and, unable to lie still any longer, Kenyon got out of bed and walked to the wash-basin. Above it was a mirror. He sluiced his face and then stared at himself.

His face was puffy and of the white that comes with working in windowless rooms. His eyes were cold, sunken. He smiled for the mirror, but only the mouth changed. He was thirty-nine years old. It was said that by the time you reached forty you had the face you deserved. The face he saw was that of a stranger. He had no doubt it was deserved, but it was not one he liked. He still saw himself as lean, quizzical, eyes full of life and exitement at what was to come. Not this thing in the mirror.

Christ, what had he come to? Where had he gone wrong? What was the moment it had all turned sour? When he had come out of the Army in 1947? God, he'd loved those days! When he'd got married for the first time? When he had decided to leave the police force? When he'd met Pamela – after all, he'd taken the club job because he thought the money could save their relationship. There were so many moments, so many times when he seemed to have made the wrong move.

And now, this!

He poured a drink then, but when he lifted the glass it was his own tears he tasted as they ran on to the rim. He raised the glass in a rueful toast.

'Michael Kenyon,' he said, 'ex-soldier, ex-policeman, account-ant, company director, twice-failed husband, current mobsters' front man – This is *Your* Life.'

Maudlin self-pity, it was a feeling he knew well. Not for the first time, he fell asleep warmed and oddly protected by it.

The simple acknowledgement within him of the hidden side of his world brought an increasing jumble of thoughts and dreams. Faces, events, conversations, scenes – all crackled through his mind without sense or order.

At night he dreamed of the gaming tables. Gambling was not his vice. Like many men with large weaknesses and faults, he was incapable of comprehending the different ones of others. One night he had watched a blind man lose thirty-five thousand pounds – twelve times as much as a doctor earned in a year. It had taken less than an hour. The amount was not that exceptional – a really big loser could drop much, much more. But this was gambling stripped of all pretence or glamour: bet, win or lose. Bet, win or lose. Bet, win or lose. The man could not even place the chips, watch the wheel spin, see the ball dance; just listen to a young woman companion giving a commentary in a voice that didn't alter, win or lose. Nor did the man himself betray emotion: Kenyon saw no change of expression from the moment the man began to play until the moment he left.

But in his dreams he came to understand. He was the blind man, and if he closed his mind to all else he could hear distinct sounds where before there had only been a cacophony of noise: not just the heavily accented pseudo-elegant French of the croupiers or the contrasting raucousness of the crap-shooters, not only the click of the balls, but the sliding movement of individual cards, even the sound of turning wrists. If he strained really hard he could hear numbers: a seven of spades sounded different from a jack of diamonds; a dice that landed four upwards gave off as distinctive a noise as a fire alarm.

Sometimes the dreams ended there – with individual sounds that he alone could hear and interpret. At other times they would blend and merge into a mad orchestra that would fill his head with pain. At worst, the sounds would die away without warning, leaving complete and frightening silence. Frightening because he knew how it would end. With pain like a burning poker, the sound of a single shot, and the smell of gunpowder. But this time, no waking . . .

The dreams and the thoughts took many forms. But always they concerned the club.

Kenyon's involvement with the club, the Big Wheel, had begun in 1963, two years before. To be precise, in April, T. S. Eliot's 'cruellest month'. Significant, it seemed to Kenyon. After two years, his second marriage, to Pamela, had become a battle-ground from which he withdrew only by retreating into himself, helped increasingly by booze. They had bought a mews house in Chelsea. 'My doll's house,' Pamela had called it at first, skipping from room to room delightedly. Now, suddenly, it was too small – she could not entertain. It was a side of her nature that pervaded everything. What was good today was bad tomorrow, often for the reason that had made it good in the first place. So small was desirable today, a disaster tomorrow; a car vital this week, useless next; long walks through the park invigorating this month, exhausting next . . .

Her mercurial moods had amused and delighted Kenyon when they first met. After all, he had been the focus of one. He had refused to see that the total intensity she brought to him could end as abruptly as her interest in the houses and cars and clothes. He knew there had been many other men – her past was the stuff of newspaper gossip columns. But that was over and their relationship was different. So he told himself. And, in large part, it was true. She said she had never felt quite this way before, and he was certain that it was so. Nevertheless, after a while, he had taken to telephoning the house to warn her he was on his way home. A courtesy, he told himself. But he knew it was also a safeguard against finding someone else there.

Then there had been the first terrible night. He arrived home first. When she did return, he had thought himself too full of booze to manage sex, but she had wanted him so desperately that her excitement had made him hard, brought a frenzy that he had not known for months. It was only afterwards, lying quiet as she smoked a cigarette in the darkness, that he had dwelt on how wet she had been from the first moment and how strong the smell of sex from the very start. As though they were repeating an act she had only just completed. When he awoke, he persuaded himself it was his imagination, fears born of knowing what she had been like before they met.

Then – and later – he forced all such thoughts away. In his desperation to keep her, to leave their relationship untouched and unchanged, he closed parts of himself, began to live a lie by pretence and omission.

Soon afterwards, she had raised the idea of the country: they could sell the mews, buy a small London flat and find a house out of town. But where? 'Oh, anywhere. The country. It's spring and I want to see everything growing and – you know – feel *alive*.' His first thoughts were that she was simply reacting to the winter that had just ended: smog, the worst for at least ten years, had killed over four hundred people in London. But as days went by, as she continued to talk about it, he realised that it went deeper than that. Then his thoughts turned to money – although his earnings were high, so were their outgoings. It had become a constant battle to keep on top of their expenses. A house in the country would mean more money still. Where from? His earnings were the commissions on loans to small businesses. He had already begun to allow some clients to overextend themselves in a way he would not have done before. His second thought was positive: a new house, a new start, was exactly what they needed.

And two days after that he had met Barton.

Hopper fixed the meeting. Hopper was an ambitious solicitor who had brought Kenyon's company business several times before. The company Kenyon worked for loaned out money. It had started just after World War II, lending small sums at high interest in working-class areas – a few pounds to buy a new chair or for clothes for the kids. It still operated that side of the business – legalised loan-sharking was highly profitable. But that area was nothing to do with Kenyon. In more recent years the company had branched out into what it liked to call 'private banking', concentrating on areas of business where real banks were wary. Its headquarters were in the Midlands, and the small London office, which Kenyon had been asked to set up, was one sign of the changes.

According to City rumour, Hopper sometimes operated close to the edge; many of his clients were the kind of entrepreneurs who ended up either as millionaires or fighting fraud charges – just which, detractors claimed, was usually a question of luck. But Kenyon had never had problems in his dealings with him. He suspected that the truth was that Hopper attracted such talk because he flaunted his ego and his ambition – something that was 'just not on, old boy', as the City establishment would have said. They would probably also have added that it was worse in that he was also 'letting the side down'. Because Hopper's own background was Establishment: a family short of cash now, but with two hundred years of breeding and good schools and then the military or running something in the colonies behind them. Somewhere along the way Hopper had become the black sheep. It was not clear to Kenyon whether he had broken away or been thrown out. Whichever, Hopper never saw his family now, never referred to them except to mock their genteel poverty when he saw pictures of them in *Country Life* or *Tatler*. ('They're like the fucking country, think all they have to do is sit on their arses and the world'll take care of them,' or, getting specific, 'What the bleeding hell good is a country estate if you can't even afford to light the fucking fires?')

Not only did he and Kenyon enjoy doing business together, they amused each other and enjoyed a mutual respect, albeit a slightly wary one. Their backgrounds could hardly have been more different. On one side, the Shires and nannies and seven thousand acres in Scotland. On the other, a village shop and pounding a copper's beat. But they didn't see those things in each other. They saw not where they had come from but where they were and – more important – where they wanted to go. They shared a mutual anger and frustration at the kind of gentlemanly part-timers who seemed to run everything – dinosaurs whose days were ending, but who still stood in their way when they could. Such men were holding back not just them, but *everything* – it was a time when anything was possible. It *had* to happen.

Both, too, had left their backgrounds, had made themselves their own men. Hopper's transformation was the most dramatic. Eton and a short spell in the Guards might never have been. The solicitor, striving to play down his background, affected his own version of the raw, abrasive new classlessness of his sixties heroes – figures like Albert Finney, Tony Newley, David Frost. It did not end there. Where his father's suits had come from Anderson & Sheppard in Savile Row, his were from show-business tailors; his hair was cut at Sassoon's, not Trumper's; his clubs were Churchill's and the Establishment, not White's or the Athenaeum; his restaurants were the Trat and the Beachcomber, not Rules or Simpson's.

He strove to sound East-Ender made good. He looked and acted like a man who has fought his way up through a British class system, and was still going places.

Kenyon had also left his background far behind. Not dramatic-ally and theatrically like Hopper, but gradually. Over the years he had added layers that had changed the way he spoke (a near accentless middle-class voice with an occasional touch of mid-

Atlantic), dressed (good branded clothes like Simpson's, Turnbull & Asser, Burberry), looked and acted (an easy assertiveness).

'We got it the wrong way round,' Hopper once said. 'You should have been in the Guards – natural fucking officer.'

That had started Kenyon remembering his days in Army Intelligence in the immediate post-war years; the way he had drifted on the edge of becoming a regular soldier. No doubt that if he had – if he hadn't done that stupid favour that did no one any good – there would have been a commission.

Still, he was not complaining . . . If he had stayed in the Army, he would never have met Pamela. Which brought him back to the permanent worry: how to keep her.

The moment Kenyon seized on the thought of the new house as a renewed start to their relationship, he thought of Hopper. To make it possible he would need more money. Hopper was plugged into a score of schemes. Maybe he could produce more loan candidates; perhaps there were other areas where Kenyon could increase his earnings.

As it happened, they had to meet briefly at the office of a small importer who wanted more money. A straightforward transaction, rapidly concluded to everyone's satisfaction. Afterwards, Hopper was running late, but seeing Kenyon's desire to talk joined him for a pub drink.

They talked small-talk at first – what they thought of Harold Wilson, the new Labour leader; Hopper's enthusiasm for David Lean's latest film, *Lawrence of Arabia*; was the BBC's satire show *That Was The Week That Was* going to be forced off the air by the Establishment . . . ?

At last, Kenyon said, 'I want to buy a house in the country.'

'Christ, you're not selling out. Set on becoming a squire, riding to hounds, laying all the local milkmaids.' He was laughing, not believing Kenyon, thinking he was going through one of those days everyone has.

'You'll feel better tomorrow,' he said. 'Besides, you'd die out there. Your lungs'd collapse without their ration of smog. Too risky. Go to bed for a couple of days until it goes away.' He checked his watch. It was 12.10. 'Or, better still, come to a club I know. That'll get the bits on peak again. Come on, I'll phone in, get my secretary to cancel the rest of the day. We'll kill a few bottles, fuck a few birds, smash up a few places.' He was gripping the edge of the bar and had begun to sweat at the thought of it. 'Come to think of it, do us *both* good.'

Kenyon's face had not changed. 'I'm serious,' he said. 'I need some help.' He explained.

'Pity, bloody pity,' said Hopper when Kenyon had finished. 'Too bloody long since we let our hair down.' He played with his glass, full of thought. 'There's something,' he said. 'I know someone who's looking for a finance director for a new company. You'd have to quit your present job. I don't know the salary, but more – a hell of a lot more, I'd guess – than you're getting. And it carries a directorship. Interested?'

'What is it?' Kenyon had been thinking of extra work, not a new job.

'I think it's best you meet my man,' said Hopper, not answering. 'He'll explain better than me. Tomorrow? I'll try to fix something then. I'll call you.'

Hopper gathered his papers ready to go. 'Just a couple of things,' he added. 'The man's a Yank. Play it up – your background. The Army – Intelligence, if you'd stayed on you'd have got a commission. Right? Make sure he knows. And the police. He'll like that – but maybe a little lie. No one looking at or listening to you now would see an ordinary PC. Christ, if you told them you were a commander they wouldn't be surprised. If he thought you'd been an inspector, well . . . it wouldn't hurt him. Up to you, of course, but I'd say it wasn't really a lie – from what I know you must have been inspector material, at least!'

They met that evening in the bar of St. Georges Hotel, high over the rooftops of central London. They exchanged pleasantries until their drinks arrived. Barton, Kenyon decided, was in his mid-fifties. His hair was unnaturally black, making Kenyon suspect it was dyed. He had a remarkably still quality, and Kenyon found the way the man's eyes remained on him disturbing. His suit was black, his tie a discreet stripe. The only flashy note was the cuff-links, large gold dice. His voice was ugly, a rasp as though he'd had a throat operation or had pickled it in booze over the years. It was pitched quiet, as though he was ashamed of it, an assumption Kenyon soon discovered was totally wrong: the low speech was no more than a reflection of the fact that he expected to be listened to with care.

Hopper began. 'Mr Barton is in the entertainment business,' he said. 'He and his associates in the United States have been expanding abroad and they're keen to develop interests in this country.'

'What kind of entertainment?' asked Kenyon.

Hopper started to reply, but Barton cut in, 'Gambling, Mr Keyon. Now it's legal over here we'd like to have us a big piece of it.'

It was not a subject Kenyon knew anything about. But then he had known nothing about importing Indian foods or converting disused warehouses into apartments or the recording business – and he had quickly learned enough about them to loan them all money.

Hopper explained. The government, three years before in 1960, had passed an Act of Parliament that was designed to legalise off-track betting shops and bingo games and allow members in private clubs to gamble between themselves. What the new law was *not* supposed to do was legalise commercial gaming operations. By accident, though, that was precisely what it had done.

'It's a little technical, and you'll have to take my word for it,' said Hopper. 'But to give you the guts. If you run gaming as a business and –' a nod in Barton's direction – 'that's what it is, a *business*, you make your money by the edge you have as the operator. Take roulette. Thirty-six numbers and a double zero, yet on single numbers it pays out only thirty-five to one.' He looked to Barton for confirmation.

'That's American roulette we're talking,' said Barton. 'It's got an extra zero over what you've got in Europe; guess we need it.' Kenyon and Hopper laughed on cue.

'And the edge?' Hopper went on. 'It varies, but for most bets 5.27 per cent. It might not sound much but over a night, over a year . . .'

'It sounds a lot,' said Kenyon.

It was Hopper who continued. 'The politicians wanted to prevent this, and they reckoned the way to do it yet allow friends to play together for fun was to say gaming was legal only *if all the chances for everyone were equal*. See what that means? You can't have the house having its edge, so you can't have commercial gaming.'

'So?'

24

'So – somebody got round it. Some bright lawyer. Saw a loophole – drove a twenty-ton truck right through it.'

What happened, he explained, was that casinos were told they could remain within the letter of the law simply by *offering* all the players in a game the opportunity to act as the house in turn. That way, theoretically, chances became equal for everyone.

In practice, it was rubbish – taking the bank temporarily made no sense at all. The statistical edge only works over a period of time. Anyone acting as banker for just one turn of the wheel risked a huge loss.

'But what the hell. *Offering* the chance made it all legal. And that's why it's boomtime!'

There was silence and Kenyon knew it was his turn.

'And me?' he asked.

The reply was phrased diplomatically. Barton and his associates required someone who knew finance. There was a lot of money involved; the business needed careful accounting procedures, especially as there were overseas partners involved. Additionally, a lot of people had the wrong perceptions about gambling. It was important to show them it was really just a business. They wanted Kenyon for his accountancy skills, but the fact that he had once been a police inspector and before that in the British Army, about to accept a commission if he hadn't needed to come home for his folks . . . well, it was all to the good. And, of course, he was English – the others involved were American and the authorities worried about foreigners running British companies.

Kenyon understood very well. They wanted a front man.

He had made his move when he had contacted Hopper. This had to be fate! Still, he had to play the game. He took care not to sound too eager. 'I'm flattered,' he said at last. 'Very flattered. But, as Denis will tell you, I'm doing well, and I'm happy in what I'm doing.'

Once Barton named the price he was committed. It was everything he needed! The forty-eight hours' thinking time he requested was just to impress his worth. He knew he would take it – even though he also suspected what a check through police files would reveal about Barton.

Forty-eight hours later he said, 'Yes,' and within the week he and Pamela had made an offer for the house in the country. It emerged she had already heard about a property in exactly the right area.

It really was going perfectly. It was all coming together to give them a fresh beginning. He could imagine it: country walks, pubs with log fires and mulled ale, endless time to share together . . . The house, and their different way of life, would mean an end to all the fears, all the worries of losing her. What had happened to them before had been no more than a temporary nightmare. From now on it would all be perfect again.

The day before Kenyon left the convalescent home, Poulton paid another visit. This time he brought a colleague.

'A second opinion,' he explained. 'Not that there's any need, but because of Mr Barton, you're a special patient.'

They both examined his wound. It was healing well, they agreed. The scar would be small and, in any event, hidden by Kenyon's hair.

They stayed a long time, as though reluctant to leave. Poulton's colleague talked little, but seemed happy to listen.

As they left, Poulton handed over an attaché case. It was locked, but Kenyon knew what the combination would be – he had often carried such cases. Inside there was his passport, two hundred pounds in five-pound notes, five hundred dollars in traveller's cheques, a round plane ticket to Miami.

Barton called him later. 'Get some sun,' he said. 'Get a good tan.' Kenyon understood – that's where he had been these last weeks. No doubt at some stage the dates of entry on his passport would be doctored.

His flight was an early evening one to New York. A car would collect him around 2 p.m. The driver would bring another suitcase with a few clothes in it.

The car arrived early. The driver was Hunter in his latest toy, an E-type Jaguar. 'Thought I'd see what the world looked liked in the daylight,' he said. And, before Kenyon could react, 'Like it?' He meant the car, around which he preened, pointing out features with a boyish excitement. 'I did one hundred and fifty on that highway they're still building – what'd they call it, the M1? – the other night,' he said.

Kenyon knew Hunter occasionally left the club in the early mornings and raced his latest car – it was the only thing, to Kenyon's knowledge, that made Barton afraid. ('What the hell would Meyer say if we had to scrape you off the fuckin' highway?'

Kenyon had once heard him say. Hunter had replied, 'You mean, what would Meyer do to you if they had to scrape me off the highway.' Although Kenyon tried to keep his ears closed, it was impossible to work in the club and not know who Meyer Lansky was – the Mafia's financial mastermind, the man they called the Godfather of Godfathers. And Kenyon had realised that, although he never flaunted it, Hunter carried real power too. 'I guess you'd better just pray it never happens,' he had continued, and then laughed to show he was going to let Barton drop the subject without losing face.

There was a suitcase tossed into the back.

'A coupla jackets and trousers, and a few shirts and things,' said Hunter.

'You went to the apartment?'

'Simpson's,' said Hunter. 'I looked up the sizes from the stuff you have round the club.' Kenyon, like the others, always kept fresh clothes there in case one day ran into another.

Hunter dismissed thanks. 'If you don't like them give them to some bum. They've enough where you're going.'

They drove in silence for almost an hour. They were early. Without warning, Hunter turned off the road into the driveway of a hotel.

'Tea,' he said. 'I love your English tea.'

The lounge was mock-Tudor, and it was too early for tea.

'We'll wait,' said Hunter, and they took seats next to french windows that opened on to a lawn.

Two girls peered and whispered at a doorway, and minutes later a waiter arrived with tea and a trolley of cakes and scones. It was still twenty minutes before authorised tea-time. Hunter had been recognised. Kenyon wondered if the girls could put a name to the American, or whether they just knew him as a star.

Hunter took it as his due, but acted out his role as he always did, taking great care in choosing a scone, smiling a lot and being fulsome in his thank-yous.

Finally, he drank and then pushed away the cup. 'The idea I love,' he explained. 'The reality . . .'

He lit a cigarette, and for the first time since Kenyon had met him he seemed uncertain of himself. Absentmindedly Hunter picked up his cup again and sipped before remembering what it was, winced, and said, 'Jesus Christ, d'you suppose they have

27

coffee?' Almost immediately he answered himself. 'What the fuck, the coffee tastes like piss in this country anyway.'

Kenyon watched, amused at seeing the mask slip. It lasted seconds only.

Hunter rubbed his eyes theatrically, as though exhausted, reached over and patted Kenyon's arm. 'You've given me one hell of a fucking problem,' he said.

Kenyon waited. He knew it was all he could do.

'I've got a good life,' said Hunter at last. 'A real good life.' He turned and stared hard at Kenyon. He sucked deep on a cigarette before resuming. 'You don't talk just to fill in silences,' said Hunter. 'I like that. Most people talk too much.'

Kenyon still said nothing. There had to be a point.

'One of the reasons I've got a good life is because I've got a lot of friends who appreciate that I've got a lot of talents and one of them is the same as yours – not talking too much.'

He turned to face Kenyon dramatically. 'I'm gonna talk to you now,' he said. 'And I'm gonna risk my neck, but like I said I owe you. I tell you, I don't answer questions, I don't say it twice. OK?'

A waitress appeared at the door and Hunter waved a star's wave.

'You know that maybe a half of the money we take is skimmed right off the top, never gets on the records, just sent back home? Hell, sure you know that. Seeing and not seeing, that's one of the things you get paid for. What I guess maybe you don't know is that Barton skims some more after that, and that *doesn't* get sent back. That's personal, money he keeps for *his* rainy day. The guy's not totally fuckin' mad, though. He knows one fine morning the boys back home may find it's missing and –' he paused for an actor's effect '– I heard one guy who got caught doing something like that got hung upside down on a hook in a slaughterhouse and beat to death with a baseball bat, but real slow . . .'

He went quiet, and this time Kenyon knew he had to prompt.

'Why tell me? Where do I come into this?'

'You're set up as the fall guy. The moment anyone suspects – and I tell you that moment's gonna come 'cause Barton's being greedy – you're the guy on the meat hook or trying to suck air through a foot of earth.'

The contrast with winter in England, especially after Kenyon's confinement in the convalescent home, could not have been greater. Miami airport, huge almost beyond belief with its ticket-counters five city blocks' long, was thronged with brown faces leaving, pale ones arriving.

The temperature was around 80°F, the light blinding, the hotels on Miami Beach breathtaking in their magnificent flamboyance and vulgarity. When Kenyon reached his hotel, a pair of bikini-clad women were trailing minks across the marble lobby as though their get-ups were the most natural in the world. He had been dropped down in the middle of the world's most ostentatiously rich resort and it felt like it.

Kenyon had a suite. With it came the kind of treatment he had never known before. Managers bowed, anything – *anything* – he was assured, was his, he only had to ask. A tourist, tired and short-tempered after a day shopping with a demanding wife, bad-mouthed Kenyon in the lobby one evening – and was immediately hustled away by two burly staff while a duty manager was summoned to ask Kenyon if he wanted the man and his family thrown out of the hotel. He was offered women, drugs, flights out to the islands.

One morning in the coffee-shop a short, slight man in his early sixties – lightweight grey suit, sleeked hair, wide parting – stopped by his table and said with gentle courteousness that he hoped Kenyon was having a good time. After a few other similar clichés he moved on. Only then did Kenyon note that the man was shadowed by two bodyguards and realised that it was Meyer Lansky. For the rest of that day the hotel staff were even more obsequious than before.

That night, Kenyon wondered if he should seek out the man, tell him what Hunter had told him. But it was a mad thought. There was only Hunter's word, and the greeter would probably deny he had said anything. Furthermore, Barton was a big man. Who would believe anything said against him without proof?

Anyway, Kenyon asked himself, did he *really* believe what Hunter had told him? It had seemed convincing at the time, but wasn't that because of Hunter's acting ability coupled with the feeling, why should the man lie to him? But he did believe, not just because he could see no reason Hunter should lie, but because it rekindled a fear that had come weeks before.

After he had taken the club job, Kenyon had drifted out of

contact with Hopper, the man who had introduced him to Barton. It was Hopper who had broken the silence. 'Mark Murphy's at Annie Ross's Club,' he had said on the phone. They were both fans of the young American jazz singer. 'What say you take a night off, join me?'

Some time that night, Hopper had said, 'I think you ought to know that your boss, Barton, has been asking questions about you – how much you need money, whether you've got debts . . . That sort of thing.' He paused to study Kenyon's reaction. 'You haven't been up to anything, have you?' he had continued, his voice heavy with seriousness. 'I don't know how much you know about him – enough I imagine to know he's not a man to fool with.'

Kenyon had shaken his head, not sure how seriously to react. Reading Hopper's concern, he had said, 'Nothing, nothing at all.' He had tried to grin reassuringly. 'I just keep my head down, do what I'm told, collect my money.' He didn't like what he was hearing, but he had been around the club long enough to know Barton was suspicious of everyone. Maybe for Barton this kind of constant checking was just normal behaviour.

It was obvious Hopper had not been convinced. 'Just don't do anything stupid,' he had said. Pamela, the separation, the house and its cost, lay between them unspoken. 'I know I introduced you,' Hopper had gone on. 'But that was because you had a problem. Just don't forget who you're dealing with. Ever.'

As the days passed in Miami, Kenyon kept expecting someone to summon him, ask him about operations back in London. He rehearsed what he would say. But nothing happened except that time went by in a mix of lying in the sun, swimming, sightseeing, sleeping and eating. He strolled down Lincoln Park Mall and Collins Avenue, took a rented car out to the Everglades, a plane to the Keys. He ate at Joe's Stone Crab Restaurant, tried Cuban-Spanish nightclubs in downtown Miami, enjoyed the horse races at Tropical Park.

He laid two women he picked up by the pool, but less from desire than because they were there and available and it was easier than not laying them. An envelope of bills was left in his room every night – just a little spending money. He counted it the first day, five hundred dollars, but after that he just stashed the envelope unopened in his case. Hardly leaving the hotel, there was little to spend it on.

It was early afternoon when he landed at Heathrow. George collected him in a car he had not seen before, a new three-litre black Rover. They reached central London and continued east.

'A surprise,' said George, noting Kenyon's puzzlement.

Then he sensed Kenyon's fear, remembered the shooting.

'Hey,' he added. 'It's OK. Relax. You're gonna love this.'

Kenyon sank back, convincing himself that if they were going to hit him they would hardly have waited for his return.

It had to be some crazy stunt. Maybe Hunter's idea. Maybe a party.

The destination was a warehouse deep in the Docklands. The area around was deserted, ready for demolition. It was dark when they arrived.

George led the way through a side door. The inside had been subdivided. The room they entered had a pile of discarded theatrical props.

'They once shotta . . . few commercials here,' said George.

They walked on through a series of empty subdivisions, their feet echoing on bare floor. They reached a windowless inner room and stopped. It was lit, but barely. There were half a dozen men grouped at the far end. It was too dark for Kenyon to recognise them at first.

He stood, uncertain, suddenly piss-scared despite George's earlier reassurance.

Then one man spoke. Kenyon recognised him. One of Barton's closest side-kicks.

'A present,' the man said. 'Welcome home, buddy.'

And from about fifteen feet he tossed something in Kenyon's direction.

Despite his fear, Kenyon thrust his hands out instinctively. All he could see as it curled towards him was that it was dark, ball-shaped.

He caught it, chest high. It was incredibly heavy and he staggered back with the force. Almost the moment he caught it, it began to slip. It was as cold and slippery as a lump of ice.

A huge snowball. A head-size snowball.

He realised what it was in the second before he dropped it.

A head. A frozen head. A sawn-off frozen human head. The flesh had lost its colour. The scar that criss-crossed one cheek, though, was more pronounced than it had been in life, more vivid than when he had stared at it through drunken eyes before being shot. The neck, where it had been severed from the body, was a mosaic of pressed-in tendon. The hair, long and black and wavy, was fixed firm in place. The eyes were open, exposing staring eyeballs that had shrunk in their sockets.

Kenyon was too riveted with shock to scream. All around him was silence. The head hit the floor. There was a sharp cracking noise and a piece shot off into the air, and Kenyon, with rising nausea, realised it was the man's nose.

Dimly, he heard George say, 'That'll teach the guy to fuck with you.'

Kenyon was still in shock, beginning to reach down to grope for the man's nose when George and another man grasped his arms. As they led him from the room, he heard a thud and then laughter. He looked back over his shoulder.

Two men were using the frozen head as a football, kicking it between them.

They hustled him on through more rooms. They entered one, larger, almost totally dark, and stopped. They held him straight. And then lights came on. Blinding, dazzling.

Sound hit him. The shooting flooded back, and he clutched his hands in front of him where he knew the bullet was going to hit. Then he was being held in a hug, and he realised there was a band blasting the theme from *Hello Dolly*. The room was full of the men present the night he was shot, and there was a woman advancing, tall on stiletto heels and naked except for a gold G-string and sequin dots on her nipples. As the cheers and catcalls rose over the music Kenyon saw Barton. He too was smiling, and he raised a glass in a welcome salute. There was a special look on his face. Appraising? Amusement? A knowingness? All of them – but expecially the last. A farmer weighing up a beast for the fattening? Wondering how long? That too.

And at that moment Kenyon believed everything Hunter had told him. Realised that the shooting, instead of killing him, had bought him time. But that was all. Unless he did something, he was still a dead man.

CHAPTER THREE

For weeks after his return Kenyon was haunted by nightmares filled with guns and disembodied heads. In one, he watched his own head explode in slow motion, a macabre blizzard of skin and tissue and droplets of blood.

The worst one, though less violent, was more terrifying. It came often. In it, he was awakened in bed by a pounding on his door. He woke, keyed, expecting enemies. He reached for a gun, and as the door burst open he realised it held one bullet less than the number of armed men wanting to kill him. Each time, his head pounded with the same conundrum: should he shoot as many as he could (knowing one at least would surivive), or should he shoot himself to avoid the beating and the tortures he knew would follow otherwise?

Afterwards, he would lie awake sweating, heart pounding, chest heaving. And as panic rose he would reach out for alcohol, which he used more and more determinedly, as though it were a prescription drug labelled 'to be taken as necessary'.

Panic struck in the daytime too. One morning, about to take a rare Tube ride, he had an almost uncontrollable desire to leap into the train's path. It was the strength of the feeling that scared him. He had to fight himself not to leap. Terrified and trembling, he had lurched back and pressed his body against the station wall for support before stumbling out to the street and the nearest pub.

It did not need a psychiatrist to interpret the nightmares or the reason for the panic. He was the proverbial trapped animal. Nowhere to go. Nowhere to run. And, in his case, no way to fight back.

A hundred times a day and night his head reeled with the question: what could he do? He could not go to the police – he'd involved himself too deeply for that. And, in any event, what could he tell them? About the shooting? About the head? About the skim? All that would happen, he knew, was that some fast-talking copper would offer unspecified help at some uncertain later date if, in the meantime, he stayed in place as an informer. No way out there.

He could try running. What had he got to leave that mattered? A second failed marriage (though some of the time he refused to admit that). A son he never saw whose mother said he was better off without him. But that would just be giving Barton his head on a plate. Why run if he was not guilty of something? And one thing he *knew*: if he ran, they would get him. You did not run from these people. And then? Hanging on that slaughterhouse hook, being slowly beaten to death . . .

Which was where he would end up if he did not run!

No circle could be more vicious.

He wished there was someone he could talk to. Just getting it out would help. But you'd need one hell of a buddy to share this one with. Something else he'd left behind.

On his way to a rare meeting with Pamela, he wondered if he could tell her the story by pretending it had happened to someone else. He half-persuaded himself that it would serve two purposes. First, it would bring his demons out into the real world. Second, her street instincts were good ones and from her reaction he might find some avenue of hope. But when they met, over lunch in a restaurant, it had been impossible. She kept the conversation general and superficial – had he been in the new Hilton in Park Lane yet? You couldn't believe the crowds in Carnaby Street – they were from *everywhere*. What did he think of her skirt? It wasn't *too* mini, was it? Should she buy the latest Dusty Springfield album?

They had spent Christmas apart, and she gave him belated presents (he had posted his gifts to her: perfume, jewellery, an album of *My Fair Lady* that he had brought back from Miami). She had kept them simple, a sharp and fleetingly painful contrast with the days not long before when they had used every excuse to shower each other with gifts. One, a kipper tie, looked as though it had been chosen quickly: it was not his taste, the wrapping was the store's own. But he was touched by the second, *The Tin Men*, a first novel by his favourite columnist, Michael Frayn. He had mentioned it and she had remembered. A small thing but, briefly, a warming one.

At the slightest sign, though, that he intended to be serious or personal, she erected barriers. And he drew back, terrified he would provoke the words he did not want to hear – the request that their separation become a divorce. Despite everything, he did not want that – it was his great fear, his constant nightmare. Pathetically, against all reality, he clung to a hope that it might still come right again. That, miraculously, they would meet one day like this and the bad times would never have existed, and that it would all be as it was before.

Only at the end, as they left the restaurant, did he slip by asking if she would stay overnight, a suggestion she side-stepped easily. He watched her cab draw away, wondering – fearing – where she was going, who she was going to meet. A mad panic swept over him. Without realising it, he stepped into the road and began to run, oblivious of everything except the retreating taxi which was already almost out of sight. A bus hooted and the driver leaned from his window and yelled at him. The cab had gone. Kenyon came to a halt, became aware of the traffic and the passers-by who had stopped to stare. He sucked on air and stumbled embarrassed to the far side of the road like a drunk although, because of Pamela, he was stone-cold sober for once.

He walked until the panic died. Gradually, thoughts of Pamela stilled, and his mind returned to his immediate problem: *what* could he do?

He forced himself to reduce it to essentials.

Since joining the club, Kenyon had tried not to see things; the less he had known, the better it had been for what remained of his conscience. But there were things you could not but know. That the club was owned at a distance by the Mafia. That Barton was their man on the spot, and because of that he must be a big man. That there was a deal with English gangsters. That there were other, less prestigious clubs that the Mob controlled in London. That they were developing interests in other big British cities too – emissaries went out, returned, and there was talk.

But the guts was simple: Mafia-owned; Barton their man.

And what did he suspect, what was his fear? That Barton was ripping off his bosses. That, in case they ever suspected money was missing, Barton had a plan ready to put into operation, one that would produce Kenyon as the fall guy.

Big on fear, small on detail!

35

He just *had* to know more. Most of all, he needed to know more about Barton himself. Just how big a man was he really? Was there any chance that Kenyon could persuade the Mob that Barton was cheating them, and, if so, how?

There must be a police file. Thankfully, he still had contacts. There was an inspector on the Flying Squad, a man who could usually be trusted to deliver provided the price was acceptable. Kenyon called him. But, even with his rank, the inspector could only gain access to a précis of the file from Criminal Intelligence Records without attracting dangerous attention. In itself, Kenyon realised, confirmation of Barton's importance.

Kenyon settled for the précis. He met the inspector in a Bayswater pub. The policeman was already waiting, tucked away at a corner table, when Kenyon arrived. Kenyon bought two pints of bitter at the bar, handed over 4s., took his 8d. change, and joined the man. They both had copies of the *Daily Telegraph*. When he left twenty minutes later, Kenyon had swapped them. The one he left behind had ten five-pound notes taped to an inside page. The one he took concealed the précis.

Kenyon walked across to Hyde Park to read the report. There were only two pages. 'Carl Louis Barton – alias John Bates, John Brent, James Bennett, Louis Wood. Born 22 March 1910, in New York; 5'10", 180 lbs; black hair, brown eyes . . .'

Just three arrests – breaking and entering, carrying a concealed weapon, 'interfering with an officer'. Only on the first – as a juvenile – had there been a conviction; the others had been dismissed. A string, though, of suspected involvements – from extortion to illegal gambling to murder. The place names were an atlas of Mob-controlled gaming: Nevada, Havana, the Bahamas.

The names he was linked with were a blue book of hoods: Bugsy Spiegel, Lucky Luciano, Meyer Lansky, Frank Costello, Tony Accardo, John Rosselli, Sam Giancana . . .

Barton appeared in the Nevada Gaming Control Board's 'black book' – the list of people banned from involvement in any Nevada gambling operation.

Kenyon had a ball-point pen and a pocket notebook, but he did not use them. Some of the detail was new to him – the convictions, for example. But he could have added to it – no mention of Angelo Bruno, the head of the Philadelphia Mafia, to whom Kenyon was sure Barton reported. What it did provide, though, was confirmation that Barton was the kind of man who could watch you writhing your last throes on a meat-hook while eating his breakfast without missing a bite.

And that he had a lot of important friends. No Mafia boss was going to take Kenyon's word against Barton's. All any of them would do was string Kenyon up on that meat-hook for even saying anything. That fucking circle again!

All around him, London was becoming the swinging capital of the world. Social historians would later decide that 1963 was the year the fifties ended and a new era began. The Beatles and Mary Quant. Gaudy pop-art colours. Carnaby Street and King's Road. Youth and drugs and flower power.

To Kenyon, it could all have been happening on Mars.

Only his fears and the club were real. And the great irony was that it was only at the club – with his enemies – that Kenyon felt at home.

On the surface everything was the same. The gamblers were still a mix of old money, showbiz and the new aristocracy of the sixties – hairdressers, fashion designers, photographers and models. With those who worked there, though, there was a change – a not unpleasant one. No one talked about the shooting, but most *knew*. And that knowledge was reflected in the way they treated him, the French with a new deference, the Americans as though he had just emerged successfully from an initiation ceremony.

He had always had his parts to play in the daily cycle of the club, although the lines were carefully written by his masters. A gaming club is a twenty-four-hour place, a factory devised for the sole purpose of recycling money, returning less than it takes in. Like all factories, it has its machinery – the cards, the wheels, the shoes. It has its raw materials – the punters and their money. And it has its workers and its managers – the croupiers who spin wheels, the dealers who flip cards, the inspectors who watch, the floor managers who watch them, and the bossman who watches everyone because the greatest single law of running gaming clubs is *everybody* cheats if you don't stop them. There were the cashiers in their cages, the security staff who patrolled and monitored the tables and checked the closed-circuit TV over the entrance lobby. There was Hunter, whose formal title was 'director of public relations'. And there was Kenyon.

On paper he was 'financial director' and in the files at Companies House where the owning company was registered he was listed as one of the four directors (together with Hunter, another of the Americans and an elderly London solicitor who had never been near the club). Except where it mattered, Barton did not exist.

The club operated on two planes. The first was the plush, predominantly red, deep-carpeted, chandeliered stage of the gaming rooms, the bar and the restaurant. The other – functional, often downright drab – was all the backstage offices, and staff eating and sitting-around rooms (dealers need a break every hour if they are not to lose the edge of their concentration).

It also had its own time zones, both separate from that of the world outside. The first time existed in the outer gaming world where it was always whatever time the punter wanted it to be or even no time at all. The second was confined to the guarded room where twice every twenty-four hours the notes were stacked and counted.

Like Barton and Hunter, Kenyon lived most of his working hours in the first time zone. There was a six-seater table in the corner of the restaurant from which they all operated. Barton and Hunter were normally already there when Kenyon arrived around four o'clock in the afternoon. There were often papers and cheques waiting in a blue leather and gold-tooled desk folder and he signed them at the table while they drank coffee.

Now, like the Americans, he took to asking as he arrived, 'What was the drop?' – meaning, how much did we make last night? – which was the most important single sentence ever asked and answered in the club. Usually Barton would say, 'It's in the folder,' because even though the table was distanced from any of the punters, there were some things best not said aloud. And, as part of the ritual, Kenyon would push his cup aside, open the file and study the amount, and then say, 'Pretty good' or 'Great' or 'Not so hot' depending on the figure, as though he was one of the real decision-makers. He never fooled himself that he was, but he basked in the warmth of the way everyone now acted out the pretence.

Later, he would walk through to the counting room where the second count of the twenty-four-hour cycle was under way. Only he and the Americans were allowed in there, and him only because it was necessary to pretend that he was responsible for the accounting of the money. Even then, he knew he was constantly watched. The room lay beyond the cashier's cage on the ground floor where cash or credit notes were exchanged for chips. It was locked from the inside and had a slide peep-hole, like a Prohibition speak-easy. The door was reinforced with metal plates. There were no windows, but the light from low-hung neon strips was dazzling. The only furniture was four upright chairs and a huge glass-topped table. Money and credit notes came into the room from the two cashiers' cages, and were counted in stacks – markers, single pound notes, five-pound notes (the highest pile) and the recently issued ten-pound notes. A television camera was mounted high on the wall. Four men counted non-stop while a fifth guarded the door. There was a smell of Barton's cigar – no one else was allowed to smoke in the room – and sweat. Give or take a few thousand (or sometimes a lot of thousands) there was rarely less than fifty thousand pounds on the table by the end of the count. As 'financial director' Kenyon never saw that much officially. He signed a declaration for about half that figure – the amount the club would declare as takings and on which it would, ultimately, base its accounts for the Revenue. The other half – the skim – was packed into attaché cases and removed to safety-deposit boxes and from there by courier to the club's real owners.

About all that, of course, he knew nothing.

Despite his panic and desperation, Kenyon kept trying to convince himself there had to be a way. He attempted to stand back and see things through the eyes of the cop he used to be.

Was Barton really setting him up? And, if so, where – and how – was he, Kenyon, supposed to be slicing money off the take? What was there that pinned guilt on him? Maybe if he knew some answers, there would be something he could do.

Hunter might know. But the only time Kenyon tried to ask, the American backed away hard.

'If you're gonna ask what I think you're gonna ask, don't be a wise ass,' Hunter said, his mouth hardly moving. And then, softening his tone, 'I told you all I know. That's it, the whole fucking deal. Right?' His face remained in the same fixed smile throughout.

The answer, Kenyon then told himself, might lie in Barton's office.

But how to get access?

The rooms for dealers and croupiers were on the ground floor, at the back of the building, beyond the kitchens. The half-dozen rooms for Barton and his associates, on the other hand, were on the third floor, over the second gaming room. They were approached by their own elevator and their own entrance corridor. Kenyon had a small room here too, with his name and title on the door, although it was hardly used, and never unless others were around. Like many other things, it existed primarily as part of his front to the outside world.

How to get access to the third floor – and Barton's office – when no one else was around? That was the problem. And, it seemed, an insurmountable one.

Until Barton himself solved it for him.

At two o'clock one morning, after taking a telephone call, Barton told him, sorry, but he needed a lot of breakdowns fast – like in twelve hours' time. Could Kenyon grab a couple of hours' sleep and then work straight through? At least it'd be quiet – nobody about, nothing to distract him from the figures. Why didn't he go home, come back around seven – that'd give him four hours' sleep, seven hours to do the work, plenty long enough, he'd guess. Barton would have the papers waiting on his desk.

Kenyon knew Barton had suggested the sleep to make sure he was fully sobered up – he was OK for chatting to people and carrying out routine tasks, but Barton was talking total con-centration.

Kenyon was back an hour early. Upper and downer drugs were widely available among the dealers. Although he was not normally a drug-taker (except, of course, alcohol), a barbiturate had crashed him to sleep, two amphetamines had him gut-tingling awake.

There was a flask of coffee and a couple of Danish on a tray on his desk – a nice touch, he thought. He checked Barton's note of what was wanted, made a preliminary appraisal of the papers, and decided it was a two to three hour job.

He drank some coffee and spent a half-hour getting the work under way. Only then did he make for Barton's room. Opening the main door was child's play – like the other offices it was secured

40

only by a rudimentary tumbler lock, slipped easily with a piece of plastic. Any real security would be inside.

The room was furnished more like a hotel suite than an office. The desk set against the wall was small and leather-topped, for ornament and the writing of the occasional cheque rather than serious work. Two long sofas faced each other across a large glass coffee-table. There were cabinets for drinks, files and a television set, all disguised to look like French salon furniture. One door led off to a bathroom, another into a small dining-room in which Barton occasionally entertained important visitors.

Kenyon returned to his own room, and took two items from his briefcase. One, a small leather pouch, he placed in his jacket pocket. The other was a block of well-chewed gum, wrapped in foil. He returned to the lift, opened the door, and jammed the 'Open' button with gum. The lift would remain stranded on this floor until he removed the gum. No one should enter the building before eleven or twelve, when daily equipment checks were carried out, but he wanted to feel absolutely safe from disturbance. Now, the only way up was via a back route that involved unlocking several doors. If someone wanted to come to this floor – and it was very unlikely – Kenyon would have plenty of notice: time enough to leave Barton's office, remove the gum, return to his own room.

Back in Barton's room, he checked quickly. Only three items were locked. One was the safe which he found concealed behind an elaborate, gold-framed seascape. A Tann. He looked at it with his ex-cop's eyes. A good make. The men who could open that without a load of equipment and without leaving signs of their visit could be counted on two hands. By no stretch of the imagination would he ever be one of them, even if he practised for twenty years. Forget it!

The other items were the desk and the filing cabinet. The desk looked the easier. First, during World War II in Military Intelligence and then, afterwards, on becoming a policeman, he had learned something about locks. The drawer of this desk had an old standard keyhole, the type that is opened by a small, round, hollow key, the kind known as 'pipe' keys. Some burglars, he knew, carried a selection of them – only a limited number were needed to operate most locks. But, without looking, he knew there were none in the pouch he carried. He dropped to his knees, studied it some more, tested the give in the drawer, decided picking might not be necessary.

He extracted a short length of flat metal rule from the pouch. Then, forcing a small gap between the top of the drawer and the desk frame with hand pressure, he slid in the rule and began to lever gently upwards. When the gap was wide enough he pushed in a folded handkerchief so that it would cushion the wood against tell-tale scratch marks.

The metal forced the drawer down, the desk top up. The last fraction of an inch was the sweaty moment – and then the bolt of the lock was levered clear of its socket, and the drawer swung out clear. He checked for scratches – nothing that looked new or stood out from marks that had accumulated over the years.

Then the contents. There were sheets of paper listing names, symbols against each one. A simple code – some of the marks he recognised. The names were gamblers; the ciphers signified credit worthiness, a gambler's peculiarities – whether he could be induced to drink a lot, should he be offered women, was he worth attention beyond his own spending because he brought in other punters?

Kenyon scanned the papers quickly. He was about to return them and close the drawer when he hesitated. He felt around inside. Something felt wrong. He pulled the drawer free and laid it on the floor. The back panel was built out, providing a three-inch-wide false compartment. It opened on a pair of tiny hinges. Not the world's cleverest hiding place! Inside was a small, flat key. A case? A car? It was too elaborate, too precisely cut for that. A deed box? A left-luggage locker? A safety-deposit box? More likely one of those.

Still, no good to him. If this were a movie, he would make an impression of it – use a piece of soap from the bathroom, a bit of unused gum. Just in case it proved useful later. But he knew that in real life making an impression in such a way and then expecting to have someone produce a key that worked made as much sense as trying to shift an ocean liner with a pair of oars.

He replaced the key and the papers, closed the drawer, again using the rule as a lever, and turned his attention to the filing cabinet.

It had a cylinder lock. This time he would need the tools.

Kenyon had picked up the rudiments of lock-breaking in post-war Europe when he was in the Army. His Military Intelligence sector had used the services of an elderly Austrian burglar who had bought his freedom by offering his skill. Kenyon, fascinated, had spent many free hours with the man. Under the burglar's amused eyes, he had practised hard. The longer he worked at it, the more he had appreciated the vast gap between them. Nevertheless, he had learned some basic techniques.

He could remember the other's lectures, especially the central message. The Austrian repeated it over and over again as Kenyon tried to manipulate the picks on a collection of locks the other had brought to the apartment: 'You are seeing inside the lock with your fingers and your experience . . . Feel your way, picture every part of it in your mind . . . You must be delicate: no strength, just fingertip tension.'

Kenyon had learned many things. The most rudimentary was that you cannot open any lock in the world with fewer than two picks: the bent hairpin or piece of twisted wire is a figment of the thriller writer's imagination. What you need is two bits of metal, thin but strong. Both went into the lock. One lifted the lever that prevents the bolt from moving, the other moved the bolt itself.

That, put simply, was it. The practice, of course, was harder. You might just as well tell someone that all he has to do to fly a helicopter is open the throttle, raise the collective pitch lever, and juggle the stick and rudder controls until it lifts off.

It needed co-ordination, a feeling for the precise moment the one piece of metal took up the tension of the bolt. Then, gently but confidently, a fractional movement of the fingers of the other hand to make the tiny motion that lifted the lever until the tension disappeared. All the time total concentration, but muscles relaxed, fingertips applying just the right pressure, no more. The skills of a good golfer or a racing driver. Except that if you got it wrong, nothing happened. The result wasn't the equivalent of slicing the ball or coming out of the bend too slow. The lock just didn't open. And the distance between success and failure, the gap you had to sense and manipulate by feel, was no thicker than a sheet of paper.

The tools that Kenyon now took from the pouch had come later, in the 1950s after he had left the Army and had joined the police force. They had been hidden in a filthy basement room where an old man had lain dead a week or more before being discovered.

Kenyon had been the policeman who broke open the door, found the body, searched the room. The room contained nothing of value – just a camp bed, a kitchen chair, rotten food, empty bottles, soiled clothing, a pitiful cardboard box of papers and personal belongings.

The post-mortem had revealed a massive coronary and the coroner had decided no inquest was necessary. The incident, such as it was, over, Kenyon had returned to tell the landlord he could clear the room. Standing there alone, breathing in the stink of decay and poverty and death, Kenyon had felt uncontrollable anger at the shittiness of it all. He had lashed out. Clothes crashed to the floor. Kenyon picked up a jacket, thought better of it and was about to let it drop when he felt the stiffness through the material. There were five specially constructed concealed pockets. Because it was such an open-and-shut case and because the jacket was so filthy, no one had given it more than a cursory glance before. Now Kenyon found that the pockets held a collection of tools a child would have recognised – lock-breaking implements. Some picks, three keys reduced to their skeletons (of diminishing worth now – such keys, Kenyon knew, worked only on pre-war locks, though many remained in use), a metal strip, a small screwdriver. It was an incomplete set – no pipe keys, no 'Hobbs' pick' (a device invented by an American of that name, which contained two picking rods joined in one instrument).

To have handed in the tools would have been to provoke crisis where none existed. Kenyon pocketed them. They had lain undisturbed for years until he had found them during the move to his current apartment. Jokingly, he had spent odd moments trying to refamiliarise himself. He remembered Hunter's amusement when he had seen them lying in the open one morning after driving him home.

'So this is how you make the real bucks?' he had laughed. And Kenyon had explained.

Now, in Barton's room, he removed two of the picks. Some of the ones in the pouch looked no more elaborate than stretched metal L-shapes. These two, though, were spring steel, flat, nail-file shape. The pick end of one was again a short L-bar, the other a zig-zag like a steam-rollered corkscrew.

Kenyon wiped his hands, took several deep breaths, and worked the L-pick into the lock. The other pick went in above it.

44

The lock was old, worn. That would help him – the movements would be sloppy, the gaps he needed to find widened by use. It could give him the edge he needed to suceed. Gentle pressure through the fingers of his left hand to apply tension, delicate yet firm wiggling through the fingers of the other. Trying to feel the vibrations inside, to find the exact spots to move the pins into the right position. Nothing. He could have been pressing against a solid wall. He forced himself not to apply greater pressure – *that* would not work, might even break the pick head. He broke off, tried deep breathing again. He knew the trouble: not only lack of practice, but fear he might be disturbed – even though he knew he had taken precautions against that. 'It is at least ten times as difficult under pressure,' he remembered being told. 'That's where your *real* professional shows himself – he can cut out everything except breaking the lock. You can't. Most people can't – never will be able to.'

Kenyon massaged his hands theatrically and picked up the picks again. Despite the heavy drinking and, now, the amphetamine, his hands were steady. Good. If they started to tremble he had real problems. Now again – eyes closed, telling himself he *could* do it, concentrating everything on seeing inside by touch. A little more pressure with the left fingers. Perfect. Gentle movements now. A welling of relief – he could feel it, sense that it was working. A little more, just a little more . . .

The click was as loud as a dropped tray.

He removed the picks carefully, conscious that his mouth was split in a huge grin of relief. He had beaten the bastards! He wanted to shout.

Now to see. There was surprisingly little inside. An unsealed envelope contained pictures of a man Kenyon recognised as a high-ranking London police officer. The pictures had all been taken at the same session and the man shared the bedroom scene with two very young girls, naked except for gym slips, and a soft-drink bottle that was being used on one of them. The letters and the other papers would probably have interested Scotland Yard or the FBI's man at the London Embassy. For several moments anger and nausea made him wonder if he could do anything with them – a bastard like that shouldn't be running free, let alone be operating as a cop. But he knew it was a gesture he dared not risk. He pushed them aside. No help to him.

There was one paper, though. He took frantic notes of its contents before replacing it. Apart from anything else, it told him what the key in the drawer fitted.

It was a copy of the documentation for a safety-deposit box. It included the names of the men who were to be given access. After each name was the note 'Photograph supplied/On file'. Two names were unknown to him – he suspected they were phoney. Without the photographs he could only guess at real identities. But he had no doubts. Barton and George. The third name, though, was real.

Michael Kenyon.

So that was it. Barton must have some convincing story as to why Kenyon's name had to be there. He read on and found it – the box was actually registered under his name. His passport had been used for ID.

Suddenly Barton's scheme was clear. When the fan got hit, he would claim that Kenyon had found out – and had used his access to cream off regular accounts. He would also claim that Kenyon would have been able to doctor figures.

He relocked the cabinet, removed the desk drawer again and extracted the key. It was not yet 7.30 a.m. He needed a copy of the key. He made sure the office looked undisturbed, ungummed the lift, and at eight o'clock was waiting for the opening of a retail locksmith in Edgware Road. The key was copied without question. On his return, he got the cab to drop him ten minutes' walk away from the club.

The club was still deserted. He repeated his jamming of the lift, replaced the key, clumsier with strain this time, making marks around the lock into which he rubbed traces of polish wiped from his shoe until they all but vanished.

Barton arrived at one o'clock, glanced through the figures, said, 'Great,' and took them off to his room.

Although he was sure he had covered all his traces, Kenyon was on edge when he returned to the club that night. He was nervous someone would have spotted a mistake he had overlooked, but it was a routine evening.

Back at his apartment in the early morning, he stared long at the key before hiding it deep in a tub of margarine stored in the refrigerator. It should be safe there until he found a better hiding place.

It could, quite literally, be the key to whether he had a future or not.

He had decided on his move. Barton had set up the safety-deposit box in such a way that it would be easy to convince others that Kenyon had had access to it and had robbed it.

So – that's just what he would do.

CHAPTER FOUR

Two, occasionally three times a week George had an errand.
Late afternoon, after talking to Barton, he would leave the club
and return about ninety minutes later.

Sometimes, if he was in the corridor at the time, Kenyon would
see him hiking the case that he knew must contain the skim.
George was always shadowed by one of the other Americans, and
once Kenyon saw their car pull out of the mews with a third man at
the wheel.

This afternoon, a week after his raid on Barton's office, Kenyon
had telephoned in to the club, saying he was having a tooth fixed
and would be in later. In case anyone checked, he had already
been to a dentist earlier in the day who, reluctant to let him leave
untreated, had cleaned out and replaced an old filling before having
his receptionist take the payment in cash.

Kenyon could still taste the amalgam and his tongue and jaw
were heavy with lignocaine as he sat across the street from the
safety-deposit company whose address had been on the papers in
Barton's cabinet.

His car was a Mini that he had picked up early that morning
from a rental company. He sat in the front passenger seat as
though waiting for the driver to return. It was a foul morning,
dirty grey light, drizzle that gusted through the window he was
forced to keep open to stop the car from misting up. A hoarding
across the street urged him to smoke Consulate cigarettes –
'Cool as a mountain stream'. One next to it told him that
Maltesers were 'Chocolates with the less fattening centres'. He
wished he had brought something to read. After two hours he
was wondering whether he should move the car across the
square to a new spot. Not once did he consider leaving. The take
had been exceptionally heavy the previous night; it was three

48

days since George had undertaken his last errand. He *had* to make a deposit today.

What Kenyon needed to know was, was this the genuine transit place for the skim? Or was this address a false trail or even a depository for something else?

Kenyon missed the arrival. He had decided to pull across to another spot and had had to struggle round the ungainly long gear stick into the driver's seat. He looked up to check the road was clear, and there was the 1965-registered black three-litre Rover. Despite the drizzle, there was no mistaking it. It was parked right outside the entrance. He checked his watch. George emerged five and a half minutes later – just long enough to be admitted, gain access to the box, empty the case's contents, and return to the street.

Kenyon watched the Rover leave, and then pulled out straightaway. Another car was forced to brake violently, but he did not notice. His mind was already on other things.

He returned to the club that evening, making great show of not chewing on one side of his mouth at dinner. One of the Americans removed a mouthful of false teeth, and explained he had had all the real ones extracted before leaving the US to work in Cuba: 'It was the safest thing, know whatta mean?'

Kenyon stared at the gleaming dentures and absently agreed. It was proving hard to concentrate on anything other than the plan that was forming in his mind.

He had already made his decision – at the right moment he was going to steal the skim and then he was going to get the hell out of London and England. Just how and where to, he did not know yet. But, though vital, these were technicalities. The important thing was the decision itself.

Like all men he had often made decisions that had then just evaporated away. Whether that would have happened this time had not Hunter delivered another warning was something he often wondered. Maybe not. The fears had not lessened. And, as for his marriage, after his last meeting with Pamela he had settled into a terrible flat resignation: they were finished. By not accepting this, he was simply torturing himself, nurturing what he now saw as a doomed obsession with her.

Still, it was Hunter who clinched it. He insisted on giving Kenyon a lift home, saying he looked beat.

'Come on, pal,' he said, taking Kenyon's arm after the car stopped. 'Should've gone easier on that painkiller. I'll help you to the elevator.' He nodded back to the driver. 'Two minutes,' he said.

He spoke fast as they entered the building.

'Just listen,' he said. 'I'm saying this and my owing's over. The heat's on. I'm going to Spain in two days, the big wedding, you know the one?' Kenyon did. A Hollywood star was marrying a famous matador, the papers had been running the romance for weeks. 'The word is that I won't get back in. You Brits'll say I'm undesirable or something.' He anticipated Kenyon's unvoiced question. 'I could stay put – our friends say they won't fuck with me while I'm here. But stopping me coming back in. That's different.'

They reached the elevator and Hunter leaned across and punched the button. 'So why go? Some people – you know who I mean? – some people say, "So the Brits gotta make a gesture, let them make it if it gets the Feds off everybody's back." '

'And you're the gesture?'

'Right.'

The lift arrived, and Hunter waved him inside. 'I'll ride up with you.'

He continued immediately. 'And me? Tell you the truth, it's no big fucking deal. I'm getting homesick. This way I get to make people happy and I get to be away from the action when it all blows up. Which –' he turned towards Kenyon for emphasis – 'which is gonna happen. You're still a lucky guy. The man up there must love you. First, you get hit and you don't end up in a box but you make me owe you. Now with me being kept out, nobody's gonna want any waves. So my guess'd be that Barton'll ease off, not for ever – the man's too deep in for that – but for a while. Six months maybe.'

The lift arrived. Hunter waved him out, but remained, holding the life on the 'Open' button.

'You reckon six months?' asked Kenyon.

'Maybe more,' Hunter said. He moved his hand down the control panel, punched 'Ground'. 'But maybe less.' He brought his face up to the doors as they started to close. He drew the index finger of his gloved left hand sharply across his throat. His eyes bulged and he made an ugly sound.

Kenyon stared, shocked. It was only afterwards he remembered the gesture from Hunter's last film. The American gave him a tight smile.

'And then, believe me, there's gonna be blood in the fucking street.'

Over the years Kenyon had given and taken many favours. They were a commodity like sugar or crude or coffee beans. You could sell them, or buy them, or (like Kenyon) barter them. You gave a favour; one day, one week, one year later you collected.

A prisoner awaiting trial wanted police bail, he got it unopposed; one day, you wanted the word on someone else, he gave it. For Kenyon it had started when he was a policeman, continued after he joined the loan company. Old friends, or contacts supplied by old friends, gave him police files or ran down car numbers; in return, if they wanted a cheap loan they got one, or maybe they needed a special deal on a television or a car – he'd got contacts there who owed him. And so, on and on it went, a never-closing circle, as big as man's need to cut through the crap of the system.

You didn't even have to know everyone else in the network. The right name was enough. 'I'm a friend of Mr Johnson in C11,' (naming the police section that dealt with the most serious crime), or 'Charlie Gray in Romford said I should call . . .' It wasn't even necessary to give your right name, just some way you could be contacted with the answer if need be. It was the man whose name you used who would owe the favour (and you might have to wait until it was checked back with him); you would then owe him. Nor would anyone be crass enough to want to know *why* you needed it. Kenyon supposed that if someone gave an address and saw later that the man living there had been blown apart starting his car, he might be more wary next time it came to answering a question. But even that wasn't certain. For the other important thing about the network (although that was too specific a word for something so nebulous) was that who the members were and what they did was unimportant except in that it gave them access to information that was tradable. A man or woman might, thus, be a chief superintendent of police or a safe-blower, a bank manager or a whore, a loan-company manager (as Kenyon was) or a barman.

Newspapermen have always been a part of such networks. Kenyon had links with three. There was a gossip columnist, who had provided him with unpublished (and unpublishable) rumours on some of the individuals who wanted to borrow money from Kenyon's previous company; in return Kenyon had filtered back dirt he came across. There was a City journalist, with whom he had a similar working arrangement on company matters. And there was an ageing news desk man who for twenty years had worked a night shift no one else wanted. Kenyon had been introduced to the man in a pub and for reasons that neither had ever tried to rationalise there had been immediate rapport. Perhaps, he reflected, it was because although they could smell 'loser' in the other they also saw in their companion potentials greater than had ever been realised. They met about six times a year, sometimes just for a drink, sometimes for a meal, always in the same basement pub restaurant off Fleet Street. They always finished off with large Cognacs before staggering out into the mid-afternoon, feeling (until the glow of each other's company faded) like men who could – and one day would – achieve everything. The man's name was Nolan, and the favours they exchanged were out of friendship, and mostly they were small which was good because big favours and friendship rest uneasily together.

It was Nolan who Kenyon called a few days later. 'Can I use the library some time, no rush?' he asked. There was nothing unusual in such a request; he had made it several times before.

'Sunday's the best night, late, if you want quiet,' said Nolan, just as he had on those other occasions.

The library served a daily tabloid and its Sunday companion and was, thus, in use seven days a week, 9 a.m. until 4 a.m. the next morning. But Monday's papers were small, there was less news on Sundays, fewer librarians were on duty and all but one left at 10 p.m. Kenyon arranged to be there at nine – 'We'll have a jar,' said Nolan, 'and then I'll take you in and leave you alone.'

For once, Nolan was preoccupied during their drink. There had been a plane crash in Holland and, with the deadline for the second edition nearing, copy from the paper's own reporter was overdue. Nevertheless, Nolan had insisted on them going to the office pub after arranging he should be called the second anything happened. There was nothing he could do that his deputy couldn't handle at least as well, but his mind was back in the office and he started every time the phone behind the bar rang. In a rare and frightening moment of insight, Kenyon saw that, for all Nolan's complaints about being overlooked for newspaper politic reasons, the man was already operating at the limits of his capabilities.

At 10.15 p.m. Kenyon was at work in the newspaper library. Its backbone was its cuttings files. Twelve, fifteen hours a day library staff perused and cut newspapers and magazines. The cuttings were stuck on pieces of paper and dated and filed and cross-filed. A scholarly piece on oil-tanker trade from *The Economist* went into a brown envelope marked 'Oil' and was cross-referenced to 'Shipping' and (most practically) with a bulging series of envelopes marked 'Niarchos' where pieces from *The Times* and the *National Enquirer* rubbed shoulders and from which detail was extracted by reporters with equal abandon. The files, in fact, contained it all. What they did not, could not, do was assess accuracy: guide the writer using them as to whether X had actually been in that Paris club at that time, or whether Y had indeed said 'So f*** her' about his latest wife, or whether Z had indeed made that memorable offer to a film starlet. But that did not matter. As long as it was on record (and could later be shown to be so), and provided there was no known libel action involved over it, a quote, a 'fact', could provide perfect ingredients for any article.

At this time on a Sunday night the men who wrote such articles were at home or in the pub or the Press Club; the articles themselves were written. The librarian on duty accepted an assurance from Nolan that Kenyon knew how to use the library, and left for the canteen.

The files were stored in row after row of floor-to-ceiling grey steel filing cabinets. The system was simple after you had used it a few times, as Kenyon had. Subjects were in one section, places in another, individuals a third, companies a fourth and so on. Within each section entries were alphabetical. On previous occasions it was individuals or companies that had interested Kenyon. This time he looked for the file that would cover people who vanished. He found it at his second attempt, under 'Missing Persons'. There were four fat envelopes of clippings, more than he had expected, and he carried them to one of the tables that ran the length of the room alongside the rows of files.

He worked solidly for almost two hours, leaving the desk only to walk the few yards to the nearest hot-drinks machine. He concentrated on the files with total absorption, often leaving half-

53

full cups of coffee to get cold before fetching yet further replacements. Although note-taking made him nervous, he was more concerned about not remembering the important points and he covered pages of an unlined pad in ball-point pen.

Later, back at his apartment, he reclined in a leather easy chair, his feet on a stool, and read through his notes, struggling to see what message they contained. Unable to bear the silence, he had found a foreign radio station broadcasting music. The signal kept drifting, distorting the sound of Sonny and Cher singing 'I Got You Babe', but he quickly ceased to notice.

Deciding to steal the money and run was one thing. Staying free when people were looking for you was another. He knew he had to vanish completely. But how? How easy would it be? Was it even possible? What were the problems he had to face?

Before coming up with any answers, he knew that first he had to understand the magnitude of what was involved. He had to plan his actions like a military exercise. In the Army, then the police force and finally at the loan company, he had seen how failing to anticipate one small problem could destroy the most carefully organised scheme – correction, *particularly* the most organised scheme.

Although as a policeman he had dealt with missing persons – a child who failed to come home, a wife who packed her bags when she couldn't take any more – he had not until now realised the sheer scale of it. Estimates of the number who vanished every year in Britain varied, but nine thousand – one every hour of every single day – seemed to be a fair figure. That was the number *reported* missing to some authority, like the police. If anything, he decided sipping at his Scotch, that figure had to be an *under-*estimate; a lot of people must go and never be reported.

What you could conclude, he decided, was that the nine thousand represented the people someone was looking for. Of those, it seemed, forty or forty-five out of every hundred were traced or reappeared of their own accord, the rest were never seen again.

Of the whole, about forty per cent were estimated to commit suicide – estimated, because not all the bodies were found. In London alone thirty corpses that could not be identified were found each year.

More men, he had noted from one article, chose voluntary

disappearance as a 'prelude to a new life'. And he had written in extra large numerals '39.9' – almost his age, and, it seemed, the average age of men who disappeared.

He had noted names of two famous missing people: Victor Grayson and Judge Crater.

Grayson, once a brilliant young MP, vanished in London in 1920. He fought in World War I and was severely wounded at Passchendaele. His wife died at the end of the war. Grayson, who was deeply attached to her, suffered depression. But in 1920 he began to set in motion a political comeback. He was in a hotel bar one day, sipping a drink, when suddenly he hurried out into the street calling, 'I'll be back in a minute.' That was the last seen of him – although there were rumours, most notably that he had gone to Australia, where he later died. Fourteen years after he vanished, the British Chancellor of the Exchequer took the unprecedented step of appealing publicly for him to reveal himself and claim the wartime disability pension that had amassed.

The other man was Judge Joseph Crater, a Manhattan Supreme Court Judge. He was last seen on an August day in 1930 when he stepped into a taxi mid-town.

The lesson from both of them: you *could* vanish off the face of the earth even if people really were looking for you and even if your face was well known. Although Crater was declared legally dead in 1937, New York police still checked out tips, of which there had been thousands over the years – Crater had been spotted prospecting in California, working in Africa, travelling in the Adriatic.

So what, Kenyon asked himself, did he know now? He flipped the pad and wrote down his main thoughts, just as he always had as a policeman wrestling with a case. There were as many reasons for disappearing as there were people who did it, though fear and a burning desire to start afresh (his motives) rated high. But that wasn't the important point. The important point, surely, was that over five thousand people every year – he wrote the figure large and ringed it – vanished and were never found. Conclusion: vanishing was not that hard. But the moment he had the thought he knew it wasn't true: the figures might be accurate, but the premise was wrong. He scored a heavy line through the '5,000'. It was *not* easy to vanish *if* someone was looking for you seriously enough. The majority of those five thousand, he was sure, were

Mr and Mrs Nobody. The police might note their names, but they would do nothing to help find them because it was not their job to do so unless there were clear signs of crime or of foul play. If someone wanted to walk out, that was their own business and nobody else's. So anyone wanting to trace them could ask one of the papers to publish an appeal for them (one paper, the *News of the World*, had a regular column for the purpose) or ask the Salvation Army, which had a department which helped look for missing relatives, but if the person wanted to stay lost they were of very limited use. A private detective just *might* be more effective – but how many searchers could afford to go to those lengths?

Staying lost if someone was looking for you *seriously* enough was almost impossible – the files testified to that over and over again. And people would be looking for him. Very, very hard.

The truth was, he realised, we are tied to our past in so many ways – and those looking for us only had to follow the cords. We are tied economically – unless we had wealth stashed away we had to work. That meant we needed papers of various kinds (a lead in itself) or the kind of work where no one asked for documents (which was a lead of a different sort). We are bound by other pieces of paper – from the moment we are born we become files and case numbers. We need them to travel, visit a doctor, drive a car, borrow a library book, obtain a charge card, open a bank account. And those acts in themselves create more files and give unto us more numbers. Every one of them is a link from the past we are struggling to lose to the present we are trying to live and the future we hope to occupy.

It might be difficult to find missing people, but the links were many. In practical terms the effort might be too great. But Kenyon knew that if he disappeared, *no* effort would be too much for the people who would search for him. Anyone who took Mob money had to be dealt with as an example.

He remembered overhearing two of the Americans discussing a news magazine piece about an informer who had given evidence to a Senate Inquiry into Mob power. The piece said that the Justice Department was giving the man a new identity and relocating him, using all their resources. One American had read it aloud, and the other had made only one comment. Kenyon could hear it still. 'They can give the guy a new fucking head, turn him into a broad and stick him on Mars, but he's still gonna look like Swiss cheese.'

Kenyon wrote a list of problem points:

LOOKS

DOCUMENTATION

ECONOMIC

He paused, and added a fourth:

PSYCHOLOGICAL

He stared at the words for a long time.

The ties were not just pieces of paper and possessions. They went beyond that. They were everything we are and have been. The way we look, a thousand habits, our career capabilities. The ties of places we love, of people we value, our hobbies and drinking habits. Our desires, our aberrations, our needs . . . Any one of them might provide a lead to someone searching for us.

So that, he concluded, was the minus side. Those were the problems he would have to face and overcome if he really was going to vanish.

And the other side, the plus? Was there one? He stood and walked over to the window. It was a half-hour after dawn, but the light was thin on the deserted street. He lifted his glass and was surprised at how little he had drunk of it. He drained the amount that remained, more from habit than need for once, and walked through to make coffee.

Yes, there were pluses. A lot of them. Many men must be found because they made stupid, often elementary mistakes. They had no knowledge of what was involved, what to do, what to avoid, so they acted instinctively, and instincts were often wrong. They ran to old places or old friends, not seeing the obviousness of such an action. Or, seeing and avoiding it, they ran for the unknown and the unfamiliar, not realising until it was too late that there they stood out like nuns in a crap game.

Kenyon knew how the police set about seeking a wanted man. The questions they asked, the leads they could follow . . . Other pursuers could only follow the same routines – though if they asked questions they could make certain they got answers.

He took his coffee and the pad through into the bedroom, kicked off his shoes and stretched out fully clothed on the bed.

So what did it all add up to?

He ran through the problems: looks, documentation. He could do something about those. Economic: the safety-deposit vault and the key were important there.

And the fourth, psychological? He would have to completely destroy and bury the man he was, drop all contact with his present and past life, quit all his friends, abandon his possessions, become someone completely different.

Like dying and being reborn. The thought was frightening and exciting. Dying and reborn. The words echoed in his mind as he drifted into sleep.

CHAPTER FIVE

It was not the ceremony he remembered, nor the church, for all that it was a fine Norman building with great wooden door and walls covered with early medieval paintings.

Nor was it the hillsides, lush with new spring grass, on the drive from the church to the hotel for the reception.

No, it was walking into the already crowded room where the wedding party was to take place, and saying loudly, 'Someone give me a pint, God I need a drink,' and everyone laughing, though Mary nervously and saying, 'Oh, Michael,' in a way that was resigned and understanding as she hugged on his arm.

That was May 1944, but over twenty years later it all returned to Kenyon as he stared down at the black-and-white photographs that he had spread out over the dining-table. There were seven of them, all wedding scenes. The couple outside the church, the couple with the best man and bridesmaids outside the chuch, the couple with parents outside the church, the couple with all the family outside the church, the couple cutting the cake, the bride with bridesmaids, the bridegroom with the best man.

It was 5 a.m. on the day after his visit to the newspaper library. Earlier, after destroying the notes he had taken, he had begun to list mentally all the things he had to do now that he had finally decided to vanish. At this hour it was impossible to start any of them. Yet, filled with restless energy, he had needed to do something. This was the result. At the back of a cupboard in the unused, second bedroom were two suitcases stuffed with personal belongings. Photographs, letters, postcards, theatre programmes, pieces torn from magazines . . .

The first case lay open on the floor. The contents had been stuffed inside haphazardly. Kenyon had removed several handfuls, and they now lay on the table. He had just begun to work through them. The reason, he told himself, was that it was wise to find, and then destroy, anything that might provide any lead to him after he disappeared. There was a deeper reason, although he did not admit it to himself: he wanted to relive the past, to see the present in a light that would harden his resolve for what he was about to do.

He had already tossed aside several things, but the photographs held him. He left them lying there while he refilled his glass, and then he stared down at them, feeling a confusion brought on by too many emotions. Was that him? He knew it was, of course, but the man was a stranger. L. P. Hartley had said that, 'the past is a foreign country'; truer, Kenyon thought, to say that the past was different people. The face was so young. No lines, no worry etched on those thin, slightly sardonic features. Yet there must have been worries. It was 1944 and in a few days he was off to war. And here he was with his new bride. What was he thinking? How did he feel? All Kenyon could remember was, 'Someone give me a pint, God I need a drink.'

He peered at his bride in her dress of white velvet – borrowed, he remembered that. She had lifted the veil from her face, but the edges had been blown back by the wind and the camera had caught her face creased in mock anger. He reached for another picture, showing her with her bridesmaids and he focused on her sister – Katharine ('with a "K", like Katharine Hepburn,' though they all knew it was Catherine with a 'C'). She wore a long pale-blue dress with a Juliet hat, and he doubted it was borrowed. She was twenty-one then, a year older than Mary, three older than him and she lived and worked away from home in Chester, where the streets were now thick with American GIs, and when she came home it was always laden with cigarettes and gum. Like the bridegroom in the careful, over-tailored black suit, they were strangers.

He remembered the day he had first met them. Friday, 1 September 1939. The day German troops moved into Poland. By 6 a.m. Warsaw was being bombed. But as the news spread by word of mouth many refused to believe it. Despite all that had gone before, it was unexpected by many, especially in Kenyon's home where his father had remained convinced that Chamberlain had saved Europe from war.

When the news was confirmed – and it became known that official evacuation of mothers and children had begun – no one could doubt war was near. Kenyon's mother had reacted by comforting her husband, 'Don't worry, it'll be all right, dear,' which was her routine reaction to any crisis, home or international.

The thirteen-year-old Michael Kenyon heard all this when he arrived home, glorying in the excitement. It was already shaping up as an exceptionally good day – school had been dismissed early, and where there had been a dull routine there was now a buzz of charged activity. The shop was open, but no one was buying and a group was gathered around Kenyon's father in fiery discussion which he, with his well-known anti-Churchill views, was clearly losing.

Kenyon's mother was ironing as though to prove that whatever the Germans did or didn't do a housewife's life in Shropshire had to go on as normal. His brother, Frederick, called Kenyon into his bedroom and told him, 'Now they can't stop me.' They both knew what he meant – Frederick would join the Air Force, thus in one action achieving excitement, fulfilling his dream to be a flyer, quitting helping in the shop which he hated (but which was his duty as he was often reminded), and going forth to support his country with all the glory and sacrifice that implied.

Foolishly, he then went to break the news to, first, Kenyon's mother and then – when he came in response to the screams – to Kenyon's father. Kenyon himself was got out of the way a half-hour into the fight by being sent to deliver a bicycle bought by the new woman who had come to look after the vicar and his bedridden wife.

The vicarage was on the edge of the village, isolated by high privet and expanses of lawn that came into use only twice a year for tea parties in aid of missions to Africa. The drive forked at the side of the house, one branch to the front door, the other – clearly marked by a sign nailed to a tree – to the back and the 'tradesmen's entrance'. Kenyon pushed the bicycle up the right fork. It was a girl's model Raleigh, and Kenyon had strict instructions: it was for the daughter's fifteenth birthday the next day and it had to be hidden inside the garden shed near the rear entrance to the house. No one would be there at this time.

On that, his instructions were wrong. A girl was framed in the doorway when he turned from covering the cycle.

'I thought you were a burglar,' she said, no fear in her voice. 'But it's the bike isn't it, the bike for Mary. Mum said someone was delivering it.'

She was a silhouette until he emerged into the daylight. 'I don't know what you mean,' he said, feeling he had to keep up a pretence that there was no bike, so the secret could remain.

'Don't be silly,' she said. 'It's not for me, it's for Mary. I know all about it. It's her birthday tomorrow. She's fifteen.' She dropped her eyes theatrically so that they embraced her breasts. 'I don't look fifteen do I?' she said. And, before the red gathered in his face, she spun towards the house and the open rear door. 'Come on,' she said, 'you look like you could do with a glass of lemonade,' entering the house and leaving him no alternative but to follow or look foolish.

The door led into a scullery. He waited there, among the milk bottles and piles of clothes waiting to be washed, while she fetched a jug from the pantry and poured two glasses. She drank, standing less than an arm's reach from him, and she played her lips and tongue around the rim of the glass, all the while her eyes fixed on him.

He felt the charge, and didn't know what to do or say or think except he realised that she was baiting him.

'Well,' she said at last, again looking down at herself, 'do I look fifteen?'

His breath stopped then and he began a step forward, but she was already moving, spinning, stepping sideways, dancing towards the door, which was opening again. 'It's the boy with the *groceries*, you know, the ones you *ordered*, Mum,' she said to convey who he was and why he was there in improvised code to the woman who entered.

'Oh, and you've given him lemonade. Good girl.' The woman progressed into the scullery, weighted and half-hidden with shopping bags. 'It'll get worse now,' she said out of her preoccupation to both and neither of them. A girl followed her, equally weighed down. Where the girl who had taunted Kenyon was tall and well-built with full breasts and hips, this one was slight, tomboyish, pretty enough, but to a thirteen-year-old just another girl. 'This is Mary,' said the woman. Kenyon made 'Hello' noises, but all he was conscious of was the elder girl still watching him, her eyes mocking.

So much seemed to happen from that day. Until then time had been endless. He remembered the feel of hours that would never pass as you waited for some special event to happen. It was the slowness of everyday time that was the enemy, not as later the ever increasing speed of it. But the four years after 1939 became a compression of events between which there seemed hardly any gaps. Frederick joined the Royal Air Force and got his wings. Kenyon's father forgot his opposition and strutted in the pride of him. His mother kept a scrapbook – anything and everything about the RAF and planes and flying. The news of the war got worse, but for Michael it still had all the makings of a Good Time.

Kenyon found new friends. Evacuees from the bomb-torn industrial Midlands and Merseyside, even exotic foreign children separated from their parents as they had fled the Nazis, and now brought together in the old Manor House. Many were townees, and he delighted in the easy superiority he brought to their contacts for this was his home ground and he knew all the places to go, the things to do.

Even at school, where he had always been more a plodder than a front runner, things went well. His relations with evacuees had awakened interest in geography and history and, most of all, languages. He had always been a natural mimic – as a tiny boy he had quickly learned that it was a talent that attracted attention and he had worked on it. Now he found his memory was above normal too. The combination together with his enthusiasm – cockiness even – made teachers declare him a 'natural linguist'. His School Certificate examinations neared, but it was now generally agreed by all, including his parents, that Higher School Certificate and then university would follow. If only, of course, the war didn't drag on too long.

And then Frederick died. Not in combat, not from German guns over some foreign field, but in England on a peaceful afternoon. He was on a training flight – no detail ever given – and his aircraft had crashed into a hillside. No other plane involved; weather conditions perfect; no cause ever notified. Kenyon could not remember the news arriving; his mind had completely blotted it out. What remained with him was the picture, later, of his parents sitting side by side, hands clasped, but eyes focused down on the floor. Every so often his father would open the fist of his free hand

and stare at the ring it contained. A signet ring, buckled and twisted, and a gap where it had been cut off Frederick's finger. Kenyon had it now, and without looking at it could see the elaborate inscription 'FSK' – Frederick Stanley Kenyon – that had survived the impact, but with one terrible, deep, obliterating scratch right through it.

At the funeral several young men in their blue uniforms made awkward conversation with his parents. Kenyon's strongest thought was astonishment that these were all his brother's friends and that he did not know them or anything about them. After years of growing up together, in which nothing was kept secret from each other, his brother had entered a different world of which he had no knowledge.

He neither cried, nor mourned, and he would not speak of his brother. For a time, Frederick's room remained as it had always been, but Kenyon never entered it. Nor did he take any of his belongings. It was not as though Frederick had not died, but as though he had never been. His mother tried to talk to him and he listened and said nothing; then a teacher spoke and he listened and said, 'Yes, sir,' in all the right places. The local doctor was enlisted, but all that really concerned him was, 'Is he eating all right?' and when he was assured Kenyon was, he said, 'He'll grow out of it, you'll see,' and it was left.

Kenyon's father, far from cursing the war for his loss, turned from a dove into a hawk. His hated Churchill became his hero; bombing was too good for *them*; victory was to be bought at any price. After all, though it was not said, he had already given his elder son; whatever the total cost the Allies had to pay it could not be too great.

He threw himself into every war-related activity that he could: Home Guard, raising money, organising the collection of foxglove leaves that were sent away for medicinal use. And then he was ill. Not fear-of-dying ill but just too ill to do much more than get up, exist through the basics and go back to bed. It was 1943 and Kenyon was seventeen. There was no real discussion about the need for him to leave school and work in the shop. It was just taken for granted that it would happen because it had to happen. He neither fought it, nor cursed it. One teacher, an old man who had grown younger in his excitement at discovering Kenyon's ear for languages, tried to talk to them, but his words meant nothing.

They could have been in one of the languages he taught for all Kenyon's parents' understanding.

And so, in the April of 1943, Kenyon found himself selling ironmongery and bicycles, a sideline which had almost overtaken the main business. His father looked into the shop every day, though only for minutes. But Kenyon needed no help. The shop was a machine that turned over almost by itself, and over the years he had absorbed what little knowledge he needed. The main thing apart from knowing where everything was kept was being there and adopting the right tone for each customer – a touch of deference or a tone of matiness, perhaps – or when selling a bike maybe a hint that this model might be *too* good, *too* expensive. He did not hate it; that conveyed too clear an emotion. He endured it. At home he could not, would not, complain. To have done so would have been to tempt his mother into opening floodgates of self-pitying truths about his brother's death and his father's illness. Just two things sustained him: one foreign evacuee who had lost more than he ever could and who endured more than he would ever have to. And Mary. Small, pretty, tomboy Mary.

It was Katharine's presence that had drawn him back to the vicarage. The first time, still at school, he had made the excuse that his father wanted to check the bike was all right. She had continued to goad his adolescent emotions; had even as the months progressed taught him to French kiss and let him touch her breasts, but only through her blouse and always with her in command and control.

Then she went away, to do war work in Chester at the telephone exchange. By 1943 that city was full of GIs who swaggered through the packed narrow streets in their smooth, beautifully tailored uniforms, and for Katharine adolescents were left way behind.

After his father's illness, after leaving school, Kenyon continued to return to the vicarage, encouraged by Mary's mother. They came from Manchester, and Mary's father was at sea. Even a seventeen-year-old boy could see that what Mary's mother wanted was a man – if only a boy man – around the house. And he, for his part, was happy to sit there on many evenings, joining in card games and listening to a wind-up gramophone and – always – at nine o'clock the news.

After a time he and Mary kissed too and she let him stroke her breasts which were very small. Later she let him touch her between the legs. And he did all this and it excited him because he was a teenage boy but there was no more in it. One Sunday afternoon, in the shadow of a hedgerow, she let him go all the way. The build-up was long and staged. By now she let him touch her naked breasts without argument, but there were ritual pleadings before his hand was allowed to drop lower. Even more before she consented to touch him. Today he argued and wheedled and pleaded and, finally, she lay on her back, her skirt high, and allowed him to insert himself. 'You'll take it out in time?' she asked over and over again. Her tightness and his excited fear made him come almost immediately, and he lay slumped on her, praying that he had moved to withdraw fast enough. Hadn't he been warned so many times that one drop smaller than you could see could make a girl pregnant?

For her things changed then, but he did not see that except in retrospect many months later. 'You *do* love me?' she asked afterwards, and he said, 'Yes,' and then, when he saw that wasn't enough, 'Of course, I do,' because he knew it was expected of him. She needed the pretence to persuade herself that she was not 'cheap'. Yielding your virginity for love was different from doing so for base animal feelings, which girls didn't have anyway.

Mary's mother sat with the vicar's wife every Tuesday evening, and Kenyon and Mary took to going to bed then. For reasons he never understood she insisted on using Katharine's room. It was always quick; they were never away from the living-room for more than twenty minutes. The ritual was always the same. His exortations were followed by her grudging agreement – 'But we must be quick.' (Didn't girls *enjoy* it? He was sure Katharine did.) Except for her knickers they remained fully clothed. There was minimal foreplay. They made love on top of the covers, and afterwards she went to the bathroom and wiped herself (for he always withdrew; the only way he could have obtained French letters was to steal them from his father's drawer or ask for them at the barber's, one too risky, the other too much for his teenage courage). She always asked, 'You *do* love me?' and he always answered the same. And, back downstairs, they continued listening to the wireless or playing card games until her mother returned at precisely two minutes past ten. The relationship was a heady one that more and more dominated his life. It was not just the sex, though for an adolescent boy it was a potent ingredient. But more than that, there was none of the tension that existed, even in the silences, at home. He liked Mary's mother, she managed to treat him as both a boy and an adult: the child was satisfied with treats, the man by the way she hung on to his words and asked his advice.

She usually returned home the same way after her Tuesday evenings. She left the vicarage by the front door and walked around the house to the rear. By this time, Kenyon and Mary were always back downstairs, but they heard her feet on the gravel path long before she reached the door.

On this particular Tuesday the vicar cut short his meeting because his wife had been more ill than usual. He was back by nine, an hour earlier than normal, and as it was raining hard he insisted that Mary's mother should return home through the house without going outside. She must have come up the stairs in those vital very few minutes when Kenyon's being was closed to everything except the *need*. Mary did not scream or even speak, nor move anything but her eyes. He turned his head and followed them. Her mother's face was impassive. Minutes later, downstairs, all she said was, 'I think perhaps you'd better go now, Michael.'

He did not sleep that night. The following day Mary's mother arrived while he was working in the shop. She spent an hour with his mother. Nothing was said until after supper when his mother cleared the table and told his father, 'Well, I'll leave it to you.' His father waited until she had closed the door, then he fetched a bottle of whisky – *the* bottle of whisky – from the sideboard and poured two small measures to which he added water from the jug on the table.

He handed one to Michael. The boy had drunk it once before, at a christening party, and knew he did not like it, but he sipped and concentrated on not coughing. He knew his father meant it to be significant. 'You're a silly young bugger,' he said at last. 'Still, no more than most.'

Kenyon took a second sip and was grateful for its warmth. It did not seem as if it was going to be too bad.

'Some'd say you ought to wait, but this damn war changes everything. She's a nice girl, though, and you could have chosen worse. Much worse.' And, as though exhausted by the emotional effort of his speech, Kenyon's father opened the door and called for his wife.

He poured her a port, and added a dash to Kenyon's glass and his own. And only as they all raised their glasses in unision did Kenyon realise what they were both saying.

He had resolved to tell first Mary and then them that they were all mistaken – he was sorry, but he was not serious, he did not intend to get married to her now or later. It had an unreal quality; it just could not be happening. He went to the vicarage the next day, but they had gone away – two weeks, the vicar said, while his wife was in hospital – to stay with a sister. It seemed best to wait until she returned before confronting his parents, but then there was more news. His uncle, his mother's unmarried elder brother, too old for military service, had been bombed out. He was coming to take over Frederick's room; he could run things in the shop. Michael could go back to his studies – not university, of course, not now. But there was the Tech. He could study to be an accountant, like Sam, a neighbour's son, who was almost the same age and who had got deferment to continue his studies.

But Kenyon did not want deferment. When his conscription papers arrived, he used the one weapon he knew was invincible: Frederick's death. '*He* didn't refuse to go,' he exclaimed. '*He* knew there was a job to be done. If I didn't go I couldn't live with myself again.' He said it to them, and he said it to her. The clichés did not change, but he varied the tone in which he said them – forcefully to his parents, regretfully to her.

The end of 1943 was a good time to be called up. Throughout the year the German successes had gone into reverse. El Alamein and the Allied occupation of North Africa in 1942 had been followed by Stalingrad, and in September Italy had surrendered unconditionally. The end of the war still seemed a long way away, but the tide had turned. People were no longer afraid of what would happen, but impatient for the moment when victory would come.

It was against this backdrop that Kenyon was called up into the Royal Army Service Corps, completed his intital training, transferred to Scotland for motorised training, and because it all seemed very dull volunteered for a special mission.

His new company of the RASC was part of an airborne division, and the training took place on Salisbury Plain. In May 1944,

Kenyon was given 'fourteen days embarkation leave prior to overseas posting'. Somehow he had never told Mary nor her mother nor his parents that he was not going to marry her. Once he was away, it just did not seem to matter. Because of the distances between them, he and Mary met only once for a weekend so filled with her emotions that he had not dared speak. They exchanged letters, three of hers to every one of his. His letters were prosaic where hers were full of romantic vows and hopes and plans but he said nothing in them to diminish, let alone end, the relationship. And when everyone seemed to believe it was the only right and proper thing to get married before he went overseas, he let events carry him along. It became not just the easiest and kindest thing to do, but the *only* thing. He had ceased thinking of the future. Marriage was for today, not for ever. Tomorrow, like Frederick, he might be dead.

They needed a special licence, but that was not difficult. He had put it on the mantelpiece and on the day someone had to return from the church to fetch it before they could be married.

What else did he remember? The cake – the icing was made with crushed sugar and powdered milk and the colouring was a Reckitt's blue bag, like his mother used for whitening curtains, so you had to be careful what bits you ate.

On this early morning twenty years later he lifted the photographs one by one and stared at them carefully before placing them one on top of the other in the 'sorted' pile on the side of the table.

'Someone give me a pint, God I need a drink.' That was what he remembered.

CHAPTER SIX

The house was ten minutes' walk from Turnham Green underground station, nearing the western end of the District line. It was the third he had tried and the first that looked a real possibility.

He had found the address in the advertisement columns of the local newspaper – 'Bed and breakfast, professional gentlemen only.' The other two had been advertised in similar terms, but both had been unsuitable on sight: one had a sign outside reading 'Greystones Private Guest House', the other a notice in the window saying 'B & B – Vacancies'. This one had nothing to say it was not a private house, nothing to distinguish it from the other semi-detatched Edwardian houses in the tree-lined road.

In aspiring middle-class fashion, the house had a name, not a number: 'Greenways' carved into a plaque mounted on the gate. The woman who answered the telephone had told him how to find it: 'Stay on the left and it's almost opposite the post-box.'

Kenyon hunched himself against the wind, holding down his newly bought hat with one hand, clutching the equally newly bought (though second-hand) briefcase with the other, as he walked up the gravel drive. Instead of his usual sharp, dark-coloured overcoat, he wore a fawn raglan-style raincoat. That, like the hat, had been purchased from a department store a few days before and then kicked around a little to age it.

The woman who answered the door was in her early sixties. She wore a tweed skirt and white shirt-blouse, and had a trace of a moustache. She waited until he had wiped his feet the required number of times and then led him into what was obviously the 'best room' – barely used furniture arranged with museum formality, curtains semi-closed against enemies like light and air.

He told his story: Import and Export Manager for a West Country food company, had to be in London from time to time, needed to be reasonably near the airport, fed up with hotels, wanted somewhere he could leave his belongings, use when he was here. He would pay for the room all the time, of course; still cheaper than hotel prices the way they were these days.

At what he judged the right moment he handed over his visiting card – Peter King, Import/Export Manager, Ronan & Hawkey, fine food wholesalers, Exeter, Devon, Great Britain. He had had them printed a few days earlier. The 'Great Britain' was important: it gave an impression of a company with worldwide business; it also made the absence of a full address seem normal.

In turn, he extracted the information he needed: there were two other 'guests', a 'sales gentleman in shirts' and a structural engineer whose company was working on a local development and whose home was in Worcester, where he returned each week-end. She – 'Mrs Price' with 'Mrs' heavily accented – was a widow, and she took in a few guests because it was such a big house and because it was nice to have some company. That was why there were no notices, no boards – it wasn't really a business, and she did not want just *anyone* wandering in from the streets. She made it sound like a hobby. Kenyon could not decide whether it was the snobbishness of not wanting to be seen taking in lodgers or an attempt to defraud the Inland Revenue by not declaring her earnings. Both, he guessed. It suited his purpose. She was not a woman he liked: in her tone and her expressions he sensed a small mind, a mean spirit. But he knew how to handle such people. You agreed with them, played on their snobbishness, fed the greed they would have denied existed.

He praised the room, which in truth was not unpleasant. It was at the front of the house, and contained a double bed, a chest of drawers and an ornate wardrobe, all in a shiny walnut finish. The floor was linoleum with a square of carpet, and there was one picture, an amateurish watercolour landscape.

He offered references at precisely the moment he knew that she would be embarrassed to take up his offer (if she had, he would have forged them), did not argue when she asked for £4 10s. a week (at least £1 and probably 30s. more than she expected) payable a month in advance, and twenty pounds deposit.

He left, explaining that his suitcase was at the station, that he was already on his way back to Exeter but would return the following week.

He was back in central London in time for two hours' sleep before setting off for the club. It had taken less than five hours. He now had a new address. His first steps towards vanishing were under way.

The following day he added two business addresses. This was even easier. He followed up advertisements in *Exchange & Mart*, the all-advertisement weekly – there were several offering central London mail and telephone facilities. At one, in Regent Street, he registered himself as Peter King, of Ronan & Hawkey, and at the second, in the Strand, he became Alan Carey of Carey Associates, International Management Consultants. He paid in cash. Each in return gave him a card and a number, to be used when collecting mail or when telephoning in for any messages. Both assured him that all telephone calls were answered with a number only; callers would not know it was only an accommodation address.

Next, he had headed notepaper and more calling cards printed with the new names and addresses (for safety, he used separate printers). On the first occasion that he stayed overnight at Turnham Green, he handed Mrs Price one of the cards with the Regent Street telephone number – just a precaution in case she ever tried to contact him. He also stressed that she should keep any mail that arrived for him between visits.

By early February, his new identities were growing. Using his new addresses, he opened accounts at three banks and three building societies. He applied for charge cards from Diners Club and from the more recently arrived American Express. In each case he used a fictitious executive at one of his phoney companies as his reference and he gave his salary as being just above the two thousand pounds minimum required.

Using his King name and the Turnham Green address, he obtained a provisional driving licence, and signed on for a short 'refresher course' of lessons with a local instructor whose name he found on a card in a shop window. He explained that he had learned to drive years before but had gone to live abroad before taking a test. He booked to take the test itself in a month's time. That would give him a driving licence which he could use in turn to obtain an international driving licence. If he wanted yet another identity that licence was easily altered – a change of photo, a stamp that a child with an ink pad and a potato could forge, a little work with a razor and putty rubber and a ball-point pen . . .

Under yet another name, he rented a deposit box at Harrods which he used to store the growing amount of documentation.

In what Kenyon now began to think of as 'the surface world' as distinct from the one he was creating for himself, Hunter went to Spain and did not return. There was a story in the *Observer* Sunday newspaper about an immigration clamp-down on 'undesirable' visitors; Hunter was not named, but for a few days there were press calls. One newspaperman tracked down Kenyon through the records at Companies House and was waiting outside his apartment when he returned home one morning. All he wanted to talk about, the reporter insisted, trying to block off Kenyon's path, was Hunter – 'I won't quote you, nobody will know we've talked. I'll keep you out of it if you co-operate.'

Kenyon said nothing, not even, 'Fuck off,' as he crashed the man aside. Two hours later, after telephoning Barton, he moved into a hotel.

The reporter continued to pursue him for the next two weeks, tracking down Pamela, who telephoned him in alarm.

Barton was relaxed. 'He's nothing,' he said dismissively. 'Just some fucking wise ass. Stay low. He'll wise up he's just wasting fucking time.'

He was right. The reporter's attempts to reach Kenyon stopped. No doubt, other priorities had taken over: the wave of thefts of furs, art and stamps sweeping London; the fast-developing war against drugs (police, he had read, had just succeeded in training two Labradors to pick up the scent of cannabis); even the first results of the experimental seventy speed limit on the country's four hundred miles of motorway.

Nevertheless, the extra pressure had its effect on Kenyon. For the first time he set himself a deadline – the end of May, three months away. It was longer than he liked, but there was still an enormous amount to do. Above all, there was the problem of passports. Not just one passport – to destroy any trail he reckoned he needed two, better still three so that if necessary, he could switch from one to another as he moved. Then, even if someone managed to pick up part of his trail, it would lead nowhere.

In his new double-life, he became wary of being followed,

checking the street before he left home, varying his route to the club, often using the rear doors there. Barton and the others noted his new caution, but they thought he was being nervous after the approach by the reporter and they endorsed it.

Above all, he became wary of being photographed. The newspaperman who waited at the apartment for him had had no camera, but then he had hoped to enlist Kenyon as an informer in return for keeping him out of any story. Others might try to snatch his picture. A tourist with a camera was now enough to set his senses tingling. A raised camera had him turning his head and jerking an arm across his face.

Spectacularly, Kenyon now found he had a constant alertness that he had no wish to dampen down with booze. He was not one of those heavy drinkers who deluded himself he was anything else. He had long accepted he was a lush; life had to be a constant battle at containment in order not to fuck up. Now, publicly he still drank as hard and fast and frantically as ever because he wanted there to be no sign of anything different. But at the apartment or the Turnham Green house as he plotted his moves, a drink would last an hour or more and the coffee-pot was drained faster than the bottle.

He took to spending one, sometimes two nights a week at Turnham Green. To explain arriving in the early hours, he complained to Mrs Price that part of his job was entertaining customers and potential customers – 'Bit of a bind really, but they expect it,' he said, gauging the attitude that would go down best. To reinforce his cover story, he bought the occasional tin or jar of some delicacy from Fortnum & Mason – palm hearts, apricots in brandy, even chocolate-covered bees – and gave them to Mrs Price, telling her his company imported them.

Time was the great problem. But he solved this by cutting back on sleep – and found that by splitting it into two periods, four hours after he got home and an hour early afternoon, he could make do without problems.

He evolved new routines: from the time he arrived back at the apartment early each morning until a quarter to six, he reviewed progress, plotted the next steps, sifted papers. By 10.30 a.m. he had showered, slept his four hours, drunk coffee, eaten croissants that he brought back from the club in a paper bag, and was beginning the task he had set for the day. Twice, three times a week there were the normal social events that he needed to keep up so as not to break old patterns – a lunch, a party, a preview at a gallery (a hangover from the early months of marriage with Pamela when they had shopped for paintings).

Once, briefly, he stood back from himself and wondered how much of what he was doing was vital and how much was simply action for the sake of containing his panic. But that was not something he dwelt upon.

More than once, he even worried that in his obsessiveness he was going mad. But he did not really believe that. He *had* to get it right. He could not afford to make any mistakes. Once he made his run, his enemies would have a simple, simplistic aim – to catch him and to kill him. In between the catching and the killing, there would probably be the revenge, the mindless brutality, the imposing of the 'lesson'.

Sometimes he overheard conversations. One or two of the Americans boasted about violence the way adolescents did about sex.

One had been talking about something and someone unspecified back in the United States, but Kenyon could not get the words out of his mind.

'So I broke his arms and his jaw, and I told him, "You cocksucker, how'd you like that?" and I pulled down his fucking pants and I shoved the gun right up his arse – I mean *right* up – and I tell you this guy's crying like a fucking baby . . .'

Each day now he lived in three worlds. There was the real one in which he was Michael Kenyon. There was the fantasy-becoming-reality one in which he was Peter King and Alan Carey and likely to become other men too. And there was the past which, as he sorted papers, he replayed each morning like a critic rewatching an old movie. And, just like that critic, he watched it with new eyes and he saw new things.

He and Mary had spent a three-day honeymoon in London. The train was so crowded they had to sit on the floor, and there were so many unscheduled stops that the journey took nearly sixteen hours. The three days, though, had a perfection that never left him. It was spring 1944 and the 'little Blitz' – four months of the heaviest air raids since 1941 – had only recently finished, and there was a tangible feel of relief and of being alive in the air. A ranking officer friend of Katharine's had obtained a room for them in a hotel near Leicester Square. Whenever they left it, they stepped out on to streets packed with American troops, young men who had fled Occupied countries, workers up from the provinces.

They clutched hands through *Gone With the Wind*, still drawing crowds after four years, queued for Madame Tussauds, sat outside at Chris's Restaurant off Leicester Square and dined on spam and Algerian wine. They walked in the parks, danced to 'Moonlight Becomes You' and 'I'll Be Seeing You,' and made love with the total abandon that comes only from knowing time is short and finite. For the only period during their marriage, there was no reserve, no constraint. Each instinct became action, each desire immediate fulfilment. They explored each other with eyes and hands and tongues. They fell asleep still coupled and woke with hands already touching each other, the scent of sex still heavy in the room.

Her wedding ring was too big, had yet to be altered (he had bought it on the black market for ten pounds; it was twenty-two carat, not nine carat like the £1 10s. 9d. utility models sold in jewellery shops). One night she woke to find it missing from her finger. They found it after a frantic search in which all the bedclothes were shaken and cast on to the floor. When at last the ring emerged, caught in a crease in a sheet, he replaced it on her finger with careful solemnity, and they made manic love on the floor during which she sobbed over and over, 'Don't go, don't go,' while outside the sirens howled and corridors echoed with people making for the shelters. Afterwards, as she lay asleep, he stood naked by the window, peering out at a terrifying beauty of searchlight and flame, and he felt immortal.

After their three days, she left London first. He saw her on to the train. It was packed with servicemen and women. He waved until she was lost from sight. Something was over. It was a feeling he was to know many times in the years to follow.

Kenyon's first choice on being called up was the Royal Air Force. Partly because of his brother, but mainly because it was generally thought to be the classiest service.

In 1944 the RAF did not want anyone without qualifications.

Kenyon's papers said 'shop manager'. That was why he found himself in the Royal Army Service Corps, the unglamorous non-combatant branch of the Forces which supplied the fighting men with everything from soap to boots.

It was not a total disaster. One of his fellow recruits was a German-Jewish refugee on whom he honed his knowledge of the language.

He volunteered for more active service and, an irony, he found himself airborne. He was trained to land a glider – in France on the night of D-Day – loaded with a jeep and a trailer full of medical supplies. His job then was to drive to a country house already earmarked as an emergency hospital for the invading Allies.

Kenyon's glider landed safely – pure luck. The Germans had planted posts, and all around other gliders were twisted into wrecks, tails and wings missing. He could hear men calling for help, but an officer yelled at him to take his vehicle and go. He remembered the sheer exhilaration of it all as he zig-zagged the bumping jeep and trailer across the field, out on to the road. He felt totally invincible. And then a flash and nothing else until he awoke. He was in the same makeshift hospital that had been his target. The rear wheels of the trailer in front of him had hit a mine. Miraculously, he had only mild concussion and superficial cuts.

He remained in hospital for three days and was then attached to a parachute batallion. His job was to help keep the front line supplied with food, ammunition and medical supplies. He threw himself into it with a mad passion: *his* men were going to get everything they needed. He wheedled, traded, threatened and bribed as he worked his way across Europe with them.

Life was a permanent nerve-tight high, a mix of fear and excitement. Bodies became real and then familiar, though he was never able to ignore them. He grew to know the look of faces without colour, to learn that when people meet violent death the result is unimaginable obscenity – stomachs ripped, trailing guts, disembodied limbs, skulls open like nightmarish serving dishes. Each day he aged a year. It was an ageing from which there was no going back.

One day, among burned-out lorries and tanks, he saw scores of German dead laid in neat straight lines – their colleagues had had no time to bury them, this was the best they could do. A group of soldiers began jeering at it: this German orderliness even in the mess of battle. But not Kenyon, nor the soldiers who carried weapons with the kind of negligence that comes only with much familiarity. He and they realised those retreating Germans had made the only gesture they could. Only lesser men would have done nothing.

Mail reached him, but in irregular bursts. Once there was a gap of five weeks, and then there were over a dozen letters, most from Mary. He seized upon them eagerly, but soon he tossed them aside. It was all too far away, too divorced from his reality. Others might savour what they had left behind, linger over stories of home, gorge on vows of eternal love and wanting. For him it had nothing to do with *Now*, and was better left untouched.

Ten months after landing in France, Kenyon crossed the Rhine, this time on a pontoon, perched on the front of a tank. Germany was hot and sunny. There was rubble and ruins everywhere, a permanent smell of fire in the air. Roads were filled with refugees, women pulling carts laden with household belongings. Kenyon could see *why* they were fleeing. But to *where*? There were only other places that were the same.

He carried a pistol, a 9 mm Walther P38, which he took from a body, as protection against hunger-driven refugees and deserters. A few days into Germany he chanced upon a group of infantrymen holding perhaps a hundred German soldiers while they waited for the arrival of lorries. He stopped to talk, to share their brew. The Germans looked whipped, cowed. It was a cliché, but they were boys, just like him and the others around him. There were no officers. He was ready to leave when he heard a snatch of conversation between two of them. The tone attracted his attention, but it was the words of one that held him. They were precise, educated, elegant – officer's words. He looked. The man wore a torn private's uniform, one sleeve caked with dried blood.

Kenyon sought out the corporal in charge. 'One of your prisoners is a German officer,' he said.

'Who the fuck cares? They're all bleedin' Krauts, ain't they?'

Kenyon began to argue, saw the look deep in the other's war-wearied eyes. 'I'll buy him from you,' he said. 'Two bottles of Scotch.'

'What do you want him for? Some German officer killed your

mate? Like to blow his fuckin' balls off? Go ahead if you wanna. What's one fuckin' Kraut more or less?'

'No, I want him alive.' He was not sure why. Some sixth sense – an officer who felt he had to disguise himself might or might not be important. Some gut feeling told him he was.

The corporal studied him for a few seconds. 'Where's the Scotch?' he said at last.

Kenyon had them truss the man, hands tied to drawn-up ankles behind his back. He drove until he found the command post, asked for the Intelligence Officer, was directed to a Major Cartwright, and gave his story.

Kenyon was lucky in his man. Cartwright broke into colloquial German which Kenyon answered without hesitation.

'All right,' said Cartwright, reverting to English, the test over, 'let's have a chat with him.'

The German was dragged out of the jeep by a sergeant and hauled in front of the Major.

The Major asked a series of questions to which he received bare replies.

Kenyon waited for the explosion he was sure would come. Instead, the Major pushed back his chair, stood and told the sergeant in slow, deliberate English, 'Don't think we'll get anywhere with this one, Sergeant. Call in Sergeant Powalowski, tell him to do whatever he thinks necessary.'

The mention of the Polish name was enough – every German knew how the Poles had been treated, what one would do to one of them given the chance.

The German's words now poured out so fast that the Major had to keep ordering him to slow down.

When it was over and the German had been led away, the Major gazed into space for a long time. 'So that was it,' he said. 'A scientist working at Farben. Claims he joined the Army last year after Goebbels said it was *Totaler Krieg*, Total War, and they started drafting all the people who had been exempted. Says he wanted to do his duty though he was never a Nazi.' He stretched his arms. 'Probably worked on Zyclon B gas or something similar. Joined when it was obvious Germany'd lost the war, scared what might happen to people like him who'd provided the means to better and faster extermination. Funny, thought that all his like who'd given up their exemption had ended up on the Eastern

79

Front. He must have been cleverer than most. Still, that's by the way. Main thing is that he may know a few things that'll interest our scientific johnnies. I'll pass him along.'

He turned to face Kenyon. 'Well done,' he said. 'Now where did you learn that German . . . ?'

A week later, Kenyon was in Hamburg, newly promoted to sergeant, and in the Intelligence Corps.

Hamburg had fallen at the beginning of May. Two months before, with the end of the war imminent, all British troops had been issued with a card signed by Field Marshal Montgomery forbidding fraternisation with Germans. 'In streets, houses, cafés, cinemas, etc., you must keep clear of Germans, man, woman, or child, unless you meet them in the course of duty. You must not walk out with them or shake hands or visit their homes, or make them gifts, or take gifts from them. You must not play games with them or share any social event with them. In short, you must not fraternise with Germans at all.'

About the time Kenyon was lying in hospital recovering from mild concussion, it was already being relaxed: 'Members of British Forces in Germany will be allowed to speak to, and play with, little children.'

Reality, in fact, had already made the orders unenforcible: who could stop soldiers from handing out sweets to kids; most of all, who could keep men from women, especially German women, attractive, long without men, and – unlike the French many had previously encountered – neither shy nor unwilling?

By the time Kenyon arrived in Hamburg any semblance of non-fraternisation was over. He moved into a world that jangled and sharpened his already keyed senses.

All around him there was devastation almost impossible to absorb. There *were* parts of the city still more or less intact, but mostly you could stand and see nothing but ruins. The desolation was made more poignant by the fact that weeds and grass and even flowers poked through the rubble. And, unbelievable as it was, many of the ruins were being used as homes. The only visible sign was improvised chimney stacks that poked out through the debris.

What had not been destroyed was being taken. Germany had become one vast looting ground. Allied governments dismantled and moved whole factories, even trees from the Black Forest for use as pit-props. Individuals took everything portable.

Kenyon lived and worked and breathed in the very midst of all this. He was a conqueror and, in his position, a very special one, and he enjoyed a privileged place. The job was exciting. He shared a large apartment with two others. There was always money, unlimited drink, the pick of food, servants to cook it. And women. A lot of women.

Like most Britons, Kenyon felt at home with Germans – it was a strange but true fact that even at the height of the war there had been little hatred for Germans in Britain. For the hard Nazis and for the terrible atrocities that were now being revealed, nothing but loathing and hatred, of course . . . but *ordinary* Germans . . . As for German soldiers, what fighting man could have anything but respect?

And the kids? Some without arms or legs or sight; veterans at ten. You had to recognise their spunk; they touched chords of horror and admiration. The women, too, sparked a potent emotive mix – pity and desire. And availability. Perhaps that above all. Availability and willingness. These women were Katharine – they *enjoyed.* Or, at least, they *gave.* No passivity here, no lie back and close their eyes.

Power and money and unlimited sex, and the time Now, not yesterday or tomorrow, but just Now as he had always wanted it to be. And all this against a backcloth of hell. No nineteen-year-old had ever felt this old, nor yet so young. In the same day he could experience new sensations with a knife-edge, gut-fluttering awareness, and an hour later handle an event that would have shattered others with a world-wearied familiarity.

The trams returned to service, and there was a fair and for a time a circus. Officially, he worked on shifts, but there was little division between work and play. He worked when there was work, whether at three or ten in the morning or ten at night. For a time his job concerned denazification – interrogating Germans seeking to work in public life to ensure none of them had been Nazis. His feelings of pity and admiration were strained by the countless protestations he heard: no German, it seemed, had ever been anything but anti-Hitler.

In his decisions, he held enormous power. In the midst of chaos, it was often a job for a Solomon. He learned to look for the tell-tale signs, whether of speech or eye movement, that accompanied answers to his questions. Above all, he learned to make use of silence: most people, he found, cannot cope with silence. Their minds fill with fantasies of what you might know or might do; unable to bear it, they fill the silence with words and, in time, they hang themselves. He learned when to lean hard and when to be sympathetic, when to scream and when to whisper, when to threaten and when to promise, when to give and when to withhold.

Another job was helping track down German scientists: all the Allies wanted them, and it was a race to find each one first. Here he learned about *realpolitik*. What the scientists had done for Germany mattered only in that it showed what they could do in the future for Britain or France or the United States or the Soviet Union. If a man was useful enough, what he had done for the Nazis mattered little, if at all. On the other hand, if he could offer nothing . . . In such ways, big criminals often went free and little ones were punished.

For his part, he learned pragmatic skills too – how to bribe and to lay out bait and to look honest even when he lied.

And some time in the middle of it, in the autumn of 1946, he went home on leave.

The countryside had scarcely changed. That autumn 1946, the houses still shone spick in the sun, the hedgerows were still rich, the sheep thick in the fields, the churches symbols of timelessness. But it was a drab Britain full of exhausted people. In the towns, there were queues everywhere. Everything, it seemed, was rationed – bread had just been added to the list. Prefabs – rectangular, factory-built temporary houses – were going up. There were warnings that there would not be enough coal for winter.

And he was different. After the freedom, the excitement, the glamour of Germany, Kenyon loathed it. Most of all, he hated the people. They were what J. B. Priestley was later to call 'dreary' and 'self-righteous'. They moaned and they whined, but seemed to do nothing. Why should they after all they had done and been through? They'd kept their peckers up, bashed Jerry, saved the world. That was enough, surely. Now it was time for someone to do something for them.

Kenyon compared them with the Germans, already building up from the ruin. OK, so they had nowhere else to go but up, but these bloodless, belly-aching, smug countrymen of his . . .

But it was not really that. It was the contrast in his personal life: glamour, drabness; lover, husband; freedom, constraint; excitement, routine. He had brought back chocolates and American candies, cigarettes, Bourbon and nylons. The delight at seeing how they were welcomed was quickly crushed, though, by the realisation of how much they symbolised the gulf between there and here. He had brought back French underwear too, black silk and lace, and Mary oohed over it. But when she wore it the pain was awful: she was like a bad actress playing the wrong part. He quickly stripped her and she mistook it for passion. In truth, he was embarrassed by how she looked in it; he could not kill the thought of how other women he had known would have looked.

As days passed, though, he began to relax once more in her gentleness and actually to enjoy the ordinariness of home. The night before his leave ended, they did not make love but lay awake and talked and made plans. Together they created a world and a life all the more perfect for existing in the imagination, but not so far from the possible that it could survive only in dream.

It took three days to return to Hamburg. For the first two he thought of her and of his parents and Shropshire. And then, as Hamburg neared, the excitement stirred, and by the time he stepped from the train it was all gone. As if it had been merely an interlude. *This* was the real world. Here he could be the real Michael Kenyon.

Several months before his service was due to end in 1947 there were feelers about him staying on, becoming a regular soldier. Nothing said directly, that was not the way it was done in the Intelligence Corps, but strong suggestions that if he cared to make a formal application . . .

There are moments in everyone's life when, looking back, they can say, if it had not been for . . . In Kenyon's case it was Ilse. The irony was that he hardly knew her. He had met her only twice and then briefly.

Dawson, another sergeant in intelligence, introduced them. He had been in Hamburg but was now stationed on the Czech border, interrogating refugees. He travelled back to Hamburg whenever he could because of Ilse, undertaking ludicrously difficult journeys, going without sleep for two or three days on end to be with her. His passion for her was well-known, a joke even, though not one anyone would have made in front of Dawson. Not because of his temper, but because he was the kind of person no one wanted to hurt. He was that rare being, a genuinely nice person. Or so it seemed to everyone he met. If he had an aberration that no one could quite understand – his madness for a seemingly quite ordinary German girl – well, so be it.

Ilse worked at the telephone exchange, and because of her job needed to stay in Hamburg. She made little impression on Kenyon when they did meet. Nor was he especially close to Dawson. He was surprised when the man arrived at his flat one evening still carrying the marks of having travelled across the country. It emerged that Dawson had learned that the Russians were insisting on the return to their sector of former residents who were registered as working in Berlin. Ilse was such a person. He was not sure how thorough the Russians were being in their searches, but he thought it likely they would trace Ilse: she had made no attempt to hide her movements.

Dawson knew Ilse would kill herself rather than place herself in the hands of the Russians. Dawson could do nothing to help her personally, but Kenyon could – he could access her files and mark on them the word 'Deceased'. If he, Kenyon, also directed officials at the exchange to refer all enquiries to his office, Ilse should be safe and able to remain in Hamburg. After all, she was not anyone specially important. Kenyon refused to promise. He would think on it. That night he killed a half-bottle of Scotch. Like his colleagues, he had come to see the Russians as evil beings – their troops had raped and looted their way through Germany, their armies had taken over Eastern Europe, reduced it to Stalinist rule, seemed poised to threaten the West. As Kenyon knew better than most, their spies and agitators were burrowed everywhere like woodworm. Although his training, his ingrained caution, told him he should not do what Dawson asked, all his emotions said, who would let *anyone* be handed over to such people? And Dawson was a nice guy. Doing what he asked would be easy. What would it matter?

Nevertheless, he was still undecided on the following day, and it was on impulse that, mid-morning, he visited the archives, summoned the file, and made the alteration for which Dawson had pleaded.

A week later, within the space of twenty-four hours, a great deal happened. Ilse vanished – to Berlin under the occupation of her hated Russians after all, it was said, though no one was absolutely certain. Dawson was returned to Britain, and Kenyon was transferred to clerical duties. Although nothing was said to him it was obvious his actions had come to light. But why no charge? He concluded that there was only suspicion about his part in the attempt to mislead the Russians, not hard evidence, and furthermore this was probably tinged with sympathy, understandable if Ilse were in the Soviet zone facing God knew what. But Kenyon understood that although he was safe, he had ended all hopes of making a career in intelligence. For nothing.

Demobilisation came quickly. He was flown back at less than a day's notice. After one night in a camp in Warwickshire, he was taken to a depot to choose a civilian suit, a raincoat, shirt, tie, socks and hat. After one further night at the camp, he was given five pounds and a travel warrant home. After three years he was a civilian.

His mother, Mary and the vicar with his car were waiting at the station. The shop, when they arrived, had a banner draped across it: 'Welcome Home Michael' in huge letters like a carnival bunting.

Everyone was gathered inside: his father, neighbours, friends. A drink was pressed into his hand; someone ruffled his hair affectionately as though he was still a small boy. His father tried to tell him something serious, but his mother said, 'Let it wait, the boy's only just arrived.'

He heard it later when everyone but the family had left. The owner of the small sub-post-office and general store in the village wanted to retire. Kenyon's father had agreed to buy it – for Michael. He was still absorbing the news through a cloud of tiredness, drink and disorientation when he became conscious of Mary's excitement. She tugged on his arm. 'Isn't it wonderful! And there's a lovely flat above the shop.'

He knew he was expected to react, but there was a tightness in his throat: the muscles would not let him open his mouth. The corner of his eye started twitching uncontrollably. He stared around in sudden panic, and then realised they were smiling and did not understand.

An aunt put an affectionate arm round his shoulders. 'Just look at him,' she said. 'He's so pleased he can't even speak.'

CHAPTER SEVEN

With his false name and addresses organised, Kenyon turned his attention to obtaining his main priority – passports. Without them, he could do nothing.

He discounted the most obvious methods of obtaining them. He could have stolen one by following a tourist or businessman of about his age and appearance from the airport and then burgling his hotel room. But, apart from the obvious danger of being caught, the passport would soon be reported stolen. By the time he came to make his move, its details would have been well circulated. He could, of course, alter it – but that was beyond his personal capabilities, and he would have to involve someone else. Dangerous.

Buying one was even more risky. Again, it involved a middle man who could always be traced and made to talk. Furthermore, if the passport were not stolen, it would be forged – and from past experience from the hunter's side he had little faith in the ability of forgeries to stand up to long-term scrutiny.

The best passports for his purpose were *genuine* passports. There was a fairly well-known way of acquiring one by fraud. You searched a cemetery for a gravestone for a boy who would have been about your age had he not died as a child. Then, after obtaining his birth certificate, you applied for a passport under his name. Given the volume of applications, the chances of being caught were minimal.

He decided on a variation of that – using the name of a boy not dead but confined to a mental institution from an early age.

That would give him an English passport. Useful. But what he wanted most was an *Irish* passport. First, no one who looked for him would expect the switch of nationality. Second, and more important, an Irish passport was near ideal for anyone who, like him, planned to emerge in a foreign country. To be Irish in a country not your own was a norm, not an exception. He had read somewhere that six million Irishmen had moved abroad in the previous century, and a third still emigrated every year.

His first step was yet another postal address, this time under the name Finch & Craddock. The printed notepaper described them as 'estates management' – he would have preferred 'solicitors' but that was dangerous: anyone could check the Law Society List in any library. Estates management, he thought, conveyed the right impression without being checkable.

Then, after a long morning in the main Westminster Reference Library Kenyon emerged with two lists. One was of major provincial mental hospitals. He had bought a new portable typewriter. At the Turnham Green flat, he wrote to the superintendent at each of them, typing painfully with two fingers. He used the new printed paper and explained that a client had recently died and, for personal family reasons had left money for long-term mental patients 'with the express intention of providing small comforts'. The minimum age under the terms of the bequest was thirty-five, and preference would be given to those who had suffered confinement from an early age. Awards would vary from twenty-five pounds to two hundred and fifty pounds – Kenyon gauged the higher figure large enough to produce responses, not so great as to excite undue attention. With each letter, Kenyon enclosed a very short typed questionnaire.

The second list was of just over a dozen Irish surnames. He took them with him on his second research trip, this time to the newspaper section of the British Library.

He used the journey to catch up on more recent news – he skimmed and discarded over a week's untouched papers that he had been too preoccupied to open. A date had been set for going decimal, colour television would begin next year. Labour looked set to be re-elected, early tourists were queuing to enjoy the view from the top of London's tallest building, the Post Office Tower.

The newspaper library is a large brick building almost opposite Colindale station near the end of the Northern underground line. It contains back copies of all the British and major foreign newspapers. In 1966 its eighteen miles of shelving held over four hundred and fifty volumes and parcels, many dating back to 1700. Kenyon walked out of the station into suburbia – a tiny cluster of shops, a solitary telephone box, serving rows of near-identical house-boxes stretching ribbon fashion for as far as he could see in either direction. An incongruous location for such a place.

The library had a small hallway, a curving staircase and then huge high-ceilinged rooms with enormous windows and columns of large desks. He found the newspapers he wanted in the card-index files, completed forms which he handed to a clerk, and then took a desk and waited. Kenyon's needs were relatively mundane: the provincial evening newspapers for the early years of the 1930s for Liverpool, Birmingham and Manchester – cities with significant Irish populations.

With its shiny painted walls and the echoes of doors opening and closing, the room had an institutional feel. Around him, working two each side of every desk, were serious researchers, with their pallor and round shoulders. Kenyon swivelled his eyes. The man on his right was reading the *Bewley Heath Observer and District Times* 10 October 1919. It was open at the Sports Page, and the main headline read, 'Vickers Trounce New Brompton'. Impossible to imagine what the man was seeking in its pages. But then that was one of the beauties of such a place: what you came here for was your secret.

It was a half-hour before the first heavy bound volume of old newspapers was wheeled to Kenyon's side by a porter. Kenyon lifted it into the inclined holder and started his search. He was not interested in the editorial, but in the small ads. In particular, those in the columns headed 'Deaths' and 'In Memoriam' and 'Acknowledgements' (where families often gave thanks to neighbours, priests, hospitals and workmates).

Kenyon's hunt was macabre, and several times he left the desk to try to shake off the feeling of gloom that permeated the old pages. Clichés and trite phrases conveyed everything: 'In loving memory of our dear baby son . . .', 'a little lamb folded . . .', 'aged two . . . suffer little children . . .'

He traced his finger through column after column, issue after issue, year after year. No shortage of young death. Occasionally, he switched his attention temporarily to columns headed 'House Servants Want Places' and 'Moneylenders' and the ads for Aviator Wheat Flakes and Vicks Vapour-Rub and Colgate Ribbon Dental Cream ('Don't ask any toothpaste to do the work of a dentist') just for relief.

Sometimes ages were given, 'just three months'; sometimes a word 'baby', 'child'; occasionally a little more, 'tiny brother'.

It became hateful, but he forced himself to concentrate on surnames. They had to be the right ones. Most, not unnaturally, were English.

It took three visits with his temporary short-term pass (made out in one of his growing number of assumed names) before he had what he needed: nine names that matched ones on his list of Irish surnames. All were male children. All had died between the ages of two and eight.

He was ready for his next call.

It is a feature of many democratic countries that anyone can buy copies of anyone else's birth, marriage or death certificates. In England in 1966 the central point was Somerset House, site of the General Register Office, near the western edge of the City of London. The actual registers are closed to visitors, but the indexes stand on open shelves, arranged according to the quarter of the year in which the birth, marriage or death was registered, and then alphabetically under the surname.

Kenyon spent a great deal of time in the crowded search rooms over the next week, competing for volumes and note-taking space with people from a score of other countries, all trying to trace their ancestry.

Kenyon's first task was finding entries for the nine children whose death notices he had found. Then, as was his right, he ordered death certificates. These gave the full name of the person who had notified the death, in each case the father. Working back from the children's birth dates he checked for marriage records. He found five. These gave ages of the bride and groom, which enabled him to seek *their* birth certificates.

At the end, he had set aside for further use the birth certificates of four of the dead children together with the marriage and birth certificates of their parents. In none of the cases had he been able to find birth certificates for *their* parents. It was a fair assumption that they, the grandparents, had been born in Ireland.

The four names were Rossiter, Kearon, Bullman and O'Hora. He knew from his research and his list of surnames that each was associated with only one county in Ireland.

He had now gone as far as he could alone. Using the Finch &

Craddock notepaper he wrote to a genealogical research company in Dublin whose name he obtained from the Irish Embassy. There are several such companies carrying out searches for the tens of thousands of Irish Americans who try to trace their roots each year. He had already spoken to them on the telephone, explained the gist of his problem, and satisfied himself that they would tackle it with urgency. In his letter, he confirmed he was acting for a client company. It wished to trace the Irish roots of four specified people. Birth or death certificates were required. In view of the urgency of the case, a double fee would be paid together with a bonus in the event of success.

While he was waiting for answers from Ireland, replies came from three of the hospitals. One regretted that it had no patients who might qualify, but wondered whether funds might be available for other needs. The other two both gave details of patients. He made a note to send a sorry letter to the first and cheques for fifty pounds to each of the others – but not for another three, four weeks. Swift replies look suspicious to bureaucratic minds.

The two names seemed ideal. Both had been confined to hospital since early childhood; obviously neither had ever been abroad. Again using Somerset House, he obtained copies of their birth certificates. With one, he made postal application for a passport. He forged a counter-signature on the form and on the back of the photographs he had had taken earlier. He described the signatory as 'bank officer', claiming he had known the applicant for eight years. With the second, he applied in person at a Ministry of Labour office for a British Visitor's Passport. Although this was a simplified form of travel document, it was still valid for visits of up to three months to nearly two dozen specified foreign countries. For this he needed more photographs, and a driving licence – he obtained this simply by applying at a post office for a further provisional licence under the specified name.

He now had an English passport and a British Visitor's Passport.

The first reply from Ireland came quickly. The researchers had traced one of the men – a Daniel Rossiter. Documents would be sent once payment was received. The name had been found in the records of County Wexford.

Years before, in his police street-pounding days, Kenyon had regularly paused at a small café where he drank strong tea from a mug and absorbed local gossip. In return for scraps of information, he turned a blind eye to minor transgressions – a card game in the back room, some small-scale black-marketeering.

The café owner had a hobby – tracing his ancestry. He lived at the back of the café, and one day he showed Kenyon the family chart he was building. It was from him that Kenyon learned the odd piece of information that, years later, had sent him to the Westminster Reference Library.

Late last century the secretary of the General Register Office had analysed all the births registered in Ireland during one year. The subsequent list provided a statistical breakdown of *where* people of various surnames lived. Kenyon could not remember detail, but he had remembered being told that some names were found in only one or two counties. These were the surnames he had sought. Chances were that if Kenyon wanted the papers of an ancestor of someone living in England with one of those names they would be in the records of the particular county concerned. Rossiter had been listed as a name found almost exclusively in County Wexford. The researchers would have known that, checked there first. And, sure enough, that is where they had been successful.

He paid them with an international money order and asked the researchers to continue their searches for the other names, but only for a further month. One name was all he wanted; if they came up with a second that would be a bonus. He had no intention of doing anything with the documents at this moment. That would come *after* he disappeared. These were to establish the man he was going to be.

With the documents, Kenyon would in time obtain an Irish passport – or more than one if the researchers came up with another name. Since 1956, although it was little known, anyone with an Irish-born parent, grandparent or great-grandparent had been entitled to Irish citizenship. It was the brainchild of the then Minister of Justice, and Parliament had accepted the 'once a Roman, always a Roman' argument without opposition. Not many overseas-born 'Irishmen' had taken advantage. In the United States alone some forty millions could claim Irish ancestry. The number who had Irish citizenship, as well as their own, ran into only a few thousand.

Yet, as Kenyon knew, all it took was 'proof' in the form of birth and marriage certificates (such as he would have soon) and the completion of a form (available from any Irish embassy or consulate). As a citizen you were *entitled* to a passport. To satisfy protocol you had to sign a form saying you currently held no other passport, but there were no checks. And nor, as a point of principle, did Ireland notify the applicant's host country of the application.

Once he had vanished and resettled, Kenyon would obtain his new passport to fit his new identity.

Kenyon had another worry. Money. Although he intended to clean out the safety-deposit box, nagging fear kept recurring. What if something intervened at the last moment. What would he do then? Surrounded by money as he was, surely there was a fall-back scheme he could devise?

Kenyon read somewhere that, whatever Britain's Parliament had intended, there were about one thousand gaming clubs by now, 1966. No one could be certain: because they existed by mistake and because there was no licensing system, there were no records. They ranged from discreet Mayfair clubs in Regency houses to back-street drinking dives. Décor ran all the way from cruise-liner splendour to smoke-filled, sweat heavy, white-washed basement. And the gamblers themselves varied from black-tie racehorse owners to cab-drivers, stacking sums from hundreds of thousands to a couple of pounds.

All gaming clubs had two things in common, though: they were awash with money, and nobody who ran one trusted anyone else involved in the operation.

Barton least of all. In the early days, particularly, he had relaxed enough in the unfamiliarity of the Englishman's presence to voice some of his thoughts. Kenyon recalled one now: 'In this business you gotta win two times over – one time from the punters, one time from the guys who wanna steal it.' The 'guys' were all the employees through whose hands it went.

Barton obviously saw no irony in the fact that the villainy began with his own bosses. The club – together with others with which Kenyon was not concerned – had been made possible with money skimmed from the tables in Las Vegas and from other American underworld activities.

In the early days couriers had brought it in in cash. Now that the clubs were up and running and earning, they in turn provided cash that went to fund new – and to Kenyon unknown – projects.

Nevertheless, the Americans, and Barton in particular, were paranoid about being cheated. Crookedness was like original sin: everybody had it from birth. The only piece of history Barton liked to throw out was that loaded dice had been found in prehistoric graves. It was ingrained that everyone – punter, dealer, inspector, security man – would cheat unless you stopped them. So all the time you showed you were smarter. And if you caught someone cheating, you punished. Fast and hard. The counting-room was good for minor infringements. It was soundproof as a by-product of its security. If you broke the fingers of a dealer who had been caught palming chips, one by one, not a scream filtered through the wall. Barton knew. It had been one of the first things he checked.

But Barton was dishonest himself. It was in the nature of the business, and the greed everyone brought to it, that your own thieving was different. There was a law of the jungle about it: steal or be stolen from. As Kenyon now knew to his cost, Barton was taking a further slice off the skim. It was also likely, Kenyon thought, that either alone or in partnership with one or other of the Americans he was cheating on markers.

Casino bosses do not mind giving credit to big gamblers, even if they know losses will exceed anything that the club will ever get back. Say a man has lost one hundred thousand pounds in cash, but wants to go on until he is down another one hundred thousand pounds in markers. You still have his cash. And if another night he loses twenty thousand pounds and his markers mount, he is still gambling and still losing real money. And say at a later date he owes five hundred thousand pounds but has no chance of paying, you can do one of two things. If he is an 'honest' punter who just needs helping out, you sell him back his five hundred thousand pounds' worth of markers for what he can pay. Say one hundred thousand pounds. Later you know he will come back and lose some more real money. And if he is not honest? You sell his markers for maybe twenty per cent to people who specialise in knowing how to make people pay even if it means them stealing the company payroll or selling the house.

Whichever way you don't lose. But who except you, the man

who does the deal, is to know what you accepted for the markers? How much of the one hundred thousand, say, stuck to your own fingers?

The paranoia in Barton's case was fed, too, by the fact that in all this there was one shaft of honesty: the house did not cheat the punter. Not officially at least; not at the Big Wheel. The same was not true at the other casinos in London controlled by Barton's bosses in the States: games there were often rigged. But the Big Wheel was a kind of flagship. It was the Mob's class front, a draw for everyone from visiting stars, minor-league aristocracy and English criminals who loved the dressing up and the showing off and the young women that gambling always attracted.

The Mob could afford to be honest. On an honest game the house was already taking anything up to fifteen per cent.

Barton's constant task, therefore, was to stop employees cheating the house and the punters, and to prevent the punters cheating the casino.

Although rudimentary compared with security measures that would develop in later years with electronic monitoring, Barton's checks were the best in the business.

At the end of every night's play, he personally examined cards that had been used in case they had been marked; scrutinised dice through a jeweller's eye-glass – checking by the minute marking he had made with a needle earlier that they had not been switched; made sure that wheels balanced before they were covered and sealed.

Chips were checked; wins and losses of big gamblers scrutinised; the performances of individual tables constantly monitored and analysed.

If anyone won consistently over a period, the club acted on the side of caution. If Barton watched and could not detect cheating, that probably only meant the man was too smart. He was not wanted anyway. Casinos only want losers. Somone would draw him on to one side, maybe order him a bottle of good champagne, and say, enjoy the rest of the evening, but – nothing personal – the club would prefer you don't return . . . And, if you were a sensible man, whether you were a cheat or not, you swallowed hard and tried to grin and carry it off as best you could, but left soon after, never to return.

Kenyon even recalled checks being made on a man who *lost*

constantly. He would visit the club irregularly, but perhaps every four, five days, change two to three thousand pounds into chips, gamble badly until he was down two to three thousand pounds, change back his chips and leave. Barton put a private detective on to that. The man had to have an angle. He did. He was a civil servant taking bribes for building contracts; gambling was his way of laundering the money – questioned, the money he took away from the casino could be described as winnings. That known, Barton was happy for the visits to continue.

Nevertheless, the checks, the caution, the constant watchings, only damped down the cheating. So much money, so many hands, so much greed, so much ingenuity. When, after the shooting, Kenyon was allowed into the conversations, he noted how much of the talk was about cheating – rumoured, discovered, from some unspecified past, even at the Big Wheel, though talk of it was in coded monosyllables.

At the most basic level, a crooked dealer and a crooked punter got together. The punter bet in the normal way, a small chip a time. Except that when he won the croupier paid out on a larger bet – say on twenty-five pounds instead of five pounds. At 35-1 that made a difference each time of seven hundred pounds. Provided the two did not get greedy, they could easily share five thousand pounds a week.

There had been one team who had connived to let a punter walk out with ten times that sum in one afternoon.

Questioned, the dealers swore it was one of those runs that sometimes happens. Reluctantly (because everyone is guilty until proved innocent in such circumstances) the story had been accepted – runs do take place, they are the highs that keep addicts returning, it is only in the long term that percentages adjust themselves. But the next day three employees had not arrived. Kenyon knew men had been sent to find them. He also knew they must have been successful, because although there was no mention of what had happened to the men (and he had gone out of his way not to hear) there was talk of what they had done.

The money had been lost – and won – at punto banco, a fast-betting card game and a simplified cousin of baccarat and *chemin de fer*. It uses eight decks of cards. They are shuffled together and placed in a 'shoe', a small rectangular box. The croupier removes cards one at a time from a slit at the bottom of the shoe, dealing two hands, one for the 'bank' and one for the 'player'. Gamblers around the kidney-shaped table have only two decisions to make: how much money to bet, and whether to back the house or the player.

It originated in Argentina and reached the United States in the 1950s (where it is known as Nevada baccarat). As in baccarat and *chemin de fer*, the winning hand is the one that totals nine or nearest to it. Unlike those games, though, it removes all options or decisions as to such things as drawing extra cards. It is as pure a game of instant chance as tossing a coin. No skill is involved. A game takes only seconds. As a famous American gambler once put it, 'A trained monkey could play.'

The 'bank' hand is calculated to have a slight advantage, and pays out at nineteen to twenty. The 'players' hand is at evens. Overall, the house is reckoned to have an advantage of around 1.25 per cent – well worth while with such a fast game and, usually, heavy stakes.

These dealers – there are three on each table – had fixed it that a fellow conspirator brought in a substitute shoe, identical to the one used in the casino. It was substituted for the genuine one during a diversion. Two other conspirators, knowing the order of the cards in the substitute shoe, were able to bet heavily – and walk out with sixty thousand pounds between them.

Though, as George said later, not much good to them where they went.

Kenyon heard of more elaborate methods – even of instructions relayed to 'hearing aids' or by means of minute electric shocks transmitted to tiny receiving discs fixed by adhesive to sensitive parts of the body.

Each day, for at least an hour, Barton scrutinised the returns for each table. He did it sitting in the restaurant, for the public nature of the scrutiny was meant to be part of the deterrent – a reminder of his constant vigilance.

The breakdowns would be pushed in front of Kenyon once Barton had studied them: the American doubted he missed anything, but he had developed an unspoken admiration for Kenyon's way with figures. As it was, Kenyon *had* spotted inconsistencies on two occasions. He had no hesitation in pointing them out: he felt no loyalty to the mainly French dealers. If they had been cheating and were 'dealt with', that was something they had brought upon themselves. In any event, he did not have to think on it.

There was one dealer, though, about whom he said nothing. Perhaps it was because there seemed nothing to say. The man's name was Pierre Bourset, but because of his painfully slim build and his nationality, the Americans had dubbed him 'Thin Frenchy'. Except that he *knew* the man was swindling the club. Trouble was not that Kenyon did not know *how* (he had not known that with the others either), it was that he did not even know *why* he knew it. The figures seemed all right, they were what you would have expected, almost textbook. And that, of course, was the rub. They were too textbook. No ups, downs, bad runs, good runs. Always, just right.

He tried to read Barton's eyes as he examined them. He could not be sure (who could with Barton?) but he saw no trace of suspicion. More significantly, nothing happened to the dealer. He arrived, worked his shifts, went wherever he went, returned the next day . . .

Kenyon made a point of drifting by his table, watching for a while, though not so often it was obvious. There were spy-holes in the ceiling (closed-circuit television was used only at the entrance and in the counting-room; it was still too bulky and primitive for effective concealed use). On the pretext of his new concerned involvement with the casino, Kenyon spent some time with the security watchers. He moved from spy-hole to spy-hole so as not to give away his special interest. And at last he saw it.

A roulette croupier spins the wheel counter-clockwise with his left hand and throws the ball clockwise with his right hand. Where the ball ends up depends on many factors: the moment the croupier releases the ball, the force of his throw, the speed the wheel is moving, whether it hits the ridges between the pockets and how many. Nevertheless, Kenyon had heard from men whose expertise he accepted that a very experienced, highly skilled, long-practised croupier could spin the wheel and throw the ball in such a way that he influenced where the ball finally came to rest. Not accurately enough to settle in a specific number or even in one of three or four numbers. But accurately enough to end up in a slot in a chosen quarter of the wheel. And that was what this croupier was regularly doing.

But this puzzled Kenyon even more. To take advantage of this, the croupier had to have a co-conspirator consistently placing bets on one of seven, eight, nine numbers. Yet there were no signs of that. On the contrary, when it happened, it was invariably the house, the casino, that won. Perhaps that was why Barton had not said anything; perhaps the croupier was cheating the punters for the house. But, even as he thought of it, Kenyon knew that could not be so. There was no need for the house to cheat. And, more practically, analysis of the table figures would show such a bias. And that fact also ruled out another possibility: that the croupier was cheating for the hell of it, a not unknown phenomenon – there were dealers who got a kick out of it.

He woke with the answer one morning. It was obvious. A double cheat! The croupier was cheating in favour of the house in order to make his books balance. And why did he need to make them balance? Because if he had not, they would have shown a bias against him. He was cheating *twice* – once to let his fellow conspirator win and then again, a second time, in the house's favour to counter that. That way, at the end of the day, the figures *looked* right. The two swindles balanced out each other; the house's percentage remained what it should be.

But *how*? This time Kenyon needed to know.

He found his clue not by watching but by studying bits of paper. To be precise, dockets for checks and for service work on equipment. He had already looked back through old analysis sheets (all of which were stored, though rarely consulted) and noted the date the even pattern had first become apparent. Cross-reference with the servicing dockets showed that the wheel had been taken out of service for the balancing to be checked and adjusted the week before that. Coincidence? Maybe. But Kenyon doubted it. He was convinced that, under the guise of carrying out adjustments, the wheel had been doctored in some way.

He returned to the club soon after six on Sunday morning, knowing it to be empty at such a time. He felt beyond fear. He had to break the seals to uncover the wheel, but he knew how to replace them. He had brought a powerful pinpointable light, a magnifying glass and a small tool kit. Surface examination revealed nothing, but he had not expected that it would. Anything that had been done *had* to be inside. The inner wheel of a piece of roulette apparatus is a precision instrument made of heavy metal and weighing about the same as the wheel of a car. Kenyon gripped the spindle with both hands, exerted pressure, felt suction give and carefully hauled it free and rested it on the table. The back of the wheel itself was covered with a metal plate which he unscrewed, revealing its innards. On most wheels, the pockets into which the ball fell were separated by adjustable metal plates. Because they could be unscrewed and shifted, the gaps were checked regularly – they all had to be the same width and they also had to be accurate to within a five-hundredth of an inch. That was vital.

This wheel, however, was different. The holes were separated by solid metal. Not adjustable. Therefore, not open to tampering. And, therefore, Kenyon guessed, not checked even by the paranoid Barton. He stared for a long time, already suspecting what he would find. He had to use the glass. And then he saw. There were filing marks on the side of some of the grooves into which the ball fell. He checked them one by one. Five were marked. Almost imperceptibly these five spaces had been made larger than the others. The difference in size was small, not noticeable except under examination. But enough, he was sure, to increase the statistical chances of the ball ending up in one of these five particular slots instead of any of the others.

He had his answer. The croupier's co-conspirators would bet consistently on just these five numbers. Nothing unusual in that: many gamblers had lucky numbers they followed time after time. The only difference here was that over a period of time these numbers had a greater winning chance. The advantage of play had, in effect, been transferred from the house to the punter.

Kenyon replaced the wheel, wiped the surfaces with care, fitted new seals, and left. He had not slept for twenty-four hours but he was too pumped with adrenalin to rest.

He had the croupier's telephone number. He waited until eleven o'clock, time the man would be home sleeping. Even then, though, he hesitated. Making the call would be yet another step.

Still, he told himself, he had already gone too far to worry about one more thing. Besides, it was a precaution. He let the phone ring and ring until it was answered.

It was difficult to speak with the pebble in his mouth, but it was, he knew, the most effective way of changing his voice – better than all the fictions about handkerchief pads or pinched nostrils.

'You've been a bad boy,' he said.

There was silence, but Kenyon knew the other would not hang up.

When he left the telephone box five minutes later, even the last trace of tiredness had gone. Twenty thousand, he had demanded. Enough, but not too much. Used fivers. A week from now, deposited at a left-luggage office, ticket posted to an address Kenyon gave him.

'Try to make a run and you're finished,' Kenyon had said. 'Just one call, that's all it takes. I get nothing, but you *become* nothing. Get me? There are some people you can't hide from.'

His failsafe back-up money was fixed.

It was only after the call, dead on twelve o'clock, as he eased into a pub as it opened that the irony of the words struck him.

'. . . *some people you just can't hide from.*'

He drained his whisky in one gulp. That was just what he was going to attempt.

CHAPTER EIGHT

There was a marching song recruits had chanted when Kenyon had first entered the Army.

> We're 'ere
> Because
> We're 'ere
> Because we're 'ere

Mile after numbing mile it was sung to the tune of 'Auld Lang Syne', defiantly at first, then resignedly and, finally, like a mantra to blot out reality.

In the winter of 1947 the words echoed through Kenyon's head incessantly. Taking over the store had come to pass, mainly because Mary (more perceptive than he realised at the time) urged him that she could run it with the minimum of help while he took time to decide what he really wanted to do.

Gradually, almost imperceptibly, though, the shop became his master. Not so much of his energy, nor his efforts, nor his thoughts, but of his time. As ordinary demands, like shopping and cooking and visiting, took Mary away from the shop, its confines became his prison. The one overriding reality of the shopkeeper's life, as Kenyon well knew, is that you have to *be* there. Some enjoy it, relish it, making the shop the centre of a stage from which they hold court. Kenyon could only resent it. If there were no customers, you had a choice – busy yourself among the shelves, or move out of sight into the curtained-off rear room and wait, reading the paper and sipping tea, until alerted by the shop bell. Some choice! Either way, on or behind stage, you were as confined as if you were chained to the floor.

If someone – Mary, his mother, his father – had said that it was his duty, his destiny, his lot, to stay, to be a shopkeeper, he would have rebelled. But no one said that. Rather they said, take your time, no need to commit yourself until you are ready. And they made sure he did not fail to notice all the awful things that were happening in the wider world 'outside' – the shortages, the outbreaks of vandalism that had swept the towns and cities, the desperate musical-chair games for somewhere to live.

And the truth was that the village *was* cocooned from many of the problems of post-war Britain. No bombs had left craters where there were once homes (the only bomb that had fallen within thirty miles was one jettisoned by an off-course German bomber making for home after a raid on Liverpool; missing miles of open country, it had hit a barn). True, men had gone to war and not returned, but the land and the people had centuries of absorbing and containing their own griefs and problems. True, others, like Kenyon, had come back changed, but mostly they were scattered, on farms, in rural cottages, and they wrestled with their demons secretly and alone.

Like everywhere else, the people had ration cards and clothing coupons, and for hours each day power was cut to save fuel and shops and homes were lit by candle. But there were no real shortages – no need to queue for hours for coal or coke, no need to go short of meat when there were farmers who could always kill an extra beast. Kenyon recalled the hilarity that greeted a story in the *News Chronicle* about a tailor in one of the big cities who had been fined for making a suit with more pockets than allowed by law. Such things could only happen 'out there'. No wonder his mother would sit in front of the wood-burning kitchen stove and nod her head sagely as the wireless filled the room with the sound of Gracie Fields singing, 'Count Your Blessings'.

And if Kenyon did not see that . . . Well, it was only to be expected. Time would change him. In the meantime, it was best to say as little as possible, to let it be.

There were rooms above the shop, but they had been neglected, and with the urging of the vicar and Mary's mother they moved into the vicarage. After all, it was enormous and underused, and they could have two rooms and a bathroom and a separate toilet all to themselves. One evening, when she and Kenyon were alone, Mary's mother had screwed up the courage to say something she had nursed and rehearsed silently for a long time. To Kenyon's increasing astonishment, she began to talk of

103

the shock people must feel returning home after being away for a long time, of men who outgrew wives, of the difficulty of fitting into different worlds . . . She did it, though, in abstract terms, referring to 'people' or to 'men' who had such problems. Although it was obvious what was meant, Kenyon's name was never mentioned. He listened without once interrupting; he sensed that she could not have coped with a conversation – she had things she *had* to say but needed to say them quickly before her nerve failed her. And when she had finished, she gazed at Kenyon for several seconds as though to confirm he had absorbed her words, and then she returned to her book. Her duty was done.

The result of it all was that Kenyon did as was expected, although often with ill-grace and barely concealed resentment. He opened the shop at nine, checked the stocks, greeted the reps, served the customers, closed for lunch, opened again at two, locked up at six, had a drink on the way home . . .

He did it partly because he had already thought through all the things Mary's mother had said and thought she might be right. He was prepared to accept the possibility that he was in an abnormal state of mind that would pass. Her points – the shock of being back, the outgrowing of those who had remained – were not less real for being clichés.

But that was only one reason he did nothing. The major one was that he had no idea of what else he wanted to do. That there was something *better* he had no doubt. But what?

'He broods all the time,' he overheard his mother say to his father. But the truth was that he *thought*. He thought and tried to make some sense of the world, or at least of his part in it.

He went for long walks. So it would not excite even more comment, he took a gun 'to shoot rabbits', for who but a fool or a townsman walks for fun? And, as he walked, he pondered – on what he had learned, on what he *knew*. It was surprisingly little but it seemed important.

From war, he had learned the value of intense fellowship. He had learned how to grasp pleasure and how to endure with stoicism. He had learned that there is probably *nothing* – no matter how beautiful, or fearsome, or foul – that could not be reality.

He had learned that all men are capable of magnificent and terrible things. It was not done to talk of it (and who would have listened?) but he had seen British and American soldiers wild in orgies of sex and destruction. It was not only bad men who raped and killed.

He had learned to obey without hesitation, but at the same time he had learned power. Real power. The power of commands that were followed with no questions. And the even headier power of holding a loaded gun.

He listed all these, and more things, as he walked.

And then he asked himself, what did he *know*? That was even less, he concluded. Much less. We knew but one thing: that life was nothing but contradiction; that there was no truth, only single truths that changed depending on the day or the place or the person or the circumstance.

Sometimes on his walks, a single image filled his mind. It was of a sign he had seen in Germany. Pressed by a colleague, he had visited Dachau. He remembered the lines of Germans who were being forced to witness what their countrymen had done in the name of the Fatherland. The sign was in the room to which the bodies were taken after being gassed. God knew what state they were in – emaciated, faces locked in grimace, bones snapped in agony, parchment skin soiled with fear. In this room they were burned, turned to blackened bone and powder. There were ovens – two, perhaps three, he could not remember the exact number. Day after day, it must have been a scene from hell. And there in the room he had seen the sign. It proclaimed in huge letters: 'It is the duty of Germans to be clean. Wash your hands.'

He tried to tell Mary about this sign once, but she misunderstood. She thought he was trying to express hatred of Germans or exorcise a nightmare. She could understand the first but thought it unchristian to voice it, could accept the second but believed it was made worse by exposure. He tried to tell her it was neither. What he was trying to say was, how can there be any answers, any truth, any certainty, any path forward in a world where man can erect such a sign? But he had no words for it. His head spun with confusion, and in conversation and in action he took refuge in platitude and cliché.

And he told himself sometimes, perhaps that was all there was. Perhaps life was no more than just getting on with what was there. And perhaps if you accepted it, it was no small thing.

The winter ended and he had the sense to see that he was being given special treatment, that allowances were being made for him

– but that it could not last. His father was making it clear that it was time he 'snapped out of it'; Mary's mother was muttering that if it were her, she would not be so forgiving when Kenyon announced at the last minute that he didn't want to see the new Alan Ladd film or go to the Saturday-night dance after all.

An aunt in Liverpool died, and they drove to the funeral in a borrowed car. His mother shook her head in disbelieving despair at the bomb damage, although for years she had been seeing photographs and hearing reports.

'You'd never believe it if you hadn't seen it,' she kept saying. And Kenyon, unthinking and unfeeling, had tried to tell her what bomb damage could be like – of German towns that had been completely destroyed, where nothing remained but stench and rubble. His mother continued talking as though she had not heard, but that night – squeezed into a single bed in a cold and bare spare room – Mary had finally snapped.

'It's over, you know,' she said.

'What's over?' Though he knew.

'The war. You're back here. You may not like it, you might wish you were back with your Fräuleins. But you're here, and it's over, and I've had enough.'

She turned her face into the pillow, and he thought she was crying. He waited in silence for perhaps a minute, and leaned over. Her eyes were closed and she was breathing deeply and evenly. At first he thought she was faking, but then he realised she really was asleep, as though in speaking she had used up all her consciousness.

Nothing further was said in the morning: the imminent funeral preoccupied them. But from that day he was changed, not inside (where the doubts and the unfocused longings remained) but on the outside. He stood back from himself and saw the person they would have him be and he settled himself into the part.

If they saw he was play acting, no one said. There was an unconcealed air of relief that he even found he shared. Only Katharine, on her occasional visits home, discomforted him with looks that showed she saw through the charade and which condemned him as a tamed and sorry creature.

Only Katharine had the capacity to disturb him, only she could have sparked rebellion. She came close to doing so just once. He returned home one Friday to find her there unexpectedly. She had

106

obviously been in the house some time: she wore a cotton housecoat and was ironing clothes. She was alone. As usual he reached out to kiss her cheek. Katharine moved close, and with a surge of shock and excitement he realised that under the coat she was naked. He pulled her more tightly to him and she responded, pressing her breasts to his chest, moving her head so his face burrowed in her hair. He felt himself rise and she shifted her groin so that she rubbed against him.

'You know what I want,' he whispered. And then she was pushing him away, laughing and saying loudly, 'See how glad I am to see my brother-in-law again,' and he saw that Mary was on the stairs and he realised Katharine had known she was in the house all the while.

Nothing was said by anyone, but rebellion was dead before it began – not because Mary had found them so, but because of what the encounter told him about Katharine.

It was the vicar who brought a totally unexpected source of pleasure into his life. A small party of German prisoners of war were moved into the area to work on dismantling an abandoned Italian POW camp (they, unlike the Germans, had been shipped home soon after the war ended). The vicar invited them to the vicarage. The next week, with nervousness, he asked Kenyon to join them. It became a weekly event. In addition, some days Kenyon would walk out to their camp at midday instead of going home and would share sandwiches and beer with them. It was two miles each way, and it meant shutting the shop for two, even two and a half hours, but he thought that as a piece of rebellion it was small enough.

The shop closed every Wednesday afternoon and one Wednesday, after visiting the camp, he entered what seemed to be an empty house. He poured a beer, kicked off his shoes, and then heard a radio playing upstairs. Still holding the glass, he followed the sound. Mary was lying on the bed in Katharine's old room. She was wearing the silk and lace underwear he had brought the first time he had returned from Germany. It was the first time he had seen it since. She lay on her back, hands behind her neck, legs parted and bent. She did not avert her eyes when he stared. Heaven knew how long she had lain, waiting.

He began to undress, but she beckoned him to come close. He did so, reached to touch her, ease off her clothes, but she took

107

hold, pulled him on to her. 'Don't wait,' she said, and he entered her with them both still clothed, his trousers open, the gusset of her knickers forced aside. She was barely wet, but he did not pause, and they moved in explosions of violence that hovered on frenzy.

It was soon over, but time had not existed. Just madness and warm release and then two bodies soaked with sweat, lying and gasping for breath.

For ever after, Kenyon looked back on the next months of 1948 as the Sex Period. Just as Picasso had his Blue Period, or Hollywood its Musical Period, he had his Sex Period.

He would return home and find Mary naked under a robe, or after seeing visitors to the door she would re-enter the living room, lift her skirt and show she wore nothing underneath. Or she would move aside his newspaper as they finished breakfast and say, 'Be late today.' And they would make love – on the floor, once half-way up the stairs, sliding and crashing down as they climaxed.

Always he allowed her to take the initiative. That, after all, was the game she had devised, and the one that excited him. The day and time varied. The period between her approaches was not constant: the shortest gap was five days, the longest eight. Anticipation and not knowing was part of the aphrodisiac; outside of the sex itself there was no other physical contact. All that could be said was that if the relationship was a strange one (and, not being able to read into other people's private souls, who could say what was and was not strange?), it worked.

The Sex Period ended as abruptly as it had begun. He did not know it at the time but it did so on a Tuesday evening. Earlier, he had walked around to the main part of the vicarage to share an evening with the German POWs. Only they did not arrive. Telephone calls revealed that they had been moved without notice earlier in the day, probably on the first leg of their return home.

Kenyon sat drinking sherry with the vicar, a strangely intimate evening – little was said but Kenyon felt that in their silences they understood and shared each other's burden: the vicar's sick wife, Kenyon's loneliness.

He had thought Mary would be in bed, reading, asleep even (not ready for sex – she resented the evenings he spent with the Germans and was always distant). Instead, she was sitting in front of the fire, not reading, nor knitting. The radio was on, but only as company: it was tuned to a play but too low to make out the words.

'What's the matter?' he said.

'I'm pregnant.'

'Are you sure? How do you know?' He regretted these were his first words as soon as they were spoken. Nevertheless, he thought she might overlook them. Then she began to mimic.

'Are you *sure*? How do you *know*?' Her eyes flashed with anger, her words were out-of-keeping brutish. 'Course I bloody well know. A woman knows when someone's stuck a bun in her oven.'

Silence. Then, he, 'Don't you want it?'

More silence and eyes lifted slowly. 'Of course. But do *you*?'

'Of course I do.' Too quickly.

She stood, sighing with effort as though already heavy with child. 'I'm going to bed.'

He followed minutes later. She was already under the covers. The light was out. He undressed and slid in beside her. 'I do want it,' he said. 'It was just that it was such a shock.' She was curled, her back to him, and he tried to pull her into him, to nestle her buttocks against his groin, like two interlocking spoons. But she wriggled away.

He turned on his back and lay awake a long time. He tried not to think it, but he knew now what the Sex Period was all about.

From that day, sex reverted to being a duty dispensed, a need eased. Realisation made him explode for the first time. 'You only fucked me to get pregnant,' he would scream. But she would sit, or stand, or lie, unmoved, saintly almost in her refusal to respond in kind. '*Some people* want babies,' she would say, and return to knitting or reading or whatever else she was doing.

An awful truth, though, was that the more pregnant she became, the larger she grew, the more her hips and breasts rounded, the more he wanted her. *Her*. Not just a woman, or sex, as before (even during the Sex Period). But *her*. He loved the round hardness of her belly, the sweet smell that rose from her, the life-filled glow of her skin, the darkening of her nipples. On the rare occasions they made love, he wanted to merge into her, to melt his body into hers, to become nothing and everything. But always she held him back. 'Careful!' she would hiss. Or he would become aware of her eyes, screwed close as though she were trying to blot out what was happening to her.

109

She left him in no doubt, less by words and actions than by silences and omissions, that she let him take her because it was part of her wifely role. But that was all. And afterwards, as soon as she thought he was asleep, she would hurry to the bathroom. He would hear the water run and sense her frantic soaping as she tried to wash away every trace of him. But in time that ceased to hurt, leaving just a hollowness and a relief that, for now, he no longer felt need for her.

The baby was born at 4.22 on the afternoon of the first Monday in June of 1949. It was not due for three weeks and Mary and her mother had set off early to spend the day shopping in Shrewsbury.

Kenyon took a sandwich to the shop, walked over to the pub for a beer afterwards, had an unusually busy afternoon, and was on the pavement locking up just after 5.30 p.m. when he first heard the news.

The doctor broke it. Seeing Kenyon from his car, he screeched to a halt, opened the window and yelled, 'What are you doing here, man? Should be home with your wife and son.' And before Kenyon could reply, he had slammed the door and pulled away.

'It was all very sudden,' said his mother-in-law, anticipating his anger, the moment he reached home. She followed him up the stairs, talking all the way: almost as soon as they had arrived in Shrewsbury, Mary had felt odd; they had headed back; then, when it was clear it was no false alarm, they could not reach the doctor, and then the midwife had been somewhere else, and she had just decided to telephone Kenyon at the shop and it had all begun to happen . . .

None of it mattered, though, when he saw the boy. The anger at not being told disappeared. His son was sucking on Mary's breast. She pulled him away so Kenyon could see him better. 'He's just like you,' she said. In her voice was a warmth he had not heard for a long time. 'Isn't he just like you?' The baby began to cry and she guided him back to her nipple.

'What do you think?' she said. She had the glow of pregnancy but more so and her eyes burned with pride and love and achievement.

'He's a miracle,' he said. 'A real miracle.'

They decided to call him Stephen, and on the day he was

christened Kenyon watched her holding him and said softly, 'Let's try again, shall we?'

That evening he added, 'It's this place partly.'

Later, much later, resignedly, Mary said, 'All right. Let's move. If that's what you want.'

'Where?'

'Anywhere,' she said. 'You decide. Anywhere you and I and my baby will be happy.'

'Aren't we happy?'

'We are *now*. But I can't go on the way we have. You always want something that isn't here. Go and decide what you want and we'll come with you.'

'But I don't know what I want.'

She reached for the baby. 'Well,' her voice suddenly hard, 'you'd better decide. You'd just better bloody well decide.'

The Army was an impossibility. Besides, it had lost its appeal: he had no desire to move his family to an Army base; it would be exchanging one stultifying village for another. Yet what qualifications had he? His German was OK, but not good enough, certainly not academic enough, to get a job as a translator. He toyed with the idea of returning to his education. But what would they live on? And, in any event, it would mean separation – his instincts told him that, for all the present tenderness, living apart would be the end of the marriage. How often had he lain awake longing for just that, hoping for some event that would bring about such a state? Now with a son, he wanted the marriage to continue and succeed.

So where?

He would have to break the news they were moving to his parents. Mary, no doubt, would tell her mother. None of them would welcome it; all would fight it. He could already imagine the protests.

'What about your father – you know he dotes on that boy?'

'What about the shop? What are we going to do with it?'

But all that begged the most immediate question. What?

The answer came in an advertisement in the *Daily Express*. 'Are you 5'9"?' it began. It was one of many such ads, inviting applicants for the police service. He glanced through it – 'a secure future . . . exciting life'. And, most pertinent of all, 'housing or housing allowance'.

Where to live was one of the main practical problems if they moved. Nationwide, there was a shortage of accommodation. 'Housing or housing allowance' was a definite inducement.

Policing, though he knew nothing of it, had a good ring about it too. Part of a service, but out on the streets acting alone. A doing job. Probably not all that far removed from what he had done before in the Army, though on a different scale.

This particular ad was for the police force in Birmingham. He liked the idea of a city. Birmingham was only two hours away – a useful concession to offer parents. And it was further south – the right direction, he reckoned.

He completed and posted the coupon. Detail came almost by return. He did not show it to Mary. Nor did he say anything when he was asked to attend a local police station for height and weight checks and for an elementary educational test.

Two weeks later he was summoned to Birmingham.

He opened the envelope at breakfast, felt Mary's curiosity, and handed across the letter.

'You said to find something,' he said.

'But the police!'

'I'm only finding out. I haven't made any decision yet.' He noticed her eyes, added quickly, 'I didn't want to say anything until I knew more.'

Appeased, 'So this is going up to look?'

'And to see if they'd want me. But, yes, really just to look.'

She handed back the letter. 'A house of our own would be nice.'

He could tell the interview was a formality. His Army service alone would have carried the day – there had already been a large ex-service intake immediately after the war, and these men, with their experience of discipline and group life, had fitted in well. Kenyon was told he would be notified in about a month. Unofficially, it was made clear that Birmingham police looked forward to having him, provided, of course, his exam result was not abysmal. At that there had been laughter – he did not learn until later that you had to be almost illiterate to be turned down. All forces were well below their strength and were desperate for men. (The exact level of desperation could be gauged from their minimum height requirement – the lower, the greater the need. Birmingham was 5'9", some – including the Metropolitan Police – were lower still; a few were higher at 5'11".)

Kenyon and Mary borrowed a car and drove to Birmingham, spending a day in a small 'private hotel' on the edge of the city centre.

'It's an ugly place,' she said, after they had driven around haphazardly for two hours.

'It's easy to get out into the country,' he countered. 'And there are plenty of cinemas and theatres and good shops.'

'You want to come?'

'I think so.'

'I'll tell Mum. You'd better think how you're going to tell your parents. They'll go mad.'

She was wrong, and so had he been in his fears. 'As long as you're sure, son,' said his mother. 'Thought you'd do something like this one day,' said his father. 'At least it's not back into the Army – you won't be too far away.'

It was left to him to raise the fears, them to ease them.

'What about the shop?' he asked.

'To be honest, your father would like to retire. I know it's early, but he's not been well, and if we sold both shops . . . well, we're cautious people with our money . . .' There was even, it emerged, a cottage they thought they could buy. 'It's been empty some years and it'll need some work, but . . .'

He told Mary, his voice still echoing the relief and disbelief. 'What about your mum?' he asked.

'She said she hoped I knew what I was doing.'

'What did you tell her?'

'What else? I said, so did I.'

He left the vicarage five weeks later. Mary would stay until his three months' training was completed. In the meantime, at weekends he would look for accommodation.

The training centre was on the outskirts of a village between Rugby and Coventry. It consisted of a series of single-storey buildings erected during the war as a hostel for workers at the nearby Rootes aircraft engine factory. After the war it became Number 4 District Centre, training recruits for a number of Midlands police forces.

There was a new intake every two to three weeks. There were thirty in Kenyon's group. At twenty-three he was the oldest. The flood of ex-servicemen freed by the end of the war had trickled away about three years before. Most of his fellow recruits were raw youngsters. At the time he had joined the Army, he realised with a shock, many were still not teenagers.

The training was easy, and vaguely familiar. Drill, two hours' marching twice a week, was straight from the Armed Forces. So were methods of instruction – commands, yells and sarcasm. Years before he had laboured to learn how to throw grenades, strip and reassemble sten guns. Now he studied how to handle himself in court or deal with road accidents. Law as it affected policing dominated: powers of arrest, the difference between felonies and (less serious) misdemeanours, obscure – and, in Birmingham, surely useless – legislation about sexual contact with animals. It had to be learned by heart, word perfect so that at the trigger question it came forth like a recorded announcement. It was boring and soulless stuff, but Kenyon found it easy.

Most evenings and all weekends were free. Evening life revolved around one of three pubs within ten minutes' walk. Kenyon went home the first weekend, and after that spent them in Birmingham although it was not until after six weeks that he was told where he would be posted and could begin looking for accommodation.

Because of his height (two inches above the minimum) he was earmarked for the inner city. That suited him. It gave him a wide choice of places to live: any area on a bus route would do. He found a two-bedroom flat in an Edwardian house in Handsworth, then a genteel residential area. The bathroom was shared, but there were wash-basins in both bedrooms. Mary, when she saw it, was openly disappointed. But he told her he would redecorate and, in any event, it was only temporary – he had been told that they were likely to be allocated a new police house within a year.

At the end of his training, there was a week's leave. They spent it packing and moving. His father pressed an envelope into his hand as they left. 'I got a good price for the shop,' he said. 'You buy something to please that young woman of yours.'

It was a cheque for seven hundred and fifty pounds, a massive amount. They decided on a three-way split: two hundred and fifty pounds on furniture, another two hundred and fifty pounds on a second-hand car, the remaining third to be saved in a building society.

Kenyon, like all newcomers, began with learning beats. For the

and the pursued was often a narrow one: whether a man was a detective or a villain, he decided, often depended on chance events earlier in life. As it was, in practice, the division between right and wrong, good and bad was often indistinct.

He imagined a police examination based on the *real* world of being a detective.

QUESTION ONE. Criminal A is a persistent offender against whom it would be easy to secure a conviction. However, in return for turning a blind eye to his activities, he will supply information about other criminals. Do you a) arrest him anyway, b) allow him to remain free, c) encourage him to increase his information flow by providing helpful advice on how to maximise his criminal returns?

QUESTION TWO. There have been four break-ins on premises. There is no evidence that would stand up in court, but 1) there is great pressure for a 'result', and 2) you are fifty per cent sure you *know* who is responsible. Do you a) search your suspect's home and plant stolen goods, reckoning if he has not done these break-ins he is guilty of something else anyway, b) as before, but make sure you write down that he says 'it's a fair cop' or 'you've got me this time, copper' as an added precaution, or c) decide it's too risky and persuade someone already under arrest to add these break-ins to his list of guilty pleas in return for a good word to the judge?

QUESTION THREE. You seize a quantity of stolen cigarettes, hidden under floorboards. Do you a) turn the man loose in return for becoming an informant, b) charge him with possession of them all, c) declare only part and keep back the rest for buying information?

In many areas, Kenyon learned to be as pragmatic as other officers. He drew the line at bribes that went into individual pockets. But, as for the rest, he recognised it was a realistic business. For later generations of policemen it might become more complex, but for now there were simply baddies and there were goodies and generally it was easy for a good copper to see who was who. What wasn't easy was proof and conviction, and if evidence had to be doctored or the law helped along, then that's how it had to be.

There were real dishonest cops – Kenyon, like his colleagues, soon learned who they were. He shunned and despised them.

117

But, such was the siege mentality of the department, that no more than anyone else would he have dreamed of exposing them.

He had only one clash with one of these bent coppers. It began after he spotted a stolen Ford in a pub car park one night. (In those days it was still possible to memorise a list of stolen cars, so few were there.) He kept watch from his own car, and then followed. The driver picked up two more men and they drove to a factory estate on the south of the city.

They broke into one of the buildings. Kenyon found a telephone, called in for help, and two of the men were caught still in the building. The third, the driver, escaped. But Kenyon had had a clear view of him and was able to pick him out from a book of mugshots.

Case over. Except that the next day Kenyon was taken aside by a detective sergeant called Tremble, a man well-known as being bent.

Kenyon was asked, was he *sure* about his indentification? It was dark – couldn't he have been mistaken? Say, a ton mistaken. Well, two ton then. You could buy the wife a nice little present with two hundred pounds.

A week later there was a second attempt to change Kenyon's testimony – this time a warning of the kind of harassment he could face. An anonymous letter was mailed to the superintendent accusing Kenyon of having had sex with the wife of a man he had helped jail (untrue, but enough to get him dismissed if she backed the story – for a terrible day, he thought someone might have bribed or threatened her to implicate him, but it was only meant to frighten him).

Still he did nothing. The third approach was even less subtle. On the night before the case was due to come to court, petrol was poured through the letter-box of their home. The bomber made a lot of noise.

Kenyon dowsed the fire himself, stopped Mary from calling the brigade. 'But *why*?' she screamed. 'Someone did it on purpose.' Neighbours came and Kenyon told them it was an accident – a heater had overturned, everything was under control. And because they knew he was a policeman they accepted it reluctantly.

Mary refused to sleep until Kenyon talked. Gradually under pressure, he told her part of the story, mainly to stress that the petrol bomber had not really meant to harm them, only to warn Kenyon of what could happen. Immediately, he knew he had made a mistake.

'You mean they'll come back,' she said. She had brought Stephen into bed and was holding the boy close. 'You mustn't go into court. Tell them you're not sure. It's not us. It's Stephen. He's only four.'

Kenyon telephoned her after the court case. 'Did you?' she asked.

'Yes,' he said. 'But it's all right. Nobody gains from doing anything now.'

She put down the telephone on him.

He arrived home at 2 a.m. the next morning. She heard him fumble with the lock, stumble on the stairs, curse as he fell. Drunk! Exactly what she had expected. She hugged Stephen and pressed into the pillow. She heard him turn the knob for the bedroom door, swear as he found the door locked. She steeled herself, but he went away.

Next morning she heard him in the bathroom early. Downstairs, she composed herself for his appearance.

'Just tea,' he said, and she took in the sight of him and held everything she had been about to say.

She made tea, poured, and still did not say anything. There was a three-inch bruise across his forehead, a split on his cheek, his lower lip was swollen and misshapen. When he picked up the cup she saw his knuckles were torn and raw.

'What happened?' she said.

'A slight accident.'

She returned to the bedroom, heard him go.

'I fell,' Kenyon said at the station. The sergeant sent him to the police surgeon.

'Funny injuries for a fall,' the doctor said. 'But that's not my business unless someone asks me, is it?'

Back at the station, the duty sergeant gave him advice. 'Find things to do away from the nick. Don't want the inspector worrying about his coppers, do we?'

The sergeant called after Kenyon at the door. 'Sergeant Tremble's accident-prone too. He's in a worse way than you, though. General Hospital. Couple of thugs. Something tells me they'll never find them.'

*

Two months later, as a matter of course, Kenyon's attachment as a detective came to an end, and he returned to uniform. The move pleased Mary. She saw 'proper' policing as a safer and more socially acceptable job.

Since the night of the fire, there had been a further, subtle change in their relationship. She drew Stephen closer to her, and she gave out an unspoken but clear message that what she wanted was a relationship without worry, without disturbance, without upheaval. If that meant it had to be all surface and pretence, fine. If it also meant that part of his life had to happen elsewhere, that was fine too provided it remained separate and discreet.

Kenyon saw the change, but did not fight it. It made for an undemanding relationship that suited him. He stayed out a lot. Often he put in extra hours, though increasingly he saw that, though better than the shop, the police service was not going to lead him anywhere – at least, not for a very long time.

Soon after the return to uniform, Kenyon began moonlighting. Although it was against regulations, most married constables took other jobs to supplement their pay. Some were plumbers or builders' mates, others drove lorries or baked bread. One even worked as a hearse driver. For Kenyon, extra money was only one reason, and not the main one. He needed a fresh avenue for his energy and his increasingly frustrated ambition. He *knew* that he deserved better than being a rank-and-file copper. He *knew* that because of the system he was being wasted. Objectively, he could look at himself and say that if anyone was officer material he was. One day, he was sure, men like him would be accelerated through the ranks. Ability and hard work would count, not age and time-serving and keeping your nose clean. But that did not help him. As it was, it was impossible to make sergeant, let alone inspector.

Kenyon sold insurance on commission. He was very good at it. After years spent assessing people, salesmanship came easy. To his surprise, he also discovered he had a facility in dealing with figures.

And, whether it was the main motive or not, there was no doubt that the extra income was useful. It coincided with a decision that rent allowances could be used towards buying a house on mortgage. They bought their first house, a 1930s semi-detached about four miles from the city centre.

By now Kenyon was studying for his promotion exam – despite the knowledge that, whatever the result, he was unlikely to make sergeant for another four to six years because of bottlenecks and internal policy.

The studying, the job itself and the time spent selling insurance, meant that he saw less and less of Mary and Stephen. He raised no objection when she suggested that her mother should come and live with them. She would help look after Stephen, enabling Mary to take a part-time job.

Kenyon took the promotion exam and passed. He felt elation as the results were read aloud on parade. Over half had failed. It quickly faded, though, as he remembered that in practice it meant nothing for a long time (and, even then, did he really want to be a sergeant, up to his neck in paperwork and under more pressure than any other rank in the station, and all for an extra twenty-five shillings a week? And after sergeant, what? Just more years of waiting – no one made inspector until they had been in the force at least fifteen years.)

Suddenly, though, with no studying to do, there was spare time. He had no idea how to fill it. Just 'being at home' did not appeal. He felt guilt at not wanting to spend his new-found time with his son, but the truth was they were awkward in each other's company. Kenyon loved him, but both found togetherness a strain. It was not helped by the habit the boy had developed of seeking Mary's reaction every time that Kenyon made a suggestion or asked a question. The awful truth, though Kenyon would never have admitted it, was that at home he never felt a true insider; there was always something of the visitor about him.

A colleague solved his problem. The man was one of the small number of more ambitious police officers studying by post for a law degree. Kenyon visited one evening and found him completing his latest lesson from a correspondence school.

'Pour yourself a beer and give me ten minutes,' said the colleague. Kenyon fetched the drink, sat down and picked up a college prospectus from the top of the man's pile of papers.

'Success is Ability Plus Training,' said the brochure of the Rapid Results College. 'Founded AD 1928' – he liked the AD. He turned the page. 'An income of £1,000 a year! That is what you can earn. If you doubt it, read the official income tax statistics . . . 835,000 PEOPLE EARN £1,000 A YEAR AND MORE in Great Britain alone.'

Kenyon's colleague finished writing, put down his pen. 'Why don't you do it?'

'Why? I've had it up to here with studying.'

'Stop your brain rusting.'

Kenyon snorted derisively. But next time he saw an advertisement in the *Daily Telegraph* he clipped the coupon.

When the brochures arrived, he disregarded law. Other subjects were also quickly dismissed – Public Administration, Credit Management, Secretarial . . . He finished reading, and realised that the truth was that none of the subjects really appealed to him.

He paused, rubbed his eyes and stared into the distance, suddenly lost in time, back in the days before his brother died. He remembered the plans for university, the talk with his teachers, the excitement of a world opening up. And suddenly he saw that what he was seeking now was the chance to study that he had never had. The subject itself scarcely mattered. It was the *act* of learning that counted – affirmation that he was still ambitious for something *better* (that old word again!).

He read the brochures once more. This time he paused on Accountancy – useful knowledge, surely, over a whole spectrum of careers. There were several courses, for many different qualifications. Most, he noted, involved the student being employed or 'articled' in the profession before being allowed to take the examinations. That was no good. There was an exception, however. The Association of International Accountants. Three examinations and then, if successful, the right to call yourself 'International Accountant (Inc.)' and add the letters AAIA after your name. He checked the curriculum – accounts, company law, income tax, auditing. And the price. He completed the form, wrote a cheque for the first stage – £16 16s. – and posted them the same day.

It had to be a measure of how far things had drifted that Mary did not notice for a year what he was studying – not that he ever told her. She thought it was a continuation of the police promotion exam, and he preferred to let her believe that.

'You're not thinking of leaving the police?' she asked, horrified, when she learned.

'I just thought it would be a useful extra string.'

He was happy to talk more about it, but she shrugged. 'It's all going so well,' she said. 'Don't let's spoil it.'

Ten hours a week. Nearly two years. Three examinations. A buff envelope. Success!

And immediate deflation.

'But what will you *do* with it?' she asked. Then remorse. 'I do think you're clever.' But too late.

A week later he had to make enquiries at a local, family-owned company. An employee had absconded; money was missing.

Kenyon knew the firm by repute. It had been started in the 1930s to lend small sums of money to individuals, mainly housewives, at high rates of interest. That was still part of the business, but the present generation was trying to move into bigger and more socially acceptable areas such as loaning money to small companies. Again, though, it charged high interest – after all, the companies they attracted were high-risk borrowers who had often already been turned away by the banks. Kenyon was wary of the firm; he had seen some of its victims.

He was surprised to find how quickly he warmed to the managing director, Geoffrey Burrows. Perhaps it was the flattering way Burrows confided the problems he was having with the rest of the family in trying to alter the firm's direction – 'Don't get me wrong, I know it's been a bloody good profitable business in the past and I'm not saying my old man did anything wrong, but times change . . .'

In the past, he added, the family would probably never have called in the police. They would have dealt with matters themselves. 'But, as I say, times change.'

A secretary brought the absconder's books, and Kenyon flipped the pages. He already knew this would be one for the CID. Suddenly, some figures caught his eye. He stared for a while and then commented on them.

'Already checked it,' said Burrows. 'He lent the money to himself – or rather to a phoney firm that I imagine will turn out to be him or some of his friends.'

But he looked at Kenyon with new interest. 'You know your figures,' he said.

Kenyon explained.

'And I've seen you before,' Burrows added. 'You sold some insurance to a neighbour of mine – nine, ten months ago.'

Later, as Kenyon was leaving, he said, 'Come and have a drink.'

Then, later still, he asked, 'Ever thought of going into commerce?'

Kenyon walked the streets alone that night, replaying the conversation, trying to make decisions. What did he want? Where was he going? The awful truth was, he did not know. He had lost his way. He had no maps. All he did know was that, handicapped and untutored, he had to keep striving, to find something more worthy of himself. The moment he had that thought, his mind asked: and working for a loan company is 'more worthy'? But the answer was already there: it would be a new world with a fresh chance. It would take him in a different direction.

Two days afterwards the formal offer was delivered by hand. One thousand and five hundred pounds a year plus commission. Job: to check out and make recommendations on company loans.

He and Mary celebrated with a rare visit to the cinema – *Rock Around the Clock*. The film was stopped twice as people left their seats to dance wildly in the aisles.

'It's a new age,' said Kenyon as they came out into the darkness.

Neither of them was sure whether he meant for the world, or just for them.

CHAPTER NINE

By the beginning of May, Kenyon was almost ready.

He had a visitor's passport which he would use first, an ordinary passport to which he would switch, and then, when the time came, all the documents he needed to become Daniel Rossiter, an Irish citizen.

He also had supporting pieces of paper – from certificates of vaccination to visiting cards to driving licences.

He had decided how he would alter his appearance initially – what he needed was the greatest change possible with the minimum of preparation. And he had worked out what he now began to think of as his 'escape route'.

The exact day of vanishing would be determined nearer the time. A key factor would be when George deposited money. Obviously, there could be no dry run here. However, posing as a potential client, he had written to the deposit company for literature, and he now had a mental picture of the layout and mechanics.

Suddenly there was less to do – but more to juggle in his mind. Too much. He would arrive back home each morning with his head echoing. At times it threatened to overwhelm him and he would slump, glass in hand, and shake between sips until alcohol quietened the clamour.

He acknowledged the irony of what was happening. His relationship with Pamela – and then the struggle not to lose her – had started this. Only he no longer wanted her as she was now, and as they were now. He longed for her as she had been, for what they had had together. But that was impossible. Time could not be undone. But, generally, he had no room for such thoughts: the act of running had become a reality in its own right, and his plans a total obsession. Just as previously he had been totally engrossed by Pamela, now everything was directed towards his disappearance. At times he could see that what he had done was replace one obsession with another – like the mass murderer who becomes ultra religious or the drug addict who gives his being to some exotic sect.

The threat, as relayed by Hunter, had been the trigger for his newer, total preoccupation. But even without it, the idea of disappearing, starting again, was a heady and inviting one. He would not have had to go to these extremes. But, at heart, didn't he just want out anyway? A chance to begin again? To wipe clear the last twenty years and to pick up as though they had never happened? From the moment he had returned from Germany, he had taken the wrong road. His marriage to Mary, born out of cowardice and inertia, had been a mistake: he should have ended it then. Better for both of them. It had finished anyway. Stephen's birth? Even if he could relive the past, he would not want to change that. But he was no real father – he had failed there, and now there was no going back. And his love for Pamela, her love for him, their time together, their utter happiness? That too was wonderful. But finite. And again reason told him it was over, even if sometimes he still clung to pathetic hope. Nothing remained for him here. Maybe, just maybe, somewhere else, as someone else, it would be different. Maybe he could get back on to the right path . . .

Now he had got this far, it was tempting to move as soon as he collected the money from the roulette croupier. That was only two days away. In fact, it was tempting to move *now:* the roulette money was a refinement, a fall-back. He could not really see he would need it. If he had misjudged the safety-deposit situation, they were going to get him. If he was right, he would have all the money he needed.

But he told himself there were still things to do – if he was to have the best chance of remaining free and undiscovered.

One of them was photographs. He did not want any left around. He had sweated over plastic surgery, but decided against: plastic surgeons were obvious avenues for Barton's associates to check, no matter where in the world they were. So photographs had to go.

He never appeared in those taken at the club: show-business personalities and local gangsters had always wanted to pose with

Hunter, but there was no kudos in being pictured with him, Kenyon.

He was included in a few of the family photographs he had inherited when his parents died. The most recent shots of him were over ten years old but, in his manic caution, he destroyed them.

Mary had kept no photographs after their split. He knew that. He had seen her destroy them. It was the night he had finally got together the courage to tell her.

She had been in the garden feeding weeds on to a bonfire when he arrived home. They went inside.

'I *knew*,' she'd said. 'The moment you came back. But why the hell didn't you write a letter or tell me on the phone?'

Then it had hit her. 'Oh God, no!' she'd cried, throwing out her arms dramatically. 'You thought you ought to do the *right thing*. Oh my God, Mr Great Lover thought he ought to do the right thing.'

She had stormed past him several times in the next half-hour, her arms laden. But he had not realised what was happening until a neighbour banged on the door and complained that they were going to set alight the garden fence.

Outside, he saw that the bonfire was licking the sky. Huge choking clouds had brought out neighbours. In the flames, he made out the sleeve of one of his overcoats, some shirts, a statuette he had bought on holiday because she liked it. And papers and photographs. Albums of them. Card boxes of them. A small suitcase of them. As he'd watched, she'd tossed on a pile of letters, still held together in ribbon – letters sent while he was in Germany. He had moved to save them. But, so what? If this was how it ended . . .

She had been kneeling by the fire, head bent as though praying when he had left minutes later. He saw her only once after that.

And Pamela? She had photographs. In the early days they had delighted in being photographed together. He doubted she would have thrown them away. More likely, she had simply set them aside. They would be in the Yesterday file. She didn't destroy, she simply put out of mind.

He telephoned Pamela around ten o'clock, got a cleaner who said Mrs Kenyon was in the bath, could she take a message? He waited a half-hour before calling back, rolling the words 'Mrs

Kenyon' around in his mind although he knew the fact she still used his name had no real significance.

He was afraid of talking to her, nervous of how she would react to him, but at the same time he longed to hear her voice. Over or not, the thought of her still made him as apprehensive and excited as an adolescent with a crush.

She was wary.

He tried to engage in small-talk to prolong the conversation, hoping against hope that she would say something he could take and hoard away, a few words he could replay in his mind.

But nothing, except polite chill, as he rambled on.

And then, at last, the dagger: 'Are you drunk? You don't sound drunk. But is there a reason for this call?'

He screwed his eyes against the pain. He forced his voice to sound calm, unconcerned.

'I need a favour,' he said.

Silence. Still wary.

'The tax man's after me. He's trying to reopen some accounts. I think I can head him off, satisfy him.' He paused and waited. He was sweating, and it was an effort to keep his voice under control.

'Why me?'

'I need the papers. The ones I want are all stuffed in boxes, still back at the house.' He dropped his voice, made it apologetic. 'I never got round to moving them.'

'There's a lot of stuff in your room. I haven't touched it.'

Your room.

'That'll be it.'

He waited for her to speak, but she didn't.

'Can I come and collect them?'

'They're your papers.' Flat.

He made one more try. 'I thought maybe you'd like to talk too.'

'I'm going away straight after lunch. Richard and Diana have invited me to Florence, they've an apartment there.'

Another stab – but this time he had steeled himself. His voice was under command. 'I need them soon.'

'You've still got a key.'

'I think so – if you haven't changed the locks.'

She acted as if she had not heard. 'I'll put Mrs Mellon on the telephone – you spoke to her first time you called. Tell her when you want to come; she'll arrange to be here.'

He started to speak, framing words that did not mean anything deep, words just to end the conversation with a not-bad feeling. But all he heard was a new voice; she had already handed over the phone.

They had been pictured together the first time they had met. The date and the time were written on the back of the print together with the name of the photographer and a number for re-ordering. 31 July 1958. (A Friday, but only just.) 1.15 a.m. Candy Photographs. 00321

There were five of them seated around a dining-table, faces and champagne glasses raised to the camera. Two of them were Kenyon's clients – half a day earlier they and Kenyon had concluded the loan deal they were now celebrating. The fourth man was an acquaintance of Kenyon's they had chanced upon in the club, and who had just joined them for a drink. The sole woman in the group was Pamela, the man's companion. Kenyon had used the club for entertaining before; Pamela was vaguely familiar – Kenyon had seen her with different groups of people, and noted her once in a gossip column, shown with the owner of a growing chain of trendy hairdressers.

The photograph made it look as though the group had been celebrating together all evening and would continue to do so for many more hours. In reality, Kenyon's acquaintance and Pamela had sat down only minutes before – they had been on their way out of the club. The seats they occupied belonged to two hostesses who were visiting the cloakroom before leaving with the clients. Ten minutes after the picture was taken Kenyon had been alone in the debris, settling the bill.

He paid from a wad of five-pound notes, noting without comment that he had been overcharged by a bottle of champagne (he kept track of such things, but one bottle even at the prices charged here was not worth protesting about after the commission he had just made). He tipped heavily – it might be weeks before he returned, but he wanted to be remembered. On the way to the door a hostess held out a cigarette in a long holder, requested a light, but he was past before he saw her. The euphoria of the deal was already dying, the booze lay sour on his tongue. The faded red-and-gold glitz of the club looked just that – faded.

At first, the rain was a relief after the sweet, hot, stale scent of the club, and then an irritation as he realised there were no cabs and that a couple were already ahead of him in the wait for one.

The doorman waved at a cab caught at traffic lights; then, to be sure, he ran to intercept it. He returned, triumphant, running beside the vehicle. Kenyon saw the man fumble for tip money, fail because he was too drunk. The girl opened her bag, handed over a note, helped the doorman ease the man into the cab. She turned into the light a second before the door was closed on the couple. She was the woman who had sat at his table for the photograph. 'You won't get much out of him tonight,' he recalled thinking. The venom in the thought surprised him.

On his way back to his apartment he remembered the newspaper photograph he had seen. And what the caption had called her – 'girl about town'. He had noted it as a neat euphemism. So she was a tart, maybe not a professional, more likely a paid-in-presents amateur. But so what? Why should tonight's encounter have produced any feelings in him at all?

The answer come to him a half-hour later as he yanked at the sofa base that converted into a bed. Jealousy, straight jealousy. As simple as that. He had not looked at her much in the club, but he recalled the newspaper photograph: there was something haunting about her. Jealousy, because he wanted a woman. Full point. His marriage was now little more than name. He and Mary slept together perhaps once a week, sometimes less. She never rejected him, never pleaded tiredness nor headaches, nor failed to respond. But he always sensed a holding back, a clinging to control; he suspected that if he stopped wanting sex she would not object. As it was, it sometimes felt as cold and mercenary an arrangement as going to a prostitute: his work and income were the payment.

He drank an Alka-Seltzer and two glasses of tap water – he had a 9 a.m. meeting, had to feel good by then. He took covers from a cupboard, tossed them on to the bed, crawled under them naked.

An hour later he checked his watch. Just after three. It was obvious he was not going to sleep. He was still tired, but everything was adrenalin sharp. His mind raced with the previous day's events – the deal, the biggest he had concluded yet; the call to Mary to say he would be away another couple of days and the way her tone had said, why tell me? Geoff Burrows's congratulations and the suggestion that maybe they should make the London operation full-time with Kenyon in charge.

In the two years since he had joined the loan company Kenyon had done well. Some salesmen simply pushed loans at any cost. Once the papers were signed, that was the end. Kenyon took a different line. Before he okayed a loan, he satisfied himself that the man could and would keep paying – *and* would stay happy with the arrangement. High interest – very high interest – Kenyon found was something clients could live with happily, provided they felt you were dealing with them straight and were in there pitching for them to succeed. It did not endear Kenyon to his bosses in the early days; only the fact Burrows had appointed him personally and that he could check police records with ease through old buddies kept him in the job. Soon, though, it began to pay off. Kenyon's customers topped up their loans; furthermore they provided good leads to other potential borrowers. And so on it went. Almost all the company's business was local, but Kenyon was encouraged to follow his customers to wherever they might be found. The London area, not surprisingly, had proved the most lucrative hunting ground. His nose for backing winners was so good that already some of his early customers were being wooed by the big banks who would not have touched them when he first said yes.

He now spent an average of two nights every week in London, though not evenly – some weeks it might be four, some none at all. The company had taken the apartment in part payment from a client who had had problems settling his debt. Apartment was too grand a term. It was a single large, low-ceilinged room, with a kitchenette and bathroom, in a 1930s block on the edge of Soho. There were seven such flats, all occupied by the kind of people who did not ask (or answer) questions about their neighbours. Two, Kenyon knew, owned clubs; another was a hooker (though she did not work here). He knew nothing of the others, but the rooms would have been hard to sell or let to anyone with a more conservative life-style or needs. The road outside was one of the main north–south arteries through central London and was heavy with traffic noise twenty-three hours a day. The fumes turned the windows black within days of being washed, maybe a reason why there was no sign any were ever cleaned (although it was more likely that none of the occupants ever noticed, using the rooms as they did as simply places in which to crash out).

131

Mary had visited once, had thought it squalid, had tried to persuade him to move. But it did not worry him. He now saw it – and his job – as transitory. He had begun to think of where he would go next. He knew he was good at what he did. Most important, he had proved several times that he could spot trends and opportunities early: a key ability and one rare enough to have a high value in the market-place. His successes were already being noticed by others. He thought it only a matter of time before one of the merchant banks approached him. He was determined to be ready – despite the workload, he tried to devote at least an hour a day to studying books that would round out his knowledge.

At 3.45 a.m. he accepted that he was not going to sleep, got up, dressed, checked the window (he thought it had stopped raining), and was swept by a great desire to walk through the empty city.

The rain had slowed to a drizzle, but it ceased as he walked. He passed the Phoenix Theatre, lights dimmed now, Cambridge Circus, traffic lights performing without need, the bookshops of Charing Cross Road. The day began to lighten as he neared Trafalgar Square. He debated whether to cross into The Mall (and St James's Park) or turn eastwards and into the Strand. The Strand won; he would make a circle, grabbing tea from a stall in Covent Garden.

There were few cars; the only people on foot were a couple in the square and a man who had paused on his way out of the all-night post office. Dawn broke strong; the sun glittered on huge puddles turning them to magical lakes; buildings shone with a whiteness they would lose later in the day. Kenyon paused opposite the post office, turned back to watch the couple now running hand in hand across Trafalgar Square. His face took on a sad smile. He felt happy for them, but they touched chords, reminded him of what might have been and what was not.

He shrugged off the feeling, and he breathed theatrically deeply, savouring the fresh, newly washed air. It was then that the sports car came into view. He saw it only in the fraction of a second before it stopped in the centre of the empty road. The driver slid out with an easy grace as though the movement had been choreographed. The car was an Austin Healey Sprite, bright yellow, its hood down. The driver left the door open wide while she scampered around the puddles to the posting box.

The woman was not tiny, but she was swamped by a huge

man's sweater which she wore over a full skirt. They did not
match; given the hour, she had probably dressed carelessly,
grabbing what was nearest and most practical. Her feet were
bare, and they were what held Kenyon most. She began her
return to the car, and they danced among the golden lakes. She
reached the car, sensed his gaze, lifted her head defiantly almost.
And then she gave a smile of recognition. He remembered the
smile: it was the woman from the club.

He walked over. A van from the market pulled past and honked
at the way the car was parked, but she seemed unaware.

'Couldn't sleep,' he said. It was a statement, meant to explain
his own presence, but she heard it as a question.

'I didn't try,' she said. 'Some nights I know I won't sleep.' She
shrugged and then gestured back towards the mail-box, again in a
movement that flowed. 'I get all my letters done.' She giggled.
'When they get a long letter from me at home, they can say, Pam
can't be sleeping.'

Another car swerved around them. 'I think maybe you'd better
move,' said Kenyon.

'I guess so.'

But she seemed reluctant to go. 'Can I give you a lift?'

'Depends where you're going.'

'Where do you want to go?' Enjoying the game.

'I'd like breakfast. Would you like breakfast?'

She slid into the car, closed the door, turned the key. Again,
movements that flowed into one.

But she didn't drive off. He stood there uncertain.

'Come on,' she said. 'I'm hungry.'

They ate at a shared corner table, and she did not talk until her
plate was half-empty.

The pub – dark old wood, long narrow rooms, smoke and voice
filled – adjoined Smithfield's, London's meat market. It was
packed with meat workers, still in overalls, grabbing pints or
taking breakfast.

Pamela – Pamela Stacey; she had introduced herself, and he'd
said, yes, I saw you in the paper once – had ordered mixed grill.
'You'll never eat that,' he'd said when it arrived. The steak looked
as though it weighed a pound. In addition there was a lamb chop,
kidneys, slices of liver. Plus fried potatoes and a plate of toast. 'I

will – I always do,' she said, and for no good reason that hurt: childishly and unreasonably, he already wanted to think of this as a 'special place'.

She paused to drink beer: a pint glass of draught Guinness.

Kenyon's food arrived. She began laughing and he looked down: a steak twice the size of hers, topped with four fried eggs.

He began to laugh too. 'I'm glad I ordered the snack,' he said.

Throughout the meal he was conscious of other men's eyes on her, and he basked in their envy (how different, how very different, it would become).

He drank bitter, a drink he realised he had not touched for a year, maybe two (at another time he would think back and try to remember when he had ceased to be a regular beer man and become a hard-liquor man).

They emerged to a day that had already begun. 'I think I'm drunk,' he said. The beer had topped up the alcohol of the previous night, but this time it had lifted him. He really meant, 'Are you safe to drive? Should you leave your car?' But she didn't reply – she was already making for the car which was parked across an exit bay, surrounded by angry workmen.

He watched from across the street as she talked to them. It was too far away for him to hear or even to make out facial expressions, but he could read the situation through gestures. He sensed the anger begin to go, and then acceptance or resignation replacing it, and then, finally, a complete about-face as the men jostled to reassure her, help her into her car, clear a pathway, and shout and wave her goodbye.

'You've left some fans there,' he said as he climbed in.

'Fans? Oh, there.' As though the event belonged to years rather than seconds before. Something else he would come to know.

She accelerated into Holborn, turned and shouted above the roar, 'Do you want to walk?'

'Where?' He was checking his watch. It was almost seven. 'I've a meeting at nine.'

'You'll be in time.'

Traffic was still light and she wove through it with the same smooth ease he had noticed in her own physical movements earlier. Her feet were bare on the pedals. It had begun to rain again, and the day's early promise was fading fast, but the hood remained down and she appeared not to notice. He turned and watched her. Her concentration on the road seemed total. He had guessed she was in her late twenties, but with her face scrubbed clear of make-up, her hair loose below her shoulders (it had been coiled earlier), and the enormous khaki-coloured sweater, she looked almost childlike. Later, he realised it was one of many contradictions – a grown, worldly (too worldly?) woman who could look as untouched as a child; someone who moved with such grace and lack of effort that she seemed small and delicate, yet when you looked hard at her in repose you realised her features – her nose, her mouth among them – were large, almost out of proportion. Her voice would change its accent: mid-Atlantic, a trace of West Country burr, a touch of hard north Germanic (which accorded with one of her stories that her father – now dead – had been a South African diplomat). Yet, whatever, in its caressing softness it could make poetry from staggering strings of obscenity. He learned it was her contradictions which excited and held him, part of her magic.

All that was in the future, though, and this rainy July morning she parked the car on the north edge of Regent's Park and scampered towards the grass, calling back to him, 'Come on, I want you to meet some friends.'

He paused, wondering whether to lift the hood, lock the doors. Then he shrugged, and followed – if she wanted to leave it unattended and vulnerable . . .

It wasn't far. He caught up with her kneeling close to the double bars of the wolf run on the edge of the zoo. Two had come as close as they could. They held her in their white near-human gaze and he shuddered at the look. But she was talking to them, so softly he could not make out the words. Others came. Despite the bars, he found their nearness terrifying and wanted to leave. He looked down; she was holding the outer set of bars, still talking. It was silly, theatrical, child-show-off stuff. Except he realised that the wolves, for all their look, were still; none growled.

She stood so quickly he was unprepared. She linked her arm in his and made for the car. 'I used to feed them,' she said. 'But they stopped me.' He waited for her to explain who 'they' were, but she did not say anything else.

They reached the road and he was about to step back into the car when she suddenly darted forward, her hand raised. A taxi stopped in response, and Kenyon looked at her quizzically.

'Your cab,' she said. 'You've got a nine o'clock appointment. Remember?'

He wanted to call her several times over the next week. He went as far as getting her address and telephone number – she lived in one of the South Kensington squares. One night he even found a reason for passing her block of flats.

But he did not contact her. His relationship with Mary had settled to one that they could both sustain, even, after a fashion, welcome for its lack of demands. Mary had taken a part-time job as a receptionist in a local hospital. Through it she had developed a new group of friends and acquaintances, which made him feel less guilty about the time he spent away from home. He worked horrendously long hours now – even evenings like the one at the club, where he had met Pamela, were work. Not for a minute on such evenings did he forget what they were all about.

His only relaxation was the cinema to which he went alone. Not just the cinema, but the 'art' cinema. It began when he went to see Bergman's *The Seventh Seal* – partly out of curiosity, partly because it was the only film showing nearby that began at a time that suited. *Nuit et Brouillard* followed, and *The Cranes Are Flying, Quiet Flows the Don, Les Diaboliques*. Wajda, Bergman, René Clair, Resnais, Bardem. He saw them all. Indiscriminately. All that he demanded was that the film should be foreign and exotic. They were his escape to another world. No matter whether they were joyous or sad, fearful or heart-lifting. Only that they should be different from his reality.

What he did not do was sleep with other women. By time and practice, Kenyon and Mary had worked out a way of existing together. It had habit (a drive into the country each Sunday, a visit to Shropshire every two or three months), and it had rules, no less rigid for being unspoken. Not sleeping with other women, he saw as one. Their own love-making had a sameness and a regularity that, though he resented its lack of passion, was almost comforting. Saturday night. After she checked Stephen was asleep. Almost always the same beginning – the uncovering of her breast in the darkness, the tracing around her nipple with his finger-point, her 'uh, that feels good' to confirm the night was right. But afterwards, while he slept, the clambering back into the night-dress so that, by morning, he alone was naked.

Kenyon did not contact Pamela because he knew that to do so would be to take a step towards breaking that rule. Fate helped him. The suggestion that there should be a full-time London office became reality. It took him little time to make the decision. He considered whether the time had come to move on, decided it was too soon to branch out. He needed one or two more successes, more up-market contacts. London would help with both. The decision made, office accommodation had to be found and rented, staff engaged. Mary did not want to move to London: she had her job, Stephen was happy at school and had friends, they had only bought the new house fifteen months before. They agreed that he would live and work in London during the week and return home for the weekend. The only new 'rule': 'You must do something with Stephen. That boy's growing up without seeing his father.' Saturday afternoon, they agreed, would be Stephen's time.

He doubted he would be in the London flat more than a year. Nevertheless, he bought a few things to make it more of a home – a large gaudy abstract painting from a young artists' co-operative, a pile of classics from Foyles (all books he had vowed to read over the years but had not), a compact stereo gramophone and a selection of modern jazz albums.

With the new office, he found a growing stream of would-be borrowers directed towards him. Many were too risky. But all of them needed checking out – commercially, Britain was changing fast. There might still be austerity, but there was also the start of better times. What had Harold Macmillan, the Prime Minister, said last year? 'Most of our people have never had it so good.' Whether that was true or not, things were happening. British Overseas Airways Corporation had just launched a transatlantic jet service. The first stretch of British motorway was due to open before the year end, admittedly only eight miles and in Lancashire at that, but nevertheless the start of a new motoring era. Within weeks it would be possible to telephone anywhere in Britain direct, without having to call the operator. Stereo was all the rage. Television was becoming commonplace. Even coal had come off ration. Fortunes were being made from the craziest ideas – who would have thought there could be a craze for the bubble car? He found he was working most evenings and – despite the promise – many weekends. Any time he had free, he worked through a list of books compiled for him by a lecturer he had met from the London Business School. Perhaps once a fortnight, he went to the cinema.

A month before Christmas, he telephoned to apologise that he could not get home until Saturday evening – a young entrepreneur wanted money to convert a deserted cinema into an antiques supermarket. Kenyon wanted to see the area on Saturday morning. His interest extended beyond assessing whether to grant the loan – although it was a substantial one. He had begun to wonder whether he should turn entrepreneur himself, capitalise on his ability to forecast growth areas by actually getting involved with one. Instead of lending out money, he would borrow and invest it. The idea appealed more and more. Think of the people who had invested in the boutiques and restaurants that had transformed King's Road from a quiet street of grocers and pubs into the centre of the Chelsea set in less than two years. All he needed was the right opportunity. When the Saturday came, however, he awoke filled with remorse: what he was doing was crazy, he would go home.

It was his first – and last – concession to trying to re-establish the family. During the train journey, he anticipated taking a pleased and surprised Stephen to the park or to a football match, perhaps meeting up with Mary later for a meal. But when he arrived Mary was out. She did not return until late afternoon – after his call earlier in the week she had decided to help out at a Christmas fair being held in aid of the hospital. Stephen was away for the weekend – Mary had persuaded the mother of one of his friends to invite him to stay. A young doctor drove Mary home, and they all sat and drank tea formally. Mary and the young man talked in shorthand about an area of her life Kenyon did not know – the hospital – and Kenyon felt awkward and an outsider. He sat, listening mostly, realising how little he now knew about her. She too was changing, had changed, but he had not seen.

'I'm sorry,' he said later.

'About what?' Genuinely surprised.

'That I'm away so much.'

More surprise. 'But you can't help it. A new office doesn't set itself up. It'll be better when you've got it all organised.' There was a moment of terrible realisation that *this* was what she wanted.

He left on Sunday evening – an early meeting the next day, he said.

138

That day, Monday, was the day Pamela called.

Nine o'clock in the evening. The room was heavy with the smell of wet clothes that had not yet dried. He was drinking rum and hot water because he thought he had a cold coming. He was slumped and tired after a bad day, but edgy and unable to concentrate. *The Times* lay open beside him. He had flipped the pages, but none of the stories held him – Randolph Churchill was demanding a retraction from an MP who had called him a coward, British troops had killed four EOKA terrorists in Cyprus, Senator Hubert Humphrey had had an eight-hour meeting with Khrushchev and was convinced that the Soviet leader was not planning to start a war . . .

Kenyon had half-watched *The Phil Silvers Show*, then turned to the *The Goon Show* on the radio when faced with *Wagon Trail* on television. Now Stan Getz on record was playing in the background, and he was wondering whether to go to bed despite the earliness of the hour.

His doorbell rang and he went to answer with annoyance – whoever rang had got past the outer door without announcing himself on the entry-phone. He slipped on the chain: a neighbour had been attacked a week before. The door opened on to an open catwalk at the rear of the block. The December sleet and wind gusted in the open well of the building, and Kenyon's caller was bent forward in self-protection. The face was invisible, most of the head obscured by a newspaper held like a rain-hood.

But he recognised her immediately.

Inside, he reached to take the raincoat – it was soaked, she had been walking – but she shrugged him away. 'I can't stay.' She giggled. 'I'm at the theatre.' She did not say which one, but most of the London theatre district was within ten minutes' walk. 'I was sitting there and remembered you lived near by and I thought I'd look in.'

'Just like that?'

She smiled. 'Just like that.'

His mind whirled. He imagined her getting up from her seat, working her way down a row of people, tiptoeing out because, surely, it was too early for an interval. What excuse had she made? Where was she supposed to be now?

She confirmed his reading. 'I said I felt sick. But I must get back.'

He stood, awkward. 'How did you know my address?' He felt self-conscious about the room and its sordidness, but she appeared oblivious and without curiosity about the surroundings.

'Andy told me where you worked.' (Andy was the acquaintance she was with the night at the club.) 'A nice girl there gave me this address.' (He found out later that it had happened weeks before; Pamela had got the girl to break the rule that his home address was never given out by claiming she had a surprise present to deliver to him.)

The fact that she had come to see him like this created a charge that lay between them, but he felt lost and tongue-tied. He had to wait for her to lead him.

'Andy told me you're married, don't go with other women.' He could imagine Andrew telling it: a coarse joke, this provincial hick ex-copper scared to do anything that might disturb his *Daily Telegraph* life-style.

He remained silent.

She took in the room at last. 'Don't you get lonely?' But as soon as she said it, she raised a hand to cut off any answer. 'Would you like to go places with me sometimes? I don't mean sleep with me. I've had all that. I mean just *go* places, do things together. Just sometimes. I've never had anyone like that. I'd like it. Would you?'

'You came to ask that?'

'Yes. Am I crazy?'

'You mean like brother and sister?' He was trying to be flippant now because it was too much for him to absorb, but she took him seriously.

'That's it,' she said excitedly. 'I hadn't thought, but that's it. I always wanted a brother.'

She was already moving towards the door. 'I'll phone you,' she shouted, suddenly in a frantic rush, and then she was gone.

As it was, he telephoned her three days later – stomach-churning days during which he stared at the telephone and willed it to ring.

At first he thought he had it wrong. She greeted him without emotion, as though her visit had never taken place – for a few seconds he even wondered whether she could have been spaced out on drugs and no longer remembered.

But almost at once she changed. 'You phoned!' she exclaimed

girlishly, as though she were the one who had been waiting for a call that was long overdue. 'Where shall we go? You choose, you say. Anywhere. When shall I be ready . . . ?'

He found he was laughing down the line. 'Hold it, hold it, I haven't said why I called. It might be to sell you insurance . . .'

'Don't. Don't tease me. Just tell me when . . .'

Over the next six weeks, with a gap of a week over Christmas when he returned to Birmingham and she flew to join unspecified friends abroad, they lived like tourists.

Not all the time. He carried on with his work (though more often than not it ended at office-hours time) and she (he imagined) continued to see all her friends. But three, four times a week they 'went somewhere' – the Tate, Greenwich and Hampton Court, Richmond Park, tourist pubs on the Thames. Very occasionally they went to the cinema (*Breakfast at Tiffany's*, which made her cry), once or twice to the theatre (*My Fair Lady* with Rex Harrison and Julie Andrews at Drury Lane, which made him feel guilty because he knew Mary wanted to see it.)

'I like having a brother,' she said one Saturday morning as they worked through the crowds at Portobello Market (his weekends were down to one day, Sunday). And for a moment he felt a stab of remorse – minutes before his eyes had paused on hard nipples showing through cotton shirt, and if he were a brother the feeling would have been incestuous. It was a feeling that surprised and worried him. Surprised because, despite the incongruity of the situation, it had worked as she seemed to intend. Going places together had in fact been *fun*. Sex, until this fleeting moment, had been absent. There had been something almost childishly inno- cent and appealing and liberating in their togetherness. Against what he had previously always believed, it *was* possible to have a platonic relationship.

That was where the fear entered. First, because he suspected that if sex did suggest itself, Pamela would flee – she had really meant what she said the night she had visited his flat. And, second, he was sure that even if he were wrong about that – if, in fact, she allowed an altered relationship – it would be the beginning of the end: their union would be doomed.

And so, he pushed the feeling aside, viciously and guiltily. And for the rest of the morning, until he left her outside her apartment, he took care not to fix his eyes on her for too long, nor to press too close.

He spent the afternoon alone – there was a train he would catch shortly after six. Partly to appease his conscience, he started on paperwork he had brought home. That completed, he decided to catch up on bills – he still had a half-hour before he needed to leave for the station. It was then that he realised that his cheque-book was missing; he remembered immediately that he had given it to Pamela that morning, asking her to carry it in her handbag because, wearing a sweater instead of a jacket, he had too few pockets.

He cursed – having started the chore he would have preferred to finish it. He picked up the telephone and dialled her number: he told himself it was to check she had the book, but he knew it was to hear her voice.

No reply. He tried again just before he left. Nothing. A deep-down voice whispered it was just as well.

He arrived at Euston to find the station at a standstill. Passengers and luggage filled the concourse. The atmosphere was of resignation and anger. An accident outside the station had blocked the lines; no trains were entering or leaving. It was not known when services would restart.

He queued in the bar for a drink. A half-hour passed and then an hour. No change. Finally, he stood in line for a telephone, called Mary and explained.

'So you won't be coming?' As though it were his decision.

'There's no trains!' And then, 'I could try to hire a car.'

The concession was enough. 'No, that'd be crazy.'

'I'll catch an early train tomorrow.'

'See how it is first.'

He carried only a document case. Not worth leaving it at left luggage or taking it back to the flat. He bought a stack of newspapers, took a cab to an Indian restaurant where he was known, ate alone at a corner table and read.

It was nearly ten when he emerged. He had no desire to return to the empty flat. He could check the station, he supposed: still time to travel. But he did not.

He went into a pub, ordered a whisky, checked his paper, decided on a late-night showing of a Fellini.

Although he stayed until the end, the film did not completley absorb him as a good movie usually does. Perhaps it was because of the train situation. Maybe it was because it had been a tougher than usual week and he was finding it hard to come down. But he knew it was neither.

A beautiful, crisp, clear winter night when he emerged just before 2 a.m. A fine layer of fresh snow on the streets. He took a side road, taking childish delight in making footprints.

He walked without thinking – along Piccadilly, through Knightsbridge, an hour or more, but not tired. He moved in a daze, as though drawn by a siren song that only he could hear. Finally, he stood looking up at her flat. The windows were dark. He did not know whether he would ring the doorbell.

The car stopped only moments later. He thought the man was going into the block with her, but they talked animatedly on the pavement, and then she went in alone. There were two, maybe more, people still in the car, and one called to the man, who rejoined them quickly, slamming the door. Pamela turned at the door, watched them go, but did not wave.

Kenyon caught the door before it locked. She was already out of sight. Lights showed the lift was moving. He took the stairs, reached her floor as she did.

'You've got my cheque-book,' he said. He could not think of anything else to say.

'I know. It's inside. I put it somewhere safe.'

'Can I have it?'

It was after three, but they both acted as though it were the middle of the morning, and as though his visit was nothing out of the normal.

She opened the door and he followed her inside. It was only the second time he had been inside the apartment. The small hallway led into a living-room, the only room he had ever seen – he had spent a total of not more than two minutes here, after seeing her home. Doors off it led to a kitchen and the bedroom. The bathroom, he imagined, was beyond that.

She opened a bureau drawer, handed him the cheque-book. Her eyes were unwavering on him.

'It's not going to go on working, is it?' she said, very quietly.

She walked to the front door and opened it wide, as though asking him to leave. But before he could react she had returned to the living-room, opened the door to her bedroom.

143

'I'm going to bed,' she said. She left that door open too.

He stood for long seconds that he knew would determine his life. Years later he could recall every moment, and he would remember that he had a choice. But he knew in his memories, just as he did at the time, it was no real choice.

Two doors. Both swinging wide.

He continued to stand, although it was only delaying the inevitable. It was no real decision. He was already spellbound.

Finally, he moved. He closed the door on to the corridor, quietly but with certainty.

And then the bedroom door. Behind him as he entered.

CHAPTER TEN

Kenyon had ordered the croupier to deposit the money at the BOAC air terminal and then to send the left-luggage ticket to E. F. Simpson c/o the main post office at St Martin's le Grand in the City of London.

The parcel, concealed in a locked travel grip, would be safe for at least a week. He could bide his time, choose his moment. The danger, of course, both in collecting the letter and, then, the parcel, was if the croupier had talked.

The British weather helped him, as he had hoped that it would. It rained heavily the third day into the week. Kenyon had already decided the best time to act was around four in the afternoon when messengers and office boys descended on the huge post office with mail, making it hard for any observer to linger at the counters. He wore an ankle-length black plastic mac over his normal raincoat, hood raised and pulled forward. Once at the counter, another of his false provisional driving licences provided the required identification. He was back in the waiting cab two minutes later. He left it at a tube station, took the escalator to the Northern underground line, doubled back and crossed to the Central line to make sure no one was following, dumped the plastic coat in a bin, and was at the club only forty minutes later than usual, blaming the weather.

The parcel itself at the BOAC air terminal presented more difficulties. It would be harder to spot anyone keeping watch, he knew. And anyone who was waiting for him would have vital minutes when the case was lifted into view to pick him out.

He decided on shortly after noon. The time when the area's hookers started work. The Street Offences Act, seven years before, had forced prostitutes off the streets: now, large numbers of them operated via cards in doorways and windows. The side

145

streets around Victoria, site of major railway and bus stations as well as an air terminal, had many of them.

It was a question of synchronising a girl and a mini-cab. He telephoned a cab first, asked it to pick him up at a pub near the terminal. When it arrived he told the driver that he was waiting to collect a friend whose plane had been delayed, but was now expected within the hour. She would be in a hurry to get away. He gave the driver ten pounds as an advance and asked him to wait.

The car in place, he rang the first of the doorbells. A door opened at the top of the stairs, and a voice called, 'Come back later.' The second had an entry-phone: a voice told him to climb to the third floor for 'Yvette'. She was around thirty, anorexic thin in a black negligee. Her eyes were weighted with so much green shadow he was surprised she could keep them open.

The room contained nothing but a double bed pushed against the wall and a chair. There were two curtained-off alcoves. A large photo album, the kind sold for wedding pictures, lay on the bed. He flipped a page – porn shots for customers who needed it.

'How much?' he said.

He hadn't taken off the raincoat, collar turned up, nor the hat.

'You're not a copper are you?'

'Copper? Not me.' He laughed. 'So how much?'

She began to reel off the list: 'Straight, five pounds, oral, four pounds . . .'

He stopped her. 'Twenty quid,' he said. 'No sex. Just come with me, collect a bag, hand it over. Ten minutes most.'

'Ah yeh, an' I end up bleedin' nicked or half me face missin' because someone wants to know who you are and why you came to me.'

'Nobody'll hurt you. This is just a precaution. I don't want to be seen. I came to you because you're across the road.' He offered, lit cigarettes. He smoked rarely, but always carried them. 'I'll level,' he said, 'but then I need your decision. Can't wait longer. I've quit my wife; the bailiffs are after me, trying to serve summonses. I've got a case I left at left luggage – I'm getting out of the country. Maybe they've tracked me, maybe they haven't. I doubt it, but I can't risk it.'

'Fifty.'

'Thirty.'

'Forty.'

Greedy! It took a worker on a car assembly line two weeks to earn that kind of money. His fault. He had started too high, alerted her to the degree of his need. Still, too late to argue now. He was impatient to get on.

He took out eight five-pound notes, tore each of them in half. Handed her one set of half pieces. 'You make a tough bargain. You'd better dress.'

Her clothes were in one of the alcoves. He escorted her to within a hundred yards of the terminal, gave her the ticket. 'It's sign-posted inside. You just hand over the ticket. It's a small grip.' He pointed to a spot about fifty yards from the exit door. 'I'll be there.' She started to move, but he called her back. 'Don't get curious or ambitious,' he said. 'There's nothing in the case but personal belongings, and I know where I can find you.'

She shrugged. 'I'm not a bloody fool.'

The moment she was gone, he waved over the waiting mini-cab, slid into the back, directed it to a position where he could cover the exit – and a second exit door.

'OK,' he said a minute later, saddened but not surprised. The whore had taken the other exit, and was hurrying to reach a side-road and vanish from sight. No one was following her. 'Pull alongside that girl. She's the one.'

She gazed about for an escape, but realised immediately that she was cut off. He took the case without opposition, nodding his head in mock censure.

'An' I don't even get my fuckin' forty quid now,' she spat.

He got back into the car, holding out his half of the fivers towards her. 'No hard feelings,' he said.

To the driver. 'She's not coming. Let's go. BEA Air Terminal, Cromwell Road.'

He gave the driver another ten pounds there, walked into the terminal as if about to catch a flight, took the ramp to the taxi rank and had a cab drop him at Kensal Green Cemetery – the biggest of London's graveyards, green with shrubs and woodland, an ideal place to be alone and unobserved.

He had brought a carrier bag in his pocket and he transferred the parcel to it, dumping the grip under a hedge.

He found a bench. There were people in the distance, but they had their own preoccupations.

He examined the parcel. Brown paper, sealed with sticky tape.

He wanted to tear it open immediately, but he was cautious. The package would have been doctored. He used his pocket-knife to cut a small entrance hole at one side. He probed with the blade, but could only sense paper – which was what he wanted. Finally, he made a slit across the bottom and peeled back layers with care. Too many layers. The cardboard box inside was surely too small to hold twenty thousand pounds. It too was taped. In his haste to see, he disregarded caution this time, cutting the tapes, levering off the lid.

He looked around to make sure no one else could see before digging his hands into the box to attempt a rough count. He thought five thousand pounds. The note confirmed it.

SO I GIVE YOU TWENTY AND YOU COME BACK FOR MORE. SO I GIVE YOU FIVE NOW AND ANOTHER FIVE IN ONE MONTH AND ANOTHER FIVE IN ANOTHER MONTH AND . . . GET THE PICTURE? THAT WAY YOU GET MORE MONEY AND I GET TO FEEL SAFER.

On the way back to his apartment, Kenyon made a detour via Harrods where the five thousand pounds joined the growing number of documents in his deposit box.

The note had left him indecisive. He thought he could tell what the croupier planned to do: pay perhaps one more instalment as a holding operation, and then run. In the meantime, he would probably take the casino for as much as he could as fast as he could.

Hard to know what to do. Try to turn the screw tighter? Or back away?

Five grand was something. Better than a poke up the arse with a stick, as his brother had used to say. But more was better. Did he press hard, or did he walk soft?

He made up his mind that evening.

'Ten,' he said, on the telephone. 'Not five. Ten. Each month. Same arrangement until I change it.'

'Ten's too much.' Too unconcerned. The voice of someone who know's he's getting out, though he still needs to buy time.

'One phone call. That's all. Think on it. Just don't be late.'

Kenyon came out of the box into the bustling morning. He reckoned he would be around for one more delivery. If the croupier paid up, OK. If not, what had he lost?

It was all small change compared with the big stuff, anyway.

Another bride, another June, another sunny honeymoon . . .

Certainly, another bride. Not June, though almost. A honeymoon this time, a holiday house on a Bahamian island loaned by a friend of Pamela's.

They were married on Friday, 19 May 1961, seventeen years to the month since Kenyon's first marriage, thirty-three months after he and Pamela first met, twenty-eight after they had first slept together.

They married at Chelsea Register Office, with only four friends present. Kenyon was thirty-five years old. Pamela, he was astonished to see from her birth certificate, was only twenty-six. He knew very little else about her either. Her parents were either dead or they were abroad – she simply refused to talk about them. Certainly, she had no contact. Her life before they had met was largely a mystery. Occasionally, she would refer to some happening, some event, but pressed she would switch to something else, saying, 'Not that, it's boring,' or 'Oh, let's not talk about the past, it always depresses me.'

Somehow, it did not seem important. If he paused to think, it was of himself – how far he had come from his Shropshire village and the sub-post-office to this dazzling woman and a world of seemingly limitless possibilities. His life was like the decade: young and new and bursting with promise and excitement. With the end of the fifties had come a new era, with a feeling that everything was possible. London was the centre of a new liberated world.

He knew he was totally fixated with Pamela. But that was good. She was his inspiration. With her, nothing was impossible.

They left for the airport straight after the ceremony, flew to the Bahamas via New York and Miami, consummating their marriage with giggling childishness in the First Class toilet of a Boeing 707 thirty minutes out of Heathrow.

Looking back five years later, as he weeded through his papers, Kenyon relived the intensity. They spent every moment together, treated every experience or happening as though it had been created for them alone. They shared the same plates of food, drank from the same glasses, smoked the same cigarette; they burrowed into the same section of bed, drew chairs closer in restaurants, held hands like children. It was not only on honeymoon: it had been like that for twenty-eight months before, a half of which time they had lived together. He recalled one dinner in Prunier's restaurant in St James's. They had savoured and praised each course as part of their shared experience. And yet their absorption in each other was so apparent to everyone that, at coffee, Madame Prunier herself joined them, carrying liqueurs, and had said, 'I hope the food had a little something to do with your happiness.'

They were as irresponsible as the teenagers who had claimed the 1960s as their own decade. Although Kenyon was in the second half of his thirties, he identified with them and not their parents. He bought Dylan records, rushed to read every issue of the new *Private Eye* magazine, danced the Twist, raved about pop art, and smoked joints through cartoons at the news theatre at Victoria Railway Station.

That menu from Prunier's was here now along with other menus from other restaurants they had shared: the inn in California designed the way the owner thought an English pub looked (antlers and oils and photographs of Winston Churchill), Sacher's in Vienna, Bailey's in Dublin (where they had talked of moving to that country, planning to hide themselves away in the Wicklow Hills, so certain were they that they needed no one else.)

Those first few months with Pamela made him feel wonderful, gave him a new image of himself. Like all lovers, he saw himself reflected in her eyes: successful, independent, amusing. Beyond all those things, they were wonderful together. The sex they shared could be passionate and intense – or hilarious. He never knew until her that it was possible to feel lust one moment and dissolve into fits of laughter the next.

He learnt the landscape of her body. Every fold and crease, every curve and hollow, the smell of her, the taste, the little golden hairs on her thighs, the pale scar on her knee, the mole under her left breast. The look on her face when she came.

Familiarity did not breed contempt. Far from it. The more intimate his knowledge, the more he craved her. Driving to work, walking to a meeting, he would think how he felt when he entered her, the grainy secret silkiness enclosing him.

They would lie for long minutes on their sides, facing each other, him inside her. She would crinkle her eyes in warning and very slowly tense her inner muscles so they gripped him tight and he would moan aloud with the ecstasy of it.

Once, reliving one of those moments, he stopped dead in the street and the man behind bumped into him. He told her about it that night, making her an offering of his obsession with her, his need.

'It's a trick. Pelvic floor exercises.' She held his hand on her flat belly and he felt, just below the line of her pubic hair, the smooth rippling contraction inside her. 'I should've been a courtesan. It would have suited me. Making a different man happy every night.'

She laughed to show she did not mean it, but he fell silent. He didn't want to hear it. It reminded him of the way she had been when they first met, the photographs in the papers, the captions. 'Girl-about-town Pamela Stacey with friend . . .' The way she had posed so easily with his group in the drinking club for the photographer.

It started him thinking of how little he knew of her, of the titbits of information she let fall, only to contradict them later. Almost the only thing he did know was that she had been born in South Africa – he had seen it on her birth certificate. But as to whether her father was a diplomat as she had once said? The section for 'occupation' carried the words 'landowner'. He had asked her about the diplomatic work and she had said, 'Oh, *that*. That was later. Daddy wouldn't regard it as an occupation.' Very occasionally, there was a letter from South Africa. 'Someone I grew up with,' she'd say. 'Lots of boring chat.' Once he searched for the latest one, but it had gone. Most likely thrown into the garbage or burned – she did not keep written ephemera in the way he did.

Her friends? He could have asked them, even though it would have been difficult – they would have expected him to have known at least as much as them. But, in any event, the chance never really arose. She rarely saw them now, and when she did it was mostly when she was alone. He insisted they invite a half-dozen of them to dinner one night, but it was not a success – stilted, often forced, long periods of silence. Once he caught two of them exchanging meaningful looks at the way he had reached out to hold Pamela's hand across the table. A not nice look, a kind of 'Look at him, look at the poor fish's desperation for her.' Then Pamela had noticed their expressions, and sent her own message by reaching out and placing her other hand on top of his.

He knew they joked about his obsession. But let them! He was lucky to be crazy about her, to have her crazy about him too.

151

Not that there were not stabs of fear. Their preoccupation with each other had no place for the past, little room for the future (except a certainty it would get more and more wonderful). Letting friends go was part of that. So too was having no place for his son, Stephen. Kenyon could think of him with love – often did – but all the spaces were occupied. Practical things, too, almost ceased to matter. Money remained important in that it allowed them to do mad, spontaneous things – fly to Vienna on a whim, go racing, buy a picture they saw and had to have. But increasingly what mattered was cash *availability*, not earnings. He began paying himself commissions early, ran up a larger overdraft, started to depend on deals before they were finalised.

His love for her sometimes made him conscious of his own shortcomings too. He had been jealous of her before he even knew her name. How could he not be now, when she was his wife?

Gradually, he became aware of subtle changes. Uncertain where he stood, how much he really knew her, he was often irritable. The feminine squalor that once had so delighted him – discarded silk underwear, crumpled tissues bearing the imprint of her lips – annoyed him visibly. She watched his face and deliberately left magazines open on the floor, milk out of the refrigerator, to offend his sense of order.

When he bought her presents, it became not just for the sheer pleasure of her response, but because he felt he must. To apologise for being late, or away on a business trip. To make up for being angry. To placate and please her, to amuse her. To woo her.

Now, Kenyon sat on the bare, polished boards of what, on the telephone, she had called '*your* room' and remembered all this and more. There were heaps of paper around him. As he sorted he raged silently and wept dry tears for what was no more. For all the things he had been. For all the failures. For all the times he had believed tomorrow would be wonderful. For the person he had become. For the contempt in Pamela's voice on the telephone.

He was alone in the house: Pamela had gone to her friends, whoever they were (more likely, friend, though he did not dwell on it), the cleaning woman had returned to her own home, too embarrassed to stay. ('Give me a call when you've finished – that's my number – and I'll come and lock up.')

A few photographs. Not many. Only five of them together, one or two others with him a blur in the background. He placed the ones that showed his face in the pile marked for destruction, the others in the stack to be kept. A hotel bill for Mr and Mrs Thomas Edison, the Feathers, Oxford; their first weekend away together – the way they had waited, her giggling, to see if the receptionist reacted to the name they had chosen. The sex? He remembered it so vividly. They had begun tearing off their clothes the second they reached their bedroom, hurling garments across the floor theatrically before collapsing on the bed gasping with laughter. And then, gradually, as he had lain there she had taken the initiative. 'Keep still, pretend your hands and feet are tied,' she had whispered, her face suddenly serious with desire. And he had, enduring the agony of being brought time after time near to peaks of ecstasy that were suddenly moved away. Until that final moment when he could not play the game any longer, and they had careered around the room linked like weirdly joined Siamese twins, reaching screaming orgasms sprawled impossibly across the dressing-table/writing-desk. And then, after that, a meal in the bar, filling time, until the return to their room. Then gentle, slow, drawn-out love-making, each of them concentrating on pleasuring the other. She had brought joints, but they did not light them – *nothing* could have made their night better.

He found a sealed envelope, which he tore open. His divorce papers, ending his marriage to Mary. 'Certificate of Making Decree Nisi Absolute (Divorce) . . . whereby it was decreed that the marriage solemnised . . . be dissolved . . . and it is hereby certified that the said decree was made final and absolute and that the said marriage was thereby dissolved.' Three names on the form, inserted in ball-point pen next to single printed words: Mary – Petitioner, him – Respondent; a name he had long forgotten against Co-Respondent.

The private detective he had engaged had supplied the woman and arranged the provincial hotel room in which they had spent the night – a farce to prove adultery to the court without publicly involving Pamela. Kenyon tried to picture the woman, but could not – except that she was in her thirties (deliberately so in order that the private detective did not lay himself open to risk of a charge under the Sexual Offences Act of procuring a woman under twenty-one to have unlawful sexual intercourse. Not that there had been intercourse, just a lying under the sheets until a maid had seen them in bed together.)

It seemed more sordid now than it did then – a necessary stage on the endless road of joy. After all, his relationship with Mary had ended. After the initial shock and trauma, he and Mary had talked and agreed – for years their marriage had endured, no more; it was not the fault of either, only of time and of life; all that mattered was Stephen, and he would be better with a loving and stable relationship, albeit with only one of them. It was Mary with whom he was so close. As to practical things, she could keep everything. To him, money was of no matter (how different later). And so Mary had agreed, and the play had been staged.

He replaced the form in its torn envelope – such a cheap and miserable piece of paper to embody so major a happening.

Kenyon rose from his knees, walked to the window and lit a cigarette. The room was at the side of the house. The garden below was well tended – lawns smooth, flower beds weeded, trees cut back. An ordered world they had briefly shared, and then only when the dream was ending.

He needed a drink, found bottles in the living-room, poured a tumbler of Scotch and drank it fast before refilling the glass. The house was heavy with her and with their past together. This was the house that was going to save their relationship, take them back to where they had been. Part of him verged on a panic brought about by the atmosphere and by the memories he had activated. Yet he did not want to leave. There was a sharp pleasure in the masochistic pain – something else he remembered: the arriving home, not knowing whether she would be there; her returns and the involved stories about where she had been; the telephone that rang unanswered because he was afraid that when he answered the line would go dead or a strange voice would say, 'Sorry, wrong number.'

He remembered two terrible instances, early on when he had only begun to suspect. He had been away in Birmingham for two days seeing Geoff Burrows. Back, alone in the house unpacking as he awaited Pamela's return from shopping, he had dropped a handful of change. Some had rolled under the bed. He found it. He also found a single cuff-link, a silver Georg Jensen piece in the shape of a fat half-moon. It was not his. He had never seen it before. He put it back, said nothing. The next day he checked. It was gone.

Worse though was the shower. Again he was alone in the house. An evening appointment had been cancelled. Pamela had gone to see *From Russia with Love*, the second Bond film and a massive hit. They had already seen it together, but she had agreed to go again with an out-of-town girlfriend. He was in the living-room, sipping at a Scotch, reading a book when she returned. He waited for her to enter the room, but he heard her feet on the stairs, drumming, moving fast, like a woman who is late or has forgotten something. Not shouting, he followed her, curious, worried though without knowing why. Inside their bedroom, she had squeezed all her clothes, everything including underwear, into a tight pile beside the rubbish bin, as though ready for destruction. He moved to touch them, but stopped himself. Instead, he walked on to the shower that led off their room. He was silent on the carpet and her back was towards him and she did not see him. The water was turned on full heat and at full power. He could only make out her outline through the steam, but he could imagine her skin smarting and reddening under the blast. He doubted she would have noticed his presence even if he had called out. She had a back loofah, but she was using it to scour the whole of her body with violent, frenzied movements as though trying to rub out stains. Suddenly, unexpectedly, obscenely, she moved it between her legs, began to rub her crotch viciously. He heard her gasp with the pain, but still she continued.

He could not watch any longer. He could not cope. He returned to the living-room quickly, retrieved his shoes and jacket, removed evidence of his early home-coming, and went out.

When he returned at midnight she was asleep. He could not stop himself searching. The clothes, expensive, designer clothes, had been stuffed into a plastic bag, rammed down with the rest of the rubbish in the garbage bin outside. He had drunk a lot, but he was cold sober. He poured himself another drink, prayed for it to work. At last it did. He slid into bed beside her. She did not wake. She was lying on her stomach. She normally slept nude. Unusually, she wore a nightdress – white cotton, faded, too large on her so that a shoulder became uncovered as she moved. He saw the beginning of a mark, hesitated, and then reached out. Pulling gently, he revealed the upper part of her back. The blood was dried. But there were three long gashes. They could have been nail wounds. They could have been whip marks.

Because of the booze, he slept, but a restless sleep full of dread and foreboding. When he woke, she was burrowed under the sheet, and he did not dare uncover her. 'The alcohol,' he told himself. 'I imagined it.' And he pushed it deep into the hidden parts of his mind. Except he knew he had not dreamed it.

The memories brought bile to his mouth. He began to walk the house, glass in hand, to re-experience her, but the rooms had been changed – they were oddly impersonal, products of design, not of living.

Her bedroom was lemon and white, clean, pure and yet soft with touches of lace. That was the same. But where there had once been chaos, beautiful chaos, it was now almost unbearably tidy, as though in leaving it she had wanted to remove every trace of herself because she had known he would look. Yet the façade crumbled as he opened a door: clothes, crammed inside in a frenzy, spilled on to the white carpet. He tried a drawer and it would not shift, overpacked as it was. Another gave, revealing fluffs of underwear, all white (she had never worn any other colour). He ran his fingers through it and then, quickly, nervously, he raised a pair of knickers and smelled the crotch to see whether even a trace remained of her.

The smell they, and the whole drawer, exuded was not of her body but of her perfume. His fingers probed and found what he had remembered would be there – an empty bottle of her scent. She had always placed the empty bottles among her clothes, so that the smell accompanied her, clinging to her body when she was naked. He did not need to look at the label, he knew the name – Caron's Narcisse Noir. It would have been a consolation if he had first bought it for her, but she had used it from before they met. He had tried to wean her from it – had tried gifts of Dior and Balmain and even Patou – not because he did not like it, but because he wanted her perfume to be *his* perfume. And because – and he could admit it now, though not then – because he had always wondered who had first bought her Narcisse Noir and what *their* relationship had been. He did not resent her having other men, there was no jealousy in that thought. But had she brought to it the same totality, the same completeness of giving? Love would not let him believe that true – *this* was Hemingway's earth that moved, mythology's two half-parts that had found each other. And yet another voice within him, one that grew, told him such

156

intensity could not endure long; like a rainbow its span had to be limited. And the same voice murmured that with her nature each period of intensity must have had a predecessor, and just as surely would be followed by another.

Slowly, he raised her garments in his fingers and let them drop like snow. The perfume filled his nostrils and suddenly he felt he could bear no more. And then he saw the picture. It hung beside the bed, part of a carefully arranged group of charcoal sketches. He could not read the artist's signature, but he recognised the style. He remembered that he had even met him. At the Goya exhibition at the Royal Academy – Pamela had introduced him. There were four – three of them work sketches of goddesses for a series of sculptures; he had read of them. The fourth was of Pamela. The artist had resisted the temptation to depict her as a goddess – or perhaps he had tried and been unable to decide whom she should be.

She was shown standing full-length, naked, face on, her legs apart and her head thrown back. The shape of her body spoke of knowingness and defiance and sexual aggression. It was drawn in bold, almost violent strokes. The face, in contrast, had been completed in more careful, gentler, more draughtsmanlike lines; the eyes had dropped their gaze and the mouth, less full than in life, had the smallest trace of a smile; it was girlish almost, and it hinted and half-promised where the thrusting pelvis offered. The whole was not a Pamela he knew. It repelled and yet of all the objects he had seen in the house, it was the only one he wanted. It touched emotions deeper than he thought it possible to reach. They permeated his being as strongly as the perfume filled his breath.

Memories suddenly flooded, disjointed, staccato.

Those breasts. Like cones. Ordinary in their size, yet like no other breasts he had seen. They rose, small pyramids, with hardly a curve, milk-white against the brown of the rest of her body, yet with nipples as dark as a nursing mother's. A balcony over the sea, and honey smeared on them, and the sweetness being replaced by a tang of salt and then another taste like no other as his mouth moved over her.

Memories.

Skin shining with sweat as they lay uncovered after making love. Eyes feasting on her, delighting in every curve, every crease, she not self-conscious but happy in his worship.

Memories.

That mouth, and words – like 'never before' and 'for ever' and 'always', words both had used before but just as words, but now suddenly made new and golden again by what they felt.

And they did feel. Not just Kenyon. Looking at the sketch, accepting it was over, knowing that the drawing itself was proof she had moved to some other man, he remained sure of that.

From that first night they slept together – she had been huddled coy under covers drawn high when he closed the bedroom door – there had begun a relationship that had seemed perfection. Not just sexually, though that was a large part. But everything – big things, small things. Walking without the need for thought, content in each other's presence. Communicating without words – *knowing* which particular painting, which bottle of wine, which play the other would like. Feeding on each other's happiness, so that contentment grew and grew until sometimes it seemed it was too much.

Occasionally, he remembered, it had frightened him. How could it go on so perfectly? He recalled a road death from his early days of policing. A car containing a couple had crashed on an open road. No other people, no other vehicles were involved. The road conditions were perfect. Examination showed that the car itself had no mechanical problems. Post-mortems on the bodies revealed no illness, no drug nor alcohol – nothing that would explain how the driver had come to swerve off the road, hitting a tree head on. Their friends, family, workmates, had all agreed that the couple – recently married – were supremely happy, had everything to live for. The coroner recorded a verdict of Accidental Death, mentioned various possibilities that could never be known – a sudden blinding by sunlight, a bee or wasp bringing distraction for a vital second . . .

An old police sergeant, though, reckoned he knew. 'Suicide,' he said to Kenyon in the pub that night. 'He drove into that bloody tree on purpose.'

But why? How do you know? Kenyon had asked, not believing. The answer when it came produced peals of mocking laughter from Kenyon and his companions.

'They were so bloody happy they knew it couldn't bloody last,' said the sergeant. 'They didn't want it to fade.'

Now, at last, Kenyon believed. All he wondered was how the

sergeant had known; what, in his own life, had given him the insight?

But with Pamela it had lasted. Not days. Not weeks. Not months. They had been wary, frightened it might burn out – sensible almost. It had been nearly three years before they married and even in the madness and certainty of their passion they had discussed that step prosaically. Would it alter things? Should they remain lovers? Afterwards, when they were married, they had been cautious with each other, determined that familiarity would not blunt the edges of their passion.

So when did it change? How many times he had wrestled with that question. He *thought* he knew – or, at least, he thought he could now recognise the first sign. But he could not be sure. He had to accept that despite their closeness there must have been things he never saw, layers he failed to reach, messages he never understood. He *thought* it was the day she told him she had bumped into Andy – 'Remember Andy, he brought us together I suppose; he said he was angry we never asked him to the wedding.' Andy, she said, had invited them both to a party. Kenyon had thought nothing at the time, but a few days after they had attended the party Pamela had received a phone call – an old friend, a woman she had not seen for years, Pamela had said. They had fixed lunch. It had been fun. They had repeated it several times, following it with shopping expeditions. Only long afterwards had he realised that he had never taken any of the phone calls himself, never spoken to the woman, never seen her. He had thought nothing of it: mistrust was long dead.

Memories.

For him, the astonishment of loving her never paled, even after their marriage. He told himself it was because he must not repeat the pattern of his failure with Mary, but it was not really that. He would bring home flowers for no reason other than the pleasure of seeing her face as she opened the paper of a single crimson rose, a heavy-headed Chinese chrysanthemum from the over-priced florist in Berkeley Square. Or a box of the handmade Belgian chocolates that she ate immediately, one after the other, licking her fingers like an exotic cat.

His love for her fed on proximity. He came to depend on her: how he felt each day was dictated by her morning mood. If she awakened smiling and receptive when he nuzzled her sleep-warm

159

breasts, he was buoyant for hours. If she drew up her knees and buried her face under the sheet: 'Darling, too early, I'm still asleep,' he would mock-grumble and bring her coffee and a cigarette before he went out. But the morning could stretch featureless until he rang her at midday to hear her voice, make her promise to be home when he got back.

He never knew when his love turned into something that frightened even as it exhilarated him. The realisation that he had gone further than Pamela, that she was no longer beside him, was like swimming on and on in a warm sea and suddenly finding himself out of sight of land with nothing to hold on to.

For a long time he did not – could not – admit to what was happening. It wasn't just flowers now, but offerings that cost him dearly.

One Sunday they walked in the early hours along a deserted Bond Street, arms round each others' waists, pretending to be drunker than they were.

'Oh,' breathed Pamela, stopping in front of a jeweller's window. 'Look at that. I've never seen anything like it, ever.'

The window was almost empty behind its fretwork security grille. On dark velvet lay a piece of rough stone, curved like a hand and spotlit. And in the palm a single ring, stunning in its simplicity. Two slender oblong stones, one set higher than the other on a narrow platinum band. A diamond and an emerald.

She never asked him to buy it, she wasn't interested in its price. He already knew that she was not avaricious: she just loved beautiful things, and she stared with covetous eyes, momentarily thoughtful. And then they walked on and looked at silk scarves in Hermès and silk pyjamas in Sulka.

He rang the shop on Monday morning and winced when they told him what the ring cost but he asked them to set it aside. He had not bought her an engagement ring: they had agreed it would be silly, as they were living together anyway, and she wore only her gold wedding ring.

He was still sending Mary money for Stephen, and his life with Pamela was proving more expensive than he could ever have anticipated: his bank account was drained before the end of each month. To raise the two thousand pounds, he granted a loan to a non-existent customer, making out the papers with his customary care, signing a made-up signature with his left hand and a ball-point pen. It was the first time he had done such a thing. He ignored his misgivings, anticipating her face when she saw the jewel, how she would thank him.

A week later, after they had made love, he kissed her navel, then put the small leather box on the rounded curve of her belly.

'A little something,' he said, 'to keep the wind off it.'

Her awed silence would have been thanks enough. The fury of love-making that followed made him gasp even now at the recollection.

'Tell me what,' she had murmured as she stroked and sucked him, 'what can I give you, my love, for this wonderful emerald ring?' And she had whispered just what she would give him, and his flesh rose as he remembered.

Three months later, he noticed she was no longer wearing the ring. He found it by chance, lying dusty on a windowsill behind a curtain with a couple of the big hairpins she used to hold up her hair in the bath. When he gave it back to her she was puzzled for a second: he saw she had not even realised it was missing.

Memories.

Another party, months later. He remembered it well. It was a week before their second anniversary; he had bought her another present that afternoon – a Victorian necklace he knew she would love; he went to join her at the party, feeling smug. She did not see him arrive. A group in a corner, drinking, laughing, among them a man he vaguely recognised from Andy's party months before. As Kenyon neared, still unobserved, he saw Pamela turn her face towards the man. Her eyes burned on him for the briefest moment before being lowered, almost guiltily. Kenyon stopped, not certain what he had seen. Then she noticed him, rushed forward to draw him into the group, and he told himself that he was mistaken. Ashamed of such a thought, he gave her the necklace that night – an impulse because he wanted to show how much he loved her, he said – and he bought another gift for the anniversary. Years later, though, he could recall that look, brief though it had been, and he *knew*.

Memories.

Phones that echoed in an empty apartment when he called because she was 'shopping' or had decided to 'catch a movie matinée'. A ring she started wearing, saying she had found it deep in a case years after she thought she had lost it, though she touched it constantly as though it were new and had special meaning. A weekend stay with an old friend in Kent; she had accepted for both of them – but at a time she knew he had to return to Shropshire because his mother was ill.

Memories.

Spending more time in crowds. Touching less. Seeing and not seeing. Hiding what was happening in carefully structured pretences. The afternoon he returned unexpectedly from a conference that should have lasted another day: their bedroom, shades drawn, bed in disarray, the feel of someone who had just left. Her naked body, half-turned, back offered to him, together with the belt in the outstretched hand. 'Hit me then, beat me if you don't believe me.' The contempt as he turned and left the room.

Memories.

And then the confession, and the promise it was over, and the trying to forget everything in the sweet pain-filled reconciliation. And then the same pattern. And again.

And then finally, 'I've said I'm sorry. I can't say it any more.'

Two years of being torn apart, put together, ripped in two again. Afraid to be away, afraid to come back home in case . . . Frightened to throw too many hours into his work but needing to work longer and longer days as the cost of holding her grew. Finally this house – the house that, away from everyone but him, was going to solve it all. A crazy, naive belief – too stupid even to be explained by the change brought about in him by his desperate need not to lose her, the lies he lived, the effect of the drinking that began earlier and earlier each day. This house that Barton's appearance and offer suddenly made possible. He stood in the room and screamed inside at all the mistakes, all the delusions, all the false turns.

And yet . . . The awful, the frightening, the dreadful truth was that if she returned to this room now, if she said, 'Let's try again,' he would be as lost as ever.

He reached out his hand, not sure whether to bring the drawing of her naked body closer or to dash it across the room.

The sound of the downstairs door opening and then of the cleaning woman's voice stopped his movement, spared the decision.

He retreated on to the landing, towards the room that was *your* room.

She was calling. 'Are you there, Mr Kenyon? Can I lock up soon?'

'Five minutes. Just bundling things up.'

She held the door wide, watched as he placed the suitcase in the back of the car.

He looked back before he pulled out of the drive. She had turned away, but he could still sense the look of pity in her eyes.

CHAPTER ELEVEN

Kenyon knew there were problems within minutes of walking into the club. It was the Thursday of what had been an unusually quiet week. Barton was not in his usual place but that was not surprising – if the American was to take a day away this was the time.

'The races?' he asked one of the other Americans, nodding to Barton's empty seat as he sat and signalled a waiter to bring his coffee.

'Upstairs,' said the other.

That, of course, need not have meant anything. But the tone and the man's expression told Kenyon something was wrong. It was useless asking further questions – even if the American knew the answers he would not speak.

Almost immediately Kenyon noted that two or three other faces were absent. Something *was* afoot. The only question was: did it concern him?

He concentrated on drinking his coffee – his hands had begun to tremble. The American noticed them. 'You're gonna have to cut down,' he said. He was grinning, and for once Kenyon was grateful for his reputation as a drinker.

'You're right,' he said, rising cautiously. God, he needed a drink right now.

Trying to appear normal, he took a turn of the floor. Although the club was quiet, there were already players at the roulette table. They hid the croupiers until he was almost there.

Not the usual men. Not the man he was putting the bite on. It was hard to finish his lap of the room after that.

He tried to persuade himself it was nothing. He did not even know whether it was the man's day off. In any event, people got sick. But, coupled with the absence of Barton and the others, he knew. He just knew.

He smiled and nodded his way around the room, feet and grin muscles on autopilot, mind trying to review the situation quickly. The croupier's latest letter should have arrived at his post-box during the day – fortuitously, Kenyon had not checked the mail drop because of a more pressing need to visit Turnham Green and clear up there.

Suppose the croupier had been caught, had talked, what was there to lead anyone to Kenyon? He had been through this a hundred times in the planning, making sure he was safe. But theory was one thing. This was another.

Nearing his table, Kenyon was hailed by Hunter's replacement: he had two punters who needed massaging, would Kenyon share a drink with one, entertain him, until he got rid of the other? Kenyon grabbed the opportunity – it gave him an excuse to order the drink he needed. He talked in overdrive until he was relieved. He felt calmer, more able to cope. The drink and the enforced socialising had eased him.

Barton appeared an hour later, said nothing, acted as though everything was normal. Kenyon was OK now. He had decided the only sensible course of action was to do nothing. He could not see that he had been exposed. And if he had . . . well, there was nothing he could do this minute.

Kenyon finally picked up the story around 3 a.m. Not from Barton but from another of the Americans. Three of them were discussing it; they continued talking after Kenyon joined them. Since the shooting that was not unusual.

'We're talking about Thin Frenchy,' said one. Kenyon shrugged, struggling to hide his mounting fear. 'He's the guy at table seven,' the American went on.

Christ.

He managed to ask, 'Trouble?'

'You could say that.'

Kenyon realised the other was watching his reaction. This was more than letting him into gossip. The man had been told to tell Kenyon, note the impact. Still, Kenyon reassured himself, that did not mean much – if Barton was looking for someone, he would be checking on everyone. This was one way.

'So?' Kenyon nursed his drink, taking care not to gulp it back.

'So Thin Frenchy turns out to be a junkie, you know that.' His voice was shrill with surprise.

'Balls. Someone'd have noticed.' Kenyon felt easier. So that was it.

'Naw. Not this one. Turns out he'd been shooting shit for years, knew just how much to pump in to keep the engine running over . . .'

Kenyon waited. There had to be more. He had to prompt. 'So what happened?'

The other shrugged. 'So what always happens to shit-shooters? He got unlucky. His source got busted. He was way off his fuckin' head. Tried to score from some guys he didn't know, got busted up. Cops found papers on him, linking the motherfucker with this place.'

Kenyon took in the rest, the fear easing all the time. The police who had found the croupier smashed up in an alleyway had quickly realised the possibilities once they stumbled across the links with the club. They had called people who had called Barton. The croupier, in hospital, might or might not live. It was no big deal to them – who cared about a junkie being beaten up, especially a foreigner?

Deals had been made quickly. The papers tying him to the club had disappeared, and would be handed over later in exchange for cash. That payment would also reflect Barton's appreciation for the four hours that the police officers were prepared to wait before going to the croupier's apartment. Plenty of time for anything embarrassing to vanish.

It looked as though the panic was over. There would have to be an inquest, of course, on how a junkie had got a job in the first place. Whether the man was stabilised on drugs or not, Barton would figure someone must have seen something – and was covering up. Then there was the fact that everyone knew feeding a habit was expensive. They would have to turn everything over to see where the man got his money – which, in practice, probably meant how much he'd stolen from the club and how.

Kenyon tried to sound casual. 'How is he?'

The American shrugged. 'Breathin'. That's 'bout all.'

Kenyon hated himself for the increased surge of relief. No one would be questioning him, at least for some time.

There was one more question. Just asking it was a risk, but he had to. 'And the pad?'

The American waited a long time before answering. 'Barton'll tell you,' he said. Kenyon thought he had finished.

But the man decided to answer after all. 'Nothing,' he said. 'Like a cell.' His eyes were on Kenyon, and Kenyon knew there had to be more. There was. 'Except a tape. He had the phone wired. Some wiseass putting the bite on for screwing this place.'

The next twenty-four hours were tough. All Kenyon's nerve ends yelled, run. Yet he knew that, even if Barton did not suspect him, everyone at the club would be under some observation. The only sensible thing to do was to try to act normal. Thanks be, all the preparations that had had him zig-zagging across London were completed. It was a question of running things down now. He had given notice on Turnham Green, explaining he was being posted abroad. He had only to remove the few items that remained. There were bank accounts to be closed. Mail addresses could simply be allowed to lapse. No question now, of course, of checking whether the croupier had done what Kenyon had instructed before the beating and deposited the money as ordered. Too risky. If Kenyon's calls were among those taped by the croupier, both the mail drop and the luggage drop were blown. It hurt, God how it hurt, the thought of ten thousand pounds maybe sitting waiting, but he knew he would be mad to try to collect it.

Time for sitting it out. And for making sure that there was nothing left around that would incriminate or lead to him. He combed his apartment, checking for papers, notes, anything that might provide any clue. Nothing. He had been scrupulous in destroying material as he had gone along, or else lodging it on deposit in his Harrods box. The only items still to be destroyed were photographs, mostly the ones he had brought back from the house.

He had not burned them yet, telling himself there was no rush. That was not the real reason he had delayed – Pamela appeared on most of them. It was all that he had left of her now. Destroy them he would – but not just yet. Rationally, he knew that it was over for good, emotionally he was almost drained of obsession. But . . .

He had Sellotaped the photographs to the wall. He sat facing them for almost two hours.

In one, he and Pamela stood in front of the house. They were staring straight ahead, grinning inanely, like kids fooling. He remembered taking it. He had balanced the camera on the car bonnet, set the self-timer, rushed to take up his pose before the shutter clicked.

It was the day after they had moved into the house.

By that time it was obvious their marriage was crumbling, though neither would admit it. There were terrible times – whole nights when she did not return home. He fought, he argued, at times anger possessed him and turned him into a madman without control. He found a note from one man, traced him, waited outside his house until he returned home. He remembered the man grovelling to his madness, protesting he had thought Pamela and Kenyon had split up. Then, sensing Kenyon was easing off, in a burst of drink-fuelled bravado he had added, 'It's not my fault if you can't satisfy her.' And Kenyon had dragged him back to the car, opened the door and coldly broken the man's arm over it.

The next day Kenyon had been sober, contrite, the lunacy gone like pus from a lanced wound. Pamela had heard of it. She had not seen his act as heroic jealousy but as the behaviour of a crazy drunk. 'You could have killed him. You ought to be in prison. You ought to see a doctor.' He tried to tell her he could not help it, that it was her. If *only* she would stop torturing him . . . Not for the first time he pleaded, but she turned away. At other times he pretended not to care. Sometimes he wooed. He suggested they should both see a therapist. He tried to understand. He failed.

He tried to lose himself in work (increasingly necessary because living costs had soared, earnings had fallen to the point where Burrows was making warning noises). And in drink, of course. As he drank, he became more a pitiable creature.

And yet, between the terrible times there were still good ones, sometimes only hours, sometimes whole days, when everything was perfect again. As months passed, such times became fewer, but there were still enough of them to keep hope alive.

Before they moved, the house in Chelsea had come to represent to Kenyon all that was bad. Her friends were always drifting in; it was here, he knew, that he had fucked her still wet with another man's sperm. Everything was wrong. He was a drunk (he had begun getting black-outs). Her friends, on the rare occasions he met them, patronised him or treated him with gentle scorn. Yet he had nowhere to run – without realising it, he had gradually cut off the whole of his own past. He had never had really close friends; now all he had was a changing parade of people who were barely acquaintances.

When he heard that she was tired of London and wanted to live in the country, it was a sudden lifeline. He realised that what she was also saying was that she too wanted to try again. Suddenly he *knew* that this was the chance for which he had cried out. He must not fail now. He had to grasp it, make it happen, make it all come true. Filled with thanks and hope, he told himself that he would curb his drinking, work around the clock three or four days a week, spend the rest of the time at home. Or maybe he would start his own business locally. And Pamela? She would visit London still, of course, but the country would absorb her. He did not think it through, but he saw her drifting around the country fairs, maybe designing clothes for sale at some trendy local shop – she had always said that she would like that.

The only problem was money. On his divorce, he had given Mary everything – house, furniture, savings. Life with Pamela was expensive. His debts were large. They had not worried him – he earned money fast. To move to the country, though, required capital. The Chelsea house was on a short lease, and would fetch only enough to buy the small flat they would need in London (not only for him to function, but also because Pamela would insist on it). He would have to find the money for the house – and quite a substantial house if the dream were to work. A problem, but not a huge one – his credit was good, and if *he* could not raise a loan . . . Whatever happened, whatever he had to do, money would not get in the way. His future – no! *their* future – depended on it.

The Barton job had solved all the problems. Or so it seemed. It made buying the house and the apartment easy. It provided Kenyon with income large enough to take care of all the bills without worry. The only problem was that the work kept him in London five, six days and nights a week.

Still, they had the house. The first time he saw it he was as captivated as she was. She had already seen it, known it was for sale (just how and why was vague, and he did not probe; it was not the time). They drove out to look at it. Out past the airport, west, countryside growing lusher all the way.

'This is great,' he enthused as they turned off the main road.

'Wait a few minutes,' she said. 'You won't believe it.'

He had a map open on the dash, but she knew the way. 'The

right fork,' she said. The road ran straight, fields either side, for about a mile and then began to twist and rise steeply.

'When we get to the top, stop and look!' Her voice was raised with childish excitement.

They crested the hill. And he saw. The road snaked down through hedgerows high and white with cow parsley. The fields were a dozen shades of green, and at the foot lay the hamlet and on its edge a red-brick house.

'That's it,' she said excitedly, tugging his arm.

'I know,' he said. And he did.

They had stood for a long time, arms entwined, taking in the view, smiling at each other, hugging and then laughing.

They had driven through the white hedgerows – 'It's like a wedding,' she said, very quietly. They parked in the drive, got out to study the house. It had a solid, welcoming feel.

'We're going to be so happy here. I *know* we are,' she said.

In the first weeks they had gloried in the new house, squeezed in every moment there. It was their house and they raised the drawbridge against the rest of the world – neither of them wanted or needed it.

And then reality. The truth, though neither saw it, was that they had exchanged one bad situation for nothing more than a mirage. They tried. They both tried. But they failed because there was nothing there but an unrealisable dream. For Kenyon, actuality was night after night at the club fronting for men he tried not to think about. Night after night of averting eyes and closing ears. He could not hide from the fact that the club was fuelled with Mob money. He managed to justify himself. OK, maybe the proceeds did go to fund other Mob enterprises. OK, maybe people did get hurt occasionally if they got in the way or stepped out of line. Well, they were only other bad guys: he did not do anything himself. As far as he was concerned, it was just a job, and whether he did it or not would not change those facts.

But the fact was, when he really came down to it, he did it because he had to. It was his only chance to keep her, and that was all that mattered. All the plans and dreams of 'bettering' himself, of joining a merchant bank, of branching out as an entrepreneur, were gone, buried deep. Besides his need for her, they were nothing.

In the country, Pamela too was confronted by reality. She was

170

courted by her neighbours. She tried to develop day-to-day relationships, but soon she found most of them boring. She had little in common with them – farmers, lecturers from the university a thirty-minute drive away, a doctor, the vet . . . Gradually, old friends began to visit. The house became Pamela's house and the apartment in London became Kenyon's flat.

Instead of drinking less, as he had vowed, Kenyon drank more. This Kenyon, maudlin, often near-drunk, a flunky for 'not nice' people, was even less desirable. He refused to admit it: the fault, he believed, was outside of himself. He was sure that one day everything would come right again. All he had to do was wait, be there. The one thing he had to avoid at all costs was a divorce. Even living as they did, mostly apart, a fiction of marriage survived. Nothing must be allowed to shatter that.

So they talked two or three times a week on the telephone. And they kept personal belongings at both homes. Twice a month they got together, always in London now, sometimes to see a show (usually with other people), sometimes to have lunch or dinner (but always at a restaurant). Kenyon was permanently afraid that divorce would be raised, relieved when it was not. He did not understand that the situation suited her as well as any situation could at this time. He could not see that she did not know what to do. A perceptive ex-boyfriend had once said her motto should be, 'No tears, no fuss, no remorse.' From her teens it had been her nature to shut off the past as firmly and totally as others might discard a frock no longer fashionable. But this time the past clung and she was lost.

Now, Kenyon removed the photographs from the wall. He had already destroyed the negatives. He burned the prints in turn on a metal tray near an open window. It was a time-consuming job, and he kept breaking off to use an air-freshening spray to mask the acrid plasticy smell.

It was after 8 a.m. when he burned the last one, crumpled the ashes with water and flushed the mixture down the lavatory. Time to eat or to sleep, but he was determined to complete his job of destruction now. There were two other photographs, both taken with Mary. He had had them in his flat in London, kept them even after Mary's orgy of destruction and their split up. Unable to bring himself to burn them, he had stuffed them away in a case. He fetched them, and methodically destroyed them too.

He paused only once, to stare at one, remembering the last time he had seen her. It had been almost five years after the divorce hearing, and it was strange how little she had changed in appearance but how much in manner.

At the divorce hearing he had seen her only briefly. Her written statement was handed to the judge; she had only to answer a few brief questions. He had not looked at her while he gave evidence or while the private detective told of finding him in bed with a woman. All over in less than thirty minutes. Decree nisi. He had caught her in the corridor afterwards, her solicitor nervous when he saw who was advancing on them. But Kenyon only wanted to make some form of peace.

'I'm sorry,' he said. 'There're a lot of good things I'll remember. I hope you will too. You can always call me if there's anything I can do.'

Speech over, he felt a concealed glow of nice-guyness. He wondered if the solicitor was impressed. He had heard there was usually a lot of bad feeling.

Mary was already turning to go, a faint, forced smile on her drawn face.

'You really think that does it, don't you?' she said. 'Well, if it makes you feel better . . .'

He watched her walk the length of the long corridor until she was out of sight, not understanding.

And then, nothing. No calls. No notes. No news. No bumping into people who talked about her. His parents kept in touch – saw her regularly. But they said nothing. When they died in the car crash he found packages of letters from her among their belongings, some dated before the divorce. He began to read, stopped, packaged them quickly into a parcel and posted them back to her. She did not acknowledge them. He should have made contact because of Stephen, but he did not. The more time passed, the harder it became even to contemplate taking such a step. At times he thought of Stephen, but a young son had no part in his new life.

Then he had gone to see her. After five years . . .

It was after he had joined the club, after he and Pamela had bought the house in the country, before the shooting. There had been a four-day period when he had been alone at the house. He had taken a holiday – he and Pamela had planned to spend the days together on Majorca in a small, isolated hotel. But then Kenyon had discovered that a group of her old friends, maybe as many as eight of them, were planning to be there at the same time. On the last occasion something like that had happened, Pamela had drifted away from him, maybe slept with someone else. He thought with the move to the house they had escaped that, but he would not risk it. So, even though he knew he was encouraging her to do precisely what he feared, he stayed at home while she went away. Childishly, he helped destroy what he wanted because he could not have it on his terms.

For two days and nights he drank and played sad Sinatra records – men alone in 2 a.m. bars, men whose baby didn't love them any more, men left with only memories, men in the September of their years . . .

On the third day he woke clear and alert and totally sober and he decided the time had come to see his son. The only telephone number he had for Mary turned out to be a ceased line. It took much of the day to trace her. Her name was different. Granville. She had married again. A family doctor. She had not moved far: a large, rich village, fifteen or so miles out into Warwickshire.

Kenyon reached the village mid-evening, took a room at the only pub, ate in the bar (shined brass, personalised pewter beer tankards for the regulars).

Late evening, he walked round the village. It had a green with a war memorial, a well-tended church, a primary school. It was an age away from the world he had just left – no signs here of protest (no 'Make Love, Not War' badges), no crazy fashions (like see-through bras, plastic dresses), no hint of pot or LSD, no youth power. Just England the way it had been. A year or two before he would have hated it, but now he wanted it to embrace him. The sixties revolution that had so fired him now filled him with bitterness. It was a constant reminder of what he had not got.

Behind the church hall there was a new building, a medical clinic, which gave the names of three doctors outside, one of them Dr W. H. S. Granville. He made a mental note of the time the doctors would be at surgery the following morning.

Next day, immediately after breakfast, Kenyon checked the telephone book for a home address, rang and heard Mary's voice, replaced the receiver without speaking, and walked around to the house. He wore hipster trousers and a suede jacket, and he felt out of place.

She opened the door. She was swollen large.

'I always liked you pregnant,' he said.

'What do you want?' Eyes darting left and right and across the street. 'You'd better come in.'

The house was modern, spacious, at the end of a small crescent. There was unfenced lawn in front, American-style. The living-room was circular with french windows opening on to a long garden. All the furniture and pieces looked as though they had been bought from a good store at the same time – style without excitement but without worrying about money either.

'Can I sit down?'

'If you want. But why have you come?'

She was fetching coffee, more to occupy herself than to be hospitable. She was more groomed, more assured than he remembered her.

'You won't believe me if I say I was passing?'

'What's the matter? Something terrible happened? You haven't left her, have you?'

'If I had, do you think I'd come here?'

'I don't know what I'd think. It's not my business any more.' Her voice hardened. 'And I don't want it to be. If you've something to say, say it, and then I'd like you to leave.'

'I want to see Stephen.'

She stood for a long time as though she had not heard him and then she began to laugh dramatically with a touch of hysteria.

'You want to see Stephen! Oh my! You want to see Stephen! Five bloody years and you want to see Stephen! You walk out on your own son! And you want to see Stephen!'

She reached for the coffee she had poured for him and moved it out of his reach.

'I want you out,' she said. 'Gone. Now.'

He stayed his ground. 'I still want to see Stephen. Just for a moment.'

'And what would you do then? Walk away again, leaving him more confused and hurt than ever? Perhaps you'd call back in another five years . . .'

'I'd like to see him regularly, once a month say. Take him out, do things with him . . .'

She collapsed into a chair facing him. 'Oh, Mike, you're a fool. That'd never work and you know it. He'd always be waiting for someone who never turned up. And besides, it's too late now.'

'Too late? What do you mean?'

She stood, fetched a framed photograph. It showed a burly, balding man with glasses, age probably early fifties. He was standing next to Stephen. Both were in waders and anoraks; they held a fish between them. 'That's my husband. He's a doctor here. He's good to Stephen. They do things together. Bill never had children before.' She looked down at her belly. 'He says it's late, but he wants them now.'

'Stephen's my son.'

'If you want to bring him pain.' She rushed on. 'He's at boarding school in the week, home at weekends. He likes that.'

'And me? Does he talk of me?'

Mary averted her eyes, and he knew she was summoning courage. 'He thinks you're dead,' she said at last. 'He didn't hear from you for two years. He was in a bad way. Everyone was worried. We didn't know what to do. Finally, I pretended you'd gone abroad, couldn't have got in touch. I got someone to copy your writing, sent a letter from you to him, saying how much you missed him. Then –' She paused and handed back his coffee.

'Then?' he prompted.

'Then, later, I told him there'd been a phone call. You were dead. Had died saving someone from drowning in Bali – it was the first country I thought of. I don't know why. I just picked somewhere a long way away. Bill said I shouldn't, but I told him it was *my* decision.' She became silent, and he could imagine the argument that must have taken place. Once more, he sensed the strength within her. Then she added, 'It's been all right since.'

She waited for him to speak, and when he did not she focused hard on him, and said, 'Don't you see, he can live with the idea of you having loved him, unable to be with him. He can't live with you being there and not caring.'

'So I'm dead?'

The coffee was cold, but he did not want it anyway.

'I'm sorry,' she said as she opened the door for him to leave. 'You don't know how hard it was.'

It was only on the train that he realised that he had made straight for the station without collecting his belongings. He had

175

paid his overnight bill after breakfast, but had left his bag for collection later. He did not telephone or write to the pub with his address. He did not ask them to send on his clothes. He wanted nothing out of that village.

Three men vanished from the casino. Rumour said they had been entertained to the out-of-hours services of a crematorium somewhere in outer London.

The three were a second croupier, a security man, and an inspector. All of them were implicated in the Thin Frenchy fraud.

The wheel had been ripped apart after the club closed one morning. The next day the story was out. A search was on for the mechanic who had last worked on it. Obviously a long and carefully planned operation.

For Kenyon it meant the heat was off. To everyone it was obvious what must have happened with the phone call on tape in the croupier's apartment. One of the quartet had got greedy and tried to get more than his share by blackmailing the main instigator. The voice could not be identified – it was not only heavily disguised, but the recording, amateurishly made, was poor. It could be one of the four; it could be another man enlisted just to make the call. End of story.

An edgy feeling remained though. New faces appeared, Barton disappeared for twenty-four hours – it was said to meet up with emissaries who had flown in from Philadelphia. Kenyon concentrated on being 'normal' – he chased a couple of friends and fixed lunch, visited a gallery and bought a painting, took a girl he knew casually to see *The Sound of Music*, which had just won an Oscar for best film. And, between such times, he did everything else that still had to be done – bought some second-hand clothes, checked hotels, packed a case and lodged it with the porter at The Royal Commonwealth Society, paying a week's tariff in advance but warning he might need to leave it for a further week. 'No problem, sir,' said the porter, who was used to looking after the belongings of expatriates who were back touring the UK.

He saw George leave the club with a case – and, knowing that soon the safety-deposit box would be rich with skimmed cash, he spent that night sweating over whether to make his move. Everything was in place. But there was a reluctance – best wait another few days, make sure the heat really is off, he told himself.

He knew, though, the real reason was that now the moment had come, he was afraid. So far it had all been no more than a great game. Making his move would change all that, make it for real.

Barton vanished for another twenty-four hours. While he was away this time, Kenyon sensed a new mood among the other Americans. They stopped talking about Barton in casual conversation, as though he had become a non-person and even the mention of his name dangerous.

Two other Americans, strangers to Kenyon, returned with Barton and spent a lot of time with him up on the third floor. One evening when Kenyon tried to enter his office he found they had closed off the floor.

He got drunk that night, as drunk as he could remember being for years. He did so systematically, after leaving the club, propped in a chair, a stack of albums on the hi-fi, Scotch and water at his elbow, two bottles to be on the safe side.

He awoke with a rare and terrible hangover – one advantage of being a drunk was that you never got hangovers. Oddly, this one was comforting – experiencing the nausea, the headache, the revulsion to light was like being a young man again when his body knew good from bad and reacted the right way.

He fixed a weak drink – whatever anyone said, more booze was the only sure way of curing a real hangover. Then he made coffee and spread out the day's newspapers. It was already two o'clock. He alternated coffee and liquor, flipping the papers without much interest, but needing the distraction. Speculation about a rematch between Henry Cooper and his victor Cassius Clay, further searches for more bodies after the convictions of Ian Brady and Myra Hindley for the Moors Murders . . .

Then, page seven, *Daily Mail*. He stared at the story for a long time before ripping the page across a dozen times and sending the pieces hurtling across the room.

'Henry, swinging London's newest "in" hairdresser,' said the picture caption. 'Crimping it up in Cannes with friend.'

He had his arm around Pamela and both had a forced fixed grin.

It hurt as much as ever. More. The picture had not been taken surreptitiously. She had posed for it, and in doing so she had made a public statement. The past was over.

Ten minutes later he poured away what remained of his drink

and carefully corked the bottle. He would make his move after George's next drop.

CHAPTER TWELVE

A busy Saturday: a big American TV-star was the night's main attraction, Barton was back in action, but quiet. Everything seemed back to normal.

Sunday – a slow night. A good relaxed feel, though: the previous night's drop – including twenty thousand pounds from the TV-star – was the highest ever.

Monday 1.45 a.m. Still quiet. No one objected when Kenyon said he was not feeling good and wanted to leave early. Eight hours before, he had seen George leave with a case. Today. It had to be today.

The first piece of music he had heard when he had switched on the radio after getting up had been the Beatles' 'We Can Work It Out'. His mood told him it had to be an omen.

The pre-dawn drive to take one last, regretful, look at the house had not been planned. It was a sudden decision, and several times later he shuddered at his foolishness. But the rest was perfection, everything going exactly as rehearsed in his mind time after time.

First, the getting rid of the car and the changing of his appearance at the airport. Next the dumping of his old clothes in the Thames.

And then the crucial forty-five minutes of his second call.

It took the guard behind the grill at the safety-deposit company no more than two or three minutes to check his name and photograph against the files, but it was a stomach-churning age. He pushed his soft-brimmed grey hat back a bit, enough to look as if he was about to remove it, not enough to reveal his slicked-down hair. The glasses with their plain lenses were safely in his pocket.

A second guard escorted him downstairs, unlocked steel-bar doors into the vault, locked Kenyon inside, told him to ring when he was ready to leave.

It could still have been a trap.

The deposit safe was one of the larger ones. Inside was an attaché case, about five inches by twelve inches by eighteen inches. It was fitted with a combination lock. Kenyon knew the type. It was a security case designed to sound an alarm and ruin the contents if anyone opened it the wrong way. He paused, rubbed his sweaty palms along his thighs. Very carefully, he touched the catches that had to be pressed before the lock was released. He felt them give. And only then, the device deactivated, did he open the case.

The notes, fives and tens, were so tightly packed it was hard to refasten it. From another pocket, he took a suitcase strap, used it to fix the attaché case shut.

He rang the bell, waited another age.

The guard glanced down at the case, but it was no more than normal curiosity. He touched his cap as Kenyon left.

Kenyon travelled to Euston station via two changes of underground train. He was early enough to leave two stations short and walk the last leg.

He was feeling good now, adrenalin-sharp, confident. He could even smile at the poster he passed – the Home Office's new anti-crime campaign slogan, 'Watch Out, There's a Thief About'. And he's going to get away with it, he wanted to shout . . .

The train to Birmingham, the flight to Dublin . . .

And then, for the first time he really *felt* safe. It *felt* like it had worked. But he forced himself not to give way to his euphoria. He could not relax yet. Ireland, he knew, was the easiest place to reach, the hardest in which to hide.

The following day he flew to Brussels. He planned to stay only one night. His priority before continuing with the rest of his planned schedule was to deposit the money. The five thousand pounds from the croupier was taped under his shirt and would keep him for a long time. The money in the case had to be lodged somewhere safe. Switzerland was the most obvious place, but for precisely that reason he had to avoid it. He doubted Barton could move that fast, but Switzerland was an obvious country in which to look for a man with a case full of money.

Kenyon's destination was Luxembourg. Less famed but just as

full of banks willing to open accounts without question. And then, once that was done, onward . . . he had his plans.

He ate in his room, afraid to leave the case alone but not willing to draw attention to it by lodging it in the hotel safe.

From time to time he unfastened the strap, swung back the lid, gazed down at the bundles of notes, fixed tight with rubber bands.

He was curious to know how much there was – but not over so. He was as familiar with currency notes as most men are with names of football players. Give or take a few thousand either way the case held about one hundred and sixty thousand pounds.

At last, around one o'clock in the morning, just as the traffic had begun to quieten below his window, he could resist no longer.

OK. It would be hard to repack, but he had all the night. Who could sleep at such a time? He *had* to empty it out, count it, see exactly what he'd got. Enjoy the feel. That most of all. God, he'd worked for this!

He was stripped for bed, dressed only in pyjama bottoms.

He laid the case flat on the bed, unfastened the strap, lifted the lid again, waited a moment and then reached in with a triumphant lunge, tearing out a handful of bundles.

It was completely different from the shooting.

Then it had all happened in definable sequence – pain, sound, smell, all separate and distinct.

This time it all happened together, was over before he realised what had taken place.

The crash was still echoing through numbed ears. His fingers were tingling but he could not tell whether there was pain or not.

The air was full of fluttering bits of paper. All bright orange. Like the smoke that filled the air.

It filled his nose and mouth, made him gag although it had no smell.

'You fool! You fucking fool!' He mouthed the words over and over again.

Someone began knocking at the door. He went to it, but did not open it – the orange smoke was too thick. 'It's all right,' he shouted. 'A can of shaving foam exploded. It's nothing. Nothing's damaged. No one's hurt.'

Disregarding words from outside, he returned to the bed, dropped to his knees and began plucking up handfuls of the paper that was falling from the air like psychedelic snow.

181

A few notes still lay in the case. But streaked in orange.

'You fool! You fucking bloody fool!'

He had been so careful. *Why* hadn't he anticipated this, taken care?'

Christ, if he could go back five minutes!

The bag had been booby-trapped *twice*. How, was obvious. A smoke-and-dye device. A hidden switch or wire triggered a small explosive cap that set off the dye-filled cartridge.

For him? For anyone interfering with the case? It did not matter. The result either way was the same.

The dye, he knew, was impossible to remove. Every penny of the money he had stolen was gone. Completely ruined. Worthless.

PART TWO

SEEK. NOW.

CHAPTER THIRTEEN

The newspaper's Friday afternoon conference was almost over. Jordan, the editor, swung his feet off the desk-top and waited for his foreign editor to finish outlining the week's main overseas stories and how they were being handled. His résumé was virtually a tour of Eastern Europe – everywhere Communism was beginning to crumble.

The heads of departments had each run through stories for which they were responsible, making their pitches for space in the upcoming Sunday's newspapers. Outside, Britain was enjoying the sunniest summer of the century; inside, the room was heavy with smoke and the smell of breath still laden with lunch-time liquor. Several of the staff had had indulgent lunches, mostly at the paper's expense with bills that would later be charged against essential entertaining of anonymous 'contacts'. Now, as the foreign editor finished, they rubbed faces, twirled pencils, stared down at duplicated lists, crossed arms, leaned chins on hands and thought about such things as forthcoming holidays, whether the fashion editor's new secretary really wore no knickers, and when they could get out of here and have a pee.

The number of pages to fill was small – it was a slack period for the advertisements that determined the size of the paper. At the same time, there was no shortage of news. Filling the pages was easy. Normally, Friday was a tough day – food at the desk, three to four hours' sleep, then an early start fourteen-hour Saturday fuelled by foul coffee in polystyrene cups. But today the air of relaxation was as heavy as the smoke and booze.

Except for the one man who had not joined the lunchers.

Stephen Kenyon had spent the hours up to the conference hunched over a telephone in his cubicle, double and treble confirming every checkable fact in the piece of copy that now lay face down on the editor's desk.

It had not been mentioned so far. Several heads had turned questioningly when he had entered the room; he appeared at the conference rarely. No one had seen him for three weeks. But that was not unusual. Gilbert, the leader pages editor, caught his eye, and forced a half-smile that masked dislike – the reporter was too intense, too sure of his own view of the world, too often a self-righteous pain in the arse. How like him to be bringing news when everyone else was enjoying the smaller papers and the chance to ease off – fuck, the readers wanted to relax too: they still wanted their papers, but they didn't want to have to *work* at them on a hot August Sunday.

Other department heads went through their lists. The Guardian Angels had started patrolling London tube trains, more deaths were expected in the outbreak of salmonella poisoning, there were new pit-closure threats, fresh detail was emerging about a Middle-Eastern terrorist who had blown himself up in a London hotel . . .

'Pretty heavy stuff,' said Jordan. 'Hasn't anyone got anything light?'

'Annie's writing about those nuts who wrote a report attacking Bugs Bunny and Tom and Jerry for making kids aggressive at school.'

'Okay,' flat, not convinced. 'But let's keep a look out for more. We don't want to bore the readers to death.'

Then, abruptly, it was over.

Most of them left, wondering about the secret from which they were being excluded, and the door closed on the editor, Kenyon, the home and foreign editors, Gilbert and the lawyer.

'You've read it?' The editor turned over the sheets of the only copy of Kenyon's story.

Each had, but only minutes before the conference began. No one wanted to be the first to commit himself.

The editor turned to the lawyer. His comment was brief. 'Legally, no problem.'

'Whether it's true or not?' The foreign editor.

Stephen wanted to say, 'Of course it's bloody true. I wouldn't have written the fucking thing if it wasn't.' But he remained silent.

The lawyer's reply was brief. 'Whether it's true or not.' His terseness contained a clear warning – although there were no legal difficulties, the lawyer, a newspaper veteran, sensed trouble; he did not want to be involved.

Kenyon got the message too. Time-serving bastard. He hated lawyers. Spineless shits. The number of times he had had to hammer things past them. And how many comebacks had there been that had cost the paper money? None. Not one fucking one. The reason was that he got his facts spot on. *And* he knew more about the law than most fucking lawyers.

It was hard to remain quiet, but he was a good tactician. Christ, it hurt even to have to sit and hear it discussed. It was a good story. Correction, a fucking *great* story. Details about what had happened to a British and an American hostage grabbed in Lebanon two years before and not heard of since. Real details about where they had been held, how they were, where they were now. Even a copy of a smuggled note written by one of them in his own writing.

Gilbert became the first to speak. His reasonable voice, an ominous sign. Kenyon knew the knife was about to enter.

'It seems to me, there are two problems.' He began tapping fingertips together. 'The first is how can anyone be sure it's true – we're operating in an area where it's impossible to know what's true, what's half-true, what's been planted and what hasn't.' The foreign editor, who was wishing he had had a chance to talk to his friends at the Foreign Office, nodded agreement. 'The second – and I would argue this should be our major consideration – is whether it would be right to use it even if we knew without a shadow of doubt it was genuine.'

'Not use it anyway? Why?' Stephen knew Gilbert's objection before he asked it. Gilbert would claim that publication would reveal to the hostages' captors that they had a traitor among them and it would result in any avenue of communication being closed. Gilbert would argue publication could endanger the men's chance of freedom. Still, Stephen asked. He used his reasonable voice too. He knew Gilbert had a short fuse; all he had to do was make him speak out, sound like a *Guardian* leader or the kind of person who belly-ached to the Press Council or thought that journalism was printing government hand-outs. That would make the editor's mind up faster than anything. God, Stephen knew the editor wanted to publish. He was an old-time newspaperman, brought up on scoops and the belief that the best news was news someone didn't want you to print. Even if these days he had to go through the motions of pleasing the advertising agencies and the marketing men and the conglomerate that owned the paper along with hotels and an airline and book publishers and television.

Gilbert bit. 'I should think it's obvious even to *you*.' Stephen's accent, still unmistakably American despite his five years back in London, irritated him as much as the words themselves.

'Nevertheless, tell us, Gilbert.' The editor knew what was happening, was joining the game.

Gilbert was in full flow. 'Irresponsible . . . no thought of the consequences . . . worst kind of tabloid . . .' And then the big mistake: 'And all for a cheap scoop.'

No expression changed, but the mood did. *Cheap* scoop. No scoop is cheap. It's either a fucking scoop, or it isn't, Kenyon wanted to say. But he kept his reasonable voice.

'I've purposely disguised a couple of key facts. There's no way the guys' captors can trace where it came from, where the leak is. All it'll do is make them all look at each other, wonder who the hell's the traitor, fuck up their organisation.' He paused for effect. 'Personally, I'd think that was a good thing.'

'What about the poor bastards' chances of getting out after we publish?'

Kenyon shrugged his sympathy. 'These hostages have been held for two years. Nobody's got them out yet, didn't even know whether they were alive or not most of the time. This'll put the heat on the Foreign Office and the State Department to get off their arses and do something.'

Gilbert knew it was running against him. He was thrown back on querying the story's accuracy. 'But how do we *know* it's genuine? I don't suppose Stephen will tell us his source.'

A mistake. Two mistakes. Kenyon paused again, not for effect this time, but just to be sure that his opponents had played themselves into a corner.

They had. He made his moves. Move one – 'The editor knows my source.'

He opened the envelope on his knee and slid out the photograph. It had been delivered by messenger during the conference. 'I didn't mention this before in case it didn't arrive.'

Move two. He passed it to the editor who stared at it before handing it around without comment. It was a dark, grainy photograph showing one hostage standing gaunt against a bare wall. In front of him he held a newspaper. Under a magnifying glass the printing on the paper was clear. It was dated just eleven days before.

Check Mate.

The story ran across all seven columns of the front page, and turned on to page three. It was dominated by the photograph, which showed the hostage naked to the waist, head dropped forward as though its weight was too great for him.

'That'll make the bastards do something,' said the editor.

In the office pub, in the basement of the newspaper complex to which they had moved in the newspaper industry's exodus from Fleet Street, Kenyon accepted the congratulations and got gently and pleasantly drunk. He enjoyed the company of newspapermen more than any other people. He liked the mixture of naivety and cynicism, the *bonhomie* of booze and anecdote, the feeling of standing apart from the rest of the world while being convinced you understood its operation and operators better than anyone.

Around 10 p.m. a group of them ate at a Chinese restaurant a few minutes away, in case he was recalled. It was an uninterrupted meal. Kenyon returned to find the editor about to leave. The only development had been the anticipated calls from the Foreign Office lodging objections that they had not been approached before publication.

'Lawler?' asked Stephen. Lawler was the chairman of the group that now owned the paper. He was not a hands-on proprietor, but he telephoned every Saturday night from wherever he was in the world. His comments were always formal, almost detached. He knew that contact was expect of him – *real* proprietors of the old school were on editors' backs day and night. But his business was owning things. Detail was for others. His calls were a necessary courtesy; the editor sometimes thought he had to be prompted to make them by an underling who programmed them into his electronic organiser.

'Away,' said the editor. Stephen waited for him to continue, but he had finished. Stephen realised that the editor had no idea where – perhaps some secret conglomerate business from which he was excluded totally.

*

Weekend for a Sunday newspaperman is Sunday and Monday. Stephen passed most of Sunday in pleasant routine. The morning was spent in bed with coffee and toast, the other papers littered around him. All had followed up his story as best they could – but had been forced back on a minimum of information taken from his article with 'No comment' statements from the Foreign Office and the State Department, and dated library pictures of the hostages.

He worked through the papers voraciously, alternatively skimming some items at speed and reading others with brow-furrowed intensity. The other quality heavies got special attention, but his interest span was wide and eclectic – the sex change of a soap-show actor in a down-market tabloid, the psychology of football violence examined in an up-market broadsheet, a City fraud, a multimillion soccer-player transfer, fears about a new drug, a country-and-western singer talking about the size of her breasts and what they meant to her life . . .

He read them all, without discrimination. A newsprint glutton devouring his favourite meal. Some weeks he paused over a rival's story, angry it had eluded him but admiring the professional skill that had produced it. On such occasions, he would read the story several times, trying to work out how the newspaper had obtained it, which of those quoted (if any) might have been the original source and why they had a link with that paper and no other.

Such occasions grew rarer, though. Investigative journalism – digging for important facts that someone, often government or big business, wanted kept hidden – was a dying trade, at least in newspapers. Too time-consuming. Too expensive. Newspapers wanted results in days, not weeks, nor months. Too potent also for owners and editors whose new concerns were whether the market-research profiles showed enough teenage female readers or young married male B1s to feed to the advertisers. Best leave it to television.

Thinking that left a bad taste, despite his scoop. Maybe tiredness. He always felt burned out on Sundays; it was battery-recharging day. But today, suddenly, he felt lower than usual. Once, he had vowed that he would get out at thirty-five – 'Unless you glue your arse to a desk, it's a young man's game,' he had said. As thirty-five had neared, he had taken to adding to himself,

'Not that you can't still do it physically,' but he had still believed that you lose the edge, became like a boxer who has taken too many punches and hangs back just a fraction too long. And yet. Here he was five years past his get-out date, sliding downhill two months after the big Four O in a dying business . . .

Maybe he should move to television. He was pretty certain they'd want him. There had been approaches. But he didn't like TV investigation, didn't trust it. What could be shown, what looked good on film, got in the way of the facts. He was a puritan about Truth (in his mind it always had a capital 'T'). Like the CIA (which has the words inlaid in the floor of its lobby), he believed 'the truth shall make you free'. Like them, he also believed in his ability to see the truth. Certainty was one of the forces that drove him.

The mood left him over lunch with husband-and-wife doctor friends and their three other guests. There was a lone woman, a divorcee, and Stephen knew it was match-making time again. Because of his job demands, the fact that he had never married was regarded less suspiciously than it would have been in other men of his age. Nevertheless, friends, especially married women, still saw it as an abnormality to be righted. Far from irritating him, he found it flattering that they cared so much and regarded him as so good a catch. Generally too the women he met were agreeable, dineable and/or bedable, and not averse to an irregular and light relationship when they saw the alternative was no relationship with him at all. This one was a set designer, both attractive and interesting. They exchanged numbers and he said he would call her.

His pleasant Sunday ended soon after four-thirty, the time he arrived home. The men were waiting in two unmarked cars.

The house was a narrow three-storey early Victorian building in a cul-de-sac in Camden Town. It was divided into three flats. He owned the basement – steep iron stairs to a strip of yard and an entrance door to three long rooms, each leading into one another, and finally on to a tiny patio.

He had been half-expecting them – but not today. Maybe tomorrow. More likely Tuesday at the office. The story was not that important from the view of national security.

They had a warrant to search his flat. A Special Branch inspector did all the talking. Stephen was more interested in another man who stood back observing and said nothing. MI5, Stephen was sure. The man had a small but distinctive birthmark below his left ear: a raised, mottled purple stain.

The telephone rang once during the hour-long search, but Kenyon let the answerphone deal with it. He neither protested, nor asked questions. The warrant was genuine, nothing he did would stop them, no questions he asked would be answered. He had been through it before. He wondered whether they had already searched the office, or whether the visits were simultaneous. In either event, they would find nothing. Long ago, in countries where the penalties for failure were much greater, he had learned to destroy documents and never to commit names and numbers to paper. His address book and diary, which they bundled up to take away along with files from the cabinet in his study, would be of no help.

The MI5 man was the last to leave. He lingered in the doorway, his expression half-amused, half-intrigued by Stephen's attitude.

'The last one called us Fascist pigs,' he said. He had the trace of a Midlands accent. 'Pity you gave up your American passport – we could have deported you.'

Stephen shrugged as he moved to close the door. 'I guess someone's got to do your job,' he said. 'I suppose you can always say you're only obeying orders.'

Alone, he checked the rooms, straightened cushions, closed drawers, cursed them for the way they had replaced the books on the wrong shelves. The message on the answerphone said that the office had been raided. He phoned Jordan, the editor, at home. They agreed that the authorities were overreacting. He said he would talk to the lawyer as soon as they finished speaking, leave the editor to set in motion the protest lobbying with key politicians.

He sensed the unease. 'It proves it was all true,' he volunteered.

Jordan acted as though he had not heard. 'I'm just wondering when the fuck I can reach Lawler. He's never had anything like this hit him before.'

The editor was locked into his own problem, every editor's perennial one. His personal fate.

Lawler's hirelings reached him late afternoon local time on Little Paradise Island in the Caribbean, where he was unwinding after four days of confidential discussions in Washington over airline landing rights.

His first anger was over the article – at a period when he needed government goodwill in both Britain and the United States it could hardly have been worse timed. None of the considerations that had been debated in the office – the effect on the hostages, the freedom of the press – bothered him. As far as he was concerned, if it was a story that sold papers, fine. Except for now. The Americans were on the point of giving entry rights to his airline. The British were under some pressure, withstood so far, to refer one of his companies to the Monopolies Commission after persistent complaints that it was rigging market prices. A time, in short, when the company needed to tread softly with both London and Washington. Not a time to tell them to go fuck themselves. Which, in effect, publishing the article did.

His second anger was over the raids. Not at the indignity or arrogance of them, but because they curtailed his scope for action. Without them, he could have sacked Jordan, accusing him of lack of judgement in publishing the article. Lawler could thus have made his peace with the two governments *and* accumulated some goodwill. It might even have worked to his advantage. But now such an action was impossible. To sack Jordan would make him, Lawler, appear a weak figure who capitulated under threat. He could not afford that.

By the time he had arrived back in London in the company jet early Monday, he had resolved his problem. A compromise, he called it. Though Jordan did not see it that way when they met. Jordan learned he was to remain editor, though in name only because he was going on immediate sick leave; he and his wife could borrow the house on Little Paradise. After six months he would resign. The man who would edit in the interim would have the title 'Acting Editor'.

Lawler held up his hand to stem Jordan's protest. He wrote on a notepad with a silver pencil, tore off the sheet and handed it across the desk. It contained a number. A cash amount. Nothing else.

'By all means consult your lawyer,' he said. 'That figure stands for one hour. After that it falls by ten per cent every hour that passes.' He looked at his watch. 'I calculate that by shortly after ten o'clock this evening it will be down to zero, and we shall have

193

to begin again from scratch. Something tells me that the discussions will be long and painful.'

Melville had been an executive on the paper for twenty years. He was a survivor, a good professional of the chameleon school. The list of moves he had made read like a game – two down, one up, three sideways, one down . . . he had been assistant editor (features), executive editor (home), senior editor (special projects) and a dozen others long forgotten.

Lawler appointed him immediately Jordan left. The résumé of candidates on Lawler's desk showed he had three major advantages. He had been away when the decision to publish was made. As an insider, his appointment would not look like surrender. And Melville would be easy to boot out when the time came.

Stephen was at the newspaper office. He had just given a short, formal and uncommunicative statement to the Special Branch. The *Evening Standard* was reporting the raid; their reporters had been trying to reach him, but he had not called them back. The office was deserted except for a few secretaries who worked Monday to Friday.

Melville called him from the conglomerate's headquarters in St James's. Brief to the point of merely naming a meeting place, but that was enough to tell Stephen what had happened. They met in the wood-panelled lounge of Brown's Hotel. Melville was already seated at a corner table next to a grandfather clock. A waiter hovered. Without asking Kenyon, Melville ordered afternoon tea. Whether they ate it or not, it was their admission charge to the calm secrecy of the room.

'Congratulations,' said Stephen. He meant it. If Jordan was out, Stephen was sorry, but high risk was the price you paid for editorship. Besides, the golden handshake he would receive would ensure he didn't starve. From his viewpoint, Melville was as good a replacement as any – they weren't close but they had always had a good working relationship. Unless, of course, Melville had called the meeting to fire him. He doubted that – the meeting would then be taking place in the office with lawyers hovering.

Melville shrugged. 'I'm only acting Godman,' he said. 'It's probably temporary.' His tone and expression conveyed that he already half-believed he was wrong – that given time, he would show that he was the best, the only choice.

Tea came, and Melville bit into a cucumber sandwich.

'Good teas here,' he said. 'I entertain a lot here – a quarter the price of lunch and four times the impact.'

He finished the two-bite-size sandwich, dabbed his mouth, dusted his lapel for imaginary crumbs. 'You're an embarrassment, Steve,' he said. 'I don't want to lose you, but I'd like you out of the way for a bit.'

'You do? Or Lawler does?'

Melville shrugged his man-of-the-world shrug. 'Does it matter?'

'What if the police want to question me again?'

'They won't. Gerry's been talking to the PM's office. Officially, it was nothing to do with the government – a police matter. Unofficially, they wanted to show anyone who leaks that they'll tear their balls off. Now the point's made, they don't plan to push it any further.'

'What about a follow-up?'

'You think your contact'll come up with more *now* – even if there is more?'

'Who knows?'

Melville's face hardened, an expression Stephen had not seen before. Strange how many men expanded into their jobs. He thought Melville might be one of them.

'No follow-up. It's a good story. Correction. A great story. There'll be a statement in the House of Commons tonight. The dailies will keep it going a day or two. You'll get your papers back before the end of the week – I imagine they're still going through them just in case you've been careless enough to jot something down you shouldn't. Pity Jordan took sick, but that's how it goes, and officially the job's staying open for his return. And you've had a tough few weeks. I've checked the files – you haven't taken a holiday for nearly two years. Take a break. Take two weeks. No, a month. Put in a good exes claim – you must have spent a fortune getting that story.'

He finished the last sandwich. 'Go somewhere warm,' he said expansively. 'Just avoid the Caribbean. Might bump into Jordan recuperating.'

*

195

The reason that Stephen had not taken a holiday for twenty-one months was simple: he could not cope with them. Away from work, he felt lost, almost useless. A day lying around, a lunch with friends, an evening at the theatre, an afternoon at the races. They were fine. Individual treats he could enjoy – food, a concert, a night at the opera, jazz at Ronnie Scott's, a tour of some monument . . . But day after day!

It used to worry him. On one occasion not long after he had returned to live in Britain he and a woman had arranged to spend two weeks in a still unspoiled resort in Morocco. The planning, the anticipation had been exciting, a spice to their developing relationship. The holiday had begun idyllically: sex in the sand, lazy afternoons, long relaxed evenings. After four days he had turned his Sony to world news bulletins, after five he was in search of newspapers. After eight he had bribed a receptionist to give him a false message, recalling him to London.

He needed a reason to be somewhere. He knew he was like a photographer unable to look unblinkingly at the world except through a camera lens. It was the presence of the camera – or, in his case, the notebook – that made it all bearable. With it, you could see and yet remain oddly detached. He was a man who witnessed and noted but rarely felt, except in abstract terms like Justice and Evil. He described individuals, but what he really saw was man and his events and happenings as headlines and opening paragraphs. Although sociable, at heart he was self-contained, a loner *needing* no one. For him the complexity of the world was the infinite number of questions it raised and contained. But he had no doubt that for every one of them there was an answer.

A psychiatrist would have found the roots to it all in his background – he would have seized upon the early loss of Stephen's father, the difficulties he had had relating to his mother's remarriage and to his stepfather (even the act of liking him had seemed a betrayal), his uprooting as a sixteen-year-old to live with his aunt and her American husband in the United States. And then, a dozen years later, the death of Tarlach, the only woman with whom he had been able to strip away the layers of protection. Stephen, who thought such things balls, regarded the way he was as an occupational hazard, to be regretted occasionally, perhaps, but to be accepted as a cost worth the paying.

His first reaction to Melville's order was to use it as a lever to get out – if he kicked hard enough, they would have to fire him, buy off his contract, leaving him free to go elsewhere with some 'fuck you' cash. (Although he earned big money and had only himself to keep, like most journalists he lived right up to his income.)

Yet he hesitated. Maybe, deep down, he was afraid that the offers would not come. More likely, he thought, was that Melville had been right – he *was* tired. A week away – because that's all he would take – would allow him to put his decision on ice.

But where? There was a ready answer. A task that he had been putting aside since the summer.

Stephen picked up a hire car in the nearest big town and drove out to the village. His mother's house, empty since Mary had moved into the nursing home in June, had a stale locked-up smell. The hallway was piled with junk mail: the woman who had promised to check the house occasionally had obviously given up caring. He cursed her tardiness, then realised that, after he kept failing to appear, she had probably thought, if her own son can't turn up, why should I care?

Curtains were half-drawn, to give a casual impression of occupancy. He pulled them back, opened windows. He toured the house, ridiculously large even before his stepfather had died. 'His' room, used by him maybe once a year on average, was still made up ready for him. There were three other bedrooms. One, used as a storage room, was full of cases and boxes of belongings. They – together with the contents of his dead stepfather's undisturbed study – had to be sorted, given away or moved: his mother had refused to touch anything after her husband died. Then the house had to be sold. The family solicitor kept urging swift action: it was a seller's market.

Stephen had prevaricated, using as an excuse the argument that his mother might still return to the house, albeit briefly – it would kill her to know it had been sold. He told himself that there was no rush; he could not spare the time; the house was capital and when his mother's funds ran out he would pick up the bills – after all, the proceeds of the sale would come to him one day. The truth was that he wanted nothing to do with the operation – he didn't want to sort, he didn't want to root among belongings, he didn't want to find things, he didn't want to have to make decisions about what to keep, what to put aside, what to destroy. Only an awful sense of duty – and the knowledge that he had to answer to his aunt Katharine – prevented him from ordering all papers to be destroyed, all furniture to be packed and sold.

Only that and a memory of the other time he had had to sort someone's belongings. He and Tarlach had met on a LA–New York flight. He had been interviewing a retired State Department official rumoured to know the identity of the Watergate 'Deep Throat', she had been visiting friends on the Coast. Eighteen months later she had dropped dead. Literally. At eight that morning he had left the Soho apartment they shared. She had been in bed still, had a day off. Just after noon he received a call at his desk at the *New York Times*. A hospital. She had been visiting the Museum of Modern Art, one of her favourite haunts, had just stepped out of the cafeteria into the sculpture garden when she had stopped, clasped her head and said, 'Oh God, I feel funny. My head hurts. Oh, so funny.' And she had died. Almost certainly a brain tumour – sometimes it did happen like this, said the doctor at the hospital. Sometimes the person went into a coma and there was the agony of deciding when to switch off the life-support. But this time, death had been quick. He had said it as though Stephen should be comforted, and of course he had been glad she had not suffered but it had not lessened the pain. Then he had telephoned the only relative of hers that he knew, a sister in Ireland. Two days later she had arrived and they had worked silently through her belongings. Some had been left with him, and he had quietly destroyed them or given them to charity.

Twelve years ago. An ocean away. But no need to disturb it now.

He ate at the village's only pub before setting off for the nursing home. The brewery had turned it into a 'fun pub': slot machines, a juke box, scampi in a basket. Stephen bought himself a beer and a ploughman's – a wrapped square of cheese, individual foil-wrapped butter, sad leaves of lettuce, cardboard bread and a dollop of bottled pickles big enough to disguise the taste.

The nursing home was a Victorian pile with modern extensions set back from the road. The residents were gathered together in the lounge when he arrived; for an insane moment he wondered whether his life was beginning to revolve around formal teas. Mary was part of a small group in a corner. He was pleased and relieved to see she was well enough to be out of her room.

He had bought flowers on the way, and he held them out clumsily. Their first minute together always made him feel awkward. In recent months it had been intensified by the worry over whether she would recognise him. This time she did, at once.

He bent to kiss her, and he could smell talcum powder. 'Your father didn't come? I hope the car isn't playing up again.'

'No, he didn't come. And the car's fine, Mum.'

She leaned back, teacup in hand, and closed her eyes. He reached forward to remove it and she was instantly alert.

'How's your job?' Her voice was more animated. He knew she had moved planes. 'I hope you're not working too hard. You should stay a few days.'

His mother's companions were disregarding them. A pert black nurse brought him a cup of tea.

'Yes, I'll be staying for a few days,' he said.

By the time he had finished his tea, Mary was dozing. The matron, alerted to his presence, sent a message that she was in her room the rest of the afternoon if he wanted to talk to her.

Her room was off a back staircase. It was tiny, cluttered, a world away from the other office at the front of the building, reserved for formal interviews. An element of front she no longer had to adopt with him. There were some bad stories about nursing homes; this one had been checked out with total thoroughness before he had first brought Mary. If you had to live in an institution – and the doctors had made it clear that outside one his mother would not survive – this was as good a choice as you could make, he felt. The matron's report, as usual, was concise yet sympathetic: no worse, the new drugs working well, doctor visiting Thursday if Stephen wanted to talk with him. 'Much of the time, she's remarkably clear. Like many of these cases, the older the memory, the clearer it is.'

'And is it accurate?'

'Her memories of long ago? Oh yes, I think so. It's just there is no separation of time. Fifty years ago is yesterday, except that yesterday may not be remembered at all.'

He joined Mary in her room. She was sitting in one of the two easy chairs. The room overlooked formal rear gardens. It was almost unbearably hot. She wore a cardigan, and he decided not to open a window.

She was knitting, what looked like an intricate slip-over.

There was a stack of crossword and puzzle magazines on the table. He lifted one, and flipped the pages. The crosswords were all completed in the same careful ball-point writing. Every square was filled with the same letter: 'Z'. He did not know whether it was significant or whether she just liked the shape.

'I like the knitting,' he said. Why couldn't he relax in her presence, talk naturally?

'It's not for Bill.' Bill had been her husband, Stephen's stepfather. 'It's not for your father either.' She lifted her eyes, conveyed that she wanted a reaction.

'I know.'

'Of course you know.'

She was looking at him oddly. 'He's not dead, you know. Michael's not really dead. I keep lying awake thinking I should have told you. I should never have lied to you.'

He felt a chill, even though he knew she was rambling again and even though it was a subject that had long been closed.

Even to hear her use his father's name was a shock. She had not talked about him or his death since Stephen was still a boy. Even then she had said little. He could remember the day she told him there had been an accident. It was a Saturday. His stepfather was away at some conference or seminar. Stephen had been playing tennis.

His mother had looked as though she'd been crying when he got home. He was in a rush, late for his afternoon newspaper delivery round. 'I've some terrible news,' she had said.

And she had told him. About the drowning. About how the person who had telephoned had said his father was a hero. About how Stephen had to be brave. About how she and his new dad loved him.

Stephen had gone up to his room. A letter he had been writing to his father for days was on his desk. It looked as though it had been moved, as though his mother had read it. The thought made him angry. Less at her than him. He could understand her curiosity. He was cross he had not put it in a drawer – it contained phrases he would rather she had never seen. Like, asking whether he, Stephen, was to blame for what happened between his father and his mother? For that reason, he would probably never have sent it. He had written letters before that were never posted. Now, he tore the letter, all three unfinished pages, over and over again until the pieces were like confetti. Even that was not enough. He found matches, burned them in a tray from a long unused chemistry set still on a shelf. He stirred the flames with a pencil until only ash remained. Then he took a book from the bookcase, opened it and removed a photograph of his father. It was one he had taken from his mother's drawer one day and hidden. Originally, it had been a group photograph, but Stephen had removed and kept only a square showing Michael. Holding it face down so he should not see the picture, he burned that too. It was more difficult than the notepaper: the flames would flare and then die almost immediately. By the time it was destroyed, eleven spent matches lay with the ashes.

He went out then. His mother called after him, but he pretended not to hear. He finished his newspaper round as normal. When he returned, they sat and played draughts and then watched television. She talked a little, always clichés, but mostly they were silent. He was in bed when his stepfather returned home, and he pretended to be asleep. He thought he cried during the night, but he was not sure. He knew it felt bad, but not as awful as when his mother had told him three years before that Michael had left them, would not be returning. *That* had been terrible. A pain under his diaphragm like a hot blade, an uncontrollable dizziness, panic and disbelief – it couldn't be true! The nightmares! The next day there were more clichés, and after that the subject – like his father – was dead, until fourteen years later, briefly, too briefly, there had been someone to whom he could talk. And after that, no one.

He knew now why Mary had remained silent over the years.

He leaned forward and took her hand. He could feel the bones, and then she squeezed and the grip was fierce.

'I'm telling you now because you'll find things. I know you're here to go through my things, I know you're going to sell the house.'

Her voice was low and sly; she was fishing.

He held her eyes.

'You know I wouldn't sell the house without your say-so,' he said. 'I told you I'm here for a rest, here to see more of you.'

He meant to say more, but she pulled her hand away, resumed knitting frantically.

201

When he kissed her goodbye a half-hour later she had still not said another word.

She said nothing further about his father the following day, and after he left her and returned to the house he began sorting, anxious now to have the task finished.

Once he started, it was less emotional than he had feared. He found himself feeling curiously detached even though the pages were the unfolding of a life – photographs, old letters (including wartime letters from his father), birth and marriage certificates. He paused mid-evening, drove to a pub more pleasant than the immediate one, returned at eleven o'clock and continued.

He found the box at around 1 a.m., just as he had decided to quit for the night.

It was a square, tin biscuit box, the lid sealed with strips of Sellotape. It was contained inside a suitcase among a number of towels still unused within their original wrappings.

Its location warned him it was special. A riffle through told him why.

He carried the box down into the kitchen, made coffee, sat facing it, and wrestled with whether to read the contents or destroy them.

He had to read them. Not because it was important, not because he needed to, not because it would change his life. Simply because he had gone this far and was determined not to stop now. And because he was curious. His trade was answering questions. One had been raised now. He could not leave it.

Considering the story they told, the papers were suprisingly few. But they were a revelation. Until now, he had believed that his father had died abroad when he was fourteen. Now a new story revealed itself. His father had not died then. He had continued living and working in London until three years after that. And then he had vanished.

There were a dozen press cuttings about the disappearance. Stephen read them with fierce intensity. The first referred to police looking for Kenyon 'seventeen days after he was last seen leaving the London gaming club where he was a well-known figure.' The last was on the first anniversary of the disappearance, summing up what had been found. Nothing. The writer said the police had investigated the possibilities of murder, loss of memory and flight. Police, it said, were still keeping an open mind.

Stephen felt a rush of unwelcome emotions: painful anger, bewilderment. Why had he not known? How had he not seen these at the time? He checked the dates – of course, he was already living in the United States with Mary's sister Katharine and her husband Ward. He put the cuttings aside and went on through the box. There was correspondence with a lawyer and an insurance company. A legal document headed 'Presumption of Death' certified Michael Kenyon dead on the grounds that he had not been traced.

Most touching of all, there was a letter in Mary's handwriting. It was to his father. It was unfinished and undated. But one phrase –'now Stephen is sixteen' – told him the year was either the second half of 1965 or the early part of 1966. Not long before his father vanished!

It began, 'You came today out of nowhere. I am writing to try to explain why I told him you were dead.' As he read on, his anger softened, and he shared her pain. He felt astonishment that she could have carried the secret this long. There must have been many occasions dating back over twenty years in which she could have said something to him. And yet, he could see that as time went by, it would have become harder. And, in any event, why should she? His father had disappeared anyway, presumably died, just three years later than she had said it had happened. Not so nobly, it was true. What would he have gained from being told? She had lied to protect Stephen from knowing his father had deserted them. What argument could there be for destroying that fiction? Unless he would find out anyway, as now.

He put the papers carefully back in the biscuit box and left it on the kitchen table. He fell asleep finally, still replaying the story in his mind. For that was what it was. A long-ago story. Now that he'd got over the shock of reading his father's name on those cuttings, he didn't feel hurt. There had been pain once, even guilt though God knew why. But for years his father had been dead in his *mind* even if he had continued to live in reality. Now, he told himself, he felt scarcely involved, except for wondering whether he would tell Mary that he had found the papers. The people in the story were different people. It was a different world. So much had happened since then.

Still, it was intriguing. There were so many loose ends. He hated loose ends.

CHAPTER FOURTEEN

Stephen Kenyon's return to work provoked panic.

He had entered the newspaper building unobserved through a rear entrance, and had been catching up on assorted papers, when news got through to Melville that he was in the building. The acting editor summoned him immediately.

'What the fuck are you doing here?'

Stephen noted with private amusement that Melville had had the office refurnished, replacing the desk with a cluster of chairs grouped with studied casualness around a huge low table. There were new pictures, including one of Melville being introduced to the Queen at a charity event with which the paper had been associated. Stephen could vaguely remember Melville, an outspoken republican, complaining about being forced to attend. The chairman was a great monarchist. Editors adapt.

'I work here,' said Stephen. 'You forgot? Or did you fire me and forget to post the letter?'

Melville picked up a desk lighter shaped like a racing car, lit a fresh cigarette, and flopped into one of the chairs.

'Don't fuck with me,' he said, but the edge had already gone from his voice. 'I left a message on your machine.'

Stephen sat facing him. 'You won't believe this,' he said, 'but the tape had jammed. You recorded on to nothing.' His fault: he had slipped in a fresh tape before he had gone away, but upside down. The moment it began recording, it had reached the end of the spool and switched itself off.

Melville pressed the intercom, asked for coffee.

His voice became weary, the tone that of someone who needs friends.

'You're still bad news,' he said. 'The PM's still got Lawler on the rack over the Monopolies Commission, the Yanks have deferred their business with him for three months to take more soundings.' He pointed upwards. 'There's a man called Simpson upstairs – until five days ago he was deputy general manager of Lawler's hotels, now he's executive director here, whatever the fuck that is.'

He knew. So did Stephen. It was executive in charge of watching, reporting and – above all – making sure nothing happened to surprise Lawler.

'You want me to go?'

'I don't want you to do anything except stay the fuck away from here. Go sick. Stay sick. Disappear on a special assignment. Go tour foreign outposts, as long as you don't file anything. I said all this on your machine, as you'd have heard if you hadn't pressed the wrong button or whatever the fuck you did.'

One of the bank of telephones rang. Melville grabbed it impatiently, listened, and barked, 'Tell Dick to deal. And no more calls.'

Stephen kept the silence, forced Melville to explain.

'You could go to the *Sunday Times*, even the *Observer* if you were that desperate. I guess they'd both offer. I doubt you'd be happy at either. The *Daily Telegraph*? I shouldn't think they'd be in the market. You could go down-market: a couple of tabloids would take your stuff provided they could rewrite it in four-word sentences.' He was thinking aloud, but for Kenyon's benefit. 'I think you'd be happier here.'

'You're saying you'd rather I stayed? Why should I?'

Melville grinned to draw him into the conspiracy. 'I imagine Lawler would be happier. Even in your going, you'd make a wave or two.' He raised his hand. 'Don't misunderstand – nothing to set the world alight, but perhaps something in *Private Eye*, or on one of those left-wing watch-the-press programmes. Enough to make our chairman uncomfortable at a time I'd rather he was starting to relax.'

'So?'

'So stay, but take a break. God, do you know how many people would kill for that offer?' Melville leaned forward and hit the intercom button. 'Joyce?'

'Sir?'

'Type me a memo to Stephen Kenyon. Subject salary. Notification of an increase. Another five thousand a year. Back-dated beginning of the month.' He paused, looked at Stephen, who remained expressionless. 'Make that six thousand, Joyce.' Stephen nodded. 'Straight away, please. I'll sign it now.'

He turned his attention to Stephen, happy with his display of power.

'OK?'

'Fine. Thanks.' He was not sure what else he could say. They waited for the memo to be brought in. Both were uncomfortable. The business over, they wanted to go their own ways.

Melville filled time by asking about Stephen's week away from the office. Stephen found himself telling him. It was not something he felt he needed to hide. He still thought the whole story was fascinating. He told it as one professional to another.

Melville heard him out, listening intently. The memo came, but Melville was still preoccupied. Finally he signed, but his mind had moved on.

'Here's an idea,' he said. 'Let's see what you think of it.'

They had agreed Stephen should sleep on it. The idea was simple, and for both of them it could solve a lot of problems. Stephen should dig deeper into his father's disappearance, treat it as any other enquiry. Then write it up as a story. All the ingredients were there. OK, it was history, Melville had said. But that was where the twist came in, made it bang up-to-date. The angle was Stephen was doing it – not just the story that emerged, but the story of Stephen looking for his own father.

'But he's dead,' Stephen had protested.

'Is he? OK, you know that. Maybe I know that. Legally, yes. But he doesn't *have* to be. You can't be sure. If he was alive he'd only be – what? Sixty-three? Sixty-four? But is he *really* dead? Isn't that what you, as a son, can't help wondering? Isn't that what keeps you on the trail?' He threw up his hands. 'I'm not telling you how you'd write the story, but that's the way I'd guess anyone would see it. It's fucking emotional stuff.'

'I don't feel that way,' Stephen had said. It was true. For over twenty years he had locked his father's existence away in a part of himself he didn't enter. He'd no wish to go looking inside himself – by now he doubted whether anything remained anyway. Maybe a few memories, a few shards of emotion – why disturb them? Just occasionally over the years, something outside his control had triggered one of them, and for a very brief moment there had been fleeting, ghostly emotion: a flash of hatred, of bitterness, of remorse even. But the last occasion had been a long time ago.

'Don't you?' Melville had studied his face, his own expression disbelieving, before adding, 'OK, so what. You're a professional. You know how to sell it. Or couldn't you do it? Would you be too emotionally involved after all?' He knew the way to hook the reporter, by questioning his professionalism.

Melville was not sure it would ever come to anything – at the end of the day, another story for the spike. But it would keep Kenyon occupied and out of the way.

'Christ,' he'd exclaimed suddenly. Another thought had come to him. The group owned a publishing house. They could be brought in. Surely the story would make a book as well as a series of articles – it was as good as most of the junk they tried to unload on the paper. That way, they could help pick up the expenses. Melville liked it more and more.

The call from the publisher came the next morning. The speed owed more to the editorial director's desire to keep Melville sweet than to the book idea itself, though in truth he was interested.

They met for lunch at the White Tower the following day. Stephen was taciturn, noncommittal. He remained that way in the early stages of the lunch, letting his enthusiasm be fired by the publisher's ideas of how the book could be developed.

Stephen, in fact, had already decided he wanted to go ahead. He was intrigued. Not emotionally – Christ, he couldn't even remember his father, and Katharine and Ward had been all the parents he needed (handling his real mother's existence had once been a big enough problem). But it was not a mystery he could walk away and leave. Besides, Melville was right – he did not want to quit the paper, not yet.

So where next? Two lines of investigation were obvious. The first was another visit to his mother's house. He found his parents' marriage certificate filed in his stepfather's office cabinet under PAPERS, MARY, PERSONAL. It was inside a manila envelope together with her birth certificate. He set it aside to take away together with a bundle of wartime letters from his father, his mother's address book (hard to tell whether it was current or not, although from the changes and deletions it looked as though it had been in use for several years), and some photograph albums. He took the albums to the nursing home – unbelievably, he realised he did not know which, if any, of the people shown was his father, and he needed Mary to tell him. But his visit was in vain; his mother had travelled to her own secret world again, there was no knowing when she would return. Other boxes and cases revealed nothing that would help, although he was touched to see that Mary had kept memories of him, and not just his childhood – cuttings of some of his early work, even a twenty-first birthday card that she must have forgotten to mail on to him.

The second line of investigation was to the Press Association library to check whether there were any newspaper reports additional to the few his mother had kept. It was a long, boring job. His father obviously did not merit a file of his own, so he had to check and cross-check under a series of subject headings from 'Gaming' to 'Missing Persons'. At the end he knew a little more about the club with which his father had been associated, but nothing helpful about the disappearance – there were just two cuttings, one reporting a 'sighting' in Australia, another saying that police were examining a decomposed body that had been washed up on the coast of East Anglia. Obviously false leads, part of the aftermath of any missing-person report.

He spent the next few days working through mounds of paper and microfilm. Like intelligence gathering, perhaps ninety per cent of investigative journalism is tracking down what is already in the public domain. The skill lies in knowing where to look, and in sensing by intuition and experience what might be important, what pieces link together.

Thus, he checked files at Companies House, read old reference books (his father, he knew, had been an accountant – where had he qualified, and first worked?), scanned memoirs of retired London policemen who would have been active at the time. Company records showed the Big Wheel Ltd had been a private limited company, set up in 1963 and put into liquidation four years later. There were nineteen named directors during the period, including his father. Many, maybe all, could be dead. Addresses were twenty and more years out of date, but he noted the names for further checking later. Reference books produced nothing worthwhile.

What might be the first lead worth pursuing came from one of the memoirs. He had obtained permission to use the library at the Senior Police College at Bramshill, the secluded mansion used for training high-flying police officers from all over the Western world. He had lectured there once, talking about the relationship between police and press to a cynical, sometimes antagonistic audience. Ostensibly, this time he was working on an article on the same subject and wanted to research published views of senior policemen.

The college gave him a bedroom, let him eat in the mess. It took him two days to skim the books he wanted. They all had an egocentric 'I was there' tone that quickly bored. One murder gave way to another, or a gangland battle to a long-term fraud, a confidence trick to an arson. All interesting cases on their own but recounted in the same simplistic way in which the hero was always the author. Not surprising because all the books had been dictated to ghost writers with a view to serialisation in tabloid newspapers.

The pile of books grew around him in the library, a barrier against earnest, often worried-looking policemen engaged on deeper problems. The volume that interested him was called, *Twenty Years of Crime: A Detective's Story*, the memoirs of a retired ex-deputy assistant commissioner. The Big Wheel and Stephen's father's disappearance were mentioned, but only incidentally. The references appeared in a tribute to the 'foot soldiers of the force', those 'unsung heroes who never reached the top – who would not have wanted to – but without whom Scotland Yard would not have become the world-renowned and admired crime-fighting force it is.' The tribute, well meant no doubt, read patronisingly – an officer referring to other ranks. Nevertheless, there it was. Sergeant Stanley Fisher – 'thief-taker in every instinct, a man who could sniff Chummy a mile away. Above all, one of those officers who never said die, a man who never gave up in his pursuit of villains. I remember one case, a missing director of a shady gaming club . . . Long after the case had to be placed on the back burner, as our American cousins would say, he continued to niggle at it . . . Unfortunately . . .'

The 'unfortunately' was that the dogged Sergeant Fisher had got nowhere (though the author was quick to point out that this, like all other unsolved cases, would never be closed).

Back in London, Stephen decided the time had come to quiz his aunt Katharine. They had never talked of his father – his decision, he realised. He waited until eight o'clock their time, telephoned, got no reply. After two more attempts he decided they must still be away – they visited Ward's brother in Seattle every summer. He debated calling the operator for the number there, but decided against it. Katharine would interpret his call as some kind of emergency. They would be back home in St. Louis soon. It could wait.

He looked through the names that had appeared on the company records. Seven were Americans with US addresses. He called another number, Paris this time. Another blank – the man he wanted, an FBI liaison officer, was away, home on holiday still no doubt. Didn't anyone work any more? He called another, this time the State Gaming Board, Nevada, a man he'd once helped when he still worked in the States. This time he was successful. He explained he had seven names, wanted to know if they were still around. He knew it was a long shot, but . . .

His contact recognised four of the names, knew one was dead, thought two others were too. What exactly did Stephen want? Why did he need it? How fast? Kenyon knew how much help he got would depend partly on the answers. A feature, he said. He was writing an article called 'When the Mob tried to take over London'.

His last call was to a private detective he had used many times before. Ted Jarvis was a man with good police contacts that included unauthorised access to computer records. Stephen got an answerphone and left a message. The callback came early evening.

'Who, what this time?' Jarvis was not a man who wasted words.

'An ex-cop.' Stephen fumbled through his notes. 'Name, Stanley Fisher. All I know is that in 1965 he was a sergeant in the Met. I need to trace him.'

Silence. The detective was waiting for more.

Finally, 'And that's it! Christ, man, that was a quarter of a fucking century ago. He's long gone from the force. Probably dead.'

'There'll be records. If he's dead, that's it. If not, someone's got to know where to send his pension.'

'How the fuck do I get into that file?' His voice was raised, incredulous. Part of the act, Stephen knew.

'You'll find a way,' he said. 'You always do.'

'Well, don't fucking count on it.'

Stephen heard a cry in the background, Jarvis's wife calling him to eat.

'Do your best, Ted,' he said. 'That's all anyone can do.'

Ted's best produced results within forty-eight hours.

'You're a lucky sod, but it cost me a ton. Hope that's all right.'

It was.

'You got a pencil ready?'

Fisher was alive, aged sixty-three. He had retired, still sergeant, in 1970, after an injury on the job. Ted had no details. He did have an address. In Devon.

On the train, Kenyon wondered what he would find. He had nothing but the address. 'Coombe Cottage', Sughurst. Not the prettiest village name, but the area was definitely retirement-country-cottage land. And Fisher himself? Stephen wished he knew more about the man. He hated going in absolutely cold; that was not the best way to extract information. Still, he normally got on well with ex-coppers.

The nearest station was Exeter, fifteen miles away from the cottage. Kenyon took a cab, switched on to doze as the driver, learning he had travelled from London, ran through his 'I don't know how anyone could live there' monologue.

The village was just as Kenyon had imagined. A main street with a church, a few shops, a pub. One or two tourists in bright shorts wandered the narrow streets. The pub would have been his obvious first call, but it was closed for the afternoon. No point knocking – curtains above were drawn, sleep-time for the landlord. A shop assistant directed him. Helpful enough, but no interest: he'd expected curiosity and chat in a small village.

The house stood alone, about a mile outside the village. Grasses and weeds, almost shoulder high, all but blacked out the ground-floor windows. Above, ivy had grown rampant and the upstairs windows were draped with what looked like old sheets.

At first he thought he had the wrong address. Then the cab-driver pulled back undergrowth and exposed the 'Coombe Cottage' sign. Looking more closely, he saw that a path of sorts had been beaten through the undergrowth to the back of the house. There was no knocker, no bell on the door. Stephen found a stone and hammered, gently at first, then more and more loudly.

'Leave it on the step.'

'I haven't got anything. It's you I want to see, Mr Fisher. Could you open the door?'

He expected a refusal, at the least questions yelled through the closed door.

But it opened. Stephen recoiled instinctively, tensed by the spookiness of the place. For a split second he thought he saw a shotgun in the man's hand. Then he realised it was a crutch. The man swung back to allow the door to open wider. An empty trouser-leg flapped.

Fisher eyed him, took in the town suit.

'Unless you're selling something, you'd better come in,' he said.

He did not wait for a reply, but turned skilfully on his crutches and led the way through a kitchen into a surprisingly large living-room. The inside contrasted strongly with the outside of the house. Although the floors were bare lino and the furniture was sparse, everything was clean and cabin-tidy. There was a strong scent of pipe tobacco. The bright light of day was almost completely cut off by the growth that covered the windows.

'I've just made tea. You'll take a mug?'

Fisher retreated into the kitchen and reappeared a minute later, a mug held in his left hand gripped along with the handle of one of his crutches. A man who had learned to use every one of his remaining faculties to the full.

He was as eccentric-looking as the house. His scalp, totally bald, was a miniature landscape of hills and pits. In contrast, his face and arms were thick with red hair the tight consistency of Brillo pads. Check shirt-sleeves were rolled high exposing biceps knotted by years of swinging the weight of his body. Yet he wore delicate gold-framed spectacles that would have looked more in place on a slightly built watchmaker. His voice was sharp East London on to which a soft West Country drawl had been oddly grafted. He seemed to accept Stephen's presence without question, even without surprise.

Stephen took the tea and, on invitation, sat in one of three leather-cloth armchairs. The seat of one facing him was raised with piles of cushions and the ex-policeman swung his bottom into it with effortless ease, propped up his crutches against the side of the chair and reached for his mug.

'When you've drunk that you'd better tell your driver you're all right. People seeing this place for the first time sometimes get odd ideas. He'll be thinking I've chopped you up with an axe or something.'

'You saw us arrive?'

'Not many people stop. When they do they usually think it's deserted. They sometimes poke around the outside a bit – tourists full of the wonders of holiday living telling themselves they've stumbled on a place nobody wants that they'll be able to buy for the price of half a kitchen back in London.'

'What happens then?'

'If they try the door, I shout at them to fuck off. If they ask questions in the village, they get told it's occupied. Mostly, they go home and forget it all.'

'You opened up to me.'

'The taxi you're in comes from Exeter. Most likely picked up on the station rank. The train from London got in near an hour ago, just in time for a man to get his bearings, drive out here, ask directions. I reckon it'd be a rude bugger without any curiosity who wouldn't offer someone who's come three hundred miles to see him a mug of tea.'

Stephen reached over for his press card and leaned forward to hand it over.

'That doesn't tell me anything. If you want inside information I left the force twenty years ago. If you've come to interview me because I've won the pools, you've got the wrong man. I already checked them.'

'I'm looking for my father.'

Puzzlement, but he had the man's interest. Stephen saw the eyes change fractionally, the shoulders stiffen. Still a cop whatever he looked like.

'You searched for him once,' he went on. 'A man called Kenyon, Michael Kenyon. He worked at a gambling club in the West End. The Big Wheel. You'd know more than me, but Mob-controlled I understand. I guess the old man was part of the front, but I don't know that. I don't know much.'

Fisher took a long time relighting his pipe. Finally, he said, 'What documents have you got – showing who you are?'

Stephen opened his wallet, extracted his driving licence, bank card.

The other examined them. He was still cautious.

'Why now? As I said, I've been out the force twenty years. This must have been nearer twenty-five years ago.'

'Twenty-three. 1966. I was coming up to seventeen. I didn't even know. In fact, I knew nothing until just a few days ago.'

He explained. How as a boy his parents had divorced and his mother had remarried. How he had been told that his father, who never came near them, travelled a great deal and then died abroad. He didn't tell him how he had felt. The confusion, the anger, the bitterness, the way he'd tried to comfort himself with his father's heroism – and how, in his guts, it hadn't mattered one bit. It was only now coming back to him – and he didn't want to think it, let alone share it. How at sixteen he had gone to visit his mother's sister, Katharine, and her American husband in St. Louis and how he had stayed on with them, gone to college, worked there, returned only in 1984.

'It was while I was there that he vanished. If I'd still been over here I'd have read it in the papers. As it was, I saw nothing. Knew nothing. I guess my mother must have had some story to fall back on if I did see any reports. I don't know. She didn't have to bother. I was in Australia once, couple of days to spare. Thought, should I stop off in Bali on the way back – that's where he was supposed to have died – and visit his grave. And then someone told me that tourists had ruined the country and I'd hate it, and I thought, what the hell, what was he to me anyway? That's the nearest I got to finding out until now.' It was one of the rare occasions when he had taken his father out of that hidden part of himself, had briefly forgotten the resentment, had allowed himself the painful luxury of wondering about him. He had killed it swiftly.

'Why are you interested? Twenty-five or twenty-three. It's still a lot of bloomin' years. What do you expect to find? Even if there's anything to be found after all this time. I looked pretty hard.'

Stephen gauged it was time to let the other absorb what he had said. He held out his empty mug. 'I wouldn't mind more tea.'

'In the kitchen. I use tea-bags, make it straight in the mug. Get me a refill, too.'

When Stephen returned Fisher said, 'There's a spare room. You're welcome to it. Pay off your driver. You can call another cab

214

tomorrow – there's a man in the village. If you want to hear it, it'll take the rest of the day.'

They ate early, sounding each other out. Fisher explained that he had not retired because of losing his legs. That had happened later.

Stephen noted the word 'legs'. Only one of Fisher's trouser-legs flopped free.

Fisher noted his puzzlement. 'Both gone,' he said. 'The one you think you see exists courtesy of modern medical science.' He banged it above the knee hard with a crutch the sound was muffled by the fabric of his trouser-leg unmistakable: but wood on metal. He watched for the reaction and Stephen had the distinct impression this had been done many times. He shook his head in silent sympathy.

Fisher went on talking. There had been early retirement on health grounds. (Stephen read it that the man had been forced to quit – maybe a suspicion of corruption that could not be proved; half the Yard were corrupt in some way in those days, although that had not stopped them from being good cops most of the time.)

At first, Fisher explained, he could not come to terms with being out of the force. 'I spent most of my time pissed out of my mind. I couldn't face that I wasn't still on the job. I used to go back, hang around, until someone took me on one side and said, did I realise what a bloomin' pain I was?'

Three years after leaving came the road accident in which he lost his legs. Two years of surgery, and then he had inherited the cottage. After a while, he had purposely let it go on the outside. 'I couldn't handle it all, and what the hell. Besides, it keeps people away. Some in the village got shitty at first – wasn't good for the image, put tourists off their cream teas. Now they accept it. I suspect they even like the idea of having their own hermit. Some of the newcomers drive past, point it out to their friends down from the smoke.'

The meal came from a huge freezer cabinet in an outhouse: rabbit stew and apple pie. They drank cider – Fisher caught Stephen's look. 'I've no need to get drunk now,' he said. 'When you stop wanting things, life starts making sense all by itself.'

'My father,' Stephen prompted. He did not want Fisher to start bar-room philosophising: whatever the other said, he could see him lapsing into booze-aided maudlin memories.

215

When the other started talking, though, it was like a well-briefed sergeant back in the witness box in front of a tough judge.

True, there were frequent pauses as he struggled to remember sequences, occasional apologies when he could not bring back exact detail. But, in the main, his recall was amazing.

Fisher had been a detective sergeant at Savile Row police station in the heart of the West End of London. A solid, ugly barracks-like building in a street better known for its tailors. It was a tough nick – clubs, demonstrations, a lot of drugs – but, spanning Mayfair as well as Soho, a lot of up-market business too. A good place to be if you wanted action. A big nick too: maybe five hundred ordinary coppers, two dozen inspectors. Fisher, it became obvious as he talked, had been one of those permanent NCOs of the police service – a streetwise thief-taker who was never going to make the officer ranks of inspector and above.

The Big Wheel was on Savile Row's patch. It was well-known that a number of top-rank villains were regular visitors, but so too were show-business names and a handful of aristos from the House of Lords. The word was that the real ownership was in the United States, allegedly the Mob. (But you only had to get any club starting up at that time and it was the Mafia or the Maltese or God knows who behind it. Most of the time it was the guy it said it was, with money he'd got from years of running some greasy spoon mom-and-pop place.) Criminal Intelligence Branch was said to keep a permanent eye on the club – one reason why off-duty detectives from Savile Row did not drop in, as was their privilege at many other clubs. But Fisher had discovered later that observation had been desultory. 'The trouble with staking out gaming clubs was that unless you wanted to stand out you had to gamble. Which made it bloody hard.'

The Big Wheel had not attracted attention-making trouble – 'As quiet a place as you could wish. There were those who reckoned if that's what you got putting the Mob in, well, why not hand the whole West End over to them. What the hell, who lost? Occasionally, there'd be a bit of a rumble – some journalist asking questions, an MP writing to the Home Secretary. Then the word would come down to the Super . . . But most of the time you wouldn't know the place was there.'

Fisher, it emerged, did not share the general live-and-let-live attitude. The club might be smoothly run, causing no visible trouble, but from it and the men behind it oozed the pus of organised crime. Much of the money gambled came from crime – from protection rackets, hold-ups, frauds. The money that ended up with the Mob owners went to fund more villainy – extortion, prostitution, corruption.

Only one other officer seemed to share Fisher's views – an inspector, but he got promoted and moved on. Nobody told Fisher to lay off but it was clear that he was expected to do better things with his time.

It was Fisher's luck, or as it turned out bad luck, that he was in the station the day Kenyon was reported missing.

'Effin' hundreds of people get reported missing every week in London. I exaggerate, but not much. Unless it's a kid or there are suspicious circumstances, the duty man tries to persuade the caller to give it another forty-eight hours. Usually there's been a row or someone's spent their money boozing and they're back home a day later. You try to avoid the aggro of all that wasted paperwork.'

In Kenyon's case, though, the procedure had been copy-book. 'His wife turned up with a solicitor from the club.'

He paused to note Stephen's reaction to that. 'You didn't know he'd remarried?'

Stephen shook his head, but said nothing.

'I'll tell you about her later,' Fisher continued. 'She'd been contacted by the porter of the block where your father lived in London. Victoria it was. There was a house in the country where she lived. He wasn't there much. They'd all but split up. The porter hadn't done anything for three weeks I think it was. Your father was a man who came and went, but this time he missed some appointments and people kept calling for him – there was some car salesman he'd fixed to see. The porter had the numbers of the wife and the club. He called the wife first. She called the club. They gave her some story about how they thought he'd been working too hard and had cleared off for a break. Although they'd near as dammit broken up, she was obviously concerned and she travelled up, checked around with friends and told the club she was going to the police. That's when they called in their solicitor, persuaded her he'd smooth things, get some action.'

Questions formed fast in Stephen's head, but they could wait. He did not want to interrupt the flow.

'The deskman filled in form 584 – a bloody long thing, twenty-odd spaces, everything from "station where reported" to "habits, mode of life". What happened – still does, I imagine – is that it then gets sent up to the Yard where they decided whether to circulate the details throughout the Met or even publish it in the *Police Gazette* so it's seen countrywide.'

On this occasion, because of the solicitor and the club connection, Fisher had been called to carry out initial enquiries – interviews at the club, a search of Kenyon's apartment.

However, because Kenyon appeared to have a key job at the club – he was a director and by all accounts there every night and in charge of finance – the case was quickly referred to a small unit at the Yard that had been looking at gaming. Normally, that was the last Fisher would have heard of the case. But his old inspector buddy was with the unit and had got him seconded to continue with the enquiries.

'There were two possibilities. One, someone had murdered your old man. Trouble with that was there was no sign of that – no corpse, no blood, no reports. Still, he could have been hit by real professionals. At first that looked a runner. The people he moved with, they could have handled that. We couldn't find a motive, but that didn't mean anything. When there's the kind of money around you get in gaming, you don't have to look far for reasons. He could have had sticky fingers. His set-up cost money, the wife wasn't cheap.'

'And the second?' Stephen had to prompt. The other was remembering something that he was not sharing.

'That he'd simply fucked off. OK, he hadn't taken anything as far as we could see – his clothes were all there, his bank account hadn't been touched. And he'd been making plans, appointments to see people. Still, you've only got to look at missing-persons files to see that doesn't mean much. They're full of people who set off for the corner to buy a packet of cigarettes and never come back, or take the dog for a walk and end up in Borneo. It might not make sense, but then it doesn't have to.'

'But no signs of him?'

'Nothing. And we weren't the only ones looking. That's what, in the end, made me discount the professional killing. There were some phone taps. Criminal Intelligence Branch had been targeting some villains. They picked up the fact that the Yanks at the club were looking for him too. It could have been deliberate disinformation. But that kind of thing is rare. You read about it in espionage, I never came across it with your ordinary criminals. But it was possible, I reckon. Just possible.'

'So?'

'So, on balance, the more I looked the more it looked like he'd plain disappeared.'

'But you never found him?'

'Nothing. Or nothing tangible. A few reports, but none that stood up.'

'But you kept after it?' Stephen was recalling the reference in the memoirs he had seen. 'You must have had some reason.' He was beginning to doubt it. Fisher had simply seized on the opportunity to investigate an incident connected with the club. In his paranoia, he had refused to accept there was nothing to find. Instead, he had pressed on, certain that the truth always lay just out of reach. Stephen had seen it before. He could understand. He had come close to it many times himself. It was a reporter's and a cop's constant temptation.

Fisher must have caught something in his tone.

'That's what they thought,' he said. 'A fuckin' bee in my bonnet.'

He paused. 'There's brandy in the sideboard,' he said. 'Help yourself.'

'I'm OK.' Stephen knew he was wrestling with something.

Stephen did not smoke but he always carried cigarettes. He fumbled for the pack, offered them. Fisher hesitated, took one, waited for it to be lit, sucked theatrically deep. 'I smoke a pipe, but sometimes I like a cigarette.' His voice was low, semi-apologetic.

He smoked the cigarette down before he spoke again.

'After I left the job, two maybe three years, this Yank came to see me. Smooth, designer suit, grey temples. Said he was a lawyer, trying to trace Kenyon, wanted to know what I'd found. I didn't say much, persuaded him I was sick and he should come back next day – I didn't have to do much to fake it in those days. I reported his visit to my old bosses, got told to forget it. Should have listened. They thought I just couldn't leave it or the job alone.'

There was a silence Stephen had to break, to prompt. 'But you didn't?'

219

'I pushed. Said they were fuckin' trying to hide things. Said if they didn't mount observation and check out the guy when he returned I'd go to the people at the American Embassy – you know who I mean?'

Stephen nodded that he did. The FBI keep small teams of men at a number of US embassies. They liaise with the local police and, in the case of Britain, with MI5. Officially, they are listed as legal attachés. If they wish, they can exercise real clout. He had to prompt again.

'And?'

'And they said, OK, just for old times' sake they'd make me happy, what was the arrangement . . . ?' He stabbed out his cigarette. 'The Yank never turned up and I said, "Maybe I should tell the legal attaché's office anyway." And four hours later . . .'

He looked down at where his legs should be. The room went very quiet.

'It wasn't an accident, then?' But Stephen knew the answer.

'A hit-and-run. Stolen vehicle. They never found the driver. Just the car. Destroyed. A real professional job.'

CHAPTER FIFTEEN

Stephen travelled back to London early the next day, still not sure how far to trust Fisher's interpretation of events.

If the hit-and-run accident had been planned, it shifted the search for his father into a different league. It was not only that Fisher had been warned off so violently; it was that it had happened so very long after his father's disappearance. Easy to imagine viciousness in the immediate aftermath if, say, his father had run with casino money. But for mobsters still to be hunting him years later suggested either a very large amount of money or some great insult that had to be revenged.

If, of course, Fisher had been hit deliberately. Hit-and-runs by drivers who simply panicked were not that rare.

Fisher's version was that it could not have been a simple accident. He had stepped off the kerb outside his front door, edging through a gap between two parked cars. One had slammed into reverse, mashing flesh against metal. He had been in intensive care for eleven days, expected to die. He had lost both legs.

A burned-out car had been found later on the edge of Epping Forest. There were minute traces of blood that matched Fisher's. All other forensic evidence had been destroyed by the fire. The work of a professional, Fisher said. Or a lucky joy-rider, Stephen thought, but did not say.

It had been an uneasy, thought-filled night. His father remained a distant figure. But Stephen's head spun with what he had learned of him: the police years, the second marriage, the men with whom he associated. Almost all of it was new. He had had dim fragments of memories of his father in a police uniform, but he had always thought his father had been a special constable, one of those part-time volunteers. But now he knew it was a job his father had held during most of the first seven years of Stephen's life. It had to throw new light on the kind of man he was. He had thought his father had always been an accountant, had worked for an investment banking firm, had spent much of his time travelling at first in this country and then overseas, which is why he had seen so little of him. A strange change to make: cop to juggling figures. What kind of man did that? And why? Especially, why? And then the move to the club. Even without information, that was easier to comprehend. Money. It had to be money.

He realised he was thinking of it with detachment. Just another story. Good. That was how it should be.

He slept for most of the journey. His internal alarm woke him just before the train reached London. It was a knack. Once, inveigled into talking to would-be journalists, he had argued a good journalist needed just five qualities. The ability to hold an inordinate amount of liquor and still remember everything, a strong bladder, constant cynicism, a capacity to lie by implication and omission without actually telling untruths, and the ability to sleep anywhere at any time. All of it, of course, dedicated to finding the truth. The final point notwithstanding, the class lecturer had been shocked, and had devoted his summing up to thanking Kenyon for his 'jocular' account of a journalist's trade.

Stephen took a cab from the station. Home, he made coffee. It was a bad time to call the diary column at the down-market daily owned by the same group as his paper, but he was impatient to press on. He reached the man he wanted: Duncan, the number two, who told him he was almost through writing a story and would call him back. Stephen kicked off his shoes, tossed his jacket on a chair and slumped in the black leather armchair with his coffee.

His head began buzzing again with Fisher's story. They had talked until almost two. Fisher had returned to Kenyon's second wife late in his narrative. Both were drinking by this time.

'You didn't know he'd married again?' Fisher said.

'I didn't even know he'd lived long enough to divorce my mother.'

'Pamela,' said Fisher. 'Pamela. That was her name.' He pronounced it with the stress on the 'e'. 'Said it in a funny way. Like that. Pamela. A hard woman. Been around. Important friends.' He waved his glass, spilled some. 'Don't get me wrong.

222

Nothing bad about her. Just tough inside, though you wouldn't have known it to look at her. You get some people who take what life throws at them, turn it their way. She was one of them.'

'What did she do?'

'A living you mean? She looked beautiful, made people feel good.'

'You're saying she was a hooker.'

'Oh, no.' Genuinely shocked. 'Not that. You see rich men, bosses of big companies with some beautiful woman in the background . . . you've seen them?' His voice was slurring. 'She was that. You understand?'

Stephen was not sure, but he nodded. 'What happened to her?'

'She returned to the nick once after that first visit. No twice, I think. I had to call her once on the phone. Then . . .'

'You lost touch? You don't know what happened to her?'

'She got married. I know that.' Years before, while he still saw newspapers, he had seen her photograph. 'Some big event. Can't remember what. Ascot. That sort of thing. No doubt it was her. But the name was different.'

The phone cut into Stephen's thoughts, bringing him back to the present. It was Duncan.

'Remember that favour you owe me?' said Stephen.

He told Duncan the little he knew of Pamela, playing down why he wanted to find her.

It meant nothing, said Duncan, but he promised he would check around discreetly.

Stephen finished his coffee, flipped television channels, tried Katharine's number, got no reply, called Nevada again and was told his contact had had to go out of town. No, he had left no message.

It was still only six o'clock. Stephen was restless, uncertain what to do. He had just decided to go out, try to switch off for the evening, when Duncan called back.

'I didn't need to check around. It came to me twenty minutes after you called. It was what you said about how she pronounced her name. She doesn't any more, doesn't even call herself Pamela. She's Elisabeth. Her second name, I imagine. But she *was* Pamela . . .'

Stephen settled back, knowing that sooner or later Duncan would provide the information. The man was a notorious windbag, but his mind was a repository of society tittle-tattle. He had spent years on newspaper gossip columns, never the number one but always invaluable – the man who knew who X had been sleeping with before Y, or which acquaintance of Lord Z or Princess P would be prepared to dish the dirt.

Pamela was Mrs Elisabeth Chitty, wife of Hugh Dawson Chitty, stockbroker. 'A bit on file, not much,' said Duncan. 'He's a distant relative of the royals – *very* distant, nine hundred and ninety-ninth cousin, that sort of thing. But old school, family money, homes London and the Shires. The family stockbroking firm was one of the few not gobbled up in the Big Bang. Not big but handles a few tasty private accounts. Your own City Desk could tell you more.'

'No, that's enough. What about personal stuff?'

'He sixty-eight, she . . .' Duncan began calculating aloud. 'I make it fifty-four, fifty-five. Her age was given as thirty-four when they married. It's varied a lot since then. Who knows? Maybe fifty-five, maybe sixty. They usually lie.'

'But younger?'

'Oh yes, and still a looker.'

'Any more?'

Duncan read off some facts. Married 1969. (Three years after his father vanished, Stephen noted. A judge must have given permission for him to be presumed dead.) One child. Jessica. Born 1970, six months after the wedding.

'Any address?'

'I can do better than that. I've got her private number.'

Duncan explained. There was a letter on file, sent in her capacity as president of an animal charity, asking for publicity. It was dated a year before. 'I imagine she's still there – you'd have to check.'

They switched to pleasantries, vowed to meet soon.

Stephen called the number immediately. It was still the right one, but Madame was having dinner. He telephoned again at ten. He had to be in her part of the country the following day, he told her; could he call, the paper had been meaning to write something about her charity for some time?

'But it must have been two years . . .'

He stifled her protests. 'Only one. Ridiculous no one's called you before. You *are* still president? You do still want publicity?'

224

She was and 'of course'.
They settled on midday.

He picked up a car from Hertz and drove – endless north-London suburbs, the racetrack of the MI, then empty country roads. The house was on the Northamptonshire–Leicestershire border. Flat, rich, farming and hunting country. A land of big estates and class hierarchies barely touched by time.

He parked in a shaded corner of the courtyard beside a Land-rover and a Jaguar, and sat for a while admiring the house. It was a small, stone manor-house, and represented Real Money. Pamela Kenyon, Elisabeth Chitty, had come a long way since his father.

It was thirty-five minutes earlier than the time they had agreed, but that was intentional. Being early was not an endearing characteristic, but it often produced results. People prepared themselves for meetings with journalists. Caught early, defences not yet in place, they were more likely to respond honestly.

A maid opened the door. A different voice from the one that had answered the telephone, but the same tone. Madame was out, but he was expected and would he please wait in the drawing-room and would he like coffee or orange juice.

He settled on orange juice with mineral water, and he was standing at the french windows looking out on to paddocks when he heard her arrive.

He knew it was Pamela, but he took his time turning, curious but wanting to prolong the not-knowing. Of the facts he had learned from Fisher just one had scraped raw nerves: news of Pamela. The woman for whom Kenyon had left Stephen and his mother. He tried to remind himself that it was a long time ago and that he was a grown man now and he did not care – but the palms of his hands were sweating.

Stephen had not realised until the moment he turned and saw her that he had hoped she would be a disappointment. He wanted that for Mary. She was not. Not even now, nearly a quarter of a century later.

She had not prepared for the meeting. She came towards him, unselfconscious, hand outstretched, face smiling and apologetic at the same time. She had just returned from riding. She wore a white shirt and breeches. Her hair was tied back. She appeared to wear no make-up. Had he not known, he would have guessed she was in her late thirties or early forties. She radiated sexuality.

'You must forgive me. I'm not usually so rude. I had problems with Carrie. And you came *all* this way.' She took in his glass with its remains of orange juice. 'At least you must have a real drink.'

She came close to take his glass from him. She smelled of sweat and a perfume he could not name – a heady, stomach-churning mix.

She screwed up her eyes and he realised that the sun through the windows was shining straight into her face. Instinctively, he moved so that she could look at him without discomfort.

Her face changed. The smile vanished. For a few seconds there was fear and horror. She clasped her hand to her mouth as though about to stifle a scream.

Stephen took a step forward, afraid she was going to faint.

The scene had all the feel of a B-movie.

'I'm sorry,' she said. 'The sun, I think . . . It's very hot.'

She shook her head, trying to pull herself together.

At last, she gestured to a drinks cabinet. 'Please,' she said, 'pour yourself a drink. And a small brandy and lots of soda for me – I must change – I'll only be a moment.'

He poured the drinks while he waited for her return. He was bemused – not just by the effect he had apparently had on her, but by the way she made him feel like an untried, young reporter. Correction. An untried, young *male* reporter.

In less than five minutes she had produced in him emotions ranging through curiosity, anger, sexual desire and concern.

He wondered what she would say on her return – her reaction had to mean something about him had reminded her of his father. Did she realise that? Or had she just sensed a strong, but unspecified, something?

When she re-entered the room, she acted as though nothing had happened. Colour had returned to her face. Her hair was wet from the shower.

'You don't mind, do you?' she said, as though his opinion mattered. 'It will dry in this weather.'

He thought she meant to lead him outside but she took her glass and sat on a long sofa. She sipped her drink and then laughed. 'I can tell you're a journalist. Could you add more soda.'

She had changed into dark-grey Levis and a fresh white shirt. The top two buttons were undone, revealing the swell of her breasts. She was slim, hard, like a dancer. He could make out lines

226

now that he stared; they put her into the forties, not thirties, but not fifties either though he knew she was. Cosmetic surgery? He doubted it. Something told him she was simply one of those rare women born to wear well.

She sipped the new drink, nodded her approval, and placed it down not to touch it again. 'I certainly never expected anyone to come,' she said. 'I thought someone might telephone. I do hope I'm not wasting your time.'

Stephen had a notebook ready, a regulation shorthand pad, bought from a stationery store on the way. Better for this than the loose scraps of paper he usually took from his pocket.

'Just tell me about the society and how it started,' he prompted.

She spoke in short sentences, basic facts learned parrot-fashion. The charity provided sanctuary for old horses. She spoke without passion. He suspected it was a duty that went with her position in county circles. She had a slim file of literature which she handed to him. He flipped through it.

A girl looked around the door, but disappeared before he could absorb her. The daughter?

'This is fine,' he said finally. It would, in fact, make a couple of paragraphs for Duncan. The charity was arranging an auction of hats donated by famous people. The string of names would justify a piece.

'Are you sure?' she asked, the smile widening, the tone relieved with a task completed. 'Can I get you something to eat? I don't normally take lunch, but a salad, a sandwich?' Sweetly said, but barely meant, the kind of question you asked the hired help. She was already standing.

Stephen suddenly resented her, not least for feelings she had been triggering in him.

'Could I ask you just one more thing?'

'Of course,' puzzled, caught by something indefinable but different in his tone.

'My father. Michael Kenyon. Do you really think he's dead?'

She could have done many things. Clasped her hand to her face again. Said, 'Oh God,' and collapsed. Screamed at him. Attacked him for his deception. He was ready for any reaction.

Except for one. She stood expressionless for a long time. And then, as though she had not heard him, she opened the door, called a name before turning her head towards him.

'Audrey will show you out. Forgive me if I leave you, I have a host of tasks to do.' And without changing tone: 'I wondered why you came all this way on something anyone could have done on the telephone. Now I know. If you return or contact me ever again, my husband will telephone your proprietor. If you check you will find Mr Lawler would take any approach from him very seriously.'

The maid escorted him to the door. It was too late to retrieve anything, but he tried. He placed a calling card on the hall table.

'Tell Mrs Chitty that this is my number if she wishes to contact me.'

It was the best he could do, but there was no doubt he had blown it.

At six o'clock the next morning, Stephen feigned sleep as the woman slid gently out of bed.

He was touched that she was trying not to disturb him. He lay on his side, his eyes closed. But he had been wide awake for at least an hour, reliving his encounter with Pamela – and cursing himself for the fuck-awful way he had handled things.

Any punk idiot could have realised that the way he had tackled her would produce only one kind of reaction.

So, why had he done it? He knew – and that worried him more. He had done it because he had wanted to smash through that so-in-control upper-class exterior. Why? Because she was the woman for whom his father had left them. Because something about her disturbed him sexually. No one had done that since Tarlach. It shouldn't have done – it was a decade and more ago since their life together – but for a few seconds it had made him feel unfaithful.

He heard Natasha switch on the radio in the shower. Not the time for such analyses. But, leaving aside all the Freudian crap, the truth was he *had* got emotional. He had gone to obtain information. All he'd done was provoke her.

Nor was this the place to be thinking such thoughts. But it hammered him. He still felt the self-anger.

Natasha returned, pulled on waiting clothes. She sensed he was awake now.

'I'm going, then,' she said. Her voice was cheerful, full of energy.

228

He lifted himself in the bed. He was naked, covered only by a sheet.

'Christ,' he said. 'You know what time it is? Come back to bed.'

He did not mean it. It was only a game.

She laughed. 'Time and Birmingham wait for no woman. Be a love, make sure you lock the door when you leave.'

She bent, kissed his nose and retreated before he could grab her.

'Train. Cab waiting.'

'How can anyone be so pert at this time?'

'That's what they pay me for.' And, from the door, 'Phone me.'

He lay for a while trying to resume sleep, but it was impossible. He turned over, burrowed into the space she had left, breathed her perfume. Then his foot disturbed something cold and wet. A used condom. It was enough. No more sleep.

He staggered into the bathroom, flushed the condom down the lavatory, turned on the shower, changed his mind, ran the bath, poured in one of her bath oils and soaked for a full half-hour.

Natasha was a model with a constant weight struggle, and all he could find for breakfast was diet rolls, plain yoghurt and a variety of herbal teas.

His own flat was only minutes away. They had met three years before in the late-night supermarket, and had had a relationship of sorts ever since. It was not intense; both knew they filled in when there were gaps. They were a kind of safety net for each other. Being together was always good. But, mostly, they did not miss each other when they were apart. That was why it would end one day.

He had called her on his return to London, and had been glad to find she was free. He did not want to be alone. They had eaten nearby and gone to bed early.

'Therapy,' she had giggled because he had told her his story.

Afterwards, though it was pleasurable, he was not sure how much it had helped.

He picked up pastries on the return to his own flat. People passed him on their way to the tube. He felt alone, realised that he was missing having a base. The isolation was bringing home how unbalanced his life was – how totally his life revolved around the newspaper and his work. How without them, the glue that held him together started to melt.

He had thought coming back to Britain would help, that simply being near his roots would still restlessness, fill emptiness. After Tarlach had died, he had quit the *New York Times*, drifted about the world, existing on savings. For over a year he had done nothing but pack, move, unpack, pack, move . . .

Tarlach was Irish although she lived and worked in New York. Her parents had died when she was a child. She had left Clare, lived first in Dublin with cousins, become a nurse, then taken a job as travelling companion to a globe-trotting elderly film actress. Finally, she had settled in New York where she worked for the Irish Tourist Board. All this she had told Stephen on the flight from LA the first time they met. He had been more reticent – it had taken him all of a week to break his normal reluctance to talk about himself. Then, one night, it had all spilled out: how he had gone to St. Louis, stayed, attended the University of Missouri School of Journalism, got a job on the *St. Louis Post-Dispatch* (thanks mainly, he had confessed, to the novelty of his being English), and then Chicago and now the Big Apple itself (though, he explained, to anyone who came out of Chicago, New York wasn't that big a deal).

After Tarlach's death, her body had been flown back to Ireland for burial next to her parents in the churchyard in Clare. Stephen had not accompanied it. Grief had been replaced by a driving hatred for the world. All he had wanted to do was move and keep moving. Maybe somewhere on the way, death would come unbidden but natural – a plane crash, an ambush in El Salvador, a bullet from a sniper in Beirut, all places he went because, although he was not reporting, he sought out countries where there was the smell of destruction.

After a year, though, the fire inside him had been dimming. A letter from Morag, Tarlach's sister, had reached him as he lay recovering from hepatitis in Hong Kong. Come and see us, she had said. Come and lay a flower on Tarlach's grave because she'd hate what you are doing to yourself now. And he had.

Soon afterwards, he had returned to work – *Time* magazine, covering much of Europe and the Middle East out of the Paris office. Gradually, he had come to specialise in international terrorism and espionage – the Red Brigades, Barbie, the IRA . . . And then, in 1984, back to Britain after an invitation from the then editor of his current paper who had read and admired some of his pieces.

Back home in Britain after nineteen years. Except, it hadn't been home, and he had found he felt more of a foreigner than he had in the United States.

Only in his work was he 'home'.

It was not yet nine o'clock when he arrived back at his own flat. He made coffee, ate a Danish, checked the post: nothing. The answerphone had three messages. The third was the only interesting one. The call had been made at 10.10 p.m. the previous night.

'This is Jessica Chitty.' The voice was low, as though she was worried about being overheard. 'You came to see my mother today. I know what you want and I may be able to help you. I'm in London tomorrow and I could meet you if you like. Don't phone me back. I'll ring you again about eleven in the morning.'

She called almost exactly on time. He could hear the familiar sounds of a railway station in the background.

No, she would rather not meet at a hotel. Could she come to his flat? She had a lunch date, but she could be with him in half an hour. That would give them plenty of time to talk.

Jessica was disconcerting. A nineteen-year-old version of her mother. Stephen had not seen her father, but it did not look as though he had passed on too many genes. If she wore make-up, it was too lightly applied to show. Her hair was longer than Pamela's and hung loose, well below her shoulders. She wore a loose cotton sweater and had the look of a sixties student. Or, rather, the look of someone in the movies playing a sixties student because, under scrutiny, the clothes were too expensive, too pristine.

He realised at once that she could easily trigger in him the same emotions he had felt on meeting her mother. He checked himself. Not this time! But he was glad that the telephone rang as he let her inside, giving him a minute away from her to compose himself.

He took the call in the study he had converted from a second bedroom. The caller was an estate agent about his mother's house. He had received an offer. Stephen said he would call him back.

Jessica was still in the hallway, working her way along the display of photographs that almost covered the walls.

'Yours?' she asked, and he realised that she must think reporters took their own photographs.

'Friends,' he said. They were, in fact, the works of some of the biggest name news photographers of the day. He had started collecting them years before.

He gave her coffee, and she accepted with alacrity the last of the pastries he had bought earlier. He settled her on his large sofa and took the old leather director's chair, the only other seating. It was difficult to make out her shape under the soft sweater, but she looked the kind of woman who could eat round the clock without putting on weight. He found himself thinking, at that age they can.

'This is really weird. My mother and your father.' She bent her head and then lifted it quickly, flicking back her hair. It was a girlish gesture. The level stare that followed it was not: a mixture of interest and hostility.

'Yes. I suppose so.'

'It's hard to imagine . . .' She glanced round the room, taking in the bare polished boards, Venetian blinds against stark white walls, the expensive hi-fi, the steel curve of the Italian floor light. And the piles of books and papers everywhere. He thought of the close-carpeted luxury of her parents' manor-house, the manicured lawns and paddocks.

'But there it is.' His voice intentionally unemphatic, his working-reporter's tone. 'Did you know about her and my father . . . ? I hope it wasn't a shock.' He didn't give a fuck if it was. Irritating to hear himself being polite: as if something about her was forcing him out of character.

'Oh, yes,' she said. 'My mother's had a real life. She's not just a society lady in a headscarf. In case that's what you thought.' She sounded proud of her, a touch defiant.

'I certainly did not.' That, at least, came out with absolute sincerity. 'Does she ever speak of my father?'

'No. I mean, I knew she was married before, it didn't work out . . . no details. I don't think it's important to her now.' She realised how that sounded. 'Oh, sorry, I didn't mean to be . . . oh, shit.'

He smiled at her discomfiture. 'Don't worry. I hardly knew him, if you want the truth.'

'Why did you come to see Lis, then?'

He had to think for a moment: of course, she meant Pamela. 'The paper will use the hats for charity story, that was genuine

232

enough.' He chose a reason she would understand. 'And I came instead of phoning out of . . . curiosity, I suppose.'

She seemed to accept that.

'And why have you come to see me?' he asked.

She flicked her hair again, and he saw she did it when she was shy.

'Like you, curiosity, I suppose.' Repeated demurely.

'Right, then,' he said bluntly. 'Now, what are you really here for? I would like to talk to your mother again, properly. There are things I want to find out about my father, and only she can tell me.'

He got her talking. She had come with a request and a proposition. She had a friend facing trial on a drug-possession charge. She thought Stephen could keep it out of the newspapers. It was a piece of naivety he had encountered before. Mostly, reporters could not do such things – and, generally, asking them meant they made sure the story concerned *was* reported, just to prove their integrity. Nevertheless, coming from her it surprised him. Her lack of sophistication made him like her more. For that reason, he heard her out without interruption, right up to the offer at the end: if he helped her, she would try to persuade her mother to see him again.

Remembering Pamela's reaction, he thought it unlikely she would succeed.

'Is he a boyfriend?' he asked, referring to the boy she wanted to help. Polite conversation.

She looked down, too theatrically. 'We grew up together.' He waited. The melodrama of it almost made him laugh. The boy's parents knew of the pending court appearance, but not his uncle. They were afraid the uncle would read about it, cut the boy from his will.

Stephen started to ask, 'Are you serious?' but it was obvious she was.

Suddenly, he wanted no further part of any of it.

'I'm sorry,' he said. He swept her out as quickly as he could.

Through the window, he watched her clamber up the steep stairs to the pavement. Under the creamy jumper, she wore a tiny black velvet pelmet of a skirt.

As the shapely legs in black tights and Doc Martens disappeared, he felt like a lascivious schoolboy. And ancient as hell. He realised he was old enough to have fathered her – maybe that's why she had come to him.

*

Katharine was his mother's elder sister, but it was hard to believe it.

They met at the Excelsior Hotel, a courtesy coach ride from Heathrow airport. He did not tell her he had been trying to reach her. She had called him from Seattle (he had been right about that), saying Ward had had to go to Madrid for a business meeting. His company was designing a new international hotel. She was planning to join him once his business was finished, but what if she routed via London, could they get together?

'How about sparing an old woman an hour of your time?' is what she had actually said. For a moment he had felt guilt – it had been over a year since he had seen them. Then she had laughed that throaty theatrical laugh and she made him feel good again, the way she had right from the very first day he went to stay twenty-four years before and she had became his mother in everything but name.

'OK,' she said the moment the waitress left with their order, 'what d'you think?' She extended her face towards him.

He pretended not to know what she meant. She had had plastic surgery, a few tucks, a couple of wrinkles gone. She had told him that on the telephone. He could not see any signs. She did not have surgery to look younger, only to remain as she was.

'You didn't need anything,' he said, meaning it.

'That's the son talking,' she said. 'What about the man?'

'The man says you're looking pretty good.'

She leaned over, squeezed his arm. 'You too,' she said. 'Don't forget we like to see you.'

When they had first talked on the telephone, she had been planning to stay over a night. Then Ward's plans had changed – he wanted her there for a dinner. Now all she had was a few hours between connections. Katharine and Ward's lives had always been like that. For Stephen, it had been one of the excitements of his adolescent years.

Today, Stephen and Katharine had three hours until she had to return to the airport, and the first disappeared quickly in gossip.

He was wondering how best to lead in to his father when she opened the way.

'Mary,' she said. She did not say 'your mother'; her sister had renounced that right. 'How is she?'

She always asked. He was never sure how much was formality

because she knew he expected it, how much was a flickering of genuine feeling. The two women had not communicated for years.

He told her.

'Poor woman.' He could tell from her tone that she was about to change the subject. Not because it was her estranged sister, but because she recoiled from any talk of illness or despair.

He rushed in: 'She told me about my father.'

Katharine raised her eyes quizzically, but said nothing, waiting for him to continue. He told her what his mother had said, what he had found at the house.

'Silly woman,' she said at last. 'I'd have told you years ago if it had been up to me. But having buried it, she ought to have let it stay buried.'

She checked her watch. 'I suppose you want to ask me things,' she said. 'I could change my flight.'

'We've a good hour. Will it take longer than that?'

She laughed. 'Get a woman my age talking about her past and it could last for ever.'

She saw puzzlement on his face. 'I was fond of your father,' she said. 'Don't get me wrong – I'm mad about Ward, even after all these years, you know that. But I think your father and I could have been very happy if things had been a little different. God sure knows, I'd have been better for him than your mother. I wouldn't have driven him into that bitch's arms.'

She paused, attracted the waitress's attention and asked for more coffee.

'Your mother didn't tell you?' He noted the 'your mother'. She was distancing herself from him to tell him something personal; she did not want to be his adopted mother *and* his father's lover if that's what she had been.

He wondered whether he should stop her now, tell her he did not want to know.

'Are you sure you want to talk?' he said. 'If it's private . . . I wouldn't want anything to change what we've got, you and me and Ward.' He owed them a lot. They had taken him in, put him through college, encouraged him. They had never tried to smother him or be what they weren't; in some respects they had always remained oddly distant, as though danger lay in over-familiarity. But they had widened horizons and given him strength by making it clear that they were always there.

She patted his arm and laughed again. 'Oh, no,' she said. 'Not that. Nothing happened between your father and me except a few adolescent fumblings. He was a kinda shy boy to tell the truth, and when he wasn't it was too late . . .'

They remained in the coffee shop, fixtures among a constant turnover of salesmen and travellers, drinking cup after cup of coffee while Katharine talked.

She told him about how she and Mary and their mother were evacuated to the village in Shropshire where Kenyon was a boy. About the day his father delivered a bicycle – 'I was a precocious little girl.' She giggled and rolled her eyes theatrically. 'You can't believe that now, can you?' knowing that of course he could. About her going off to the city and Michael Kenyon going off to war. About his marriage to Mary, and his home-coming and the shop his father gave them – 'I've never forgotten his face and when I looked at everyone else I suddenly realised I was the only one who knew.'

She paused and the silence was a long one. 'I think I despised him a little after that,' she said. 'That's when he caved in and let himself get like everyone else. Ordinary. He could have been something special. He'd got a spark.' She leaned forward. 'You've got it – don't lose it.'

She had seen him twice after she had married Ward and settled in the United States, once with Mary, once after they had split up. 'Even when they were together you could tell it wasn't a proper match. Don't get me wrong, I'm not blaming your mother. It was both of them. They got together too young. The pressure was to marry and they did. God alone knows why they stayed together as long as they did.'

And the second time they had met, after the break-up?

They had met by chance, she said. They had literally bumped into each other in Piccadilly, opposite Green Park, near the Athenaeum Hotel, where she and Ward were staying. It was about a year before he had vanished. They had gone for a drink. He had not said much. 'He was kinda sad, a long way away most of the time, pleased to see me but wishing he hadn't if you can understand what I mean?'

'Did he ask you anything, tell you anything?'

'You mean, like someone had sent him a death threat or that he was getting ready to blow town or that he was trying to screw up enough courage to jump off London Bridge?'

He took her seriously. 'Something like that?'

She reached out for his arm. 'Don't let it get you,' she said. 'It was a long while ago. Another life. Be careful. You should have mourned when your mother told you he was dead. You didn't. I don't think she'd let you. Watch that it doesn't hurt you now. You, if anyone, should know what that can do.' He thought she was going to mention Tarlach, but, instead, she answered him: 'No nothing. As I said, he was kinda sad. Maudlin. He said he was working as an accountant – I was surprised, I didn't even know he had the qualifications. His wife was in the country, he said. I remember he tried to make it so it sounded good, as though that was how he wanted it, but it just came out a bit desperate.'

'We'd better go,' he said.

She continued talking on the way to the airport. 'I thought about it after,' she said, 'when Mary phoned me and told me what had happened and reminded me that you thought he was already dead. She made me promise to check the newspapers, make sure they carried no reports about him. We argued. I gave way. I guess that's when things got really bad between us.'

'And?'

'And I guess I just thought he was a loser.'

'You thought he might have killed himself?'

'I don't know. He was a man who'd gotten used to losing. I would have thought he'd gotten used to living with it too.'

They talked right up until the final call for her flight. At the last moment she leaned close and said, 'I lied. A small lie. I've told you the rest. I might as well tell you this. We arranged to meet again the next day. Ward had these meetings all day. Your father gave me the name of this pub.'

'You didn't go?'

'I did. He didn't arrive. I waited an hour. I guess in a way I was glad. As I said, I was pretty fond of him.'

'He hadn't given you a telephone number?'

'No. And if he had, I wouldn't have called it.'

He watched her pass through to emigration. She turned and waved, her smile broad and warm as though he had not just tried to tear away scar tissue.

She had not said whether his father had mentioned him at that last meeting. It *was* getting personal: he had not dared to ask.

CHAPTER SIXTEEN

Pamela contacted him the following day. She sent a formal invitation card to a charity lunch, with a handwritten note saying simply, 'I do hope you can come,' as though they were old friends and she had never thrown him out of her house.

The lunch was three days later, at the Cafe Royal, and Stephen shared a table with two company chairmen, an actress from a current soap, the female head of a public relations consultancy and Jessica.

There were about two hundred people present, all rich and/or well-known, and Stephen marvelled at the drawing power of animals. Pamela was half a room away on the top table with two duchesses and a television celebrity who was to conduct the after-lunch auction. The actress told him that the Princess Royal, as patron, would have been present, but she had to be abroad. Nevertheless, she had sent a hat for the auction.

'Not a crown?' asked Stephen. She took his question seriously. 'Oh, no, I don't think the Palace would allow it. But I'm sure she would have done if she could.' The PR woman gave Stephen a mind-your-manners grimace. Jessica said nothing, she was too busy listening to one of the captains of industry who, it emerged, admired her father.

The auction began with a fedora contributed by Elton John, ended with a baseball cap from Robert Maxwell. It raised seventy-three thousand pounds including five thousand pounds from the tycoon on Stephen's table, who bought a headscarf worn by Meryl Streep in a recent movie. He collected it like a beaming schoolboy going up for his house prize. It was handed around the table for admiration. A beautiful scarf, a silk Hermès, supposedly a one-off – a handsome receipt for what was, after all, a five-thousand-pound public donation.

'Do you like it?' the man said to Jessica, the last to handle it. 'It suits you, goes with your eyes.' Then bluff, embarrassed English, 'Suits you a lot better than me anyway. Here –' he pushed it towards her. 'Do me a huge favour, take it as a present. You'd please me a lot.'

The lunch was over. People were standing, making their farewells, drifting away. Stephen left the table – Jessica and the businessman were still arguing about the scarf. He thought she would accept it finally; he was to find later that men often tried to give her gifts.

He found Pamela surrounded by people congratulating her. He hovered until he could get close.

'I was surprised to be invited, but thank you – I enjoyed it,' he said. 'You raised a lot of money.'

'You helped,' she said. Then, seeing his disbelief, 'Truly. That little piece you wrote made a lot of difference. People who come feel they're under media scrutiny, that what they do will be seen by their neighbours, their business rivals, their brother-in-law, so it pays to do the right thing.'

'I did all that?'

She was leading him away towards an ante-room, and he was finding the contact easy.

'That man at your table who bought the scarf. They say his business survives on the edge of bankruptcy. That five thousand wasn't just money. It certainly wasn't a donation to charity from his heart. It was a public statement that five thousand is nothing to him. I half-expected him to hand the scarf back to be re-auctioned just to make sure no one failed to get the message.'

'When I left him he was trying to give it away.'

'There you are then! My point reinforced. I only hope he's not trying to press it on Jessica. He'd use that. He's been trying to get my husband to help him.'

A small group of women were already waiting in the ante-room.

Pamela halted in the doorway. 'We have a meeting. It's a sheer formality, but we find this is the best time to get anything sorted out. Saves people coming up to town twice.'

'Of course.' He waited. She had to make the running.

'Jessica and I thought we'd stay and do some shopping before we go home tomorrow. Would you like to call in for a drink this evening? I think that perhaps I owe you a chance to ask me things.'

The apartment block was in Victoria, one of several identical solid buildings tucked away behind the railway station. Unlike the residential buildings near other London termini, they were still expensive, upper-middle-class bastions, probably because of their proximity to Westminster and the Houses of Parliament.

Nevertheless, it surprised Stephen that Chitty should have his London home here. Given the stockbroker's wealth and background, he would have expected their London apartment to be in a grander area like Belgravia or Chelsea.

The lobby reinforced that surprise: it was as neutral as a transit lounge. On the third floor the corridors were as narrow, the doors as evenly spaced as if they opened on to cells. The apartment itself was the type where a young professional couple lived until they started having children or where an executive camped down in the week. A place where cooking meant feeding the toaster and switching on an electric coffee percolator.

Pamela was alone and wearing a dress that was obviously designer label, a sharp contrast with the setting and the occasion. While she fixed drinks, he took in the surroundings. He was in the living-room, a large, low-ceilinged rectangle with one long window looking out on to identical anonymous blocks. He thought there was just one bedroom. Obviously a bathroom. And through a half-open door he could make out a kitchenette.

She returned with drinks, Scotch for him, white wine for her.

'Is this your apartment?' he asked, taking care to keep his voice neutral – this time he was being eggshell careful.

The question did not surprise her. 'Yes and no,' she said. 'We have something rather larger and more practical in Knightsbridge. I keep this for myself. It's somewhere to be alone and get on with things quietly.'

He wondered, did she mean she kept it for lovers?

She seemed to read his thoughts: 'We occasionally lend it to friends. It's central and London hotel prices these days are absolutely *ridiculous*. My husband think it's rather a silly place to hold on to but is happy to regard it as an investment.'

'And you?'

'I –' a fractional hesitation – 'inherited it. Just can't take the step to get rid of it. Haven't been able to for twenty-odd years. It was where your father lived.'

Her words arrested him as she must have known they would. She explained that they had moved from Chelsea to a home in Wiltshire. They had also bought this flat where Kenyon stayed during the week, joining her in the country at weekends.

After he had vanished, she had left it unused and untouched for a while. 'I thought, what would I do if he came back and I'd got rid of it? When I remarried, keeping it seemed a good investment, and then I started using it for my work.'

'Your work?'

'My charities. There always seem to be papers to read, notes to write. This has always been a good place to deal with them when I'm in town. No distractions. I treat it as an office. It's a kind of self-deception, I suppose – pretending that I'm doing a *proper* job.'

Stephen walked to the window and looked out on to the street. It was curiously empty but for parked cars. Windows opposite were draped in net, making the rooms behind them as anonymous as the blocks themselves.

'You've changed the furniture?' It was Scandinavian – a lot of angles, steel and black and white, and a little dated.

'I changed everything one day. Couldn't sit here any more looking at it. I phoned Harvey Nichols, told them what I wanted. It was all completed the next day.'

'What was it like before?'

'I can't remember.' But she could. 'A lot of leather,' she said at last. 'One of those two-part chairs you sink into. One of those wall units that holds records and books and hi-fi – they were very trendy once. A long teak table he used for everything. When he went, it was still covered with papers as though he had just popped out – that's why I thought there must have been an accident.'

'Food?'

She looked puzzled.

'Food? When he vanished, had he kept the kitchen stocked up?' Stephen had once covered the disappearance of a politician who had faked his death. He had done everything right except for one thing. A week or so before he planned to disappear, he had stopped replenishing everyday items and had done without them. The suspiciously empty food cupboards had screamed out a message.

241

'I don't know. There wasn't much, but I don't think he ate in much.' She hesitated and then added, 'The refrigerator was full of bottles of whisky – that's where he kept it. Your father drank a lot.'

Stephen knew. Fisher had mentioned it.

'How much? A lot lot? Or just a lot?'

'A lot lot. That was one of the problems.'

'Will you tell me about him? I know very little.'

'Your mother must have told you.'

He explained how, when he was fourteen, Mary had concocted an elaborate lie about his father's death, one he had continued to believe for over twenty-five years.

'My God,' she said when he had finished, 'what a devious family.'

'My father was devious too?'

'Oh, yes, it was so ingrained in him I don't think he knew how devious. I think much of the time he even deceived himself. Sometimes I thought he lived in a world that owed as much to his imagination as reality.'

He misunderstood her. 'You still feel bitter about him?'

'Bitter? Oh no. Probably less than you do, or have a right to.' He started to deny it, but she was rushing on. 'It didn't work towards the end – no, to be truthful it hadn't worked for a long time before he went. But I was mad about him, more mad about him than I'd been or have been about anyone else.'

He waited while she wrestled with some specific memory demon, and then said softly, 'So, will you tell me?'

They talked until well after midnight, or rather mostly she talked and he listened. After a while, he made notes but she did not appear to notice.

At one stage they broke off and walked to Victoria Street, planning to eat a pub sandwich, settling instead for a McDonald's.

Stephen did not know it, but facing her across the Formica table, the stirrings of emotion he felt echoed those his father had experienced in a Smithfield Market pub more than thirty years before. Despite her sophistication and poise, there was something in her that invited protection. Knights must have slayed dragons, died happy for such women. There was something else, though, an even more potent contradiction: she exuded sexuality – but appeared to be indifferent to it.

Pamela felt stirrings too. Stephen touched chords. It was not so much in the way he looked – though the shape of his head was the same, as was the set of his blue-grey eyes. It was more the gestures – the inclines of his head as he listened, the wry smile that began first at one corner of his mouth. For fleeting moments it was easy to feel the past had returned.

She told him how she and Kenyon had met in a club, but not about the dawn breakfast and the wolves in the park – that was too personal, too precious. She told him much else, though. About what she knew of Michael's background, about the finance house, about the club, about the houses.

'So what went wrong?'

They had returned to the apartment, and were sharing a bottle of wine Stephen had bought from an off-licence. But for their ages, they could have been two students talking the night away.

Pamela had kicked off her shoes and was sitting on the floor with her feet drawn under her. She moved with easy flowing grace, and he thought she was like a cat. Not only physically. Even being co-operative as she was, there was something restrained, almost secretive, about her. She chose her words with care, and stopped when she had said what she wanted to say. Her eyes were opaque and he could not read what she was thinking. She did not give parts of herself away.

'Who knows? Who ever knows? I thought a lot about it when he first vanished. Sometimes I thought I had the answer. I never had.'

'What kind of things?'

She shook her head and laughed. 'My, you are persistent.' But she answered.

'I said he deceived himself, and I think he did. He always seemed to want something that wasn't there. It was as though he'd never settle for less than perfection, less than the ultimate. One less-than-wonderful instant and something was ruined or ended or never the same again. Sometimes when I saw that happening I'd scream at him, "But that's life!" but I never knew whether he understood what I was saying. Sometimes I thought he even created obstacles so things *would* fail. He persuaded himself I had lovers and wasn't content until I had. I thought sometimes there was something in his past – I don't know what, just something which he thought could have been perfect and it had gone and he wanted it back. Perhaps he didn't even know what it was.'

She laughed again, embarrassed by her own seriousness. 'I'm talking nonsense now. It's been a long day.'

'No,' he said. 'It helps. Please, tell me more. What else?'

She held out her glass and he refilled it.

'Jealousy, that was part of it. At the end. He was a jealous man.'

'There was reason?' He thought it was safe to ask. She had already spoken of lovers, but he was nervous until she spoke.

'Perhaps. Some. But it wasn't important. That's what he didn't see. It wasn't *important*.' She became silent. 'He had to be *everything*. He allowed no room for anything, anybody else. That was the trouble, I suppose.'

'His drinking?'

'Who knows? I never knew how much he needed it. How much he drank to say, "Hey, look at me I've got problems." '

She stood, placed the still half-full glass on a table.

'I must get back to Knightsbridge.' Her voice was brisk suddenly.

They walked to the station cab rank.

'Just tell me one more thing,' he said. 'Not about him, about after he vanished. What happened?'

She told him about the calls, about going to the club, about the visits to the police.

He heard her out, and then said, 'What happened at the club? Did you hear from them again?'

'Once,' she said. She stopped, waited until he looked at her, wanting to be certain he understood. 'You have to realise that I had nothing to do with the club, your father kept me away from it, that was his life, not mine.'

He could not tell whether it was an apology, an alibi, just a statement. He nodded noncommittally.

They began walking again. There were cabs waiting. They paused at the kerb.

'So what did the club want, what did they say?'

'Just that they were sorry and that if ever anyone asked about him or them, it might be better not to answer – I took it they meant newspapers. They said I should be sure to tell them I'd been approached, though.'

He waited, expecting more, but that was it.

244

She moved to a cab and he opened the door. 'Was that it?' he said.

'That was it,' she said. 'That was the end of it until now.'

He was not sure he believed her, but she surprised him to the end. She moved forward quickly, body against him fleetingly, lips fluttering on his cheek, hand finding and squeezing his. He could smell wine on her breath and that perfume whose name he did not know.

'You're a lot like your father,' she said, and then she was gone, and he felt suddenly that he had lost something.

It was hard facing his mother after Pamela. Even though he would not mention the meeting, having talked to Pamela suddenly seemed like a betrayal.

He had travelled down reluctantly. The estate agent had been persuasive: the offer for the house was a good one and the prospective buyer was anxious to conclude a deal as quickly as possible.

Although Stephen had the power to make a decision, he felt he had to see his mother first. Yet, when he did see her, he did not raise the matter: she had been moved into hospital for a few days for tests. That, at least, made the decision easier. It was obvious she would need constant nursing. It was his duty to sell the house and invest the money for her. She would never be returning to it anyway. She need never know it had been sold.

Months ago, when his younger half-sister had come from Sydney to see Mary, they had agreed that when this moment came, he would handle the details. He and Lucy had never been close; they had grown up apart, had seen too little of each other, the age gap was too great. But there was affection between them. She was a sensible, generous girl. She had trained as a physiotherapist, married a paediatrician and moved with him to Australia. She was part of his family now. Stephen had twice visited their large untidy house in a prosperous suburb. Both times he had been warmly welcomed and pressed to stay longer. The last time they'd seen each other he'd noticed, for the first time, how much she had come to resemble Mary.

Stephen told the estate agent to go ahead with the sale and spent the next days finishing sorting the contents. He saw to the packing and documentation for the mementoes that were going to

Australia – his stepfather's leather-topped desk, a bookcase, a couple of fishing trophies. And Mary's silver candlesticks, two of her pictures, the pine table and chairs she and his stepfather had bought on holiday in Wales.

On the day he was due to return to London, he called at the home on his way to the hospital – his mother wanted him to collect a few personal objects.

Standing alone in her room, the feeling of betrayal returned. Among the many photographs was one of her with his late stepfather on their wedding day. He stared at it and realised how very frail his mother was now. True, the picture was nearly thirty years old. But he could barely reconcile the image in the photograph with the old lady in the hospital bed.

He stared at the elfin face, the slightly too thin lips softened by laughter lines. This was the woman his father had abandoned. He tried to envisage Pamela then. She would have been more than ten years younger than Mary, so in her mid-twenties. An unfair contest. Or was that too simplistic? What had Katharine said about his father and Mary being mismatched? But he, Stephen, and his father hadn't been mismatched, though, so fuck that for an excuse!

Turning to leave, he had a thought so obvious that his stupidity stunned him. He had spent days searching through papers at his mother's house. But she lived *here* now. Surely, she would have brought her most personal belongings with her.

He found a number of papers in a drawer of her dressing-table. But, on examination, the letters and cards were all recent. Nothing to interest him.

Others were in a cabin trunk in an alcove. He pulled it out into the body of the room. It was not locked. Most of the contents were items of long-unworn clothing, carefully folded and packed in a number of plastic bags.

One contained a wedding dress: under the plastic the white had become streaked with yellow. She had worn a suit for the register office wedding to his stepfather. This had to be the dress she had worn when she married his father. Another held baby clothes: his and Lucy's.

Spaced among the parcels of clothes were oddments – a travelling clock, inscribed on the back 'To Mary from all the girls,' a Parker pen and pencil set, still boxed, a musical jewel case, empty, that played a few bars from *Swan Lake* when he lifted the lid.

Searching was an intrusion and it disturbed him, but he continued. The matron looked in at one point.

'I'm looking for papers on the house,' he explained. He had already told her he planned to sell.

'I just wondered if you'd like some lunch.'

He checked his watch. 'I'll get a sandwich later.'

She nodded and left him alone again.

The papers were contained inside a shoe-box; they were disappointingly few. There were letters from him and from her mother, photographs of her and Katharine as children, wedding greetings, hand-drawn and coloured birthday cards signed 'Stephen' and 'Lucy' in haphazard capitals. A cutting of the article he had written for the *Chicago Tribune* in Bicentennial Year on what it was like to have been on the losing side – an article that had got him the offer to move to New York. He remembered sending it with a triumphant letter. His excitement at finding them died away. Nothing to help him. He began to repack and stopped at one card that did not quite belong.

It was a twenty-first birthday card. No signature – just an 'X' kiss mark in blue ball-point. The picture was of a fireworks display. The manufacturer was a US-based multinational.

Why keep it? All the papers in the box had been carefully selected. They were her most valued private possessions. Many very personal items, such as birth and marriage certificates, had been left at the house.

She had brought it by mistake – that was the most likely answer.

Yet . . .

It was out of pattern. As an investigative journalist, that was always one of the things he sought. It just might mean something.

He put it on one side. Probably nothing, but just in case . . .

There was no problem tracking down the date the card had been published. No problem, that was, except the thirty-odd telephone calls it took. If he had been a police officer, it would have been easy – the makers would have co-operated immediately. The fact that Stephen was a newspaperman proved of limited help: the company's idea of press liaison was limited to circulating a few publicity hand-outs. So, although Stephen quickly found it was possible to date the card, getting someone to dig out the necessary records involved pleading and wheedling – and, above all, getting across the message that he was not going to go away.

When the company finally provided the information, at least it was interesting. The card had first been produced in 1969 and had last been reprinted in 1971. Stephen's twenty-first birthday had been in 1970. Could this be a card Mary had bought and not sent? If so, why only a scrawled 'X'? And why keep it now?

There was something else interesting. According to the card company, it was from a range that had been created to have global appeal. It had been on sale, for example, at airport shops and in hotel lobbies. The card Stephen had found could have been bought almost anywhere in the world.

Geoff Beldon was an ex-police officer whose calling card now read 'Forensic Consultant and Fingerprint Expert'.

Underneath a small illustration of a microscope, the card added:

Fingerprints
Glove & Shoe Impressions
Tyre and Instrument Marks

Stephen had met him once, after a court case in which Beldon's evidence had cleared a man. In this case, one of burglary at the country home of an international financier, Beldon had success-fully challenged the prosecution's forensic expert over how much could be deduced accurately from a palm-print found at the scene.

He operated out of Gillingham, an industrial town on the Medway Estuary, Kent – carefully chosen to be close to motorways because much of his life was spent in courts in London and throughout the country or working for major corporations.

Stephen reached him at home. He reminded Beldon of how they had met, told him he needed professional help. Beldon, as he had remembered, was matter-of-fact practical, a man used to having problems thrown at him and solving them. They arranged to meet the following day – Stephen was lucky in that a court case in which Beldon was to have given expert evidence had just been postponed because of the illness of a witness.

Stephen took an early train from Victoria for the forty-five-minute journey and was there soon after ten o'clock. They talked in Beldon's office before moving through to his small laboratory, with its assortment of chemicals, containers, pans, burners and weighing machines.

Stephen had placed the birthday card inside a plastic folder for protection, and Beldon withdrew it with tweezers.

Stephen had given him the background, and as Beldon gathered materials together he gave a précis to make sure he had it correct.

'The card's about twenty years old given a year or two either way. You've touched it recently, you know your mother has. You want to know what other prints I can find, anticipating they could be as old as the card.'

Stephen murmured agreement. He had brought another piece of card, which only he and his mother had handled, so that the expert would know which were their prints.

Stephen had expected Beldon would need to use laser technology to raise any latent prints. He had been wrong: not the best way, said the expert.

'To date, the oldest prints developed using laser have only been nine or ten years old, and we're talking double that here. But maybe if we find something, we'll need to use laser to enhance it. Maybe. I hope not – unless you've got friends with laser access or you've been lying to me and you're really working for national security, it's pretty expensive.'

Smoothly, unhurriedly, Beldon mixed a near-clear solution and poured it into a glass tray. 'Ninhydrin,' he explained. 'If there's a latent print, it should reveal it. It acts on the amino acids left in the perspiration. It will dye the marks that were left a pink-purple colour.'

Using tweezers, Beldon soaked the card in the solution and then removed it immediately. It dried within seconds. Next, still using the tweezers, he placed it inside a black box – 'To keep the light off,' he explained.

'What now?' Stephen was impatient again.

Beldon grinned. 'Now we wait,' he said. 'At least forty-eight hours. Then I'll look at the card again. Maybe there will be the prints you want, maybe not. If not, it goes back into the box for another forty-eight hours.'

'And that's it?'

'That's it. I'll look at it every two days. If and when there's anything I'll photograph it.'

'Can't you speed it up?'

'I could – I could have applied a lot of heat after I took the card out of the solution. That hastens the process.'

'So, why didn't you?'

'Because, if this process doesn't work, I'd have destroyed any chance of trying other methods.'

'There are other ways?'

Beldon sensed Stephen's frustration. 'There's a lot we can try yet – if we need to. Don't worry, if there's anything to find, we'll find it.'

Beldon telephoned him five days later, his voice noncommittal.

'Do you want the bad news or the good news?'

'OK, let's have the bad news.'

'The ninhydrin treatment didn't work.' He explained that it was not infallible. It could not detect latent prints if the paper had become damp at any time – the water would destroy the amino acids. Alternatively, there were individuals who simply did not deposit sufficient quantities of amino acid.

'Fuck. The good news had better be good.'

'It is. There's another technique. The Atomic Weapons Research Establishment developed a reagent called Physical Developer for use in cases just like this. You immerse the paper again, this time in a solution containing silver ions – I can give you details if you want them.'

'I want them. But later.'

'If there are prints, the metallic silver settles on them – it's thought it acts on the fatty deposits in perspiration. The ridges stand out quite clearly as dark-grey images.'

'And?'

'And there are two pretty good prints. Probably not good enough to stand up in a courtroom if you ever had to compare them with another print: the law wants sixteen clear points of comparison and we've only got nine here. But, in reality, that's enough to be as certain as dammit – an expert reckons to be pretty sure down as low as seven or eight points of comparison.'

'Is it worth trying to do anything else with them – get them submitted to laser illumination?'

Beldon was certain. 'You don't need it. Bring me the other prints and I'll tell you if they match. You've drawn lucky.'

Ted Jarvis, Stephen's private detective contact, was less thrown by the request for a sample of Kenyon's fingerprints than he had been about tracing Fisher. As Kenyon's body had never been found, they would still be on file.

All he said was, 'Give me forty-eight hours.'

While he was waiting, there was one further test on the twenty-first birthday card that Stephen wanted to try. Beldon had photographed the prints and had returned the card by courier.

There are two possibilities when someone sends a letter or a greetings card. The first is that the sender writes the envelope before inserting the contents. The second, which Stephen suspected was more common, was that the writer addresses the envelope *after* the card or letter has been placed inside it.

If the writer adopts the second method, there is a chance that the words written on the envelope are impressed through it, leaving marks – albeit invisible – on the paper or card inside.

That was Stephen's hope with this card, small though it might be after nearly twenty years.

Like all journalists who had handled crime stories, Stephen was familiar with ESDA. ElectroStatic Detection Apparatus is an instrument for detecting indented writing in documents. It had been used in a number of spectacular recent criminal cases. In one notorious instance, the tests had proved police officers had inserted fresh material in log-books months after the original entries and had led to the closing down of one whole Serious Crimes Squad.

Though revolutionary, the idea is basically simple. The piece of paper to be examined is placed on the top of a small rectangular machine containing a vacuum pump. It is then covered with a sheet of thin transparent film. The vacuum pump is switched on, drawing the film down on to the paper. The surface is charged with electricity by a small 'discharge unit' shaped like a hand microphone being passed over it. A special powder poured on to the surface at an angle then reveals any images.

It had been explained to Stephen when he had first seen ESDA in action that the powder is attracted to damaged fibres produced by the indented writing. These damaged areas generate high positive electric fields which attract and hold the negatively charged particles of powder. Since being produced by an English company in the late 1970s, the apparatus had been adopted by forensic laboratories and police forces throughout the world.

Stephen telephoned the company, Foster & Freeman, in Evesham, Worcestershire. He had talked to Bob Freeman before. He explained his problem. Could he help?

'Will you send it by courier, or do you want to bring it yourself?' was all Freeman asked. Another man used to solving problems.

'I'll send it if that's all right.'

Less than twenty-four hours later he had the result. The age of the card had not worried Freeman. The fact that it had a gloss finish had: 'Common notepaper works best. Papers that are less porous, like this one, generally respond poorly.'

He was apologetic. Only isolated letters were clear. He read them over the telephone.

Stephen took them down. He got to 'N', and smiled.

'It's OK,' he said. 'Fine. Just what I wanted.'

tep n K yon. No problem guessing the missing letters. The name was the one he had expected.

Stephen Kenyon. The card had been sent to him.

Beldon's call came a few hours later. He had received Michael Kenyon's print and checked. It was the same as the one he had raised on the twenty-first birthday card.

Stephen replaced the telephone and stared down at his notes, not moving. He was filled with a familiar mix of elation and exhaustion.

The forensic evidence was indisputable.

Michael Kenyon had written and sent the card to Stephen – God knew why, maybe the envelope had contained something else that was now missing. Not knowing Stephen had moved to the United States, Kenyon had mailed it to the one address he knew. Where Mary had intercepted it and kept it.

None of that was important, though, for now.

What was important was this.

Kenyon had vanished in May 1966. Stephen was twenty-one in June 1970.

The card proved that four years after he had disappeared, Michael Kenyon was still alive.

CHAPTER SEVENTEEN

'So, tell me,' said Melville.

Stephen faced his editor across the Savoy Grill dining-table.

'You took me to tea last time,' he said, gazing deliberately around the room and its collection of industrialists, politicians, and Establishment figures. He knew that – to those with the key – where each diner was seated provided a guide to status as precise as the size of carpet on a civil-servant's floor. He guessed that Melville ranked in the top third – by job, not person.

Melville was not sure whether Stephen was being serious or was mocking him. He gave him the benefit of the doubt.

'Tea-time's a bad time these days,' he said.

Stephen waited for him to explain, but all he said was, 'Tell me,' again.

So Stephen did.

The waiter came to take their order but Melville waved him away. He had just heard Stephen's news about the card and the fingerprint, and he was puffed with pleasure at his foresight in seeing the search as the basis for a series of articles and a book.

'Told you, didn't I,' he said. 'So the bastard's alive after all. You've got yourself a good story.'

'I've only got him alive nineteen years ago. Plenty of time for him to be dead.'

'He's alive. I can feel it.' Melville paused, stared at Stephen, pondered on the other's words. 'Christ,' he said at last, 'you're a cold bugger. We're talking about your father.'

Stephen remained silent. They had been through this before. Besides, he was no longer sure it was completely true, and that worried him. Pamela had talked of him having the right to feel bitter. But it was more than that. Twice recently, he had awoken with the ghostly feeling of guilt that he had felt all those years ago when his father left his mother, that awful, but undefined, sensation that he alone was to blame for their break-up. Now, as an adult, he could rationalise it: it was common, he knew, for children of people who got divorced to experience such guilt. It happened too with survivors when a death occurred. It was completely open to explanation. And yet . . . No matter how he tried to view it objectively, he could not totally shrug it away. Justified or not, suspicions that he bore blame still remained. And, if for the break-up, why not for what followed . . . ?

Melville beckoned a waiter. He ordered sautéed guinea fowl. Stephen said he would have the brill. Neither wanted anything to start.

'What about the Hon. Mrs C?' asked Melville. 'You said you think she's holding something back.'

'I still don't know why she changed her mind about talking to me. There has to be a reason.' He shrugged. 'I've a hunch.'

Melville liked hunches. 'You say she's got a daughter, the one who tried to recruit you. Why not try her again, see what she knows? Maybe Mum's talked about it.' He reached out to take the wine list. 'Take her to dinner, soften her up.'

Christ, thought Stephen. For a moment he toyed with telling Melville that Pamela claimed to have influence with their proprietor. But why spoil his guinea fowl?

Instead, all he said was, 'Good, I'll try that.'

Although he had told Jessica that there was nothing he could do about keeping her friend's court appearance out of the newspapers, Stephen had made enquiries about the case. It seemed absolutely routine, unlikely to contain anything of interest to national newspapers. The boy's only worry had to be that an agency reporter would send details to the local newspaper.

Despite what he had said, Stephen probably could have prevented this. A drink with the right court reporter, a request for a personal favour. It was tempting. Not just because he suspected that Pamela still held a key piece in the puzzle and Jessica might be the way in, but because the memory of the girl had begun to haunt him.

Although they had been on the same table at the charity lunch, they had scarcely talked. At first, he had thought it was intentional on her part – anger at his refusal to help. But when she had looked at him her smile had been warm.

And yet, tempting or not, suppressing the story was not something he would do. It would mean crossing a line. Beware the sole exception, had always been one of his personal credos. He knew that the single instant easily became a second and a third once the barrier was down. A principle was a principle. Stop. He was intelligent enough to recognise the downside: sometimes sticking with the bigger truth could result in hurting the individual, and, of course, that was sad. But if that was the way it had to be, so be it. The alternative was much more dangerous.

As it turned out, it was not necessary anyway. Luck intervened.

Stephen received a telephone call from a police sergeant he had contacted for details about the case after Jessica's visit.

'Bad news,' said the sergeant. 'Thought you ought to hear it.'

The 'bad news' was that the main witness had withdrawn his story. The Crown Prosecution Service had decided there was no chance of a successful prosecution.

'The defendants don't even know yet,' the sergeant continued. 'Hope they'll let the little bastard sweat a bit more first. Thought I'd better tell you, though. Don't want you libelling someone.' The sergeant had not known Stephen was merely curious; he thought he was putting together a dossier on the case for publication.

Stephen telephoned Jessica immediately.

'Thought you'd like to know they've dropped the case against your friend,' he said. 'Nothing to do with me. But it's all dead now. From what I've heard, he hasn't even been told yet. You can call him if you like but keep me out of it.'

As he had anticipated, she half-believed – wanted to believe – that he was responsible.

He denied it again, but added, 'If you want to thank me for something I didn't do, you can always have dinner with me.'

They fixed a meeting three days later when she would be in London. Eight o'clock at Green's.

She was already waiting when he arrived at the St James's restaurant. He was late and he swept straight through the oyster bar into the mahogany-panelled resaurant. She was sitting, back to the wall, a glass of white wine in front of her, two waiters hovering in the hope of being summoned and a half-dozen pairs of eyes of male diners admiring her.

Most of the diners were men, but not overwhelmingly so. Stephen liked the restaurant because it was solid and yet relaxed, because you could eat simple or complicated, and because it was a place you could feel at home concluding a business deal or starting an affair. It usually had a sprinkling of celebrities which was useful if you needed to stimulate easy and innocuous conversation. Most of all, he liked it because they knew him.

Without being asked, a waiter brought him a whisky and water, no ice.

He rushed through apologies for being late, thanked her for coming, and – without pause – raised his glass in a mock toast, and said, 'My father drank this I've learned. Only, from what I can gather, by the bottle rather than the glass.'

'You should be kind to the dead.'

He acknowledged the rebuke. 'Journalists aren't kind to anyone. But, for your sake, tonight I'll try.'

The two waiters had not moved. They were still watching her. He felt an odd mix of embarrassment and pride. Embarrassment because it must look like seduction – and he had been almost exactly the age she was now when she was conceived. Pride because she was regarding him with rapt attention.

'You've changed your hair,' he said.

She had rolled it into a tight pleat at the back of her head and secured it with pins. The new style made her head small and neat, accentuated the oval of her face. It was a disconcerting face. At certain angles, she looked like a boy – but a very feminine boy. Her skin was pale, devoid of noticeable make-up. The line of her nose had a barely perceptible kink, as though it had been broken and reset not quite perfectly. Her features were full of contrasts: her mouth was full and wide, yet her chin pointed and delicate.

The hairstyle made it hard to pinpoint her age, other than young. She could have been seventeen or twenty-two. It made her look less like her mother, though.

She wore a shirt, open at the neck to reveal prominent collar-bones. Like the sweater she had worn on their previous meeting, it was loose and hid her shape, but he thought her breasts must be small. She was not the kind of woman who usually excited him. He liked rounded women with wide, full faces, breasts in which you could lose yourself. Like Tarlach's had been. ('Sure an' it's only me tits you'll be after,' she'd say in a stage Irish voice, cupping her naked breasts as they lay in bed. 'I thought all you Catholics were modest,' he'd say, and she'd reply, 'Ah sure and that's some other Catholics you'll be thinking of,' although, belying the jokes, all the time they were together she ceased taking communion.) The thought came and went.

Truth was, this boy-girl, gangling and for all her beauty awkward in her youth, made his insides turn.

As soon as they had ordered – smoked fish, sausages and mash – he got her talking about herself. He was a good listener, both by nature and by practice.

For most people, Stephen had found, listening is simply that part of a conversation where you shut up temporarily and wait to speak again. Stephen made listening an active pursuit: he concentrated not only on words but on nuances, constantly analysing what was not being said as well as what was being spoken, and gauging how best to draw words out of the other.

It made a useful asset. Socially, concentrated listening is the ultimate in flattery. Workwise, it helped create contacts, produced information, and – surprisingly often – it even led to people condemning themselves from their own lips.

There was an Arab proverb, cynical yet true, which put it well. The word that is unspoken is your slave; the word you speak is your master.

There was a downside, though. Those traits that made Stephen a good listener were the same ones that made him talk in vague generalities, use meaningless words that could be interpreted in any way the listener chose. His words were too often like the balls served by a tennis coach – their main purpose was to produce the right return. Except on very rare occasions with very rare people, unguarded thoughts, bare emotions, spontaneous remarks, remained unsaid. The result was often the verbal equivalent of Muzak.

Tonight, though, was different. He lost himself in listening to her and when he did talk he did so without thought or reserve. Perhaps it was her total lack of self-consciousness. Perhaps it was because she seemed so very much younger and unthreatening. Perhaps it was simply flattery. Perhaps, though he did not think this, it was because she was a good listener too.

She had left boarding school a year before, he learned. She had no real idea what she wanted to do. Not university, though she quickly stressed that her teachers had argued she was 'good material'. Not marriage, although two of her friends were already engaged. She had been filling time by taking a series of courses – art appreciation, cordon bleu cookery, tracing the history of old houses. She was about to begin a more substantive one, on journalism, at a private college. She named it. Kenyon had heard of it vaguely – it specialised in courses for sons and daughters of the privileged of the Third World.

Stephen, who had never in his life done anything without an end in mind, listened with genuine fascination.

As to talking – almost without realising it, he told her about his life: about his mother's divorce and remarriage, the fear and excitement of being an English teenager in Missouri, entering journalism, Chicago, New York, travelling the world, Paris, returning to a country where he was almost a stranger. Everything except the year and a half he had shared with Tarlach. That was too personal.

'I could help you,' she said at last. It was nearly midnight, tables near them had been vacated and occupied by new diners.

'Help me?'

'Look for your father.'

Without realising, he started to laugh and then stopped when he saw a mixture of hurt and anger appearing.

'How?'

'You said there are lots of small things you still have to follow up. I know it's not the same as doing it for a job but I've been taught how to research. If you told me what to do, I could do it.'

'But why,' he said, 'why would you want to do it – supposing there was anything?'

His hand was on the table, about to pick up his brandy glass. She placed her own hand on his.

'It would be fun,' she said. 'And good training if I go on with journalism.' She paused, and then ruined it all.

'Besides,' she said, 'we're almost brother and sister.'

The doorbell woke Stephen, and his first thought was that he had overslept and then he realised it was not yet light.

Stumbling to the door, trying to shake himself awake, he prepared for bad news – maybe even another Special Branch raid although, surely, they would be hammering to open up.

He checked the spy-hole before he opened the door, and then said, 'Do you realise it's not five o'clock yet?'

And then, a second later as the fact of her presence hit him, he said, 'Christ, what's happened? Is it Jessica?'

Pamela followed him inside without answering.

'It's nothing,' she said. 'Should it be? You delivered Jessica safely home three hours ago.'

'So, what?' He was still emerging from sleep. Everything had an unreal, dream quality. He became conscious that all he wore were pyjama bottoms, and he tugged at them.

'Why don't you go back to bed?' she said. 'I'll bring us a drink.'

While he was still taking in what she had said, she moved to pick up a bottle and glasses.

When she turned back, her raincoat had fallen open.

Underneath, he saw, she wore nothing.

She stood silent under his stare.

'I drove myself,' she said, as though that explained everything.

Then, bottle and glasses in hand, she walked past him into the bedroom.

When he woke again it was seven-thirty. She had gone. He looked in vain for a note, for a message. Nothing. Only the smell of her perfume and her body. And an unmistakable taste that was not booze.

The huge sign outside read, 'Public Record Office Hayes Repository. This Site is not Open to the Public. Admittance by Prior Arrangement Only'.

Stephen sat in the passenger seat of the parked Sierra, the entrance in view, while Ted Jarvis slid a fresh country-and-western tape into the stereo.

It was almost one o'clock in the afternoon. They had been waiting only a few minutes. It was hot in the car, and Stephen was finding it hard not to drift into sleep.

'Any moment now,' said Jarvis. 'Civil servants keep nice regular hours.' He said it with a mix of satisfaction and malice: satisfaction because they would not have to wait long, malice because he had been up all night on another job.

'You should get more staff,' said Stephen. 'You must be earning a fortune.'

'Kids,' said Jarvis. 'You try bringing up four kids and see where the money goes. Besides, you can't trust staff.'

Stephen shrugged and bit back the obvious reply. If Jarvis wanted to play the it's-hard-to-make-a-living-down-at-heel private eye, OK. It would be unfair to remind him of the villa in Mallorca and the two other cars in the garage, one a Porsche.

He let his head fall, and he closed his eyes. There was a dull thud at his temples, and his mind kept returning to the events of hours before.

Images formed in his mind like hallucinations. He could see the shadow of Pamela's body rising and falling above him, her head now bent forward, hair brushing his face, now thrown back, mouth open, murmuring indecipherable words. He had had an erection that would never end. His penis had stood swollen, bursting, part of him but separate. He had lain and enjoyed, but he had observed what was happening as though he were two separate beings. And when he had come – long after she had begun to show exasperation – it had been with relief even more than pleasure. She had collapsed on him immediately and sweat had sucked their bodies together. She had slumped unmoving, limbs floppy, full of weight, as though she were dead. Gradually, he had become conscious of his own breathing, harsh, painful, like a long-distance runner struggling the final yards. For a few minutes he had felt wide awake. His mind had become sharp, alert. Why? He had asked himself. Why? Why? And then, without dislodging his shrinking penis, she had rolled, taking him with her. Her arms had tightened, and she had muttered something, and just as he was wondering what would happen next, he had fallen into a deep, sudden sleep.

All this returned to him as he sat barely awake, head throbbing, eyes burning, in the overheated car waiting for something to happen.

And what, he asked himself, had remained when he did wake? A taste that filled every corner of his mouth. A dark purple patch, puffed, with tiny pinpricks of red, where she had bitten into his shoulder. An ache between his thighs that he could feel even now. And a strange, jangling mix of questions and emotions – excitement, disbelief, guilt, wonderment.

'Wake up, don't go to sleep,' said Jarvis. And in the same tone, 'You look fucking awful. All the same, you bachelors.'

Stephen opened his eyes and made to reply, but Jarvis was tugging his arm.

'There he is,' he said, starting the engine and beginning to pull out.

Stephen forced himself awake and back into the present. They followed the A-registration blue Renault for about ten minutes until it pulled into a pub car park. Jarvis waited a brief while, followed the Renault driver into the pub and returned ten minutes later with a bulky packet in his hand.

'An hour,' he said.

There were two envelopes. Stephen opened the first as Jarvis set off on a circular tour of the area. It was the police file on his father's disappearance – it had been shifted to Hayes for safekeeping once it ceased to be current. It could always be summoned back if anyone needed it.

Stephen had a mini-cassette-recorder and he dictated notes as he read through. There was the formidable document Fisher had mentioned – form 584. Notes of Fisher's initial investigation. Transcripts of interviews . . .

Stephen worked through with increasing frustration. The file was remarkable less for what it contained than for what was missing. Impossible to believe everything was here.

Jarvis found a quiet side road and parked.

'Anything?' he asked Stephen.

Stephen passed him the file. 'See what you think,' he said.

While Jarvis was reading, Stephen turned his attention to the other envelope – his father's Army record. The Hayes depository was the biggest of the Ministry of Defence's collections of archives. Over eighty miles of records – personnel files had to be kept for seventy-five years from discharge. Fifty thousand people a year made enquiries about the contents – old soldiers wanting replacement medals, widows needing details for welfare purposes, family solicitors anxious to prove a death was caused in some measure by military service, thus allowing the avoidance of death duties.

Stephen could have applied in the normal way, but Jarvis, who had used the archives before, had warned him that some papers – notably medical records and anything that smacked of intelligence – would probably be withheld. Stephen doubted medical records would be of help, and had no expectation that his father had ever had anything to do with security, but not knowing what he would find, he had wanted to see everything.

The envelope's main item was a slim book, slightly smaller than a paperback, with stiff red covers and lettering in black. The words 'Regular Army' were printed above the royal coat of arms and below that 'Certificate of Service' and a warning from 'The War Office, London SW1' that 'Any alteration of the particulars given in this certificate may render the holder liable to prosecution under the Seamen's and Soldiers' False Characters Act 1906'.

Stephen turned the pages. Surname, christian names, enlisted at, enlisted on.

Page three was interesting, listing postings and dates. So was page seven with its heading 'Educational Attainments, Trade Qualifications'.

A flap in the rear cover contained a postcard-size photograph of a group of soldiers. They were in three rows, the first lying on their stomachs, the second kneeling and the third standing. It was hard to make out faces.

There was a copy of Army Form B.104–81A, addressed 'Sir or Madam' and signed by the 'Officer in Charge of Records'. It read, 'I regret to inform you that a report has been received from the War Office that (Rank) Sergeant (Names) Kenyon, Michael has been wounded.' The 'nature of wound' was given as, 'Blast injury. Head and back'.

'It has not been reported into what hospital he has been admitted, nor are any other particulars known, but in the event of his condition being considered by the Medical Authorities as serious or dangerous this office will be notified by cable and you will be immediately informed.'

The original, Stephen imagined, would have been sent to his mother. He had found no trace of it either at the house or in her room at the nursing home. There were no further papers about the wounding. It could not have been 'serious or dangerous'.

Jarvis was waiting for him to finish. He had scanned the police file.

'This one's been got at – or someone's lost half of it,' said Jarvis.

'That's what I thought. This one's more interesting.' Stephen handed him the Army file. 'Look at pages three and seven.'

Both referred to Germany. The first to Kenyon's near-colloquial grasp of the language. The second to his post-war years there in Military Intelligence – again facts unknown to Stephen.

Together, they gave a vision of a man he had not seen before. Surely, they must have been important factors in his father's life. Why had he had no hint of them until now?

Jarvis finished reading. His reaction was the same as Stephen's.

'I'd like to know more about Germany,' he said. 'Post-war. Exciting times. He'd meet a lot of people. Interesting about the language too.'

The kind of place someone might return to, Stephen was thinking. Strange – the police must have checked this file. Why hadn't Fisher mentioned it?

'I'd say something worth taking a look at,' said Jarvis, restarting the engine. They had ten minutes to return the files.

'It's a big country,' said Stephen.

Jarvis produced a rare grin. 'I'm the one who moans how fucking hard it is.'

Katharine and Ward were still in Spain, but had moved on to Valencia. Fortunately, they had made their reservation through the Madrid Hotel. A helpful reservations clerk checked the computer terminal and gave him the number he wanted.

Ward answered the room telephone. He was dressing for dinner, Katharine was in the bathroom. They were taking a few days' vacation now his business was concluded.

Stephen held while Katharine came to the telephone. 'A small one,' he said. 'Did my father talk much about Germany?'

He felt the resentment in her long silence – she did not like him asking about his father where Ward could overhear. Ward, after all, had been his father all those years.

'Look,' he said, 'I wouldn't have called like this, but I need to know.'

If she told the truth, she knew little he had not already learned from the Army file. A few oddments, but they were just background – German at school, a feeling for languages ('He used to talk to the refugees at the hall – you'd never have believed he hadn't been speaking the language all his life'), the Army, stationed in Germany . . .

'He didn't talk much about it when he came back – not to me, at

263

least. Don't forget I didn't see much of him. Your mother would know.'

She would, but there was no way of getting through. Not now. Perhaps she would improve again.

'The only thing I can tell you was that when he came back he was changed. Really changed. How? Well, he was just different. A different person.' She laughed down the phone, a signal she wanted to end the conversation. 'Still, I suppose you could say that about everyone who went to war.'

CHAPTER EIGHTEEN

'Why didn't you tell me about Germany?'

It was early afternoon and Stephen and Fisher had paused about a mile from the ex-police sergeant's house.

Stephen's voice was breathless. The hill had been steep and pushing the wheelchair was unaccustomed exercise.

From here you could see the sea, a streak of almost impossible blue on the edge of Stephen's vision. He had left his jacket in the house. The sun burned on his neck and his arms. The only sound was a gull. A hundred yards below them, Jessica was picking grasses.

'You've no soul,' said Fisher. 'You should just stand here and let it seep into you. Smell the air, feel the breeze, look at the view, admire that girl of yours . . . It's the kind of moment you should want to freeze and keep.'

Stephen checked the handbrake, found a comfortable spot on the roadside bank and sank down. He disregarded Fisher's words.

'What else did you hold back?' he asked. 'And why? You didn't have to talk to me, but when you did, why didn't you level?'

Fisher was watching Jessica. She looked up, saw him and waved.

'She's lovely but too young for you,' said Fisher. But then he answered. 'I wanted you to do some work,' he said. 'I'd still like to see the case closed, really closed. Even after all these years it still gripes.'

He operated the chair so that it turned in Stephen's direction. 'I knew if you were serious about your search, you'd find out and that you'd come back. If you weren't, what the fuck, why should I waste my time?'

'I came back. So tell me. And the girl: she's not *my* girl. She's

265

just helping out.' Fisher's assumption about Jessica irritated him. Although Stephen had agreed she could accompany him, he had been feeling stabs of regret. Her presence disturbed him in ways and for reasons he could not define. Perhaps the reason was the obvious one – that he'd fucked her mother (or – more truthfully – been fucked by her, although he could hardly plead his body had been unwilling). Surely that was cause enough? But, a quiet voice nagged, was that all it was?

Like Stephen, Fisher had been intrigued by the references to German and Germany – people on the run often headed for territory with which they were familiar.

He had found several specific links, he explained. He had pursued them as best he could. 'There were names, places on his Army records. I put in a formal request to the German police. They went through the motions, came back with nothing. How hard they tried I don't know. Not very, I'd imagine. It wasn't much of a case, and what was in it for them?'

'That was all?'

'There were a few other leads, too slender to follow up. I persuaded some local copper where your father grew up to ask some questions. He'd befriended some German POWs after he came out of the Army. I fed that in too, but as I said it wasn't much of a case.'

'None of that's on the file,' said Stephen.

The effect was less dramatic than he had expected. 'You've seen it, the police file?' said Fisher. 'It's still around?'

'Filed away at Hayes,' said Stephen. 'But it's pretty slim. Looks like the weeders have been at it.'

'Come on,' said Fisher. 'Take me back to the house. I'll show you.'

The papers were in a metal box under the floor in the utility room beyond the kitchen. The hiding place was covered by the freezer – Fisher must surely have had help moving it. Maybe he'd concealed the box first, replaced the boards and then got the freezer placed over it by some unsuspecting hireling or neighbour. Stephen needed Jessica's help and then it was difficult.

The file was a good three inches thick and it was subdivided into a succession of folders and large envelopes.

'The rest of it,' explained Fisher although the fact was already obvious.

'Other people were showing interest,' he went on. 'The file was safe while it was still active and I was still around. When I knew I was going, I started to worry about who might make use of it. I'd followed up leads as best I could. But I always knew there was more that could have been done if I'd had a free hand and unlimited resources – which is what your father's old friends would have had. The other leads might have led nowhere. But if I couldn't track your old man, I certainly didn't want the material we'd collected getting into the hands of the Mob to help them trace him.'

'So you vanished it.'

'Not all of it. Just the most sensitive stuff. Especially the intelligence file – that should never have been there anyway, it should never have left Criminal Intelligence Branch.'

In flipping, Stephen had already found it: A4-size papers between plain brown covers, the whole held together by a treasury tag.

'But you stole it?'

'I reckoned it was only safe with me. If anyone had asked any questions I would have denied all knowledge – papers are always going missing. I thought of destroying it – but I just couldn't bring myself to do that. Maybe I thought it would be useful one day. Who knows?'

'Surely someone noticed the intelligence file had gone?'

'In those days the only proof one had ever existed was a card index. I got rid of the card too.'

'You must have had a good friend.'

Fisher shrugged; not a question to answer. Instead, he said, 'Why don't you get your notebook out and start reading.'

They sat around the dining-table, Fisher sorting before passing papers on to Stephen.

Jessica had joined them.

'Can I?' she asked, reaching for one of the files Stephen had already flipped and discarded.

'Maybe she'll see something we miss,' said Fisher.

Stephen nodded assent; he was already preoccupied reading statements.

There were ones from Kenyon's former employer at a loan company, from a solicitor who had introduced him to the club, from neighbours at the Victoria block. Many painted a picture of normality, with no signs that Kenyon planned to vanish or was in danger or had come to harm. A car salesman had spoken to him just the day before he disappeared – the two men had arranged an appointment for a week hence; another acquaintance was due to lunch with him later in the week.

The one from the secretary of the Big Wheel read like a testimonial: 'Mr Kenyon was punctilious in the pursuit of his duties. There was never any indication of anything that would explain his disappearance . . . No, there was no money missing. Furthermore, Mr Kenyon had no unsupervised access to money. It is true that one of his functions was to be present at the counting each night, but in accordance with our normal security procedures at least three people were always present.'

Stephen's mother's statement included an account of the last time she had seen Kenyon. He had appeared on her doorstep unexpectedly, saying he wanted to see Stephen. Even though it was early morning, she thought he had already been drinking. They had argued and he had left. She had told Kenyon that his son was at weekly boarding school. A lie – he was in the United States, but Mary feared that if he knew this he would contact her sister Katharine for access, and he and Katharine had always been friendly. Later, through village gossip, she had heard about the man – obviously Kenyon – who had stayed overnight at the local pub and left without his belongings.

Pamela's words were formal, dry, legalistic. Stephen pushed her statement across to Fisher for comment.

Fisher understood his unspoken question. 'Reads like a court deposition, doesn't it,' he said. 'She had a lawyer present, answered like a speak-your-weight machine.'

'Hiding something?'

Fisher shrugged. 'No more than most, I think. She had powerful friends. I think they warned her the less she said, the less she'd get involved.'

Barton's was equally bald. The replies to questions were almost monosyllabic.

Again, he pushed it across to Fisher for comment. 'Another one with a lawyer present?' he asked.

'He didn't need one. He'd been taught to keep a closed mouth from the day he was born. I suspect the first time he said "daddy", his family beat the shit out of him as a warning to keep his mouth shut. I tried to question him again later, but he'd left the country.'

He noted Stephen's interest. 'Don't get excited,' he said. 'Nothing that tied up with your father. He went back to the States – he made the trip every two to three months according to Immigration. This time I heard the Home Office wanted to use it as an opportunity to keep him out as an undesirable. They reckoned the Mob would stop being interested in owning clubs in London if they couldn't put in their own men to oversee things. So keep out the Bartons and in time you'd drive out the Mob . . .'

'And that's what they did?'

'They might have done. But while all the talk was going on, Barton got himself in a car accident. He and a couple of others got smashed up by a truck. It could have been gangland. But I spoke to the Philly police and they reckoned it wasn't Mafia style – too risky, too imprecise.'

'So Barton was killed?'

'As good as. All smashed up inside. Every time I checked, the surgeons were in the middle of stitching something else together. Maybe he lived, maybe he died later – I don't know. But no way was anyone going to press for bedside interviews about something like your father.'

Stephen had saved the Criminal Intelligence Branch file until last. The fact that Fisher had stolen it – surely at greater personal risk than he let on – meant it had to contain something.

There were nine sections. The shock was that many of the pages were almost blank.

Fisher noticed his expression, guessed the reason and rushed to explain. 'Back then, in 1966, there were two categories of intelligence file – with computers, it'll all have changed now. Minor subjects got a record card. As the information grew, other cards got pinned to the first one. Major subjects, on the other hand, got a proper file – a docket, what you've got there. Your old man had just gone up in the league. He'd been transferred from minor to major. That's why there's so little – they were only just starting on him. It's still worth reading.'

Stephen began to work through steadily. The first page carried Kenyon's name – Michael James Kenyon, his date and place of birth, a blank against 'Criminal Record Number' and a Criminal Intelligence Branch number. The square set aside for a photograph was empty.

The second page had details of his family – Stephen noted his own name and date of birth. A physical description: height, build, complexion, eyes, hair, face shape. Against 'Marks/tattoos/deformities etc.' was written 'Walks with an intermittent limp'.

The third page – 'Criminal Convictions' – was blank.

Page four was more interesting. Under 'Known Associates' it listed a score of names, many Americans (with references to FBI files) but also three notorious London gangsters with the note that they were regular visitors to the club and had been observed in conversation with Kenyon.

One American name was new to Stephen, though vaguely familiar: Raoul Hunter, described as 'long-time associate of American Mafia bosses', and as 'notified excluded UK as undesirable alien, Home Office document AEX/876445/CuUK'. Source was given as 'surveillance reports' with a cross-reference to Hunter's own file. Five dates were given.

Fisher moved his chair, leaned over. 'They were obviously watching friend Hunter closely. Those dates would be times they were seen together outside the club.'

'The reason for the upgrade?'

'One of them. Not the main one. Keep reading.'

'Raoul Hunter. I know that name.' Kenyon was noting it in his book.

'Try the old movies section in your local video store.'

Stephen remembered then, 'Of course. Gangster films. Kind of Jimmy Cagney, George Raft.'

'More George Raft.'

'Is he still alive?'

'If he is he'd be a pretty old guy. He was around sixty then.'

'No one interviewed him?'

'He'd already long gone back to the US. He'd left the country meaning it to be temporary. The Home Office refused to let him back in. Looked more like a sop to the FBI – they kept pressing for a crackdown on these bastards. The Home Office . . . well, you know this country. All the bureaucrats want is a quiet life. I put in a routine request for someone to interview him but nothing happened.'

Stephen turned the page. 'Places frequented.' The club, of course, with a note of times. A couple of restaurants. Nothing interesting – except a note of a visit by Kenyon to Miami in November 1965, with flight dates and hotel detail.

The next two sections were routine – 'Vehicles used' (Stephen noted that even living as he did in central London, his father owned a car), 'Previous addresses'.

The last section – and potentially the most interesting – was headed 'Intelligence Log'.

There were three pages of notes – all of them references to occasions where Kenyon's name or presence had emerged during investigating other subjects.

A number resulted from surveillance of Hunter and of Barton's bodyguard, George Russo – the file referred to Kenyon as 'subject': 'Subject driven home by target, escorted to front door.'

And, more tellingly, 'Subject met at airport by target. Picked up at club five hours later. No surveillance en route. No knowledge missing time.'

One other note concerned a plastic surgeon, called Poulton, operating out of Harley Street. He was under surveillance on suspicion that he had provided new faces for wanted men. Kenyon's name had been mentioned during a telephone call to a man believed to be Barton –

(Transcript of part:

Poulton: 'My colleague attended the consultation as we arranged. He can't be categoric on such brief contact, of course, but overall he would say, yes, my diagnosis probably was right.'

2nd voice: 'You mean he is. Is that what you're saying? Speak fucking English.'

Poulton: 'Not dangerously so, nothing for you to worry about. But yes. He'd say, yes.)'

Kenyon asked Fisher about it. The ex-sergeant shook his head. It meant nothing to him. The inference was that Poulton had diagnosed in Kenyon an illness that an unnamed colleague had confirmed. But what had Poulton, a plastic surgeon, been doing examining Kenyon in the first place?

At least Fisher had an answer for that: to be a plastic surgeon, Poulton also had to have general medical qualifications. Kenyon must have gone to him for those – which must mean, of course, he had not dared go near a regular doctor.

An explanation that raised yet more questions that could not be answered. Kenyon snorted with frustration, and turned the page.

The section was headed 'Informant File'. All the entries, Kenyon noted, had the same code number, which must denote the same informant in every case. They all concerned activities inside the club – mainly the names of visitors with whom Kenyon had been seen to spend time. One report was of an internal fraud centred on a rigged roulette wheel: Kenyon's name occurred because Barton had been heard to wonder why the Englishman, normally ostrich-like about such things, had been showing interest.

Kenyon noted that the police *must* have had someone inside – he'd like to get time with him.

The final section was an envelope, marked 'Recent Photographs'.

There was only one, taken either early morning or at dusk. Two men were getting out of a car. One, obviously the main subject, was in focus. The other's face was a blur.

'Which one?' said Stephen.

'The wrong one,' said Fisher. 'That's Barton's minder. George something or other – his statement's there somewhere. The other's your old man – or at least he's supposed to be. It could be anyone. God knows why they put it there – maybe just so there'd be something. As I said, the file was new – another week or two and there would have been real stuff.'

Stephen brought all the papers together and squared them neatly in the centre of the table.

He spoke his thoughts aloud. 'I'll check if Hunter is still around. And maybe the doctor's worth talking to. You didn't interview him?'

'Told to lay off,' said Fisher.

He noted Stephen's expression. 'I didn't like it – orders from up high. But I had to see it made sense. If friend Poulton *was* building new faces for criminals, it was better to keep him under surveillance, unaware we knew anything. That's what intelligence believed and I couldn't argue.'

'OK, I'll see if I can trace him now,' said Stephen. He was disappointed. Again, he had a sense of Fisher seeing more than actually existed.

Fisher reached out for the Criminal Intelligence Branch file, opened it at the section listing information from within the club by the unnamed informant.

'You could try him too,' he said, leaning back to enjoy the surprise on Stephen's face.

'You know who it is?'

'I shouldn't, but it was an open secret within the Branch. If he could have done it in safety, he'd have been informing live on television – he was so anxious to get the Yanks.'

Fisher explained that the informant, an Englishman, had been the owner of a rival and highly lucrative casino, fighting a rearguard action against the Americans. 'He was a big boy himself, bit of a hard man, but he was shit scared that if the Yanks got big enough they'd move in on everything, him included. He hadn't enough muscle to face them head on, so he tried to make the government do it. He set up his own intelligence network inside your old man's club, and used to feed details to anyone he thought would help. Not just us, but the people at the embassy, journalists, MPs.'

'He didn't get his fingers chopped off?'

'As I said, he was a tough guy in his own right. Besides, he leaked it anonymously or through third parties.'

'And he's still around?'

'Oh, yes, he's still around.' And he named a name. One Stephen knew immediately. A man whose name was in the newspaper business pages most weeks. The head of one of the country's major leisure corporations.

Poulton was dead. He had had a fatal heart attack nine years before. It took less than an hour to discover that.

Finding out about Hunter was a different matter. He was listed in several movie directories. No date of death was given, but neither was any detail later than 1959. One entry included the name of a Hollywood agent.

Stephen called, finally got through to a man who sounded as though he was pacing the room as he spoke.

'Hunter. Raoul Hunter. I'm an agent, not a spirit raiser. The guy's been dead twenty years.'

'You sure. You *know* he's dead. You read something?'

He hadn't. He just *knew*.

Two hours later Kenyon gave up.

He told Jessica when she telephoned. They had travelled back from Devon separately. She had wanted to call on an old schoolfriend who now lived in the county. Stephen had been oddly relieved: her presence continued to unnerve him, made him feel old, triggered a jumble of contradictory emotions. Although she had wanted to travel to Devon with him, she had been remarkably quiet and distant – perhaps the evening at Green's had been a one-off, not to be repeated. Nevertheless, on the long train journey back to London he had found himself missing her: precisely those features of youth that made him feel so ancient – her enthusiasms, the way she had yet to learn to hide emotions, the sudden switches between childish naivety and womanly insights.

'Where are you?' he asked, half hoping, yet half fearing that she was back in London. She was – her friend had been boring, she had only stayed an hour, had caught the next available train.

'Let me try,' she said.

'Try what?' He had already pushed Hunter to the back of his mind.

'See if I can find out if he's still alive.'

'If he's not, he'll be gaga – he was born in 1905 according to the books and who knows he didn't lie.'

'You thought it worth trying,' her voice petulant and very young.

What the hell. She was right. What was there to lose?

'You're right.' He gave her what detail he had, was about to suggest dinner when she said, 'Cross your fingers, maybe I'll be lucky,' and hung up.

Stephen had copies of press cuttings sent round by messenger before calling Robert Brent's office.

The basic story of his rise and success had been told many times. It was the stuff of which tycoon legends are made. One of nine children, Brent had been brought up by a widowed mother in the East End, and sent out to work in a sweat shop at fourteen. Soon, he had begun collecting small cash bets from workers for delivery to a local illegal bookmaker. One afternoon he had cut delivery too fine, and found himself still on his way to the bookmaker *after* the race had been run. Terrified, he had waited for the result, sure he would be forced to pay out the winnings himself – or be beaten to pulp. Instead, he had found no one had won: the money was his to keep.

From that day on, he had started keeping back some of the bets, taking the risks – and the profits – himself. According to the cuttings, when the bookmaker had discovered what he was doing, instead of breaking Brent's kneecaps he had invited him into his organisation, seeing in Robert a younger version of himself.

The story from then on was of a steady rise: a sideline of a small chain of war-surplus stores, later (when they became legal) betting shops, then hotels, a theme park, and finally property. Brent was now a big man even if the City had never learned to trust him completely. In the papers Stephen read there was no mention of him having owned a casino in the 1960s.

Brent's secretary referred him to an outside public relations company who, told that Stephen's newspaper wanted to profile the tycoon the following Sunday, were back to him in an hour: Brent would see him the following day in his office. The PR man hoped 5.30 a.m. was not too early – Stephen did know, of course, that Brent was always at his desk by five. Stephen did: it was a fact mentioned in almost every article he had read.

'I'll stay up,' he said.

The PR man laughed. Good PRs always laughed at a journalist's joke even when they had heard it a hundred times before.

'So,' said Brent, 'what do you want to know? I'd have thought you fellows had enough on file now without needing to leave your office.'

They were facing over Brent's desk. Although huge, it was almost empty.

One of the few items it held was a 'press pack' – a thick folder of material on the tycoon and his companies. It had been awaiting Stephen when he arrived and he had already opened it and made a pretence of examining its contents.

Brent was small and slim. Unfashionably long silver-grey hair framed a deep-tanned, constantly mobile face; only his eyes had a stillness. When he walked over to a side table to pour coffee from an electric percolator, Stephen noticed built-up heels on his glass-shiny shoes.

Apart from a security man who had admitted him, they seemed to be alone in the building. That had surprised Stephen – he had expected that Brent would be surrounded by secretaries and assistants even at this hour. The thought struck him that maybe Brent only went to the office at this crazily early time when he was being interviewed – that it was all staged for publicity. Maybe the clear desk was a phoney, too; perhaps a few rooms away there was another office, the real one, with its desk piled chaotically high.

He liked the idea. He had already decided Brent was a phoney. The hail-fellow/old-boy greeting he had been given had been as convincing as an American accent on an English actor. The shoes and the suit were probably more the real man – dark blue, shiny, probably silk, sharp-cut with pronounced stitching, tailored to be more at home at a fight or a showbiz party than in a boardroom.

Stephen stifled any more such thoughts: he was reacting like the old City establishment. Give the man his due. He had built up an empire and a personal fortune of five hundred million pounds or so.

'I just need to fill in a few gaps,' he said.

He set down his coffee cup on a mat decorated with one of Brent's new London Docklands tower blocks, and flipped the pack biography theatrically.

For twenty minutes, he asked routine questions – what drove Brent, didn't he ever feel like quitting and spending more time on his boat? Brent answered well – he had been down this path before but he had also retained a rough honesty.

Stephen waited until he gauged the moment was right.

'But the *size* of your empire,' he said. 'Can you feel *personally* involved any more?'

He paused. 'It's not like running a casino in the sixties, is it? You must have had to be everywhere then. Know everybody. Be able to count every penny on the table.'

Brent lifted his cup and drank and then began to laugh. He knew something was happening but not what. Pushing himself to his feet he began to pace, cup and saucer in hand, without speaking.

At last he stopped in front of Stephen.

'So that's it. Brent's got big so let's see if we can pull him down. Let's throw a few lumps of shit and see what happens. That it?' He crossed the room, opened a cupboard and mimed touching buttons. 'Excuse me while I switch on the tapes. Better have a record of this. Or should I throw you out?'

He sat down abruptly, and changed his approach.

'Who put you up to this?' He named a rival company. Then, when there was no reaction, a firm of merchant bankers.

And then. 'Ask your questions. I've nothing to hide.'

'I don't want it for publication,' said Stephen. He told his story.

'Shit,' said Brent when he finished. The fact that Stephen knew he had been an informant had shocked him visibly. 'Talk about ghosts from the past.'

He looked down at the papers Stephen had brought – papers that proved the story the journalist had told. He was still stunned, but tried to make light of what was happening.

'You'd think they'd protect secrets like that,' said Brent at last. 'No wonder the poxy country's going down the pan.' A trace of East London had eased its way back into his voice.

He pushed Stephen's papers back across the desk. 'I could deny it,' he said. 'You'd never have enough to publish. I never owned anything, not on paper anyway.'

'Why should you want to deny it? It wasn't illegal.'

Brent stared at him. Too late, Stephen realised there must be more – something Brent now preferred to keep quiet must have happened at his club. He should have checked, prepared himself more carefully.

He rushed on, 'Anyway, I said it wasn't for publication. If I wanted to write something later, I promise I'd check back or diguise you so no one would ever know. This is personal.'

Brent snorted, but he had decided to speak. He launched straight into his story as though anxious to get it over. 'I had some money invested in this mom-and-pop café place and they put a wheel in the basement. The old man was raking it in. Small stuff, but lots of it, constant you know. Trouble was he couldn't stop betting. I kept buying a bigger chunk of the place to keep getting him out of trouble.

'I'd known he was doing well. But when I took a look at the figures, it was a real revelation. A few months later I got approached with a proposition. Someone I knew around – I don't think we need his name, he's dead now anyway – had heard about these premises that'd be ideal for a real class casino. We could get our croupiers in from France. We'd be in business.'

They had, and the money had poured in.

Then one night Brent had received a visit from two Americans and an English lawyer. The Americans, the lawyer had explained, wanted to invest in swinging London. They would be interested in buying Brent's club.

'One of them was Barton. Your old man worked for him later. I told them I was happy the way things were and they didn't push it. We had some trouble a couple of weeks later: some drunks tried to smash up the place, claiming they'd been cheated. I was ready for them, though; to be honest, I'd been expecting it. We'd taken on a few hard men, really hard men, and they settled it fast. I sent out the message that if it happened again, it was a game two could play. Their clubs could get demolished as quickly as mine, their customers could have accidents on the way home. From then on we got left alone. Other clubs, though, were getting picked off – either handing over a few points or closing down. I decided that it was time to think of the long-term – I didn't want these foreigners getting so strong that one day there'd be nothing I could do.'

Brent had done two things. He had infiltrated two men into the Big Wheel, the American's flagship club, and he had recruited an informant among the East End gangsters who had forged a link.

Brent used information he gathered to create pressure to drive the Americans out of the country: 'I used to pass it on to a few people – a couple of MPs, a journalist on the *Observer*, the people at the American Embassy.' From time to time he would send an anonymous note to the Home Secretary. He made sure the information was always specific and easily checked. 'I'd say things like, "Ed Fish arrived yesterday TWA flight 123, is checked into the Hilton." They could take it from there. I knew they'd find out Fish had a long list of convictions or links with the Mob. I didn't care what they did as long as they did something. I just wanted to keep stirring it.' He knew that in time it would have an effect: the British establishment wants stability; the thought of change, particularly criminal change imported from the lawless lands of the United States, was anathema. Especially if there was publicity. In time, he had been proved right. Americans had been kept out (Hunter was an early victim). Later, others had actually been deported. By the beginning of the seventies, the nature of the invasion had changed. Clubs like the Big Wheel had gone. Mob money was still in London, but invested much more discreetly.

Five years later Brent himself had moved out of gaming.

He paused here to see if there was a reaction, and Stephen

knew this must have been the time something happened. (He checked later – he was right. A call-girl operation, involving some underage girls, had centred on the club. Though Brent still ran the club, his name had been kept out of things – something that must have been difficult and expensive.)

His empire had grown ever since. The second half of the eighties especially had been good to him. The reason he was being so co-operative, Stephen suspected, was that unsavoury publicity was the last thing he wanted right now – it was rumoured that Mrs Thatcher was about to give him a knighthood.

Interesting, said Kenyon. But what about specifics? What about his father?

'It was a long time ago,' said Brent. 'He didn't interest me much. He was . . .'

He stopped himself. Then he grimaced. 'What the hell, you want the truth. No one else'll give it you.' He balanced a letter-opener on two fingers. It had a long, flat blade of silver. 'He was a nobody, a puppet, someone they needed to have around to wave at the taxman and sign bits of paper.'

'But you remember him?' said Stephen, thinking he could not have been a complete nobody.

'Oh, yes. I wondered at first whether he was worth approaching. I figured the Americans rated him so low, they probably didn't care too much what he overheard. That could have made him useful.'

'And did you?'

'No. I had him investigated, and I decided it was too risky. I found out he was probably a lot smarter than I'd thought. But he'd got real problems: his wife, drink. You know all that? The report I got said he and the wife were living apart, that he'd taken the job to get the money to try and get her back. Hadn't worked, and all that was happening was that he was drinking more. Don't know how true it was – the reason, I mean. Didn't matter. The drinking was true enough. Drunks have always worried me. And the other feedback I got was that in a crazy way he was quite close to the Americans. He and the greeter who got chucked out – an old film star, I forget his name – got pretty buddy-buddy.'

A buzzer sounded, and Brent punched an intercom and said 'OK' and a secretary entered. She must have just arrived. She carried a tray with a jug of juice, a basket of croissants and a new pot of coffee.

279

'I'll take care of it,' said Brent gesturing to the tray. And then, 'Are you happy or do we need to talk?'

'I've the Brussels memo.'

'OK, I'll be another half-hour. Let's do it then.'

There was a ritual to the exchange, and Stephen amended his earlier doubts: the man's early starts were genuine.

Brent poured juice and fresh coffee, pointed to the basket saying, 'Help yourself if you want,' and continued.

'I'm telling you everything,' he said. 'Everything I remember. Once I've told you, I want it to be over. I may want a favour one day, too, but we can worry about that when the time comes.'

Stephen reached for a croissant, broke off a piece.

'You haven't told me much yet,' he said. 'At least, not much I didn't know, or that isn't just wallpaper.'

Brent disregarded the sudden irritation in Stephen's voice and said evenly, 'I'm trying to tell it in order. It's the only way I can remember it.'

He paused long enough to make sure he had Stephen's full attention, and said, 'Now, let me tell you about the shooting and about how your old man took off with the money.'

He paused again – this time to enjoy the expression on Stephen's face.

Kenyon, he said, had been shot one night at the club, late, after it had closed. Brent had not managed to gather the detail until weeks later. Even then it had been sketchy. A gunman had hijacked a chauffeur who called at the club each morning to collect the greeter. 'There are three stories – take which you like. The gunman was going to hit Barton. He was going to shoot the greeter (though, if he was, why not wait until they were alone in the car)? He was going to shoot anyone he found. Whichever, it was your old man who got in the way.' Judging by the length of his absence ('They whisked him off to the country,') the wound must have been 'medium serious'.

'That's when I guess he got the idea,' went on Brent. 'Mind you, I'm only guessing here . . . He could have been planning to rob the club before. Something tells me he wasn't, that this was it. You know . . .' (his voice became confiding) '. . . you know how your life can change in five seconds – it's one of the truths you learn as you get older . . . I reckon your old dad's life changed in that moment. I see him like a drowning man having everything flash before him . . .'

Brent stopped, laughed, suddenly embarrassed at his own self-revelation.

'What the fuck? I'm making it up. Maybe I should be writing this story. Let me stick to what I know as fact. So he got shot. He was back in the club after nine, ten weeks – don't take that for gospel, my memory's not that good. I got reports he was quiet, withdrawn at first. I thought again about trying to recruit him. Then I heard he and the Americans were acting more buddy-buddy, as though getting shot had put him on the team, and I forgot it – and, to tell you the truth, him.'

The next he had heard that interested him was when Kenyon went missing. 'A lot of information came in then, but it was all messy and mixed up, and it wasn't for months that I got a picture. To be honest, I'd got other worries by then. I'd been moving in other directions.'

What he learned, it emerged, was that Kenyon had vanished with around one hundred and fifty thousand pounds that had been in a safety-deposit box en route for the US. Weeks later, Barton too disappeared, back to the United States, reportedly in disgrace.

What had happened to Kenyon, he had never heard. As far as he knew, he had escaped. He had never heard that they had caught him – but then he was outside such things now.

As for Barton, he had heard things over the years. He had been very sick and then, thought Brent, had recovered. Where he was now, he had no idea.

'In his grave, I suppose. He wasn't a young man.'

And the greeter, Hunter?

'Dead too, I'd think. Should be easy for you to check.'

The door opened. The secretary. 'You said thirty minutes.'

'Mr Kenyon's just leaving.'

Brent escorted him to the lift, accompanied him down to the street. 'You know where I am if I can help you again,' he said. Then he patted Stephen's arm. 'On something else, though,' he said, 'OK? I'm a businessman now. Not Jesse James.'

The searchers had left the apartment surprisingly tidy.

Drawers had been left open, the lock of a filing cabinet had been snapped, clothes and papers had been pawed through. But whoever had carried out the search had done no more than was necessary to his purpose. There was no sense of vandalism, no lingering aura of unsprung hate and fury. Stephen, standing in the doorway of his bedroom surveying the scene, knew that any detective would have taken one look and muttered, 'Professionals'. Spoken with a grudging admiration and an implied warning: such men did not leave traces – hardly worth searching for prints.

Which was one reason why, even before he found that nothing was missing, Stephen decided not to call the police.

He was still straightening up, trying to obliterate the intrusion, when Jessica telephoned him.

'Have you seen the *Evening Standard*?' Her voice was shrill and emotional.

He had not.

She read it aloud. The item was brief.

The home of an ex-police sergeant Stanley Fisher had been destroyed in a fire in Devon. Police had found a body, believed to be his. Foul play was not suspected. The cottage was old and a wiring fault was thought to be responsible.

The story merited six inches on page eight and only then because the local journalist who had filed to the Press Association had said that Fisher was an ex-Metropolitan police officer.

The cremation, ten days later, was attended by three people apart from the undertaker and a resident jobbing clergyman: a woman from the village who (it emerged) had fetched Fisher's shopping, a neighbouring smallholder who had been worried no one at all would attend. And Stephen.

The woman disappeared immediately after the service. Without speaking, the smallholder and Stephen both made for the nearest pub where they drank Scotch for half an hour.

Afterwards, Stephen had his taxi make a detour to the cottage before continuing to the station. It was gutted, a mere skeleton. He remembered the gas cylinders, the cans of fuel in the garage. It would have gone up fast.

He walked through the ruins, the smell of ash and smoke still heavy.

The walls of the utility room still stood, although the roof had gone and it was now open to the sky. A beam had collapsed across the floor. The blackened freezer cabinet was still in place, too old,

282

too damaged to be worth moving. Briefly, Stephen wondered what would happen to the site. Would it be left derelict, the ruins left to be eaten by the land? Or was some estate agent even now penning a description of 'Idyllic building plot, away from it all but within a mile of village'.

Stephen tried moving the freezer, a tough task at any time, but now the fire had buckled one side of it, shifting its weight, making a difficult job virtually impossible. He had decided he might as well take the file. He had notes. But no point leaving it here. It was no good to Fisher now. And if they developed the land, he didn't want anyone digging it up. It would still be in its hiding place. Or most of it would. Inadvertently, he had taken the blurred, and useless, intelligence file photograph of his father back to London with him. It had got caught up in his own papers. Not that it was any good.

He finally realised that he needed help to shift it. The cab-driver was curious but willing and, more important, used to lifting. 'I dropped something in here last time I came,' explained Stephen. 'Thought I'd have one last try at finding it.' An obvious lie, but the best he could do.

They moved it a few feet, and Stephen pretended to search.

The driver made sorry-we-did-our-best noises and went outside to wait. Stephen quickly prised up the loose floor-board.

He had had a bad gut feeling since the break-in, but it was still a shock.

The hiding place was empty.

Fisher's stolen file had gone.

CHAPTER NINETEEN

At 2 a.m. the morning after the funeral, too full of thought to sleep, Stephen tried to review the previous few days – and to assess what he had learned.

It had certainly been eventful, he concluded wryly as he fixed a drink. Reading two illegally borrowed files while he sat in Jarvis's car. The discovery that Fisher had stolen documents. A session with a tycoon who had once been a crook.

And the claim that his father had gone on the run with one hundred and fifty thousand pounds – a sum equivalent to around one million pounds in today's terms. Enough to go anywhere. Live without working for the rest of his life.

But where? With that kind of cash, South America or Australia were obvious places. Nearer home, Germany was a possibility: by all accounts, he spoke the language well; he had a number of contacts. Stephen imagined that in the mid-sixties Germany was still in a state of some flux. But could a man have settled there without too many questions being asked? Stephen decided he would seek advice from an old friend, Nick Benson, the paper's European correspondent who worked out of Germany.

More to the immediate point, though, who had broken into his flat? A casual burglar? Unlikely – nothing had been taken. His father's old friends, alerted to his activities? Another search by intelligence, this time illegal? Perhaps less in the hope of finding anything than in warning him they had not lost interest? For some reason, he found himself remembering the MI5 man who had been on the search following publication of his story. (Christ! *That* seemed years ago now!) If Stephen had not been so preoccupied, he would have tried to check him out. It should not be hard – the man's purple birthmark was memorable. Always best to know the opposition.

More important still, what had really happened at Fisher's cottage? Was it really an accident as the police had quickly concluded? Fisher could have removed the file from its hiding place to re-read yet again. Then, unprotected, it would simply have perished in the flames.

Yet, if so, how had Fisher managed to move the freezer by himself? And what about the metal box in which the file had been stored? That would have survived the flames. It had not been in the hiding place. Nor had it been found anywhere else in the ruins – Stephen had checked with the fire brigade.

He had no real doubt. Fisher had been killed, and the file stolen. It was not surprising that the police had come to a different conclusion – what had happened had seemed so obvious to them that no one had bothered to look hard.

When, finally, Stephen fell asleep, his head was jangling with a score of questions.

He woke an hour later, wet with sweat, his mind absolutely clear.

There were just three questions that mattered.

If Fisher had been killed, why?

It could only be because of the file.

But why *now*? The file had been hidden in the cottage for two decades.

Again, Stephen had the explanation. Whoever had killed Fisher had only just discovered the file's existence and whereabouts.

But how?

There was only one answer.

Stephen swung himself out of bed: impossible to sleep any more.

Apart from Fisher, only two people had known about the file.

Him. And Jessica.

There was no reply from Jessica's London number. She had told him the name of the school of journalism, and he telephoned under a pretext but was told she had called in sick.

At four she telephoned, excited.

'Where are you?' he said, worried and angry.

'I've found him,' she said.

'Who?' His mind was still full of Fisher's death.

'Raoul Hunter. He's alive. I have his address.'

His reaction deflated and puzzled her.

'Have you told anyone else?'

'Of course not.' Not understanding, unsure whether to be offended.

'Where are you?'

She was in the South Bank theatre and gallery complex. He joined her there twenty-five minutes later. She was in the coffee lounge on level two, looking out over the Thames, eating sandwiches and drinking milk.

'I couldn't wait,' she said, taking another bite. 'Starving. No time for lunch.'

She was flushed with the excitement of success. It made him force back the question he wanted to ask her. He realised that she was waiting for him to prompt.

'Come on then,' he said, joining in the game. 'Give. Where is he? How did you find out?'

She produced a notebook, made him sit through the story of her search. She had first examined the files of the British Film Institute, found nothing useful, but had enlisted the support of one of the staff. From her account, the man had noticed her exasperation, had left his desk and volunteered his help. Then for over an hour he had made a succession of telephone calls. She told it as though such help was simply a due.

Watching her, face and movements full of youthful animation, Stephen could imagine the man being drawn, persevering in his enquiries in order to keep her with him and to win her admiration. He interrupted her.

'Was he young, old?'

Puzzled. 'Neither. Like you.' That hurt. And then, 'Youngish,' which made him feel childishly good.

'Did he ask you out?'

Puzzled again, but impatient this time to continue. 'He asked if I went to the cinema much, but I said I didn't live in London. Can I tell you now?'

'OK. I'm sorry.'

The man had finally had success with a call to France. She noted his surprise, smiled and elaborated.

'He was a bit worried about calling, but I told him to charge it to my telephone chargecard.'

'And did he?'

'He said, what the hell, the BFI could afford it, and it was a chance to practise his French anyway . . .' She smiled, and he realised she was trying to impress him and that she was also telling him that she knew why the man had gone to such lengths for her. He realised she was sending him a message about her desirability, and it unnerved him. He feigned impatience.

'So?'

She explained that, in France, apparently, there was a cult following for Hunter's films. Several years before there had been a special showing of them which he had attended. The man who had been telephoned had arranged the event, and, as it emerged, had kept in touch with Hunter.

He had given Hunter's address without hesitation, pleased that at last the British were catching up with French cultural taste.

Jessica pushed her notebook across the table. She had devoted a fresh page to the address. It was written in studiously neat capital letters.

Apartment 105, Yaacov House, Herbert Samuel Esplanade, Tel Aviv.

Hunter was living in Israel.

It was easy to be fulsome. It was a find, and one he had not expected. Before they left, though, he had to ask the question he had been holding back.

The answer was the one his gut instinct had told him to expect. Jessica did not realise why he had asked, just looked puzzled. He did not tell her.

It was the first time he had spoken to Pamela since the night she had come to his flat.

'It's important I see you,' he had said over the telephone.

Her voice was cold, dismissive. 'I don't think we've anything to discuss.'

Whatever had brought her to his bed that night had been purged. She thought he was trying to resurrect something between them and was making it clear not only that it was over, but that she would have preferred it had never happened.

'Not *that*,' he said, using shorthand he knew she would understand. 'I think you've got something to tell me. I don't want to sound threatening, but I could just write what I know. The first you'd see of it would be in print. I don't think either you or your husband would like that.'

'I told you your proprietor is a friend. Besides, there's nothing.'

He could tell from her voice that the words were forced. She could not risk calling his bluff. He waited, silent, until she added, 'All right. But a few minutes, and only because of your father.'

Now, four hours later, he faced her. She had opened the door herself. There were no sounds within the house. He guessed she had sent the help away on a pretext.

She wore black jeans, a white shirt, a scarf at the throat. Her perfume was heavy. She led him into a room he had not seen before, a small library, walls warm with leather-bound books. Decanters of sherry, port and brandy stood on one of the two writing tables. It was, he guessed, a room for impressing rather than reading. Her use of it now was calculated.

She took a cigarette from a silver box, lit it with a Dunhill lighter, and smoked with the jerkiness of someone who indulged rarely. She was playing a part, and he wondered if she knew exactly what he wanted.

He used the silence to make her speak first.

'I haven't long,' she said.

It was an odd experience: facing a woman who had come to his bed, fucked him with hardly a word, and who now acted as though nothing had happened. He had already decided, before all this, that the man she had sunk down on was not him but the ghost of Michael Kenyon. The words she had been murmuring must have been a pet name for him. Kenyon had gone without any farewell. This had been her goodbye. An eerie thought.

Nevertheless, despite it, despite his preoccupation with Fisher's death, he felt an unbidden surge of desire.

Lust and anger merged. He wanted to tear her clothes from her, rape her, hurt her.

A tight lump formed in his stomach, his hands began to sweat, his throat felt constricted and when he tried to swallow spittle he could not.

She stood motionless about a body's length away from him, her eyes, deep but expressionless, fixed on him. Slowly, sensually, she lifted her cigarette with exaggerated movement, and then sucked deep on it before exhaling incredibly slowly.

It was theatrical but unbelievably erotic. She knew what he was thinking, he told himself. She knew, and she wanted it.

He took a step forward. It was an effort, like wearing a lead boot.

She did not move.

Another step, and this time her mouth relaxed into the bare touch of a smile.

Encouragement? *Come on, baby, you're almost there . . .*

He stopped. His mind took the look, analysed it, registered it as 'Triumph'. It broke the spell. He swallowed hard, breathed deeply, returned from somewhere he had never been before.

For a few seconds, he told himself later, he had tasted his father's madness for her. If his father had run, there had to be many reasons. But his doomed relationship with Pamela had to be one of them. Now he could feel why. It was not a feeling Stephen had ever had touch him before. His one deep relationship, with Tarlach, had been one of lightness, of contentment, of gaiety, of freedom from being driven.

She sensed the change in him, half-turned and stabbed out the cigarette.

'Well?' she said. Matter-of-fact now, anxious to get it over.

'It's about the search for my father,' he said. 'Jessica told you we'd been down to Devon. That I'd spoken to an ex-policeman called Fisher. You may remember him.' His eyes bored into her face.

She looked as though she might speak, and he raised his hand.

'Let me finish,' he said. 'I don't want conversation from you, just facts. Fisher told me things, showed me a file he'd kept hidden for years. He was a bit mad, I guess, didn't know what to do but couldn't give it up. Then I came along . . .'

He reached into his side pocket for the clipping of the *Evening Standard* story about Fisher's death and placed it on the table in front of her.

'Look at it,' he said.

She took it and read, again no expression.

'So? He had an accident. Things happen.' The hardness was not forced. He detected years of surviving and winning. Christ! She was like a cat; she gave nothing of herself away.

'It wasn't an accident. Someone found him in bed, stuck a pillow over his face. They already knew where to find the file. Then they

289

torched the place.' He lied: 'The police have already reopened the case. They've already found the fire was started deliberately and the wiring fixed to make it look accidental. They're exhuming the body. I don't know what they expect to find – there wasn't much left, but it's incredible what they can deduce these days.'

'So? What's this to do with me?' Despite the toughness, he sensed the ripple of fear.

'So you killed him. Not directly, but that doesn't matter. You killed him anyway. Jessica told you about our visit and what we'd seen, and you told someone else. What I want to know is, why? Who did you tell?'

She did not deny it. She moved effortlessly into another role. From mistress of the house she became frail woman forced to do man's bidding through fear. She cried first, and then held on to him, and finally collapsed into a chair.

'Would you give me a brandy,' she said.

He poured, and expected her to toy with the glass, use it as prop for the role. But she drained it, coughed and asked for more. Her face had crumpled and she had aged ten years.

She told it quietly and when she had finished he believed her, perhaps not every detail, but the overall story. After Kenyon's disappearance, she had received a visit from Barton. He had told her that he was convinced Kenyon was alive; either she had helped and connived or she knew something. He had threatened her, told her he would give her a week to think and he would come back – and not alone. She had waited, frightened, not knowing what to do. She had considered going to the police, but never seriously – Barton had anticipated that and had warned her. First, the police would have no proof, and second, he would be told – and she would suffer. In any event, he had never returned.

Through friends who knew the club, she had heard that Barton had left. Nothing had happened then for four years. In the meantime, she had remade her life (her words) including remarrying, and soon after that giving birth to Jessica.

One morning, when Jessica was out being walked by the nanny, Pamela had received a telephone call. The caller said he was a doctor at the local hospital. She should get there immediately: her daughter had been admitted after a bad road accident and was in intensive care, her life in the balance.

Still in her housecoat, Pamela drove there crazed. She rushed into the Casualty Department – and straight into a Kafkaesque situation: no one knew about the accident. Finally, a doctor gave her Valium, and she and a policeman returned to the house.

Although the nanny and Jessica should have returned by this time, they were still not back. The policeman was calling in to organise a search when they arrived at the door – safe and unconcerned. They were late because one of the roads they walked was closed off; they had been forced to make a detour.

A sick joke, said the policeman. And then, soon after, he discovered that the road closure was not the work of the authorities: the signs had been stolen from a site elsewhere and erected by 'a person or persons unknown'. That night an inspector called at the house and asked Chitty whether he had any enemies. Police surveillance was organised; a security company checked and strengthened the locks and alarms; a guard was employed to accompany the nanny and Jessica on walks.

After a while, when nothing happened, surveillance was lifted, security was relaxed. To the police and to her husband it remained a mystery. Both suspected it might be some client or competitor from the past although her husband could not understand why. Equally, the threat could have been a softening up prior to a blackmail attempt that had never been followed through (as to why that should be so, there were many theories, none of them wholly convincing, but all possible – ranging from the criminals having been caught for some other crime to them finding an easier target).

Finally, there was agreement that they would never know what had happened. But Pamela knew, and it was confirmed when she received a telephone call summoning her to a meeting. The tap was off the telephone by then, but in any event nothing was said that was remotely sinister. Just something about Mr Barton being sorry he'd never come back to her as he had promised, but the caller was a friend and was passing by and could he invite her to lunch.

When she arrived at the restaurant there were, in fact, two of them, one English, one American, both middle-aged, well-dressed, respectable, professional-looking.

They had heard about the fright she had had. A terrible thing. Just showed you what a dreadful world it could be. One second someone could be alive, the next dead. One moment, a mother could be happy, the next stricken with grief. Still, that was by the way. Nothing to do with their visit. They just wanted to let her know that Mr Barton was still interested in her ex-husband. Had she heard anything? Was she sure? They had ways of checking. They heard things. Phones got tapped. People got followed.

If it had not been for the incident involving Jessica, Pamela would have found it laughable. Instead, she strove to convince them that she knew nothing, had heard nothing since Kenyon had vanished. They did know things: that Fisher had contacted her; what was that about? Finally, blank-faced about whether they believed her or not, they had left, giving her a card with a name and number.

Over the years the phone calls and the meetings had been repeated. The men had changed, the number she was told to call had altered. At first, it had been every year. Then the gaps had become longer and longer. More recently there had been only telephone calls.

Until a few days ago.

Again, two men. One of them the Englishman she remembered from the first visit. Much older, of course, but unmistakably the same.

She had gone to the meeting incredulous that the whole subject was not long over, dead, buried. And she was no longer so afraid. Jessica was a grown woman, or at least a grown girl. She herself was now a woman of powerful position.

They had some photographs of her, they said, taken long ago admittedly, but not pictures they thought she would like anyone to see. (She stared at him defiantly, daring him to react as she told him this.)

The son was buzzing around like a mad bee, they said. And Jessica was involved too. What was going on? That's all she had to find out. The photographs would then be destroyed.

Pamela's voice was so small now that Stephen had to move closer to hear. 'How would I know? I asked them. How could I be certain?

'One, the Englishman, just shrugged. I couldn't – but if I didn't find out anything, I could be sure copies would be posted to a few important people.'

She had bought time, she said, by saying she would see what she could do. She knew that whatever she did, the threat would remain; she was not foolish enough to believe blackmailers went away.

She convinced herself that her husband would understand: it *had* been a long time before and her background was no secret to him. Best then to tell him, to bring in the police, to fix another meeting, let the men be caught in the act.

Two days later a Recorded Delivery envelope arrived for her. One of the photographs together with a typed note. It said a dozen copies were already in envelopes. One hint she was not co-operating and they would be posted.

Then Jessica had returned home and without prompting had wanted to talk about the search.

When the men telephoned, Pamela had told them what she had learned. She had persuaded herself it did not seem much. A visit to an old policeman they must have known about, a file that was nearly a quarter of a century old . . .

'I'm sorry,' she said when she had finished. 'I didn't think, I didn't know.'

She reached out for his hand, and he held it for a while.

There was no feeling except regret and sadness. No vibes, no stirring. Her face was still aged, her body crumpled with years.

He wanted to feel something. Even sorrow. But he could not.

He left a few minutes later, and she did not move.

CHAPTER TWENTY

The temperature outside was in the low eighties, but inside the apartment the heating was switched on, making the room feel like an orchid house or a Turkish bath. Through the window that stretched the full length of the room, Stephen looked down ten storeys to the sunbathers on the beach. Only a naval launch on patrol on the horizon showed that this was Israel.

Jessica, in a plain shirtwaisted dress, sat in a bentwood rocker, looking relaxed and very, very young. A young man, who had admitted them, stood near the door, making no pretence at not watching them.

There were two such men, Jessica had told him. She had managed to make direct contact with Hunter the day before, after two days in which the American had refused to come to the telephone or return Stephen's calls.

'Let me try,' she had said. 'He was big in pictures, right? He won't be able to resist a star-struck little girl who's been reading all about him at the British Film Institute.'

Stephen, smiling at her tough-guy talk, had been sceptical, but what was there to lose? He had already found out that Hunter rarely left the apartment.

Jessica had returned triumphant, reported that she had simply turned up at the apartment block, sent up a note, answered some questions on the house phone and had been admitted.

'Top floor, apartment 105. I only went into one room. Enormous, looking out over the sea. But hot, you wouldn't believe it. And, oh, there are two kind of nurse figures, but they're more like bodyguards.'

'And Hunter?'

'He's nice. But *really* old. Not just because he's eighty-five – I've got an aunt who's ninety-two and she's not *really* old. He's so

294

frail they have to half-carry him.' She had shuddered theatrically, and she could have been a twelve-year-old telling him about a horror movie. 'If you told me he'd died and they'd managed to bring him back, I'd believe you.'

She had talked to Hunter for an hour, about his films and about his admirers – she had absorbed a lot of background detail during her BFI visit. What Stephen had not known was that, curious, she had also obtained two of his old films on video and watched them.

'He really came alive.' She'd giggled. 'I shouldn't have said that – you know what I mean.' And then to soften it, 'I liked him.'

After about an hour, one of the nurse-guards had entered the room, reminded Hunter gently but firmly he should not tire himself, and gestured to Jessica that she should leave.

Hunter had told him quietly but surprisingly firmly, 'Ten minutes. Just ten more minutes.'

And then, once the nurse had left the room, he had leaned forward in his chair, switched on the old screen-Hunter smile, and said, 'Now, young lady, tell me why you really came,' and she had.

The man entering the room now was Hunter.

Jessica's description had prepared Stephen, but not enough. Hunter walked without help, but only just. He moved with breath-catching slowness, a leg sliding forward stiffly like a badly controlled puppet, and then the whole body resting before the other limb moved. One arm hung limp and the other fluttered jerkily to help him keep his balance. One side of his body remained rigid, forcing the other half to twist with each movement forward. He was skeletal thin, and his eyes were dark deep holes. His slow advance towards an elaborate special chair was followed equally slowly, as though in mime, by one of his nurse-guards with hands outstretched, ready to steady or catch Hunter if he fell.

The other nurse-guard moved in to help as Hunter neared the chair, but Hunter managed alone – with a quick twisting movement he sank back on the bottom-high seat. He pushed a button on the arm, and the seat slid down.

Stephen took a pace forward, ready to speak, but the two nurse-guards had moved in well-practised choreography. One swung out a tray fixed to an arm of the chair, the other placed on it a pair of spectacles, a glass already filled with what looked like plain water, a remote control which might have operated anything from the blinds to a concealed television, and a small pad with a gold pencil.

As one, the men pushed forward two chairs into a position four to five feet in front of Hunter but to one side, adding to Stephen's suspicion that the American had had a stroke and was part paralysed.

One of the men nodded to Stephen that he and Jessica should take the seats. As they left, one spoke, softly and with great formality. 'It's ten after eleven now. At noon Mr Hunter has to take his medication. Please don't tire him too much.'

Hunter appeared to have forgotten them as they took their chairs. He stared down at a fingernail, rubbed it, twisted it so it caught the light, totally absorbed. Nearer, Stephen saw that the mane of white hair was a wig, the tan was make-up.

When Hunter finally raised his head, the movement seemed as slow and painful as the walking.

'So you're the boy,' he said. 'Your father was a good man. But for him I'd be long dead, not sitting here now waiting for the Big Man to come get me.'

His voice was still deep, firm, unmistakably that of an actor. Stephen looked away and he could imagine a young man sitting there.

'Do you smoke? Go ahead if you want. I like the smell. Can't smoke myself any more. Can't drink either. Can't do anything. Can't even die. Wake up each morning, open my eyes, stare up and see this mark on the ceiling and know I'm still alive.'

Then, without changing tone. 'What happened with your father's the only thing I ever felt bad about. One morning there's going to be no staring at the mark on the ceiling. Just the Big Man.' He tried to laugh and it became a cough. 'I'm a hangover. Do you believe in hell? I did as a kid, and then it went away, but now I *know* there's one. You know what they say, once a Catholic . . . ?'

So that was the reason Hunter was prepared to talk. He had returned to his Church, guilt-laden and desperate for absolution. Hunter raised his eyes. 'You think Mike'll be waiting for me, that he'll be in hell too? I think he sure will be unless they've got no booze down there. Heck, he was some drinker, your father.'

The tone was jokey, but Stephen sensed it hid a real fear of damnation.

'Tell me,' said Stephen.

Hunter beckoned him closer and Stephen moved forward to the edge of his seat and then, when he saw the American was reaching out, he took his hand. Cold, skin hard and scaly like dried bark.

'This is my confession,' said Hunter, staring into Stephen's face with those dark sockets, confirming the journalist's suspicions. 'You're the priest. You can give my absolution. Make it OK for when I meet the Big Man.'

It began, Hunter said, after Kenyon got shot. Barton had already arranged that Kenyon's name appeared on documents allowing access to the safety-deposit box where the skim paused on its way to the US. He had done so on the pretext that Kenyon's name was essential to satisfy the façade that the club was English owned. In reality, his intention was that any suspicion Barton had been creaming off extra money for himself could be deflected: Barton would make sure any blame was shifted to Kenyon.

But by the time Kenyon was shot, Barton was already under suspicion. Not from Philadelphia, which was the city to which he reported and to which he was directly responsible, but from another Mafia don. This man, who had points in the London operation, had become suspicious during a visit to London to take a look at his investment.

That time Barton had considered having Kenyon killed and faking his death to look like suicide. Money stolen from the club would then be found hidden in Kenyon's apartment.

Barton delayed though. He was not a man to panic. He had no qualms about hitting Kenyon, he just wanted to be sure it was necessary. And there were two big problems. First, Barton knew the Brits were looking for excuses to clamp down – no knowing what chain of events Kenyon's death at that time could set off: his 'suicide' could trigger uncontrollable press publicity for the club. Second, maybe more important, the faked suicide and the hidden money would be a confession that the club had been ripped off, and under Barton's eyes. However cleverly he handled it, Barton would not be able to stop the suspicious family putting in its own man. Whatever happened, Barton's days of ripping off money would be ended.

So he waited. And he was proved right – his friends in Philadelphia decided, in the jargon, to back him one thousand per cent. The heat was off.

For a time.

Then came the shooting. Hunter *had* been the target. That much the gunman had admitted. Why Hunter? The gunman didn't know. Just as he did not know who wanted Hunter dead – nor the identity of the man who had approached him.

The shooting had nothing to do with Barton's long-term problem. But it started him thinking again. The heat could be back on any time. All the more reason for taking as much money as he could while he could. But was there any use to be made of the shooting? Reluctantly, he decided not.

A plastic surgeon – the only doctor Barton could trust – treated Kenyon. One of the plastic surgeon's close colleagues was a psychiatrist, with whom the surgeon insisted legitimate prospective patients should discuss psychological implications before he operated. This, Hunter thought, was less for medical reasons than as a gimmick to help justify the surgeon's ultra-high fees.

The surgeon had been intrigued by Kenyon's post-trauma reactions, and on one occasion he had asked his psychiatrist colleague to sit in. Barton had been furious when he found out – but, then, fascinated by the information that emerged. Without detailed tests, it could only be a provisional diagnosis, he was told, but Kenyon was almost certainly suffering from alcoholic paranoia.

Stephen realised that the diagnosis must have been the subject of the tape transcript he had read in his father's intelligence file. What had Poulton said to the man believed to be Barton during the taped telephone conversation? Something about his colleague having attended the consultation and thinking that Poulton's diagnosis was right?

In Kenyon's case, Hunter continued, the paranoia took a classic form – the conviction that people were after him. It had been fed by his marriage break-up, even more so by the shooting. Again, it could only be an informed guess on so short an observation, but it seemed as though, like many paranoics, Kenyon would continue to behave in a normal manner outside the area of his delusion.

Barton pretended to be uninterested, but he had been given the germ of an idea which he began to put into practice. What if he fed Kenyon's paranoia, scared him into making a run for it? For Barton it would be the ultimate alibi for the missing money. In the meantime, he would milk the casino for all he could.

Using Hunter, he planted the idea on Kenyon that his days were numbered; that he was being set up by Barton as a sacrifice.

Next, Barton laid various trails to lead Kenyon to finding the papers that would reveal details of the safety-deposit box. They soon saw that Kenyon had bitten. From then on, it had been a matter of feeding his paranoia, tightening pressure until he cracked and ran.

At last, almost to Barton's surprise, he had done just as they had wanted.

By this time, Hunter was back in the United States, more worried about other matters (although he was not directly involved, a periodic battle between rival dons was under way). He did not say, but it was obvious to Stephen that Hunter must have been involved with Barton in his theft, at least in the earliest stages. From his tone, it seemed certain, though, that he had gone along with the plan to frame Kenyon after the shooting only with reluctance – and then, as he now pleaded, only because he had always believed it crazy and unlikely to work. He thought that in practice any extra pressure would make Kenyon drink more and more – and then simply quit, unable to take it any longer.

He had, Hunter assured Stephen, wanted that. Kenyon had saved his life – even though he'd done it drunk and by accident. More, he liked the man. They were both to some extent outsiders: Kenyon in the tight community of the gaming club, Hunter in England. Both, though they did not show it, felt vulnerable.

'Hell,' said Hunter, 'I'm getting too deep. I guess I just liked the guy.'

When Kenyon did make his break, though, he surprised everyone – not because he ran, but because he managed to disappear.

That was not in the scenario.

'He fixed it better than anyone expected. The wiseguys tried for a long time to pick up his trail. I heard they found he'd built up at least one false ID – they backtracked him to that one after checking around safety-deposit boxes. I heard he'd made it real tough: not one photograph of him left behind. Nor any papers that mattered.'

Barton, far from being let off the hook by Kenyon's flight, found himself under new suspicion. Surely, argued his enemies, Kenyon must have had inside help.

And then the missing Kenyon delivered his blow.

Out of his paranoia he had decided to get Barton, whom he must have seen as his main enemy.

The day he had vanished, he had posted two identical pieces of paper, one to Philadelphia, the other to Miami.

The papers contained only dates and figures. But to anyone with inside information, it was obvious what they were: details of the casino's takes – gross, after being skimmed, and after being skimmed again by Barton personally.

Philadelphia could protect Barton partially. But some punishment had to be administered. He was recalled on a pretext. And then he was beaten. Trouble was, said Hunter, either the beating went wrong or someone deliberately interfered with the orders: what should have been a painful lesson got out of hand. Barton survived – but only just, and with severe internal injuries that resulted, among other things, in Barton having to have a colostomy, an artificial anus, and in having to use a kidney machine.

Hunter confessed – confirming Stephen's earlier suspicion – that he had only escaped because he was already back in the States, having been barred from re-entering the UK.

All this came out on the second and third visits that Stephen made.

Surprisingly, after the beating Barton had not only survived physically, but in time he had even prospered. He had set himself up in a cross between a home and a clinic and with nothing to do except hate and scheme he had become an increasingly sought after adviser and, then, arbiter of Mob disputes.

Hunter, himself, had long ago drifted away. He had married for the fifth time at seventy-two a Jewess, and moved to Israel. She was dead now. It was after her death that he had returned to Catholicism – 'Where better, this is where it was all at?' He still had occasional visitors. Barton, he thought, was still alive – at least, no one had told him he was dead. Last time he had heard of him, he was still like a spider at the centre of a web of evil.

'Every time he needed to take a pee or a shit he thought of Mike and what the fucker did to him. You wonder why he never let it go?'

Then, on his fourth visit, Stephen was told that Hunter was at the hospital. No, no emergency, just regular treatment.

The next day Hunter was low. His voice had joined the rest of him. Stephen had to lean forward, strain to catch the words. Nevertheless, the American insisted on continuing.

'I want you to know it all,' he said.

There was not much more. But Hunter had kept back a surprise right until the end.

'The bag,' he said. 'Mike took the bag full of money. That wasn't planned. Barton thought he'd transfer it down in the vault of the deposit company. Stick it in a hold-all. Made sense.'

That had been the last part of Barton's plan. The case was fitted with a security device. Unless the catches were worked in a specific way, a dye device was triggered, staining the notes irrevocably, making them worthless. The explosion would also have brought a guard running – thus setting up Kenyon just as planned.

Barton had even anticipated that Kenyon, a man used to dealing with money, might have been familiar with such devices. For that reason, Barton had had a second trigger fitted. Even if the case was opened properly, taking out money would release pressure on a spring, activating the dye. He had, effectively, sacrificed the money to fix Kenyon. Chances were, said Hunter, even though Kenyon got away with the bag, he ended up with a load of worthless paper.

'The poor bastard fucked up to the end.'

CHAPTER TWENTY-ONE

Stephen had seen little of Jessica for three days. Having found Hunter and persuaded him to co-operate, she had been hurt when Stephen told her he wanted to talk with the American alone.

He had tried to appease her: Hunter would play up to her youth and beauty like the old actor he was, he argued. And two people would tire the sick man more quickly.

'So you want me to fly home?'

'No, of course not. Stay. I *need* you here in case he's difficult – he could change his mind about talking. But not at the meetings, that's all I ask.'

So she had stayed. But to show her resentment, she had kept out of his way. Each day, early, she had left the hotel to explore like any other tourist – not just Tel Aviv, but the rest of the country on tour buses. Each night she had returned late. They had talked – but on house phones as though they were divided by a continent and not just a few rooms.

An uneasy relationship. But one that suited him and the moment. Certainly, he wanted her to stay. She might be useful. Her presence was a precaution. And he owed her – though, in time, he would have found Hunter himself. But he felt easier with her at arm's length. He could concentrate better.

The truth was, her presence continued to disturb him. She triggered a host of conflicting emotions. They were complex beyond any he had felt before. The simplest was that she touched feelings that he had not felt for over a dozen years. But beyond that she was Pamela's daughter. Pamela, loved by his father, briefly his own bedmate, the woman who could almost have been his mother. This girl resembled her in more than looks: when he was with her, he could have been with Pamela. Yet his father had been married to Pamela: so Jessica could easily have been his own sister.

Because of their respective ages, she was young enough to be his daughter.

It was like the families of painted Russian dolls, one inside another. All different and all the same.

Stephen, who except for one all too brief period had always handled close emotions by avoiding them, just could not cope. And, especially, not now. Because the truth, whether he liked it or not, was that the search was affecting him in ways he had not foreseen. Subtly, it was changing him. His belief in absolutes – in black and white, right and wrong – was beginning to falter.

Reluctantly, he was finding himself forced to face the possibility that his belief in certainty and order was an illusion. It was the way his eleven-year-old mind had found of coping with his father's desertion and the loss of love.

After what he knew would be his last meeting with Hunter, he emerged from the American's apartment block with no idea of what he would do next.

For days he had been absorbing Hunter's story. He thought it rang true. In any event, he had to accept that he had now learned everything the American knew – or was willing to tell him. There would be no more meetings.

Hunter had made it clear his account was at an end. The nurse-guard who had seen Stephen to the door had asked, pointedly, when he was leaving the country.

'Maybe tomorrow,' Stephen had said.

And the nurse-guard had said, 'I shouldn't make it later,' neither changing his tone nor trying to look tough, which had only given his words more force.

Outside, in the early afternoon sun, Stephen walked aimlessly. There was nothing more he could do for now.

He turned off the coastal strip with its ugly concrete hotel blocks overlooking the Mediterranean. On this visit, he had seen little of Tel Aviv, but he had been here before and it was not a city he liked. It had vitality. But when you had said that, what else was there?

He took another turn north, into the jumble of twisting tiny streets. It was easy to get lost here, and he allowed himself to drift. He stopped twice, once for a beer, once at another pavement café for a meal he found he could not eat when it arrived.

He pushed it aside, and ordered another beer. It was cool under the shades and he was reluctant to leave. Mentally, he chalked up one other plus for Tel Aviv – you could sit around the cafés for hours for the price of a drink. All around, there were people reading, talking, writing letters. Seeing him alone, a group nearby tried to draw him into their conversation. He was polite but cold, and they left him alone.

Now he was beginning to feel anger at his father growing inside him. Not for leaving him and Mary – but for putting him through this search.

God, why couldn't he have been left alone? He had told Melville that he did not feel anything, and that had been true. Before this search, he'd honestly believed that his father's absence had never affected him. He'd never felt the need to rush around seeking a father substitute. Ward had been great in his growing-up years, but Stephen had never made him anything he was not. He and Katharine were people he loved who had helped him grow up until he could handle things himself.

And now . . .

And now, he did not know. Michael Kenyon was getting through to him. Whether the man was alive or not, he had become a constant presence. Shaking his innermost convictions. Rousing anger. Rekindling long-buried guilt.

Stephen could not stop thinking that he was almost exactly the age now that his father had been when he felt he had to run.

A chilling thought.

As was the sense that he was reliving his father's past. Even living in his skin: Pamela had not been making love to him, but to his father.

It was as though in uncovering his father's tracks, he was uncovering feelings of his own – feelings he had never allowed himself to acknowledge. Feelings buried so deep, it hurt physically to look at them.

There were no photographs of Kenyon – in his paranoia and his fear he had destroyed them all. And neither had Stephen asked anyone directly, 'What did he *look* like?'

But he knew there were things about them that were the same – he only had to remember Pamela's initial shock. The blue-grey of their eyes. The way they held themselves.

At one moment Hunter had interrupted a question:

'Heh, you looked just like he did then. The way you kinda

dropped your eyes for a second and then stared me right out as you got to the point. Kinda accusingly. He used to do that.'

Stephen finished his beer, and began walking again. Thoughts clattered around. He imagined Kenyon planning, plotting, scheming, not knowing he was being manipulated and that in running he was doing what Barton had wanted. And yet, having the last laugh, evading them at the moment they had expected him to be trapped. Or did he really triumph? What about the booby-trapped case? Did it work as planned? Did he lose everything? And, if he did, what of his careful schemes then?

Suddenly, Stephen realised he was thinking of it not just as a story, as an article, as part of a book – but emotionally, sympathetically, caught up in it, seeing his father's fallibility, sweating with him, suffering with him. He even found himself thinking, if my life had been like his, what would I have done?

And then he thought, what *had* he done at his own moment of truth when Tarlach had died? He had done the same thing – he had run. Not in a planned way, but then he had not had warning. Nor did he disappear. But he had no one chasing him. Because he was running from himself it had not worked. Had the same happened to his father? And had he, like Stephen with his work, then found something in which he could hide and become lost? Or had he survived only to destroy himself?

He shook himself back to the present. He found that he had returned to the hotel without noticing his path. Mid-afternoon now. A few stragglers in the bar, only the most dedicated sun-worshippers at the pool. He paused for another beer, exchanged inanities with a barman, wanting distraction.

Suddenly, he felt sick, tired, drained. He waved away the barman who was about to bring another drink and walked through to the lobby to collect his key.

Waiting, he saw Jessica's key was missing. The key tags were large, unwieldy. Unlikely she had taken it with her. Maybe she had returned early.

He took the elevator to the eighth floor. He had to pass her room on the way to his own. He stopped and tapped on the door. When she opened it, he saw she had been sitting on the balcony. An opened book and a can of Coca-Cola lay beside a canvas director's chair. She wore a floppy T-shirt over shorts. The motif on the shirt was a devil with horns and the word 'Horny'.

'Lucky it was me,' he said.

She did not reply at first and then, when he was thinking it was a stupid thing to have said, she looked down and connected and said flatly, 'Oh, I'd forgotten I'd brought it.'

He followed her inside, and she opened the mini-bar and passed him a beer.

'I think I need to get drunk,' he said.

'There's whisky,' she said, but he was already drinking the beer.

He sat on the edge of the bed and told her what Hunter had said. When he finished, he sat silent, his head bent forward. She thought he was concentrating and she said, 'So where next?'

Then she realised he was crying, softly. She watched for a while, at first unbelieving, and then uncertain, and finally tender.

'I'm sorry,' he said, embarrassed. 'The drink and the heat.'

He began to stand, but stopped when she moved beside him.

'Here,' she said, and she lifted his head and dabbed at his eyes with a tissue. Then she pulled his head on to her shoulder.

'Let it out,' she said. 'It'll do you good.'

The depth of her concern broke through, amused him. He turned to stare at her. 'Do I call you mummy?' he said.

Her eyes were green, and they pulled like the sea beneath a high cliff. He waited for her to turn her head, avert her eyes, but she stared him out. Then she kissed him, first under one eye, then the other.

'Shut up,' she said.

He reached for her, but she took his hand and placed it on her crotch.

'I'm . . .' She left it unfinished, but he could feel the bulge. 'Do you mind?'

In reply, he started to draw her close, but she broke away, stood and made for the bathroom.

'A minute,' she said. 'You've made me wait, now you can wait.'

He was still absorbing the words when she returned, and slid naked beneath the sheet. He tore off his clothes and uncovered her.

'I want to look at you,' he said.

'Not now,' she said. 'Later. Just do it. We've all day, all night.'

She splayed her legs, and he rose over her.

And then he couldn't.

'Christ!' he swore.

'What is it?' alarmed. And then, moving her hand between them to touch herself. 'Is it *this*? I've nearly finished.'

'No. It's me. I'm sorry. I don't know what it is.'

She pulled his head down on to her breast, and then she wrapped her arms around him, blotting out the light.

'Just sleep,' she said. 'Sleep. It'll be all right later.'

Sleep! his mind said. Sleep! Like hell! And yet he did, sliding into the blackness as though drugged.

When he woke, he was still lying across her, and she still held him. He felt a cool wind across his back. He moved his head, and saw the curtain billowing in the breeze. The sky was dark, although it was not yet night, and he realised that the sound he could hear was rare October rain.

He freed himself without waking her and closed the balcony doors. The road below was a streak of colours from reflected car lights and neon signs.

He walked back to the bed and saw Jessica had thrown off the cover. She lay on her back, one arm thrown behind her head. He sat and stared in the half-light, absorbing her body like scent. It was a young body: long, tight, slim. A flat belly, slightly flared hips. Her pubic hair was long and gold. He trailed a finger through it and she murmured but did not move. Her breasts were larger than he had imagined; the nipple of the left was noticeably higher than the other.

He bent to take it gently into his mouth, holding it loosely with his lips as he brushed the tip with his tongue. Her hand moved and rested on the back of his head. His lips moved to her other breast, worked down her belly, jumped to her toes which he sucked one by one. And then the insides of her legs and her thighs with the merest taste of blood and, cautiously, her sex.

She pushed her fingers hard through his hair, and then pulled on his shoulder.

'Come on,' she said.

She was very tight, and he thought it was fear and he paused but she increased the pressure of her hands on his back and thrust herself high, her legs locked behind him.

A long time afterwards, when they had slept some more, she went to the bathroom and came back with a wet cloth which she dabbed at the undersheet.

'I should have put a towel down,' she said, practical, matter-of-fact.

He reached out, pulled her back to him.

'We'll buy them a new bed,' he said.

'Let's take it home,' she said.

And then, very quietly into his ear. 'Was it all right?'

Something in her tone worried him, delayed his reply. There was no sound, but he felt the tears.

'What's the matter?' he said. 'Of course it was all right. You were wonderful.'

'Nothing's the matter,' she said, and with one swift movement she swung over him, thighs wide.

She reached and held him with her hand, eased herself down gently until only the tip penetrated her.

Her eyes were mad with laughter.

'The first time,' she said as she sank on to him, turning his insides to fire.

'The first time.'

And then when she saw the understanding dawning: 'The first time. The fucking first time. The first fucking time. The first time fucking . . .'

And she threw her head back and opened her mouth in silent laughter and he bucked his body to meet her and realised he was laughing and crying too.

CHAPTER TWENTY-TWO

They held hands the whole of the flight home.

Yet, although the touch of each other brought excitement and desire, they talked not of love but of the search for Kenyon.

It was, after all, what had brought them together. But more than that, as it had developed, it had bound them closer and closer. Jessica had seen the 'real' Stephen emerge – one known only to her. For Stephen, Jessica had become the only person other than Tarlach to whom he had ever bared raw emotions.

More practically, the search let them continue living for the moment. It pushed aside more abstract concerns, let them bind themselves together without thought of mundane practicalities that might now arise. Like, where would their relationship lead; what of the age difference; what would Pamela and Jessica's father think and do . . . ?

From Heathrow, they took a cab to Stephen's flat. When they had made love and slept, they returned to the search.

There was a message on the answerphone from Melville. He wanted a written update. He sounded relaxed, but Stephen suspected that soon he would have to justify himself.

A succession of other calls produced little in the way of information but set off yet more enquiries. He asked the paper's stringer in the Midlands to try to track down anyone who had been at the refugee home in Kenyon's village at the start of the war. He spoke to Nick Benson, the paper's German-based European correspondent who, it emerged, was due in London in two days' time, summoned to see Melville. They agreed to meet – 'Always better to talk face to face, don't you think,' Benson said. After thirty years in Europe, West and East, he worked on the assumption that his telephone was tapped routinely.

At a loss, Stephen made one more call, this time to an old

contact, a psychologist, whose help in unravelling problems he had sought before.

'Come to dinner, stay the night,' said the psychologist, Donoghue. 'It's been too long. Cissie'll be glad to see you.'

'I need advice,' said Stephen. 'And I've someone with me.'

'A woman?' said Donoghue. 'Someone special? One bed or two?'

'Yes, and yes, and one.'

'I can't wait to meet her,' said Donoghue.

'She's too young for you,' said Donoghue thirty hours later. 'How old is she? We're not helping you break the law, sleeping together, are we?'

'Shut up,' said Cissie. And to Stephen, 'He's jealous. His students have stopped fancying him, and that was the only reason he became a teacher in the first place.'

Stephen knew it was only jest – and Donoghue had waited until Jessica had gone to the bathroom – but he felt irritated. He had been unable to stop himself thinking of what he had been doing at Jessica's age. He had been at college in Columbia, a small town dominated by the Missouri University campus. As a foreigner, he had enjoyed a certain cachet. After a year in dormitory, he had moved out and he shared an apartment with two others in a ramshackle, wood-frame house that had been turned into student accommodation. Like the other journalism students, he and his flatmates stood apart from the rest of the University, seeing themselves as a little bit arty, a shade superior. Most of all they saw themselves as the one group who did *not* plan to stay in Missouri when they graduated. There was a large fraternity influence, but consciously neither he nor his flatmates joined. They regarded frats as insular – people who had swapped one family for another. People who couldn't bear to strike out and be alone.

Being alone was one thing Stephen could handle. At nineteen he had good friends, an active social life – but he had also built invisible barriers. He knew already that *never* would he allow himself to need others to be whole. He'd broken that vow once years later. He could not regret it. But look what had happened! Remembering what he had felt all those years before at college, recalling events since, accentuated the age gap between him and Jessica in a way nothing else could. It was not a good feeling.

Donoghue let him alone with his thoughts before becoming contrite. 'Cissie's right,' he said at last. 'Nothing but jealousy. She's a lovely girl and if I wasn't a happily married man I'd envy you.' He laughed. 'Mind you, careful she doesn't give you a heart attack – she's not the problem you want to discuss, I hope.'

'Everything you say is making it worse,' said Cissie. 'Take him in the study, and Jessica and I will act all prefeminist and stack the dishwasher.'

Donoghue's study was the most chaotic room Stephen had ever been inside. It was furnished with a desk and chair, and an old leather *chaise-longue*, cracked and stained with age and misuse. These stood like islands, though, in a sea of books, magazines, old newspapers, files, boxes of stationery, and items ranging from three portable typewriters to a shop-window clothes dummy, all piled haphazardly on the floor.

Donoghue found a bottle of whisky, poured two large measures, and sat on the edge of the desk.

'Take the couch if you want to unburden your soul,' he said. 'We'll play psychiatrist and patient. I need the excitement. I'm going to seed, dying with boredom. I just hope it's something to do with sex.'

Donoghue, despite his words, looked a contented man. He sat, mass of unkempt curly hair, shirt sliding out over beltless baggy cords, face flushed and beaming. Stephen had always regarded him as one of those rare people who had known what he wanted and had found it. For a moment, though, he wondered whether it was not as much a surface cover as Donoghue's stage Irishness which he adopted to hide a deep and sharp intellect.

'Just shut up and listen,' he said. 'It's serious.'

He told the story from the beginning: the discovery that his father had not died when he believed he had; the assignment from his paper; the search since. The only thing he left out was Pamela's coming to his bed, not because he wished to hide it from Donoghue but because it had no place in the main narrative.

'And that's it?' said Donoghue at the end. He had lit a pipe and the smoke hung round.

'That's it.'

'And what do you want from me? Fresh thoughts on where to go next just in case you haven't thought of them? Or advice on whether to go on with it at all?'

Stephen grinned. Donoghue had read him, as he had hoped he would.

'Both,' he said.

'OK,' said Donoghue. 'Although I'd really like to know a whole deal more, there's a lot we can deduce. The first thing you've got to remember is that what he did was a kind of suicide. That's what he was doing – killing himself, without actually pulling the trigger or putting the rope round his neck. Having said that, where it gets you I don't know.

'The second thing is how important Germany was to him. That's where, for the only time in his life, he seems to have found himself. That's what he'd want to get back to – not necessarily the place itself, but the *feel* of it. The problem is that could be almost anywhere – a place he's read about, seen in the movies, heard someone discuss. A place he felt he could make a fresh start. Be born again.

'The third thing is that he's obsessive. Lots of things you said make that obvious. We can go through them if you like. I'd need to know more to be certain, but you can be pretty sure that whatever he decided to do would have been worked out to the last degree. He'd be like an electric hare at a greyhound track – once he was running there was only one way he could go. Unless something went wrong, of course.

'And that's the fourth thing. If something did go wrong, disrupted his carefully laid plans, like, say, the money suddenly not being there, he'd be lost – I'd say he'd go running for help to someone he knew.'

He relit his pipe. 'But I imagine I'm only telling you what you've already thought. If I were you, I'd be chasing up the people he knew back in those wartime days. But you're already doing that.'

Stephen held out his glass for a refill.

He was disappointed, but what had he expected.

'You think I should go on?'

'That's up to you. Seems to me you have to.' He poured more whisky, and added, 'You care? You worry you might find him alive, and whether you can handle it?'

'For the first time, yes.' Stephen paused, debated whether to continue. Then, hesitantly, he went on, 'He's already got me hating him, being sorry for him, wanting to beg his forgiveness . . . Christ knows what.' He tailed off, tried to lighten it by knocking his forehead with his knuckles, saying, 'Thanks to him

I'm a fucking mess in here.' Then, suddenly serious again, 'I've been getting this growing sense that a part of me is missing. That I'm not only looking for him, but that I'm searching for that too. Trying to make myself whole. Does that make sense?'

'Sounds like the kind of crap us psychologists speak,' said Donoghue. 'But yes – it makes sense. You know what's happening, don't you? You should have mourned your father a long time ago when he went, and you didn't. That's why you're such an uptight bastard.'

Exactly what Katharine had told him.

'Thanks.' Stephen gave a wry grin. 'And all this *without* even finding him. Fact is that I've got a gut feeling he *is* out there. I may never find him. But if I do – do I want to?'

'No one can help you there.'

'No, you're right. I guess I just needed to bring it out into the open.'

Donoghue switched on his *bonhomie* again. 'As long as I'm some good to somebody. Let's go back to the women . . .'

And then a thought struck him.

'I'm a fool,' he said, 'and so are you. He told us something without meaning to. Remember what you said about the photographs? About how he destroyed them all? Quite deliberately. Quite obsessively.'

'Yes.' Stephen could not see what Donoghue was driving at; the significance of the destruction of the photographs was obvious, and he said it: 'He told us he was planning to disappear – he didn't want any photographs around to help the search.'

'No!' said Donoghue, impatient and excited. 'He told us more than that.' He jabbed his pipe to make the point. 'He told us that he was not going to change his appearance.

'I don't know about you, but I took it for granted all the time I was hearing the story that somewhere along the way there'd be a discreet plastic surgeon and a new Michael Kenyon . . .'

'You're right. But I still don't see.' Stephen was finding it hard to absorb the information.

Donoghue was laughing with triumph. 'You said there was one photo, the one you found in the Criminal Intelligence Branch file, but it was too blurred even to make out the features.'

'Yes,' agreed Kenyon, puzzled. He could not see where this was leading.

Donoghue was already continuing.

'Forget all this clever stuff about following up lead after lead, of trying to second guess. Remember the Gordian knot – no one could undo it, then Alexander said, "Stuff this," and just sliced through it with his sword? That's what we're going to do, Stephen my boyo, cut the bloody knot.'

They took a cab from Cambridge station. There was a Christmas tree in the forecourt, and its coloured lights flashed forlornly on and off in the murky rain.

Jessica was wearing a man's trilby hat and a Burberry; surprisingly, the outfit only accentuated her youth and femininity. She looked desirable and vulnerable and in the cab Stephen lifted her hand and kissed it gently, overcome by a wave of tenderness.

'You'll have to wait,' she whispered, misunderstanding. She had wanted them to travel the previous night, so that they could spend the night in an olde-English hotel she had found in a guidebook – 'I've always wanted to do it in a four-poster bed,' she had giggled. But Stephen had wanted to stay in London and write the memo, as much for himself as for Melville. Now, he wondered whether his priorities had been right.

The cab took the causeway across the Cam, and turned right to pass the Backs, the famous stretch where the gardens of the colleges slide down to the river. Today, the bankside greenery was a sea of mud; beyond it the twin towers of King's College were sad grey against an even sadder, wide sky.

For all its beauty, for all man had done with his wonderful building and landscaping, Stephen found the flat lands of East Anglia full of depression. He turned his eyes from the view, and was amused to see the taxi-driver was still watching them in his mirror. Even in a student town, as a couple they stood out.

Perhaps if they had been heading for a private address or one of the colleges . . . But their destination was a research centre, the Cavendish Laboratories, where Rutherford had first split the atom.

If they were lucky, one scientist there was going to take Stephen's blurred photograph and make it recognisable . . .

It was Donoghue's idea. A year or two before he had met a Cambridge physicist who had helped devise a way of improving the quality of radio astronomy pictures using a complex mathemical formula and high-speed computers. Donoghue and the physicist had both been delegates at a conference of scientists whose work had, or might have, crime-solving potential. Donoghue had done work on psychological profiling – working out from the facts of a crime the kind of person who might have committed it. The physicist, a young man called Steve Gull, Donoghue recalled, had demonstrated how his work might be adapted for forensic science. Donoghue especially remembered before-and-after pictures of a speeding car. In the first, there was nothing but blurred lines; in the second even the number plate had been readable.

Donoghue had found it so interesting that, later, he had asked his secretary to check for articles: she had quickly found one in *Nature*. Almost miraculously, Donoghue had been able to retrieve the photocopy for Stephen from among his stacks of material. 'Image reconstruction from incomplete and noisy data', it was headed, and although the text – including its mathematical equations and its examples from radio and X-ray astronomy – was beyond Stephen, he noted the claim that the technique was immediately applicable to 'virtually any type of optical image processing'.

Donoghue had reached the physicist on the telephone, talked him into helping, and then set off the previous afternoon with the photograph. 'He can't guarantee anything,' said Donoghue. 'It depends how bad it is, he can't do magic. That said, if it's normal camera shake or bad focusing . . . Anyway, he's willing to try.'

Donoghue was with Gull when they arrived. He must have felt at home in the organised chaos of the room. Slides, books and the innards of electronic apparatus looked as though they had been grabbed and tossed aside by an intruder. There were five computers, one of them on the floor. Gull himself had the keen youthful boffin look captured in a thousand Hollywood movies.

They fetched coffee from a communal kitchen, and Gull explained that they had waited for Stephen's arrival. 'We thought you'd want to be here,' he said.

Gull looked into another room on their way back. A half-dozen young men were working at computer terminals. 'What news?' he called to one.

'It's done. On its way over. Should be here any minute.'

While they waited, Gull explained his work, pausing patiently for Stephen's many interruptions for explanations of words that were part of Gull's workaday vocabulary but as alien as Mandarin Chinese to him.

It was based on a mathematical principle called maximum entropy, and involved the theory of probability. Gull and a colleague had begun to develop it in 1972 to improve pictures obtained by radio astronomy.

As Stephen understood it, it could cope with what astronomers called 'noise', graininess strong enough to obliterate detail, and also with blur caused by poor focus or camera shake. With the second problem – the one presented by Stephen's photograph – it worked by providing the mathematical basis for the computer to make a *guess* at what the sharp image was like. It then blurred that image and compared it with the actual blurring. It did that over and over again until it produced the right image – one shown to be accurate by the fact that the artificial blurring and the actual blurring were the same. A massive task made possible only by the combination of very advanced theoretical mathematics and the computer.

For all that to happen, though, the original picture first had to be scanned and reduced to numbers that could be handled by computer. That was what they were now waiting for. The photograph had been sent over to the Institute of Astronomy, put on the big scanner machine used to measure stars, translated into a million numbers which were then stored on magnetic tape.

A head poked around the open door. 'It's here.'

'Go ahead,' said Gull.

Stephen was already moving, but Gull slowed him down. 'Finish your coffee,' he said. 'It'll be at least ten to twenty minutes before there's anything to see.'

Then, sensing Stephen's impatience, he said, 'Eight years ago you would have had to wait days.' Now, he added, not only were computers faster but these particular machines were speeded up by the addition of special processor boards. That way, they had machines that could handle a staggering ten million numbers a second. By the time Stephen had his picture – provided it worked – the computer would have juggled around with over a billion numbers.

They walked through to the larger lab and to a terminal in the far corner. A succession of pictures was flashing on to the screen, one after another.

At first barely perceptibly and then without any doubt, shapes, real shapes, began to form from the photograph's badly blurred images.

Stephen became oblivious to anything but the screen. His father, he knew, was on the left. He concentrated on that image.

Slowly but steadily features became clearer. A grey patch became an eye, a shadow gave way to a nose; an eyebrow emerged, and then another.

At last, Gull moved his hand, tapped a key. The image froze.

He turned his head to look at Stephen. 'That's it,' he said. 'The best we can do.'

Stephen was barely conscious of him. He was as fixed as the picture on the monitor.

For the first time in twenty-five years he was gazing on his father's face.

CHAPTER TWENTY-THREE

That night he dreamed. He was a small boy and he was at a railway station, clutching a tiny cardboard case. There were people with him, but he could not see their faces, only sense them. The train arrived, but as he began to climb on board he realised that he had forgotten something and he turned back to find it. He returned too late – the train was moving and although he ran it was moving too quickly. Nevertheless, he kept running, faster and faster. His heart was bursting and his legs were filled with pain. His mouth was wide open, but his screams were silent. Gradually he began to make up the distance. He reached out to grab a rail, to swing himself aboard.

But then the platform ended, and the train was disappearing into a tunnel. And as it vanished all he could see was a face at the window, shining white as though lit by a searchlight.

His father.

He woke, sweating, the face and its expression still vivid in his mind. Fixed, staring, devoid of any feeling.

Jessica was cradling him and making 'easy, easy' noises, and he realised he must have been crying out in his sleep.

'It's all right,' she said.

Gradually, the veils cleared. He could feel his heart pounding as hard as it had in the dream.

They were both naked, and she pulled his head into her breast.

'What is it?' she asked at last, though she knew.

He waited a long time before answering.

'Him,' he said. 'I don't know if I want to find him.'

Like Donoghue, she answered, 'You have to. I don't think there's any going back.'

*

It was good to see Benson again. It had been over a year. They had known each other for well over a decade. At various times they had competed, co-operated, got drunk together, cursed the same people together, even chased the same women although Benson was twenty years Stephen's senior.

The moment Stephen walked into the Cock Tavern and saw Benson, though, he knew it was going to be a cursing-the-people day. Benson was drooped over the bar, a whisky and a beer chaser in front of him.

He did not see Stephen arrive.

'The same – twice,' said Stephen to the barman, pointing at Benson's two glasses.

They carried the drinks over to a corner table and sat before talking.

'*Salut*,' said Stephen, draining one of the whiskies.

'Fuck the bosses,' said Benson, tossing down the other.

He picked up his beer. 'Good to see you,' he said. 'Nobody drinks any more. The kids coming into the business live on designer water.' He shuddered. 'All that fucking gas. No wonder they're such little farts.'

He fetched more whiskies, walking back to the table with the measured dignity of someone with an honours degree in hard boozing.

'What's up?' asked Stephen.

He had fixed the meeting to ask Benson's advice – but now that he had the photograph and his plans for using it, the need for the correspondent's help had already faded.

Besides, for now this would have taken precedence anyway.

'Melville,' said Benson, switching to the beer. 'Acting editor prick. Offered me early retirement. Some fucking choice – my successor's already about to file from Prague.'

Benson, it transpired, had thought he was being recalled to London to give an on-the-spot briefing about the situation in Eastern Europe – already this month the Berlin Wall had fallen, the Communist leadership in Prague had been forced to resign, and Bulgaria had seen its largest post-war street demonstrations.

Instead, Melville had told him he wanted 'a new pair of eyes' looking at the developments. He had decided to shift the paper's young Washington number two to Europe – in fact he was already on the way. Benson was welcome to stay on with the paper if he liked – but they'd want him back home. Of course, he was sixty-two, not a bad time to retire . . .

'Back home!' spat Benson. 'I haven't lived *back home* for thirty fucking years.'

'So?'

Benson spread his hands. 'So,' he repeated. 'So provided we can work out a deal – I retire. Slippers by the fire. Choosing lawnmowers. Walking the dog.'

'You're not that kind of man,' said Stephen. 'Anyway, you're too young. You'll find things.' He did not know what else to say.

Benson sensed his unease. 'You're right,' he said. 'I'll manage. I've got lots of things I've been wanting to do.' He laughed. 'Anyway, fuck it. You wanted to talk to me. Give.'

Although Stephen now knew what he was going to do without Benson's advice, he ran through the story – Nick might see something he had missed.

When Benson spoke, though, his thoughts only echoed Stephen's own conclusions: Kenyon's destination when he ran in 1966 was probably somewhere far away – South America, Australia maybe. Not Germany – he had gone to enormous lengths to leave no trail; he would know Germany was too obvious to anyone who delved into his past.

They agreed, too, that if the money had been destroyed, the situation had probably changed dramatically – Kenyon might well have been thrown back on his old friends and German background.

But where, if anywhere, did that get them? Where, in Germany, might he go?

Benson had thoughts. Berlin could have been Kenyon's best bet. Given time, that might be checkable through intelligence records – the arrival and settlement of an Englishman would almost certainly have resulted in the opening of a file.

'What if he tried to pass himself off as a German?' asked Stephen: his father's use of the language had been excellent.

Benson was dismissive: almost certainly impossible. Only rare individuals could really speak a foreign language day in, day out as a native: 'You'd have to be brought up bilingual.' *If* Kenyon had masqueraded as German, all the more chance there was a record. 'But we're talking time to find out – and with what's happening in Germany, you couldn't have picked a worse moment to try.'

What about Kenyon passing himself off as German somewhere

other than Germany itself, Stephen had persevered. This time, the correspondent had been less adamant. Possible, he conceded. Maybe Switzerland – though it would be hard to settle there for other reasons. Czechoslovakia, except that was well behind the Iron Curtain in 1966. Austria – that's where he, Benson, would have gone. Accents varied throughout the country. And in the mid-sixties people were flocking in from outside. Its philosophy had always been live and let live . . . Yes, maybe Austria.

And, although there was no evidence, it made some sense to Stephen too. He decided he would call the Midlands stringer again – ask him to look out in particular for any connections with Austria. A long shot, but crazy not to take it.

Donoghue was right though – it was knot-cutting time.

He realised that Benson had returned with fresh drinks. He reached out for one. Knot-cutting could come later. This was a time for helping a friend get drunk.

The key to 'cutting the knot' was the photograph of Kenyon. Donoghue's idea was simple. Stephen should get the photograph reproduced all over Europe. *That* would flush his father out.

Get it reproduced, how? Donoghue was dismissive: a minor problem. 'Make up the right story and you'll get dozens of television stations showing it. Or stick ads in papers. Christ, you're the expert there. That's just mechanics . . .'

To Stephen's protest that if such an approach succeeded it would be by blowing his father's carefully developed cover, Donoghue was contemptuous: 'Don't tell me you really care about that! He's the bastard who ran off. You keep telling me that. All you want to do is find him and lay the ghost. Then you write the story, and get on with your own life. Period.'

Stephen did not voice another worry: that it might also help Barton's hirelings. There was no reason Donoghue should know about them.

The more he thought about the idea, though, the more – as a reporter – he liked it. The search had to have a time limit: Melville would be pushing soon. The leads he had were slender. And – as a son – Donoghue's idea held out some hope of finding Kenyon. The alternative could well be not finding his father at all. Even as he thought that, he realised he was now taking it for granted that Kenyon was still alive. That was a big assumption. After nearly a quarter of a century there had to be a real chance Kenyon was dead. Nothing spectacular. An accident. An illness. Perhaps a genuine suicide. But if that were so, he'd like to know: the ghost would be laid to rest.

Publishing the photograph with an appeal for information, maybe a reward, might flush him out. It might bring evidence he was dead. Either way, it would be worthwhile. Besides, what would he really be telling his father's old enemies by publication? That he suspected Kenyon was still alive? They already knew that. All Stephen had to do if it did yield any leads was to make sure they didn't get word of them – which meant seeing Jessica did not communicate with her mother and that, if he went anywhere, he was not followed.

The decision made, his professionalism told him that good as it was the photograph by itself was not enough.

It showed Kenyon the way he was aged in his late thirties. What was needed was a picture of Kenyon as he would look now – a seemingly impossible task, but he thought he knew how to obtain one.

Stephen had first met Arthur Headley two years before. Headley, a medical artist at Manchester University, had been called in by police to help them reconstruct the skull of a girl whose skeleton had been found buried in an unmarked grave. Stephen had spent several days with him, watching him build up a face in clay on a cast of the skull, using human facial thickness measurements determined by research and his own knowledge of human anatomy.

The day after his decision, Stephen sat in Headley's office at the University's medical school. The illustrator sat perched on a stool, glasses half-way down his nose, peering at the pictures Stephen had handed him. On the walls were photographs of reconstructions of skulls thousands of years old found by archaeologists and worked on by Headley.

A partial reconstruction was on a tripod, covered with a plastic bag to stop the clay drying out. Shelves held a variety of skulls. In the casting room, off the larger outer studio, Headley had just checked the cast of a lung, on order from a drug company to distribute to physicians. A foetus floated in a plastic container. On the top shelf the skulls of ancient Greek warriors waited to be worked upon.

322

'Who is it?' asked Headley at last. 'Someone I should know?'

'My father. Aged about thirty-eight. Taken about twenty-five years ago.'

He explained the background.

'And me? What do you want me to do?'

'Can you work on it? Show me how he'd look now?'

Headley whistled. 'You don't ask much,' he said. He sat for a long time, deep in thought, and then added, 'Yes. Yes, I think I can.'

Although, obviously, people changed as they aged, Headley explained, some key factors remained the same – like the distances between the fixed anatomical points at the inner corners of the eyes, the bottom of the nose and the mouth.

To illustrate, Headley placed a piece of tracing paper over one of the close-ups of Kenyon's face and drew lines between the points – a triangle to link the eyes and nose, a straight line down to the mouth. 'Excluding disease and trauma and provided you don't lose your teeth, there is little that can change the shape and size of the head. Those proportions will stay the same whatever age the person is – and that, I strongly believe, is what matters.'

Some assumptions would have to be made. 'Has he gone bald? It ténds to be hereditary. Do you know about his family? If not we can illustrate him both ways.'

Stephen remembered his grandfather during visits as a boy. He had a good head of hair, he told Headley.

'Good. And you haven't started to go thin on top, and neither had he as far as we can see in the photograph. I think we can gamble he's kept his hair. To be safe, I can do one picture with it thinning.'

Another assumption was, where he had lived since he vanished. 'In the tropics, to give an extreme, the skin gets dried out and wrinkled. Fairly modest wrinkles become pronounced. From what you've told me about him, though, I think we can safely assume that his life remained reasonably middle-class in a benign environment.'

As to other changes, they were common to all ageing processes. 'Soft tissue is not supported and tends to drop back. Wrinkles become more pronounced. There's less elasticity in the tissues of the face – the outer corners of the eyelids droop, pouches form under the eyes. The soft tissues round the jaw become heavy and sag. Everything falls. There's a fattening up around the lines of the jaw . . .'

He grinned. 'Sounds inviting, doesn't it. Still, you know what they say, think of the alternative.'

'So what would you do?'

'First, I'd need you to find out as much as you can about his family – whether they look young or old for their years: how fast a lot of things happen is genetic. Could you do that on the phone?'

Stephen nodded. He would check with Katharine. She would remember. He would also ask whether his father had had good teeth.

Stephen had two questions. 'What about weight? People get thinner – or fatter.'

'Not a real worry. Weight up or down, unless it's really spectacular, doesn't make much difference with regard to whether he'd be recognised.'

'What if he's kept his hair, but gone grey, or white?'

'That's one reason we should stick to black and white in the modified picture. With colour you're more likely to have errors. In black and white, if hair's not black you're just saying it's not dark. In colour, you have to decide exactly what colour. Besides, we don't all see the same balance of colours. Some people see a beautiful red sky, to others it's nothing special.'

Stephen was lucky. Headley was intrigued enough to start that day.

'Can I help?'

'Just make your phone calls, and keep out of the way.'

An hour later, the call to Katharine made and details passed on, Stephen was in the basement cafeteria killing time drinking his third cup of coffee. It was there Headley found him.

To Stephen's bemusement and embarrassment, he began running a pair of callipers over his face.

'What's happening?' asked Stephen. Headley seemed oblivious to the amused interest of students at other tables.

Headley's voice was decisive. 'Come on,' he said. 'We're going to London. There's a train in forty minutes.'

Their destination was one of London's major teaching hospitals, University College, and a slight man with glasses and greying tight curly hair.

Dr Alfred Linney, a consultant medical physicist, had devised computer methods of showing how patients would look after face-altering surgery. Headley had talked about him on the train and explained the reason for the dash. Stephen's skull shape, he said, was very much like his father's. There was good reason they should take advantage of the fact.

He had spoken to Linney, who was willing to produce a three-dimensional reproduction of Stephen's skull using laser and computer graphics. This had the advantage that the skull could then be called up at any angle on a computer screen. Facial tissue could be added to the computer image together with details from the photograph. Some ageing changes could also be made by computer. The jaw, for example, could be moved forward. Finally, Headley would take the computer images and add his modifications and provide illustrations based on them.

In all, they would get the best of both worlds. 'An illustrator can produce pictures more immediately understood than computer drawings – years of conditioning have made people more familiar with them.'

They had to cross the street from Linney's office to the laser room. Behind a locked door was a chair with a headrest. It stood on a metal stand. Four mirrors were placed around it, and facing was a small table with a computer keyboard.

Linney arranged Stephen in the chair, positioning his head against the rest. 'Sorry it's got a bit of a do-it-yourself look,' he said. 'But I assure you it works.'

Linney took up a place at the keyboard.

'In a moment I'll start your chair rotating,' he said. 'It won't take long. Just keep absolutely still. As it turns a laser line will be projected on to your face – it's very low energy so there's no danger. The scanner and the video camera are interfaced with a computer. As you revolve, it will take measurements of your skull at thirty thousand different points, and record them in the computer. All right?'

'All right.'

It took less than five minutes.

Next, an X-ray to reveal the bones supporting Stephen's face, and an hour later they were all in front of a monitor in Linney's room, a 3-D reconstruction of Stephen's skull on the screen.

With touches of his fingertips, Linney made it turn and tilt. He changed the angle so that the viewers were staring at it from above, and then he straightened and spun it so that it was in profile.

Knowing it was his own skull gave Stephen a weird feeling. 'What next?' he asked.

Linney called a menu on to the screen, zoned in on the jaw segment, cut it and moved it forward 3 mm – the amount that corresponded to ageing the shape to Kenyon's present age, he explained.

Next, marking points on the skull, he added thicknesses of tissue. Finally, he called up the photograph of Kenyon, transplanted it on to the skull image and instructed the computer to merge the two images.

Within minutes, they were staring at a number of computer drawings, showing full face and profiles to each side.

'It's going to take me some time,' said Headley.

And to Linney, 'Can I use a room?'

They met for breakfast. Headley had not slept. He pushed the pictures across the table. There were front and profile pictures of Kenyon at the time he had vanished; front and three-quarter views of him as he might look now.

Stephen sat staring at them, his plate pushed aside.

Headley mistook his silence for concern.

'They're the best we could do,' he said, almost apologetic.

Stephen looked up, grinned. 'You've got me wrong,' he said. 'I'm stunned. They're uncanny.'

And then, 'If they don't flush him out . . .'

All reservations were forgotten.

The *International Herald Tribune* wanted reassurances before agreeing to run the advertisement. Being asked to publish what was in effect a 'Wanted' notice made them nervous.

Stephen told them his father had disappeared months before, and was suspected to be suffering from amnesia. The reconstructions were necessary ·because no photographs existed. He produced documents showing Kenyon was his father. More to the point, he produced a letter from a doctor backing his story.

'We will have to check,' said the clerk.

'Of course. But can you phone? This is urgent.'

The clerk was cautious and meticulous. He made three calls. The first to the British Medical Association to confirm that the doctor did exist at the number given. The second to the doctor himself. The third was to the paper's head office in Paris.

Stephen waited, unworried. The doctor was real. He owed Stephen a favour. A big favour. He was repaying it now.

The clerk returned.

'We'll get it in Thursday,' he said.

'And Friday and Saturday,' said Stephen.

The clerk was smiling now.

'I don't think we've ever run an ad like this before,' he said.

'You'll go down in history,' said Stephen.

The ad took up a prime space on the back page, 20 cms across, 15 cms deep. The size, let alone the content, made it an attention grabber.

'Michael Kenyon,' it read. 'The family misses you. Please phone home.' The telephone number given was a line he had had specially connected to the flat.

He and Jessica would man it day and night.

The first call came two days after the first advertisement appeared.

CHAPTER TWENTY-FOUR

The first call was a hoax. So was the second. The third was from a wire service reporter checking whether there was a story (Stephen persuaded the journalist that he was only manning the phone but would pass on a message).

The first one of real interest came at 8.20 a.m. on the third day, Saturday. The caller spoke in English with a German accent – a good start. Stephen was shaving. Jessica called him to the telephone, but the man rang off before he got there.

The man telephoned again twenty minutes later, and Stephen answered this time.

'You wish to contact someone. It is possible I may help. But I have to know why and who wishes to make the contact.'

'Do you know the man concerned?'

'I need to know more before I speak.'

Stephen did not answer directly. 'How do I know you are genuine? What proof do you give?'

The line went dead.

Stephen shrugged at Jessica.

'What do you think?' she said.

'It sounded kosher. He obviously rang off the first time in case we were trying to trace the call. But who knows. If he's genuine, he'll be back.'

He pressed the tape button, replayed the conversation. He could hear traffic noise in the background. A public telephone. Still, that meant nothing.

He was speaking and acting more relaxed than he felt. Jessica was not deceived. She reached out and squeezed his hand. 'You're getting to know me too well,' he said, but he felt warmed and strengthened by her understanding.

There were two further calls that day. An educated-sounding

drunk who said he was staying in London and had been sitting in his hotel room staring at the ad on and off for hours and just *had* to know what it was about. And an optimistic or desperate salesman making a pitch to sell life insurance.

The German caller telephoned again on Sunday.

'Although it has faded over the years, the scar above the right ear is still visible.'

'OK,' said Stephen. 'Where do I find him?'

He knew what the next step would be; he had played it through in his mind many times. The man would ask for money, and they would haggle over the mechanics of exchanging cash for verifiable information. Only when that was settled would they move on.

It did not happen that way.

'You must fly to Köln. Check into the Hans Lyskirchen Hotel. That is on Filzengraben. A room is reserved in your name.'

Stephen began to speak, but the other pressed on as though reading.

'You should stay in the hotel. You will be contacted.'

'When?' But the line was already broken.

Again, he played back the call. Jessica listened, and then said, 'Will you go?'

'That's what it's all about. I just hope to God it's not some elaborate con.' Except, he thought, who would know about the gun wound except those who had shot his father or had been with him since?

'I'm coming with you.' Her voice was determined.

He clutched her hand. 'Who'll mind the phone?' he said. 'There may be more calls.'

'We could get someone else.'

'I don't trust anyone else.'

The kind of phrase that comes out without thought. Like 'have a nice day' or 'pretty good weather' or 'how are you?' Yet, as he spoke, he realised he meant it. Apart from Ward and Katharine, and them in a different way, Jessica was the only person he would trust totally. An admission that said a lot about himself, he realised.

'I want to go to bed with you,' he said suddenly', voice low, nervously boyish.

She began to laugh before realising the intensity that lay behind the words.

'Let's confirm the hotel and get you on a flight first,' she said, as though she were the one twenty years older.

And then, smiling, she added, 'Then we'll see. Your father's waited twenty-five years. I suppose he can wait a little longer.'

He took the late-afternoon flight out of Heathrow. The Airbus was packed with identikit businessmen with attaché cases.

The Lyskirchen was on the banks of the Rhine in the old part of the city. It was a medium-size hotel with a mainly German business clientele. There was no message waiting for Stephen when he registered.

His room overlooked a nondescript side street. He threw his overnight bag on the bed and returned to the ground floor. The restaurant was still serving food. He and a woman of about thirty-five with short black hair were the only two people eating alone. He stared and she lifted her eyes and allowed a brief smile to break the severe look on her face. He had never been a man to proposition lone women in hotels but this time he sensed that an approach would be welcomed. It could have been tempting: she had a hard, handsome look that excited him. But he finished eating and left without looking her way again. It was not the time for such distractions, he told himself. But the real reason was different: Jessica. He did not want anyone else.

He slept fitfully, waking several times throughout the night, once from a nightmare filled with grotesque visions of Stanley Fisher's burning face. Flames devoured flesh; tissue melted and ran away in streams like lava. At last there was only skull – except that the eyes remained intact: staring and full of accusation.

After that, he lay awake. It was a relief when the room started to lighten and trucks began to rumble in the street.

He walked through to the shower – and then the telephone rang. Instinctively he checked his watch as he lifted the receiver. It was 7.40 a.m.

'I hope the room is to your liking,' said the voice. He recognised it immediately.

'When do we meet?' asked Stephen.

'You are impatient. It is a pleasant morning. You should see the city. Take a stroll to the Cathedral. There is a very fine hotel facing it. The Dom. Have breakfast there – by then you will be hungry.'

The man hung up.

Stephen stifled frustration at not being in control and told himself, at least there was activity. He shaved and dressed quickly, consulted a map for directions, and then hovered at the hotel door while he tried to check the street. The inference was that he would be contacted again at the Dom, but that could be a blind: they – whoever *they* were – might be meaning to snatch him on the way there. With Fisher's fate so clear in his mind, he would not risk that. True, he wanted to make contact – but it had to be somewhere public.

There were cabs parked nearby – but there was no way of knowing whether they were safe. While he waited, uncertain what to do, he saw a chain of schoolchildren and nuns come into view on the far side of the street. He waited until they were directly opposite, crossed the road and quickly joined their tail. As he walked, his eyes raked the street ahead. After a few minutes, he saw what he wanted come into view – an alleyway which the children would pass. Quickly, he worked his way along the inside of the crocodile, so that he was hidden from the rest of the street. The moment he reached the alleyway, he broke into a run. He came out into another street, stopped and looked back, breathing heavily. Clear. No one was following. Immediately, it seemed melodramatic. Then he told himself, crazy not to take precautions.

He checked his map, and twenty minutes later Germany's largest cathedral loomed ahead. It was one of the few buildings that had survived Allied bombing. Its towers raked the sky. According to legend the building had been spared because the Allies wanted it standing to guide the bombers that had razed seventy per cent of the city to the ground.

He turned towards the Dom Hotel. The square was slowly coming alive. Groups of sightseers were beginning to gather on the Cathedral steps, a juggler was getting ready to perform. The only vehicle was a garbage truck cruising the edge of the square. As it neared, he stepped aside to give it room. It was travelling so slowly that he barely noticed at first that it had stopped beside him. Then it was too late. The truck hid him and his attackers from others in the square. Two men held him while a third plunged home the needle. Nothing clever, nothing too delicate, just the large muscle on the outside of his right thigh. It would take longer

331

for the drug to work than if it had been injected into a vein, but they had no need to hurry. The two men kept him pinned until the drug took effect. Then, effortlessly, they lifted him and rolled him on to the floor of the cab. A rug was thrown over him, and it smelled like cat pee. Stephen's last emotion before the darkness was not fear but anger that he had allowed himself to be caught so easily.

They were standing over him when he awoke. He was lying on a stone floor and there was a damp, cellar smell. By the faint light from a caged bulb, he could just make out bare, whitewashed walls.

One man was kicking him, but without any real venom. A hot sourness rose in his stomach, and, without warning, he vomited over the man's foot. Through blurred eyes, Stephen saw his attacker examine his trouser-leg, and then raise his foot to deliver another kick, but this time to his head. Stephen waited shivering for the blow. It was a long time coming. He heard muffled argument, and when it finally landed, it was more a token – the other two men had cooled the man down.

Stephen's relief was short. One man spat orders, and Stephen was pulled to his feet. Again two of them held him. He saw the third clearly. He wore a green loden coat and a Tyrolean hat, and he had a thin moustache so black it looked false. Stephen wished he could see his eyes, but they were behind tinted glasses. With careful deliberation, the man hit Stephen across the face with the back of his gloved fist, like a Gestapo interrogator in a bad film.

Stephen was beginning to think, I can bear this, when the man took a short cosh from his pocket and hit him three times, twice across his upper arms, once on the side of his face, tearing skin from his cheekbone.

'Fucking Englander,' the man spat. He nodded an instruction, and immediately Stephen felt his wrists being lashed together in front of him. A gag was rammed into his mouth and a blindfold tied over his eyes.

'Soon you will meet someone who knows how to ask questions,' the voice said.

He heard the door open, and then he was being guided out. He could hear sounds of clatter and of talking in the distance, and he was conscious that one man was walking ahead, clearing the route along corridors. Another door opened and he could smell cooking

– he thought he was probably in the basement of a restaurant or small hotel.

Then air. He heard one man climb steps, shout that it was clear. He was manhandled to the street, lifted and thrown into the back of a vehicle which pulled away almost immediately. He waited for someone to speak, but there was silence. After a few minutes he wormed his way to the side of the vehicle and worked himself into a sitting position. He could feel blood clotted on his cheek and forehead. He lifted his tied hands, pretended to rub his face in case anyone was watching him, and managed to shift the blindfold a fraction. By tilting his head, he had some vision.

He turned his head slowly towards the front of the vehicle. A barred window separated the back of the van from the driving cab. The bars were about six inches apart.

While Stephen was absorbing the information, the van stopped violently and he shot across the floor with a crash. From the corner of his eye, he was conscious of someone in the cab turning to see what was happening. The man spoke and they all laughed.

The van moved forward again but with a series of stop-starts. Stephen could hear bustle outside. At first he could not place it, until his blindfold permitted a half-glimpse of striped awning. Then he realised it was the sound of stalls being erected. His cab-driver the previous day had told him about the pre-Christmas markets that were a feature of the city.

Once someone banged on the side of the van. Stephen cursed inside with the frustration of help being so near and yet so far. He knew he could rip the gag clear – although tied, he had a lot of movement in his hands. But screaming would be no use – it would be just another sound in a cacophony of noise.

Stephen was shivering. What had he got himself into? Until now, it had been like working on some complicated, academic problem. He had even been able to walk away from it when he wished. His only worry about involvement had been about *emotional* involvement. Now he was part of it – and of all its dangers.

The van shot forward and stopped again. The driver's technique was accelerate, slam on the brakes. Stephen slithered and hit the side again. This time no one even bothered to turn to look at him.

The shivering had stopped and a calm anger possessed him. He had been in bad situations before – held for three days by secret police in Iran, once pinned down by gunfire on the hills of Lebanon. He had an in-built toughness and he kept himself moderately fit. But he was no Action Man. Survival in those bad times before had meant taking what came and enduring. It had called for a passive, albeit real, strength. Yet he knew that this time that was not enough. This time he had to act. He thought he knew how.

He was lying on his belly, his hands under him and as he moved he could feel the belt of his raincoat, untied and loose. Gingerly, he wriggled himself to his knees, and then tugged on the belt. It moved freely. Within seconds it was free of his coat and in his hands. He worked the material so that it was looped in the fingers of his tied hands.

The car kept shooting forward and stopping in a series of kangaroo movements. The men upfront were laughing like small children. Stephen struggled to his knees, arms high as though protecting his face. The barred window to the cab was inches above him, and he could see the back of the driver's head tilted back in exhilaration. The car jerked forward again. Stephen sensed they were almost free of the congestion. Then the van started to accelerate.

Time!

He struggled upright. Although his hands were tied, he could move his arms freely, and he swung the loop of the raincoat belt through a gap in the bars. The back of the driver's head was only inches away, and it was not a hard movement to complete even in Stephen's weakened state.

The loop went right over in one so-easy movement. Stephen yanked the moment it cleared the man's face. He feared he had moved too quickly and that the belt had snagged on the driver's jaw. But the man panicked and tried to turn his head and that was enough: the loop slid down on to his neck. Stephen pulled, using all of his weight, and the belt bit deep into the man's throat.

The man's head hit the bars, and then twisted to an almost impossible angle. A scream began and was choked off almost immediately. A hand, grasping at air, appeared in Stephen's view and then vanished as the van lurched to the right and shuddered its way through a series of obstructions until it smashed to a juddering halt.

Stephen was cushioned by the partition. He let go of the loop, and the ends of the belt shot through the bars with the weight of the released head. His movements had loosened his own binds and he pulled a wrist free and tore away the gag and the blindfold. There was screaming outside and someone was trying to force open the rear door.

Finally, it gave. Stephen clambered out. The crowd parted and he realised he must look a terrible sight: the blood from his beating had been joined by a fresh outpouring from a gash on his forehead.

He tried to smile, to frame words in his rudimentary German to explain that he was all right. Then a hand took his arm, and a man said, 'I'll take care of him.'

He did not have to look. He knew the voice. One of his captors. The hand began to pull him away. A woman in the crowd tried to intervene, saying, 'Wait for the ambulance.' Her words had a strange echoing sound.

Stephen used the diversion. His captor had relaxed his grip and he broke free. He burst through the crowd of onlookers, mad strength propelling him.

He ran with painful, disjointed movements, knowing only that he must get far away. Blood was running down his face and people leapt aside to clear a path.

Cries pursued him: 'Stop him, stop him, he's sick.' But he had a lead.

Soon blood mingled with sweat, and pain racked his side. He had to suck harder and harder to get air into his lungs. But still he managed to keep going, frantic, driven.

All he needed was a policeman. Surely one must come into sight soon.

He could hear his pursuers behind him, still shouting for someone to stop him. He fought the desire to turn to see how close they were. He slipped and righted himself, but knew he must be losing ground. He turned into another street. Then another. He was nearly done now. His strength had almost gone.

For God's sake! he screamed inside.

A store, bursting with shoppers, came into view. There must be guards inside. They would protect him until the police came.

He crashed through the doors, sending customers spinning. He fell, forced himself upright again. A hand grasped his shoulder. For a second, he thought it belonged to a guard and that he was safe. Then he recognised the face – the man who had hit him. He managed to tear himself free and stagger on.

An escalator loomed ahead, soaring upwards, visible for floor after floor. With nowhere else to go, Stephen threw himself on to it. Surely the man would not follow him any further. Stephen was moving purely by will-power now. All feeling had gone from his body. He sank to his knees, looked back.

Unbelievably, the man was still coming, clambering up the escalator, scattering people as he came. He had a knife in his hand. All Stephen could think was, he must be mad, why doesn't he give up.

Stephen staggered off the last step and skidded round the corner to the next section of escalator. Between the banks of escalators was a wide well sheer to the ground floor now far below. Christmas decorations added a surrealistic element: huge snowflake-shape lights hung in the well, suspended from long chains that began two further floors above.

The man reached him, and Stephen kicked out, forcing him back. He knew now that his pursuer had to be mad. He was going to kill him even if it meant certain arrest.

Stephen kicked out again and the other slipped back. The man was regaining his breath and his strength ready for a final effort. Stephen knew he was too weak to fight any more.

The escalator had carried him about two-thirds of the way between the second and third floors. Through swollen, blurred eyes, he could see the chains holding the lights hanging about six feet away to the side of him.

His only chance!

Only panic and the knowledge that he had no other chance of survival made him do what he did next. In the few seconds he had left, he used his remaining strength to drag himself on to the escalator rail.

Too late then for second thoughts – he swung himself out into space, a good thirty feet above the ground.

His arms were outstretched to grab one of the chains. A gymnast or even a fit, trained soldier might have made it. As it was, he came close. One hand made contact. But he had no real grip. Searing pain tore through his palm. Immediately he was spinning and twisting madly as his weight sent the light arching through the air. Instinctively, as he plummeted down, he grabbed at another length of chain. Again, he could not hold it, but at least it slowed his fall.

A micro second later he crashed into a ground-floor counter while screams erupted through the store.

No one was kicking him this time. He was in bed. Two faces peered down at him. As they came into focus, he realised they belonged to a doctor and a nurse.

He tried to say, 'Don't let them get me,' but nothing would emerge.

A third face joined the group.

'It's all right,' it said in English. 'You're safe here. No need to speak. Take your time.'

It withdrew, and Stephen turned his eyes in an attempt to follow it. He saw a door and near it a man in uniform, and he realised he was under guard.

The face returned, alone this time.

'The doctor is going to give you something to help you sleep some more,' it said. 'Then we'll talk, you and I.' His smile was conspiratorial, as though they alone shared a secret.

Stephen felt his arm lifted, the needle penetrate. He did not struggle. He allowed himself to go with it, welcoming the darkness as it rolled over him.

The face had moved out of vision, but he could still see and hear the man in his mind. It was strangely familiar. He remembered who he was a moment before the blackness came. The intelligence man with the flat Midlands accent and the vivid purple birthmark. The silent MI5 man who had stood and watched as his apartment was searched all those months before.

The man's name was Miller. Or so he said. He returned an hour after Stephen woke again. A nurse had taken Stephen's pulse and blood pressure, another had brought him soup and bread. Neither had spoken, and they had feigned not to understand him when he tried to question them in his halting German.

Propped up in bed, watching the man enter the room, Stephen felt curiously disembodied. He raised his left arm. The wrist was bound in plaster.

'If that's all that hurts, I shouldn't worry,' said Miller. 'You broke your wrist doing spectacular circus acrobatics. From what I hear, you're lucky not to have smashed everything.'

Stephen tried to test the rest of his body. He flexed muscles. There were no stabs of pain, but everything felt heavy, deadened.

'How long have I been here?' he asked.

The intelligence man carried a chair to his bedside and sat down.

'I wondered when you'd ask that,' he said. 'Three days.' He looked at his watch. 'Three days all but four hours. The police had been called to a road accident, heard about some half-crazed survivor running amok, finally found him in the Kaushof department store spread across the cashmere sweaters. I gather you didn't do them much good: lots of blood. At least you didn't hit some bloody passer-by. Then we'd have had a real Anglo–Kraut incident.'

'Can I ask, where am I, as well?'

'Why not? It's traditional, isn't it. You're in the city hospital – the local police didn't like the idea of us spiriting you away out of their jurisdiction. But they compromised – you're in an isolation wing.'

'And you?'

Suddenly a wave of nausea came over him and he began to shake.

Miller saw and was surprisingly solicitous.

'Easy,' he said, leaning over, pressing a buzzer to summon help. 'You've had a tough time. We'll talk later.' And he vanished from view the moment the doctor appeared.

They spoke the following day. Stephen had been helped to a chair where he sat supported by cushions. His body was a continuous ache – only bad bruising, he had been reassured.

A doctor had told him more about his injuries. His fall had been cushioned by a feet-thick pile of sweaters which had probably saved his life. He had struck his head but almost certainly only after the landing had absorbed most of the impact. The wound was not severe. X-rays had shown nothing sinister. However, there was a slight chance of undetected internal injury. Because of that, they wished him to remain under observation for a few more days.

'How few?' he had asked.

The doctor had shrugged. 'Perhaps three. Maybe four.'

The doctor had become stern. 'You should be glad to be alive, not worried about how long you have to remain. From what I have read in the newspaper, your survival is a miracle.'

'I was in the newspapers?' was the first thing Stephen asked Miller when he returned. What he really wanted to know was, had Jessica been told, would she have read about it, had she been in touch? But he drew back from introducing her name.

Miller read his mind. 'We told your girlfriend, and your paper. At least, the embassy did. Said it was an accident, though – it was, in a way, wasn't it? Assured them, no need to worry. The girl's here now in Cologne – she's taken over your old hotel room. We've told her the doctors won't let anyone see you for a day or two, but she was adamant about staying nearby.' He opened his hands. 'See, I'm levelling, telling you everything.'

'Tell me about the newspapers?' Stephen said.

'Oh, that. You were in them. Not every day someone hurtles three floors in Cologne's biggest department store. The police persuaded them that you were concussed after a street accident, didn't know what you were doing.'

'But what about the man with the knife? People must have talked.'

Miller shrugged. 'Surprisingly few – everyone was watching you. It wasn't hard to persuade them they'd got it wrong, thought they'd seen something they hadn't. As for the man, he got away. Officially, the police know nothing about him. Unofficially, they're looking out for him – for us.'

He pulled his chair closer to Stephen. He had answered enough questions. Time to start asking.

'You remember me?' he said.

'Oh yes, I remember you.'

'Then listen to me, and let's see if we're on the same side.'

Miller had accompanied the raid on Kenyon's apartment, he explained, because he was already interested in the Kenyon family.

As he continued, Kenyon realised he had been wrong on one point. True, Miller was not Special Branch. But he was MI6, not MI5.

Certain people had known for a long time that Kenyon had resurfaced after his disappearance in London in 1966, Miller said. They had not known who he was at first – they had been interested in a man known as 'The Irishman' who had emerged as a small-time operator on the East–West border, working out of Austria.

'People got especially interested because they didn't know who he was, where he'd come from. His nickname threw them for some time. They were checking the Irish connection. Turned out he wasn't Irish, but English. He'd got his hands on an Irish passport – clever. The Irish are everywhere – before the IRA thing blew up again they were almost everybody's friends. An Irish passport was the nearest thing to a world passport you could get.'

The Irishman's speciality, it had emerged, was running counterfeit medicines from the West into Eastern-bloc countries.

'He bought from clandestine factories in Italy and Germany mainly. Bootlegged. Mainstream stuff. Wide-ranging antibiotics, birth control pills, ulcer drugs. I'm told it's not hard to produce. And manufacturing costs are low – the price of drugs is in the research and, of course, these people don't have any. So, cheap to turn out. Not so cheap, of course, for the people who have to pay for them. They need to hand over their antiques, granny's jewellery, hard currency if they've got it, sackfuls of forints or lei or dinars or crowns or whatever if they haven't. And if they haven't got anything, they can always steal it of course. One museum has lost a lot of paintings from its vaults over the years to pay for its director's ulcer drugs.'

He paused. 'And that's what your old man's been doing.'

Stephen tried to remain impassive. Even if Miller was telling the truth he did not trust him. Still, it made sense. With Benson's help he had already thought of Austria. Even if he had lost the one hundred and fifty thousand pounds he had stolen, his father probably had access to some money – perhaps a few hundreds or even a few thousands. Not enough to retire to Brazil – but useful funding for the kind of operation Miller was describing . . .

Stephen said, 'If people knew – and I assume you mean your people – why didn't you stop him?'

Miller smiled a huge grin. 'My, my,' he said, 'we are being naive, aren't we? Why should we stop him? We didn't mind medicines going in. If they're good and save lives, that's humanitarian. If they're not – if someone's done the old Harry Lime act and diluted the penicillin – it's not our fault and you could say they'd probably have died anyway.

340

'And, as for the other side, why should they stop it even if they found out – which I have to tell you they did. For a few well-placed people it was just another juicy pie for their greedy fingers: "Want to swap some medicines for a few icons? Fine. Just leave an envelope with our commission under the loose brick on the wall behind the third house. Dollars would be best, but we're helpful sods – Deutschmarks or sterling will do instead." '

'The operation was useful to you too?'

Miller poured more water, clearly buying time while he wondered whether to answer. He decided he would.

'To both sides,' he said. 'It meant people going in and out of the East all the time. A regular little delivery service if anyone needed it. Got to be sure you know who's working for who, of course, but then that's always true, isn't it?'

'So,' said Stephen, 'everyone's happy. The gang –' he could not bring himself to say Kenyon's gang – 'and the West and the East. Sounds a perfect set-up.'

'Right,' said Miller. 'You've got it in one. Except we're talking in the past. It *was* a perfect set-up. But the world's been changing. The walls are falling down, the comrades are on the run. The goodies are winning, but the whole of fucking Eastern Europe is going to be in more and more chaos. State planning's going down the tube, and the market economy's on the way. You know what that means? Every woman wants to be out whoring for hard currency, and the really hard boys are moving in – the Moscow Mafia and the New York Mafia. Nice scenario.'

'So?' Stephen did not understand.

'So, nearly a year back your old man must have seen the end was coming. It was already getting nastier. He looked into his crystal ball, didn't like what he saw, and he made his plans. He planned it well – but then he always was a good organiser wasn't he? He gathered together three consignments of medicines and then made them vanish.' He paused for effect and then said, 'Together with himself and two or three trusted buddies.'

Miller paused again, grinned and added, 'Sound familiar?'

Stephen was having to concentrate hard to absorb what he was being told, but he had to smile too. 'It does have a kind of *déjà vu* quality,' he said. 'So what now?'

'So now we have a man many powerful people would like to see – except nobody knows where he is.' He began ticking fingers.

'First, there's all the friends he left behind. They know a load of drugs are missing and there's no share of the proceeds coming their way.

'Second, there's us. We see someone with a lot of secrets that might embarrass a lot of people. Like, who helped who? Who took money? Who passed messages to who? All those things.

'And, three, just to complete it, there are all those bastards in the East who're kicking their Commie bosses out of power. Trouble is, they may be goodies now, but some of them have a few skeletons they'd like to keep hidden. Including a few your old man probably knows. As I said, a lot of people helped or connived over the years.'

'And don't forget a fourth – the people he fled from in the first place,' said Stephen. 'Hard to believe, but I'm ninety per cent sure someone's still chasing him after all these years.'

Miller looked deep in thought, as though wondering whether to admit something.

At last, he said, 'You mean Barton. Thanks to you, he's probably the only person your father doesn't have to worry about any more. Your visit to Israel and calls to Nevada set off ripples the Mafia didn't like. Our information is that his old enemy has been told to quieten it. No more personal vendettas. Let bygones be bygones.'

Stephen had another question. 'And you?' he said. 'You knew I was coming. You thought I'd lead you to him.'

'You went public,' said Miller. He gave a rare smile. 'And for a man who doesn't trust anyone you were certainly free on the telephone.'

He shrugged. 'But we lost you outside the hotel. Nicely done, that. But I doubt anyone'll contact you again after what happened. We both blew it.'

He smiled again. But this time it looked forced. 'At least you don't have to justify yourself to anyone for what happened. I'll be two weeks just writing reports.'

He became solicitous again. 'You need rest.' He stood to leave. 'I'll get word to your girl. And I'll talk to the German police. Get them to finish their questioning, let you see her. OK?'

He turned at the door as though to say something, but thought better of it. This time, he did not even try to smile.

CHAPTER TWENTY-FIVE

The ambulance to transfer Stephen to a private clinic arrived shortly after six o'clock in the morning.

The two male nurses were accompanied by two police officers. The night sister who escorted the group to Stephen's room was visibly flustered. Although the men showed all the necessary documents, she was annoyed at being given such short notice: she had been informed of the move by telephone only twenty minutes before.

One policeman tried to pacify her as they neared Stephen's room. Information received suggested there might be an attempt on the Englishman's life, he said. Better to be safe than sorry, hence the move to a place where he could be better protected. Best not to frighten Stephen, though: perhaps she could tell him it was a transfer to another branch of the hospital preparatory to being released. They would tell him the truth later.

Stephen wakened slowly, heavy from drugs given to help him sleep.

The night sister's presence reassured him. He heard her explanation, still too groggy to make any move himself. The male nurses helped him into a wheelchair.

The clock in the corridor showed it was only 6.10 a.m., but that did not surprise him. Things moved early here. The sister accompanied them to a rear exit where an ambulance stood waiting.

At the last moment, he thought he saw a flicker of concern cross her face, but he was already being lifted into the ambulance. It pulled away almost immediately.

The message that Stephen had left the hospital reached Miller at 6.16 a.m. He could make out the luminous orange digits on his travel clock as he answered his bedside telephone. He listened without interruption.

'You know what to do. I'm on my way.'

He swung out of bed, already dressed.

What Stephen had not known as he had passed other nights in his isolation room was that for Miller the hunt had been far from over. As Miller saw it, Stephen's actions had started to stir the waters and, given help, might still lead somewhere. What no one who had seen Stephen's advertisement knew was that the hunter was Kenyon's own son – and that included Michael Kenyon himself. If he, Miller, could just get that fact back to Kenyon . . .

He had lied about the man with the knife making good his escape. He had been arrested, held incommunicado and questioned, though with little success – he and his companions had been hired. They did not know who had sent them – it could have been Kenyon himself, anxious to learn about his pursuer, or one of his enemies. Nevertheless, the man had been fed the truth about Stephen and allowed to escape.

That was only one of the ways Miller was trying to reach Kenyon with information. Informants in half a dozen countries had been enlisted. All were being used to spread the story that Kenyon's son Stephen had been badly injured while seeking his father and that he now lay in hospital in Cologne.

OK – it was a longshot, Miller was the first to admit. But if you had bait, why not use it? If Kenyon had been behind the attempt to kidnap Stephen, he might now try again. If he had not, he would learn his son was in danger because of him. Either way, Miller had hoped, Kenyon would make a move.

Now it looked as though it had worked.

The ambulance stopped after about half an hour. Stephen was helped out of the vehicle.

One of the policemen was already standing guard, pistol in hand. Stephen was still sleepy with drugs. It took him two or three minutes to register the fact that they had stopped on a deserted patch of wasteland and that the pistol was pointing at him.

He did not fight the needle this time. There was nothing he could do, nowhere he could run. Nevertheless, he began to struggle when he saw his destination – a false compartment in the boot of a Mercedes. But by then the drug was working and it was too late.

Stephen's captors stopped the car and checked him several times during the journey. The compartment was padded to absorb shock and there was a supply of air, but they were afraid he would be sick and choke on his own vomit. Because of that they had kept the drug dose low, and long before they reached their destination Stephen was conscious enough to know what was happening.

He thought later that the drug they used was probably a tranquilliser. Otherwise, he would not have been able to control his panic in the confinement of the coffin-like prison once he became conscious. The dark was total. There was space to move no more than three or four inches. The padding absorbed some of the noise, but the constant drum of the road inches below him was still a nightmare soundtrack. His nose was filled with the smell of rubber, petrol and sweat and once, when he could not contain himself, his own urine. The constant movement churned his stomach and brought bile to his throat. He had lost track of time – even if he had a watch, there would have been no way of looking at it.

He was afraid that the constant thudding noise would harm his hearing, but when the car stopped he could still make out individual sounds. At one halt he heard the car's trunk being raised and then desultory thumps and scrapings that could have been searching movements: perhaps they were at a frontier.

He decided he must concentrate and note any sounds that might help him retrace his journey. He also tried counting the minutes. Both were almost certainly useless tasks but they gave him a feeling of doing something. After what he calculated was about an hour he made out train noises that seemed to come from below him. The sounds went on for a long time. He guessed the car must be passing over a wide bridge with a railway below. Another hour later, by his rough counting, the car stopped again. This time he was hauled out.

They had to hold him upright or he would have fallen. Gradually, he became conscious of his surroundings. The Mercedes had pulled off the road. There was no light other than a pale moon which illuminated a thin layer of snow covering rough ground.

After the trunk, even that seemed blinding. There was nothing in sight but open country. Nevertheless, a blindfold was slipped over his eyes.

'Let him sit a minute,' one of the men said in German, and they helped ease him down on to the edge of the opened trunk.

The movement brought stabs of pain. A wave of dizziness set his head spinning. His stomach lurched. Suddenly he knew he had to throw up. He began to gag. Cramp tore at his guts. He needed to crap too.

It was obvious what was happening.

'Get him away from the fucking car,' screamed one voice.

Hands dragged him upright, hauled him down a slope. He fell to his knees, vomited and then, in panic, struggled to pull down his trousers with his one good hand.

'Jesus,' he heard someone say.

And then another voice, 'Leave him be. He'll be all right. Just let him get it all out.'

Afterwards, he remained squatting, trembling uncontrollably, feeling the bitter cold for the first time. There was nothing on which to wipe himself. He felt around gingerly, found a handful of soft snow. He did the best he could with it. Then he pulled himself to his feet, feeling soiled and humiliated. He desperately wanted to lift the blindfold, but did not dare. He took a hesitant, awkward step in what he thought was the right direction and slipped. He fell painfully, one leg doubled under him. The snow and the earth moved under him and he began to slither down the hillside.

He heard yells, and he dug at the ground blindly in an attempt to stop his slide. His uninjured hand grabbed what felt like a wet rope and he swung to a halt. The blindfold had been torn away and in the dim light he could see he was anchored by a piece of woody taproot trailing in the thin snow above the hard ground. He noticed that there was a lot of it on the hillside – surface root and the thick decaying stalk of some unknown plant that had lost its leaves.

When they reached him, his captors were solicitous and frightened. It reassured him: they did not want him harmed. At least, not yet. He tried to memorise the face of the man bending over him, but sweat and panic blurred his vision; he could make out only a stocky figure with a woollen hat low over heavy features. He was half-carried, half-dragged back to the car. The stocky man helped him brush snow and mud from his anorak. The hood was of the kind that rolls up into the collar. It had become undone and soaked during the fall. Standing behind him, the man painstakingly rolled and refastened it in place so that its cold wetness would not rub against Stephen's neck.

Then the blindfold was replaced, but not before he had managed to focus on a huge shimmering snow-covered plain in the distance below and strange dark circles of shadow on the hillside: he wondered if he was hallucinating. He slumped down on the open trunk again, and was listening to the two men debating whether they should give him brandy when he heard the other car arrive.

This time he was pushed into the back seat.

He was no longer cursing himself or asking what he had got himself into; now it was just a matter of holding himself together minute to minute, trying to cope with whatever came along next. During the journey, he forced himself to count again – it might be useless but he needed something to hold on to. He had reached eighteen minutes when the car stopped. He was bundled out immediately and helped up wooden steps and into a building bursting with warmth and the smell of food.

Others were waiting. He could sense them. Hands stripped off his clothes. He was too exhausted to struggle. Gentler hands checked his bruises, his wrist: certain, knowledgeable. A doctor? Instructions were muttered. A voice started, was interrupted and then spoke again, a different tone. Doors opened, water was running, he was lifted into a warm bath, held there until heat returned to his body, dried, placed in a bed already warm. A mug was pressed into his hands. He drank: hot, sweet milk.

It was all unreal. All a dream. Except for the needle when it entered. That was always real.

The blindfold had been removed. He opened his eyes expecting to find someone else in the room. In his dreams a face had stared down at him as he slept. The face, in deep shadow, was no more than a shape, but he had known who it was and what was happening. But when he awoke he was alone. He had been dressed in an old but clean track suit.

He lifted his head and looked around. The room was wood-panelled, rustic, like a hunting lodge, and the only furniture was the bed and a kitchen chair. The one window was shuttered, but a weak shaft of light penetrated. Obviously day, but without a watch there was no way of knowing the time.

His mind was surprisingly clear and sharp. He shifted in the bed, tensed his muscles one by one. There were a thousand aches and his stomach was still sour, but suddenly he felt that there was nothing he could not handle. What he had been through no longer frightened him; that he had survived so far gave him strength.

He decided to try and stand. He pushed away the duvet, rolled down on to the floor. Gingerly, he stood. OK so far. He took two tentative steps towards the window – and an alarm went off. Nothing happened for about two minutes. Then the door opened, and a man carried in a tray. He was about Stephen's age, and he was bearded and had a mass of wild, black curls. His expression was neutral. He placed the tray on the end of the bed, and then switched off the alarm – a simple battery-operated infra-red device hooked on to the wall.

He left the room without speaking. On the tray there was a mug of coffee, bread, cheese and fruit. Stephen ate, suddenly ravenous, but forcing himself to eat slowly. He did not want to throw up again.

Finished, he checked the window. The blinds were locked. Through the gap, he could make out trees. The hut was in a clearing.

He heard the door open, turned but too late to see anyone. On the floor was a bundle of clothes: dark-green cord trousers, a check shirt, woollen socks, trainers. Like the track suit, which he discarded, all well-worn but clean. The trousers were loose, the shoes tight, but they fitted more or less.

He sat on the bed trying to assess the time. He thought they had probably arrived at the hut some time during the evening of the day he had left Cologne. That meant a journey of maybe twelve to eighteen hours. There had been a fresh smell of cooking suggesting a meal had just been eaten, which could have meant late evening. Then they had drugged him again, but he could not remember further doses during the night. The clarity of his mind now seemed to confirm there had been none. So it was unlikely he had slept more than twelve to fourteen hours. Which would make it the following day any time from early light to four or five in the afternoon. The fact that they were surrounded by trees made it impossible to see the sky through the gap in the blinds. But the light seemed real daytime light, not that of early morning or later afternoon. He decided it was probably somewhere between 10 a.m. and 3 p.m.

He waited for the man to return. He burned with questions, but he was amazed at his patience and his inner calm. After a while, though, he stood and tried the door. It opened. There was no one the other side to stop him. He walked through into a larger room. Here too shutters were drawn, but there was more furniture including a scrubbed pine table. A lamp hung over it and a man, sitting with his back to Stephen, was bent forward, writing.

Without turning, he said, 'Come in. Sit down.'

There were two empty chairs. Stephen took one. He felt shaky again. The seat was cold and damp as though the open fire in the room had not had time to have effect.

He realised the man had spoken in English.

The man turned, and he knew it was the face in the dream.

The most startling thing was how accurate the reconstruction had been. His father looked younger than in Headley's picture – Stephen would have put him in his fifties instead of sixties. But, as far as likeness was concerned, only the hairline and the nose were wrong. The hair had receded at the temples further than in the reconstruction, and the nose was longer.

Stephen absorbed all this with a curious and unexpected detachment. Though unbidden and unwanted, thoughts about this moment had jangled his mind many times since the search began. It was a moment he had both sought and feared. He had imagined many scenarios. All they had had in common was the assumption that the meeting would be emotional – after all, it had been twenty-nine years. Either it would be hate filled or warm and forgiving or nervous and gentle. But full of feeling.

Instead – he felt nothing. No emotion at all, only a kind of deadness. The title line of a Peggy Lee song went through his mind: 'Is this all there is?'

Almost unconsciously, he started noting and memorising Kenyon's appearance for his notes: thin, drawn face (a man on the run?), long fingers nervously playing with some small object he could not make out. Hair still dark brown, only streaked with grey at the temples. Reading glasses set aside. Dark clothes: grey sweater and trousers.

They locked eyes. In the light from the hanging lamp, Stephen could see Kenyon's eyes were blue-grey. For a moment, he wondered where he had seen them before. In Headley's drawing? No – that was in black and white. And then he realised. Looking back at him in the mirror.

His father, nervous, suddenly relaxed his mouth and at the same time dropped his head to one side, giving him a quizzical expression. It was obviously an involuntary movement, a part of the man, a piece of body language adopted a hundred thousand times. And then he began to laugh.

Stephen did not know why at first, and Kenyon shook his head at his son's puzzlement and pointed. Stephen still could not see – and then suddenly it dawned on him. He was sitting facing Kenyon with his head perched on one side, expression quizzical.

A mirror image of his father!

Kenyon saw understanding dawn, began a movement towards Stephen, as though he wanted to reach out for him – but he sank back on his chair.

'I looked at you in the night,' he began. His voice was deep, hesitant.

'To make sure I wasn't dead, ensure you hadn't killed me?'

Kenyon was perplexed by his son's accent – soft but unmistakably American – and hurt by the tone.

'To see what you looked like.' His voice was tired. 'Don't let's fight. I'm not sure I wanted this. As I understand it, you pushed it. It just happened this way.'

'And?'

'And what?' Kenyon had lost his thread.

'And: you looked at me in the night. You were going to add something.'

Kenyon smiled. Still cautious, but suddenly boyishly appealing as he warmed. 'You looked like your mother. That's what I thought. Like your mother. You've got her chin.' He touched his own with the tip of a finger. 'Gives you a resolute look. *Steife Oberlippe.*' He saw Stephen's puzzlement. 'It means stiff upper lip,' he explained. 'What the British have. You don't speak German?'

'Some French, some Spanish, even a few phrases of Russian. But no German. Sorry.' Not true. But he had heard his captors talking in German – better to let them think he could not understand them.

Kenyon began talking again, this time too loud and too fast, trying to create something between them. 'How is she? All right I hope. Do you see her much?'

Stephen wanted to say, 'She could be dead for all you fucking care. And, why the hell do you want to know now? You haven't wanted to know for twenty-five years.' But he did not want to fight either.

He told Kenyon: an abridged, slightly optimistic version of Mary's illness. 'But she's OK,' he concluded. 'A lot of the time she's perfectly lucid, and there's still a lot of things she enjoys – they have a choir, she likes that.'

Kenyon had leaned forward to show his interest, but Stephen could tell he was finding it hard to connect with a world he had left long ago.

Stephen tried to think back twenty-five years, at all that had happened in that time. Not only to him personally – though that was an enormous amount – but to the world. Twenty-five years ago had been pre video, VAT, fast food, couriers, armed police at British airports, the computer except as an oddity, Aids, condoms on open sale . . .

He realised Kenyon was still asking about Mary.

'She's a widow?'

'Yes.' Stephen had forgotten to tell him that. 'He left her OK. Some investments. They're nearly gone now, but there's still the house.' He was about to add, 'And then there's me,' but instead he added simply, 'He was a doctor. A caring man.'

'I know,' said Kenyon.

'You met him?'

'No, I went to the village not long before I did my disappearing act. I suppose I still thought I could work something out. It was too late. I saw his photo. He looked a fine man.'

A silence came over them. They were strangers. There was nothing between them. Kenyon put down the object with which he had been playing and fetched a bottle from a shelf. Ballantines, about two-thirds full.

He poured two glasses. 'Do you want water? There's mineral water somewhere.'

'Just neat.'

Stephen was trying to make out the object his father had placed on the table. It would make a good touch for his articles – that's how he was thinking about the meeting, part of a story to be written. Some kind of worry bead? Impossible to see. It looked like a small coin. He lifted his glass, wondering whether his father still hit the bottle. It was hard – impossible some said – for alcoholics to revert to normal social drinking.

Kenyon read his mind (it was getting disconcerting how his father seemed to be able to see into him). 'You've done your homework,' he said. 'First today. At one time it mightn't have even been the first bottle.' He sipped self-consciously slowly. 'This one. One, two more. That'll do me.'

'You haven't asked about Pamela,' said Stephen.

'Does it get bloodier now?' Again, the boyish grin to soften the words. 'I know how much you've done, how many people you've seen. But tell me, how is Pamela, my beautiful Delilah?'

'Still beautiful.' He patted his pockets with a mock gesture. 'If you'd given me notice I'd have brought you photographs.' He did not add, 'And still wonderful in bed.'

'It's best you didn't.' And then, face serious, voice more intense. 'It was a different world. No! Not just a different world. A different *life*. It's good to see you – I haven't emotions enough to show you how good. I'll have to joke, say, why'd you want to make a grown man cry? And there are things I'd like to know about you. But I have to tell you – and you have to remember: it was a different life.'

Stephen remembered the psychologist's words: 'What your old man did was a form of suicide really.'

'How's your head?' he said, for once not being able to bear the silence.

Kenyon touched it gingerly. 'So you know about that? Of course you do – you're a good investigator, I read you when I can get the papers. It's OK. I get headaches occasionally, but I suspect they're psychosomatic.'

He picked up the coin-like object from the table, held it out for Stephen to take.

A thin, jagged, irregular circle of dull grey metal. Hard to make out what it was at first. Then the weight told him it was lead. His father confirmed his guess.

'The bullet,' Kenyon said. 'Smith and Wesson .38. I can tell you everything about it. I read it up so many times. Length .63 inches, diameter .359, weight 145 grains – though you'd never know to look at it now. The manuals tell you everything except what it feels like . . . Some quack took it out – quarter inch from my brain, he said.' Kenyon laughed. 'Probably exaggerating – doctors do. Makes them more godlike and the patients more grateful.'

Stephen could see that whatever he said he believed it.

'You kept it.'

'The only thing. I destroyed or left behind everything else – you know that too, I imagine. At the last moment, though, I couldn't bear not to keep this.' He laughed again, embarrassed. 'My lucky charm, I guess. It goes wherever I do. Wherever it is, I am. Lost it once in a hotel in Milan. Didn't find out until I was four hundred miles away. Turned round and went straight back, even though it cost me a big deal!'

He held out his hand to retrieve it. He stared at it for a few seconds, and then reached under his sweater and placed it in his shirt pocket.

There was a knock on the door, oddly formal in such a setting. *'Ja. Eintreten!'*

The man who had brought food earlier carried a tray with bowls of soup, cold meats, bread and wine.

'A simple repast,' said Kenyon, still trying to keep the atmosphere light.

He spoke to the man rapidly in German. The words were fast and low. Stephen could only make out, 'Warn them both that it will have to be the last run. It's important. Don't forget that.'

They talked little as they ate. They had too much to say, too many things to ask. So, not knowing where to start, they said almost nothing.

Finally, Kenyon asked the one big question.

'All I know is that you've been looking for me seeing a lot of people, asking questions. What I'm wondering is, why? Why now?'

Stephen picked up the wine bottle. It was still half-full.

'Finish it,' said Kenyon. 'I've had enough.'

They moved to the easy chairs.

'Perhaps we'd better talk,' said Stephen. 'Me first? You first?'

'You first,' said Kenyon. 'I've lost the habit.'

Stephen began with his informal adoption by Ward and Katharine, explaining how and why he had known nothing of Kenyon's disappearance until years later. How he had continued to believe his father had died in Bali and how, finally, only months before, his mother had talked to him and the search had begun.

'I didn't know whether to believe her at first. Then I found the twenty-first birthday card.' He explained how it had seemed out of place and how he had had it tested for fingerprints and hidden writing.

He could see his father was remembering.

'A mad thing to do – I can recall it like yesterday,' said Kenyon. He had been travelling and his flight was delayed. He had got maudlin drunk. He had bought the card at a news-stand, sent it unsigned with a handful of dollar bills from his wallet. 'I don't know how much. I think five hundred dollars. The next day I realised how crazy I had been, but I thought, what the hell? And I had not written anything. There was the stamp on the envelope, but that only revealed the country where it was posted – and I was only passing through.'

He paused. 'Sometimes, I wondered what you had bought. I tried to guess. Some clothes? A camera? A motorbike?'

Stephen realised Kenyon was asking him now.

'A holiday,' he said. 'Mexico.' He did not want to say he had never received the cash.

He expected Kenyon to ask how his mother had explained the money when she had given it to him. But all Kenyon said, smiling, was, 'Good. A good choice at twenty-one.'

He leaned back, and Stephen realised that he was expected to continue.

He did so, keeping to the main points. He explained the search was journalistically motivated, but not the problems that had launched it. He told about Pamela, but not about her visit to his bed, nor about his involvement with Jessica.

At the end, he said, 'And that's it,' watching Kenyon's face and wondering how much longer it could remain in its half-smile.

'They weren't my men,' said Kenyon. 'The people who grabbed you first. I wouldn't want you hurt.'

'You know them, though.'

A shrug. 'From what you say, people I left behind who would still like to see me.'

Stephen waited for further explanation, but Kenyon had moved into the past.

'You were right,' he said. 'The money. It exploded. You should have seen it. Five-pound notes fluttering through the air like snowflakes in a blizzard and all turned bright orange and bloody worthless. Smoke everywhere and me trying to get the windows open. Someone at the door yelling in Belgian and me thinking, fuck, everything gone, everything wasted. I'd forgotten I'd got some more – a few thousand under my shirt. Even when I remembered it, it didn't seem much, but without it I think I'd have blown my brains out.'

He had gone to someone he had once known – he was still circumspect. The five thousand pounds, in sterling as it was, represented a lot of money for starting an enterprise. As Stephen obviously knew, they'd smuggled things across the border.

Stephen couldn't hold himself. 'Fake medicines. Bootleg stuff. Lousy counterfeits.'

Kenyon did not bite. 'Is that what they say? Yes, medicines. And, yes, counterfeits sometimes. Sometimes drugs that had been diverted. It was a needed business.'

The door opened. No knock this time. A man Stephen had not seen before. He wondered how many were in the house.

His face spoke of emergency.

'*Wichtig?*' asked Kenyon. 'Important?'

The man nodded and they left the room together, leaving the door ajar.

Stephen moved closer to it, strained to hear. He caught a few words. He thought he heard 'last run' again, and then a hand closed the door.

Kenyon returned within minutes, face set, body tensed with stress. Three men, including the two Stephen had already seen, were with him. The third, the new man, wore outer clothes: a parka still dotted with snow.

One of them tossed him the old anorak he had worn on the journey. Their faces were hard.

'Put it on,' said Kenyon, his voice low, sad almost.

'What are you doing with me?'

'Sending you back.' He poured them both another drink from the Ballantines bottle.

'Just do exactly what you're told. They don't trust you, but they'll do what I've ordered – provided you don't try to get away from them. Please, for your own sake and for my conscience, don't do anything clever. They'd prefer you vanished for ever. I've told them as long as you are blindfolded – '

He paused, struggled for more words. 'Perhaps later this will seem real – to you as well as me, I suspect. Perhaps then we'll be sorry we did not have more time. Perhaps. I think so. I think I am sorry now.'

He lapsed into silence. His face screwed into thought. Finally, decision made, he took a wallet from his hip pocket, removed a square of paper and passed it to Stephen.

'I lied,' he said. 'I took two things. The bullet and this.'

It was a passport-size portrait of Stephen as a boy, probably from a school photo session. His hair was carefully parted and brushed down. His mouth was fixed in a 'cheese' smile, exposing protruding front teeth, the way they were before they were fixed.

Kenyon took it back immediately, handled it with gentle care, replaced it in the wallet.

'There's a lot I'd wanted to tell you. I'm like the Austrians – I go with the current. *Biegen, nicht brechen*, that's what they say there – "Bend, but don't break". That's something I've learned. Hate ideals – have always thought the world would be a better place without most of them. They're what kill and enslave people. The Nazis, Leninists, Muslims, Christians . . . All the big believers. They're the bastards that have slaughtered millions – always for the people's own good, of course! Not your just-trying-to-get-on-with-living pragmatists like me. You know what Koestler said? "Statistics don't bleed." Good, yes?' His voice was racing, throwing out half-formed thoughts that he suddenly wanted to share.

Tiredness clouded his face, and his voice dropped. 'Only half-true, though. You've got to have some ideals. I've been learning that. You've got them. I can tell that from your pieces I've read. I've admired that. Maybe you're the me that wasn't . . .'

One of the waiting men cleared his throat, noisily, a message that time was passing.

Kenyon snapped into another mood. He raised his glass in a theatrical toast. 'I hope we both have a safe and happy journey.'

He drained his whisky, waited for Stephen to do the same.

The first two men were pulling on their parkas. One took Stephen's arm and they led him to the door.

As he reached it, his father took a step towards him.

He half-turned, wanted to go back. But hands tugged him

through the door. Then a hood was pulled over his head, and he could not catch his father's farewell look.

This time there were no needles and they changed cars twice before they reached their destination. Stephen estimated that they had been travelling for four or five hours. He had kept thinking back on the meeting – trying to get it straight for the story he would write, but at the same time regretting, feeling something was over that had not even had a chance to begin. The end of the journey was sudden. One moment they were driving fast on an open road, the next the car pulled over and stopped. The door was opened, and, still hooded, Stephen was yanked out.

He waited to be grasped and led again. When nothing happened, fear returned: they were going to kill him and that was why his father had avoided taking a final look at him. But almost immediately the car door slammed, the engine revved hard and the vehicle skidded away.

Stephen continued to stand, transfixed, as the sound died in the distance. Finally he pulled off the blindfold. He was on an autobahn, no other traffic in sight. There was a turn-off in view, perhaps one hundred and fifty metres away, and he started towards it. He heard a rumble and minutes later a truck passed him. At first he remained warm from the car, but soon the cold began to bite despite the anorak he wore.

The turn-off had a sign, 'Flughafen. 1 km'. Traffic was almost non-existent. There was no sign of aircraft in the black sky. He guessed it was the middle of the night. He wished he could be more accurate. He was almost certain he knew where he was. He had not travelled long enough to have reached Germany. Schwechat Airport, Vienna. The road he was leaving would be the A4 Autobahn. Instinctively, he knew that if he tried walking to the airport at this hour he would be spotted and picked up. He did not want to be picked up by a police patrol suspecting that he was a terrorist.

He left the road, made a crude matting of branches he tore from bushes. Then, curled into a tight bundle, he waited for the working day to arrive. It was cold but the ground was hard and not sodden. He remained there, hidden, until the traffic turning off to the airport began to increase.

Then he walked. At the edge of the airport he passed a police car, but its occupants did not stop him. He sensed their eyes following him, but at this time of day he could be a workman on an early shift.

Inside the airport, he found a telephone. Nick Benson was his best bet – he should be back home in Bonn. He asked for a collect call. The phone was answered by a woman. Benson came on seconds later.

'I've a problem,' said Stephen.

'You've always got a problem.' Benson's voice was full of sleep, but not angry. He was used to being wakened by the telephone.

He listened and then said, 'Give it twenty minutes. Then go to the Austrian Airlines Desk. I'll have a ticket and money waiting for you.'

And then, confirming, 'For London?'

'Cologne,' said Stephen. 'I've unfinished business'.

Benson met him at Cologne airport. 'You look fucking terrible,' he said. 'I'm surprised they let you on the plane.'

'I need coffee,' said Stephen.

He waited until they were seated in the airport bar. Then Benson said, 'OK. Tell.'

Stephen talked; it still seemed unreal.

Benson kept shaking his head. 'What did he look like?'

'Exactly as I thought.'

'And you didn't feel *anything*?'

Stephen struggled with the answer. He wanted to be honest. 'I don't know,' he said. 'It just wasn't real. At the end, perhaps. A little. He'd kept my photograph. I must have been ten. Imagine that.' He paused and added, 'I think for him too.' The truth was, he had been feeling more since he had left his father. Emotions had crowded in on the flight, so many that he could not separate or define them.

'So what now? asked Benson.

'Back to the hotel. Find Jessica if she's still here. Talk to Miller if he hasn't fled. And then back to London.' He paused. 'And start writing, I guess. That's it.'

Benson used words he had used before. 'Christ,' he said, 'you're a cold fish.'

This time it got through. It was not even true any more. Stephen was talking tough guy out of habit and tiredness.

'What else can I do?' he said. 'It's over.' His voice snapped with exhaustion and frustration. 'I've almost been knifed to death. I've been locked in the boot of a car. I've been turned loose on an autobahn in the middle of the fucking night. I found him. He wants to stay lost. You tell me.'

Benson shrugged. 'I guess you're right. As you say, what else?'

Miller picked up Stephen moments after Benson dropped him outside the hotel.

'It's all right,' said the MI6 man gently, leading him to a car. 'She's all right. She's up in the room. Doesn't even know you've been away. This won't take long.'

The phone, thought Stephen. Benson's phone. He should have known it would be tapped. He had stopped thinking straight. The reason was not just tiredness. It was because he cared. Emotions were scrambling his mind. Still, what the hell! What did it matter? He let himself be eased into the car, too exhausted to protest. Anyway, he had wanted to see Miller, to tie up a few loose ends.

They took him to an anonymous apartment only minutes away. What surprised him was the desultory nature of the questioning. There was one man other than Miller present. Neither of them kept notes, but Stephen took for granted that the room was fitted with recording apparatus.

He had determined to keep to himself his thoughts about his journey, not revealing any of the things he had seen or heard that just might help identify Kenyon's location, although it was obvious to him that the meeting had been somewhere in Hungary. Nor did he say anything about the words he had overheard about 'last run'.

But Miller had scarcely probed.

At the end he had hinted why. 'Sounds like he's finished,' he said, dismissively. 'I guess we can all call it a day.' His eyes were probing. 'You and me both,' he added.

Jessica held Stephen for a long time and then helped him undress and bath. She said 'later' when he tried to talk, and then cradled his head and eased him into sleep.

It was three-thirty in the morning when he woke, still bleary but alert. Jessica was beside him. She had fallen asleep still clothed. His mind was cartwheeling with the events of the previous days.

He could feel the blackness and the thudding of the road, the skidding on the hillside and the stomach-lurching sensation of sliding and spinning, see his father's face the moment he turned. Pictures and thoughts and feelings kaleidoscoped without sense or order. Suddenly, stronger than ever, he again felt full of anger and regret at the way it had gone. Why hadn't he reached out? Fuck! Why hadn't his father reached out?

Taking care not to wake Jessica, Stephen got out of bed, found the Scotch he had bought on the plane from London, and drank straight from the bottle, hoping the alcohol would soothe him. He felt it bite, wanted another, but decided to fetch a glass from the bathroom. He reached for one, and it slipped from his fingers, crashing into pieces on the marble tiles.

The accident triggered the release of all his suppressed emotion. He clenched his right fist, pounded his forehead against the wall tiles. He smashed one hand down on to the wash-basin, realising too late it was his injured wrist. The cast struck the porcelain, sending agony through the whole of his arm. He cursed and felt tears of pain and frustration fill his eyes.

He had wakened Jessica. She tried to calm him.

'I'm OK, OK now,' he said, letting her lead him back into the bedroom.

He was worried about his wrist now. What a stupid bastard he was! He sat on the bed, cradling it in his good hand, examining it. The remnants of the cast remained. Funny thing was that the wrist did not feel broken.

Jessica had switched on the light, and something shone in the broken cast. It lifted out easily. A metal disc, about an eighth of an inch thick, an inch diameter. Like a large version of a watch battery. But with threadlike wires trailing out from it. Suddenly he knew why Miller had shown so little interest in what he remembered about his journey.

Stephen had been fitted with some kind of tracking device from the moment he had been grabbed from hospital.

He had led them to his father.

CHAPTER TWENTY-SIX

They sat up until dawn.

'What are you going to do?' she said.

'What can I do?'

And then, angry, 'What the hell should I do? It's over.'

Trouble was, he knew it was not. He had thought it was, but that was before he had learned that he had probably led his father's pursuers to their quarry. That changed everything.

They ate breakfast – rolls and coffee – in the room. During the night, he had chipped away the rest of the cast: the wrist seemed fine. He stared at the bug, wondered if it was still active. Even if it were, he doubted anyone cared – its use was over. He imagined it was a simple tracking device, enabling someone to follow from a distance. How far? He could only guess from what he had learned of bugging over the years. A mile, two miles, maybe more, depending on the terrain.

Other thoughts crowded in. The meeting with his father had been ended abruptly. Was that because suddenly he had been alerted to pursuers? Impossible to know for sure. But the truth was that by his actions he had betrayed his own father. In addition to the guilt, though, there was something else. After nearly thirty years he and his father had been reunited; he had been through a lot to achieve it. He couldn't just let it go like this.

The hotel radio carried limited stations, but he found a news bulletin. He had had a sudden irrational fear that there would be a report about his father being found dead. All the news, though, was of grander events: the secret police were to be disbanded in East Germany, six people had died in an attack on a Syrian post south of Beirut, there was growing support for Václav Havel as Czechoslovakia's next president, protests were continuing about the involuntary repatriation of Vietnamese boat people from Hong Kong . . .

He switched off the radio. Jessica sat silent, knowing they had said everything there was to be said.

Suddenly he leaned forward, took her hands.

'I've got to find him again,' he said.

'I know.' And then, 'I'm glad you said that.'

The next two hours were filled with fresh activity. Stephen called Benson's number in Bonn from a telephone box. All he got was an answering machine. He left a message asking him to make contact.

Jessica went shopping and returned with large-scale maps of Europe and Hungary. Stephen laid them open on the floor and tried to remember everything he could about the journey, seeing if he could match recollections to details on the maps. After a while, he pushed them aside, beaten. He had already decided that the destination had almost certainly been Hungary. But that was small help: it could have been anywhere in that country.

Benson called him shortly after ten. Stephen cut him short, gave him the number of the telephone box he had used earlier, and was there when Benson called back ten minutes later.

'Are you in a box?' asked Stephen.

Benson snorted. 'What is this cloak-and-dagger stuff?' he asked.

'Where are you?'

Benson was still in Cologne. He had picked up Stephen's message on his answerphone remotely. 'I wanted to see you anyway,' he said. 'I stayed over, talked to a contact, discovered something you ought to know.'

They met, a half-hour later, in the huge entrance hall of the Ludwig Museum of Modern Art. Both had taken precautions against being followed. Stephen followed Benson to the top floor and out on to the roof. They were alone in the shadow of the Cathedral.

Stephen had left the hotel by a fire exit and was wearing the old anorak his kidnappers had given him – he had decided it provided some disguise.

'So?' said Benson. 'I thought you said it was over.'

Stephen told him about the bug. He felt embarrassed. He found it necessary to explain himself but he played down his emotional involvement. It was hard enough trying to come to terms with the

362

change in himself without having to voice it. 'So I've got this guilt thing,' he said. 'He may be a fucking crook, he may have been poisoning half the Eastern bloc with watered penicillin, but I still don't want to be the man who kills him.'

'You may be too late,' said Benson. He added, 'Even if you can find him, and I don't see how the hell you're going to do that.' He pulled his coat collar up against the wind. 'Christ, it's cold,' he said.

Then he added, 'Anyway you're wrong about the watered penicillin.'

The reason he had stayed overnight, he said, was that he had a good contact with the BfV, the Federal Office for the Protection of the Constitution. 'You know what that is?' Stephen did. It was roughly the equivalent of MI5.

'I'd got him checking about "The Irishman". Couldn't resist it. Thought there might be something I should know.' He paused, ready to deal with Stephen's protest at him hacking into his story, but all Stephen said was, 'And?'

'And he found out a little. The Irishman first came to their notice in 1967. That fits in with your dates. Lots of small-grade smuggling, including a few people East to West, at first. Medicines came later and became a bit of a speciality. There was an Austrian doctor who seems to have provided the first contacts with a small plant in Italy. From then on it grew.'

'So?' Stephen's voice was loaded with impatience. It was useful material for when he came to write, but of no help now.

Benson pressed on. 'It wasn't a very safe operation. My contact reckoned almost everyone infiltrated it and made use of it somehow over the years. The BND, probably MI6, the Czechs. They all tolerated it because it gave them something.'

Again, only confirmation of what Stephen already knew.

'One more thing – and this I thought you'd like to know,' Benson continued. 'It wasn't watered penicillin. The stuff they smuggled in was good stuff. OK, it was mainly bootleg, although I'm told some was bought in on the grey market, and it wasn't one hundred per cent. But it was good counterfeit, did its job. And if you think about the alternatives . . .'

'So?'

'So I'm saying it wasn't that shit-awful a trade. OK, people had to be rich to pay for it or they had to get the money some other

363

way. But that's just the real world. Do you have any conception of what medical care was like over there if you weren't a party bigwig, what it's like even now? Dickens had nothing in it. A tumour? Lucky to get an aspirin. Need an operation? Hope to God they've got enough anaesthetic. Die in hospital and the first thing they'll do is whip away your bloodstained bandages and stick them on the man in the next bed who hasn't got any at all. You don't know the East like I do. Without the black market, life would have been even more of a fucking hell-hole than it was. Mostly, it was the only thing that made it liveable.'

Stephen waited, but there was no more.

'Thanks,' he said. He meant it. Although he had never admitted it, the lie of his father's heroism in dying to save someone's life had helped sustain him over the years. When he had discovered it was a fable, even that had gone. Then Miller had told him Kenyon was just an immoral crook, killing people with substandard medicines – a man with no pity, no other point in life but his own survival. Another blow, shattering the image that was all he had of his father. Relief flooded over him. OK, his father might be a villain but he was one with a deep-down core of morality.

Time to go but neither moved.

'I've got my man checking some more,' said Benson. 'But it's like you heard – your father vanished nearly a year ago. A lot of people would like to talk to him.'

It began to rain. Without thinking, Stephen unbuttoned the hood on the anorak and pulled it over his head. Something fell out and hit the floor.

He stooped to pick it up. He stared at it puzzled. A piece of old stem or stalk, a good inch thick, some four inches long. It must have been there when he was handed the jacket. Then he remembered the fall on the slope on the way to his father after he had been sick. He peered more closely. The stalk was like the one he had grabbed to halt his slide. There had been a lot of it on the hillside. A rotting piece must have been torn away, got caught up in the hood.

'What is it?' asked Benson.

'A bit of wood.' He explained its background.

'Can I see?'

Benson examined it. One end was still encrusted with soil.

'Remember the Standler kidnap?' asked Benson.

'Vaguely.' Stephen recalled a terrorist kidnapping that had gone wrong. The victim had been found murdered.

'They convicted someone after linking him with the body because of soil on his shoes. To the forensic experts, it wasn't just soil, it was a particular soil.'

Stephen was sceptical. 'So what? So they scrape the soil off this and come up with the revelation that in all of Europe there's one little place it could have come from . . . ?'

'OK,' said Benson, 'it's a longshot. But let me keep it. Let me try. What else have you?'

They finished their conversation in the square. People passed with bulging shopping bags. It was a little over a week to Christmas.

'Where next?' asked Benson.

'Back to the hotel. I'm going to persuade Jessica it's time for her to go home. I guess I've run out of leads. I think I might go to Budapest. God knows what I'll do there, but there might be something.'

He stared down at the damp pavement. He knew that Benson had good contacts throughout Eastern Europe. The correspondent had spent years cultivating them. As the least repressive of the Communist regimes and lying, as it did, at the very centre of Europe, Hungary would have been one of the countries he would have known best.

'The place is still in turmoil,' said Benson. It had been in Hungary that the breakdown of Communism in Eastern Europe had really begun the previous May. After four decades, Hungarians had begun tearing down the Iron Curtain along the country's border with Austria. In September it had allowed the passage of tens of thousands of East Germans to the West. In October it had ended forty-one years of Communist rule.

Still Stephen said nothing. His plea, though unspoken, was clear.

When Benson finally spoke he was decisive. 'We'll do best taking the train to Vienna and a flight from there,' he said. 'Your friend Miller may have people keeping watch at the airport. There's a train, via Munich, just before four. I've caught it before. These days they'll issue a visa when you arrive at Budapest airport.'

He turned to face Stephen. 'That's what you want me to say.'

365

'I owe you again.'

'Just make sure you're there on time.'

They reached Vienna at six the following morning after a fourteen-hour journey. There was a train for Budapest ninety minutes later. Catching it would save them over three hours as against taking the next available flight. The only fear was over whether Stephen would be allowed to cross the border without a visa. They decided to risk it.

Time was important. And they knew now where to go.

Benson had only just caught the train at Cologne. Stephen could see he was elated, but he had refused to say anything until the train was moving.

Checking no one else could see, he had taken the piece of stalk from his pocket. It was now contained in a transparent sample bag. He had taken it to a forensic laboratory, he explained. There, a scientist had confirmed that soil, composed as it was from dead plant and animal matter and minute particles of rock, was one of the easiest substances to identify and place within a few miles. That was the good news. The bad news was that identifying an area would need the help of specialist geologists – and it would take time, possibly a great deal of time. Even then it might not prove possible in practice. Differences in soil were often destroyed when it was treated with fertilisers – and that might prove to be the case here: the stalk looked as though it came from a cabbage or cauliflower-like plant.

Not so, Benson had protested – it had been growing wild on a hillside.

At that, the scientist had shown fresh interest and he had made a telephone call. Benson had been passed to a colleague at the Botanisches Institut on Gyrhofstrasse.

The botanist there had carefully examined the stalk, asked a few pertinent questions, and had then told Benson he was lucky. The stalk came from a plant called *Crambe tataria*. Local people knew it as 'Tartar bread' – legend said that the fleshy roots had been roasted and eaten during the Tartar invasion of Hungary in the thirteenth century. A relative of the cabbage family, it was covered with small, white flowers in May, followed by tiny grape-like fruits. By now, though, most of the plant would have died down. The roots would remain, and also, depending on the weather conditions, the tough, chunky stem.

'So it came from Hungary?' Benson had said at the end of the lecture. At least, that was useful confirmation – but no more.

'Yes,' the botanist had added impatiently, 'but you don't fully understand. I am saying it is *rare*. It occurs only in Hungary, yes. But even there, only in a few localities.' He was already consulting reference books.

Benson moved the sample bag and opened a map of Hungary. It was already marked.

'Just three places,' he told Stephen triumphantly.

An hour later they had pinned it down to one. The hills above the towns of Balatonkenese and Balatonfüzfö on the north-eastern corner of Lake Balaton. It fitted Stephen's timing. It also meshed with the oddments he could recall.

The crossing over of railway lines had probably been at Györ, fifty-five miles from the Austro–Hungarian border at Sopron. The large circular 'shadows' Stephen had seen on the hillside above him after he had fallen could have been the dark holes, known as 'Tartar caves', again special to the area. And the snow-covered plain below that Stephen had thought part of his hallucination? Not a plain, but water – the lake itself, thick with ice.

A pack of Marlboro and his press card got Stephen across the border. At 11.35 a.m. Budapest station was bursting with crowds. Cab-drivers jostled for fares; other Hungarians, capitalising on the shortage of hotel accommodation, fought to rent out rooms in their homes to incoming Westerners.

More Marlboro bought Stephen and Benson a cab ride to a garage where they hired a nearly new Russian-built Lada Samara 1300, tank already full of petrol. They drove for more than an hour, taking the M7 motorway, passing the northern shore of Lake Velencei Tó. As they neared Lake Balaton they turned north on to Route 71. The first sight of the lake was spectacular: the ice-covered water stretched out into the far distance and hills soared on the horizon. A group of skaters traced elaborate patterns, the sun flashing on the blades of their skates.

The shore they followed to Balatonkenese, though, was silted and monotonous, and the town itself when they reached it had a deserted feel. Even in season, Benson explained, it was not one of the major resorts. Most of the hotels had closed for the winter. They found one on the waterside still open. The owner/manager was effusive: plenty of time for lunch, he said, even though it was late. They ate a kind of pike, and then they began their search.

Benson had been optimistic on the train: although there were luxury villas used year round, Balaton was primarily a summer resort area. The building in which Stephen had met his father had seemed like a fishing or holiday lodge. In the summer such places would have been occupied by thousands of shifting tourists. In the winter, their occupants would be almost as rare as the plant that had guided them there.

In the event, it took a lot of walking and driving, a lot of questioning and showing of photographs – and the rest of the Marlboro – before they found the hut. It was a summer cottage, one of a number scattered in a forest of pines and oaks.

It had taken them two days. And they were almost too late.

The man was lying on one of the beds when Stephen and Benson broke in. He was barely conscious, and at first they thought he was dead. Despite the injuries, Stephen recognised him immediately – he had driven the car one leg of the journey to Vienna.

He lay naked, hands and feet still tied to the frame of the bed, though it was now an unnecessary precaution. He could barely raise his head, let alone move his body. His toes and fingers had been broken, crushed beneath a stone which still lay blood-smeared on the floor. His face and stomach were pocked with cigarette burns. Even that, it seemed, had not been enough. His eyelids were torn where they had been taped back so that he could not close his eyes. Then, judging from the injuries and the discarded burned spills on the floor, naked flame had been held to his eyeballs.

The ultimate torture, though, had been in leaving him alive. Unless Stephen and Benson had arrived he would simply have died – which, Stephen feared, he might do anyway.

Stephen fought back anger and nausea. What kind of men could have done this? What had they done with his father? 'We'd better get him to a doctor,' he said at last.

'Not yet,' said Benson. 'A little longer isn't going to make any difference to him. Ask your questions. You can't save him now. You might save your old man – if he's still alive.'

Stephen lifted the man's head, supported it with his rolled jacket. He wanted to give the man water, but Benson stopped him – 'We don't know if he's injured inside. Best leave it.' Stephen placed his mouth near the man's ear. In his halting German, he talked gently, reminding the man that he was Kenyon's son.

They *must* know what had happened, what the man knew, he said. Soon, he promised, they would get him to a doctor.

The words when they came were faltering. It was obvious that what he knew he had already told his torturers. Kenyon had left before his pursuers had arrived. He was headed for Romania with a truckful of medicines. There were a number of drop-off points in the country, but the man did not know where they were. All he did know was Kenyon's final call: a carpet warehouse in Bucharest, where he was due on 21 December. Painfully, he spelled out the address.

'The last run!' said Stephen suddenly. That's what it was. That's what his father and the other men had been discussing in German, not knowing Stephen could hear and understand the words. This last trip into Romania.

Stephen saw the puzzlement on Benson's face. They were kneeling either side of the bed close to the man so as not to miss his words. He explained.

At Stephen's words, the man on the bed tried to speak again. Stephen bent closer. 'Take your time,' he said. The man collapsed into silence and then tried once more. At first the words were inaudible, but suddenly the man found some strength.

'No,' he said. '*Not* the last run. Your father saying "No more last run". He had decided . . . we should depart, leave the medicines . . . too dangerous. After you left, he changed his mind. Said the medicines should not waste . . . people need them. Romania. There was argument. Only one man went with him. The others left. I . . . stayed here . . .'

Stephen waited, but there was no more. The effort had drained the man's remaining strength.

For a few seconds, Stephen and Benson stared at each other across the bed. Neither spoke though the man's words hung between them: Kenyon had gone into Romania *because* of his meeting with Stephen. Something in his son and his search had made him change his plans to quit, take his dangerous decision. Hadn't he spoken about Stephen's idealism? '*Maybe you're the me that wasn't . . .*'

Silently, they busied themselves with the man, his injuries now their priority. They wrapped him in blankets, gently carried him to the car, and then drove him to Balatonfüred further west along the north shore of the lake. That resort, a renowned centre for treating cardiac patients, had a state hospital, said Benson.

They left the man on a bench less than fifty yards from the main entrance. It was freezing cold, but they had wrapped him in every layer of material they could find. They drove off immediately. Minutes later they alerted the hospital by telephone. It was the best they could do.

Time to move on.

Stephen and Benson used the return drive to Budapest to review what they had learned. Kenyon had left before his pursuers had moved in. At this moment, unless something had gone wrong, he was somewhere in Romania. He was due in Bucharest in three days' time. There, at an address they had, he would hand over what remained of his consignment. The trouble was, Stephen and Benson were not the only people with the information. When Kenyon arrived, he would find his enemies waiting for him.

A waste of time speculating exactly who they were. It was Miller, no doubt, who had had the bug planted and who had found the hut. Stephen suspected that at that stage Miller, and MI6, might have passed on the information to others seeking Kenyon – people who, they knew, would dispose of him without any mercy. That way, British intelligence would achieve its aims without bloodying its own hands.

Stephen had just one advantage. The man Kenyon's pursuers had found at the hut had not been able to keep back anything from his torturers. But in his agony he had repeated over and over again *exactly* what Kenyon had told him: that he would arrive at the Bucharest address on the *22nd* December. To Stephen, though, the injured man had added further information; he had explained painfully that, to Kenyon and his closest confidants, this was a routine code for the day before, the *21st*. Over the years, Kenyon had used an elementary security system of always speaking of dates and times a digit out. Thus 2 p.m. on the 3rd was really 1 p.m. on the 2nd. A legacy, Stephen and Benson suspected, from his wartime intelligence days.

Where did all that leave them, though? Both men fell into silence.

Benson was the first to break it.

'Ever been into Romania?' he asked.

Stephen hadn't. 'You?' he said.

'Once or twice.' Benson paused before adding, 'One of the few places that gives me the shits even to think of it.'

He spelled out why: even by Iron Curtain standards it was brutal. The Securitate had one hundred thousand men, more secret policemen per head of the population than anywhere else in the Communist world. Thanks to the megalomaniac Nicolae Ceauşescu, people had no rights, no contact was allowed with the outside world – Romanians who talked to foreigners had to report details to the secret police within twenty-four hours. Every typewriter had to have its face on file to prevent it being used for secret anti-state propaganda. Duplicators were illegal. There was barely any food. Even the centre of Bucharest was mostly in darkness because electricity was heavily rationed. Women had it even worse than men – it was their duty to have at least five children: contraceptives were illegal, women who did not conceive were subjected to compulsory medical examinations to find out why.

Benson himself had a special problem. He knew through contacts inside Romania that he was on the Securitate's wanted list. They believed that he had names of anti-Ceauşescu dissidents. On his last visit he had got out just ahead of them. Even in normal times it would be dangerous for him to return to the country. Now, with reports coming through of rebellion and unrest – there had been killings at Timisoara – it would be complete madness.

'It means I'd put you at risk too,' he said apologetically. He took it for granted that Stephen would try to get into the country.

'God knows if you'll make it,' he said. 'You'll need a visa.' He paused. 'I can get you that, I think. What do you call yourself on your passport?'

'Consultant,' said Stephen.

'Good. Despite all that's happening, they want Western businessmen. God knows, all the years they've been destroying their own people they've kept on sucking up to the West. They probably want to show the world they regard everything as normal too – that could be in your favour.'

Benson dropped Stephen at a bar near the railway station.

'I'll be back as soon as I can,' he said.

There were about a dozen people in the bar. Stephen took a seat at a corner table, ordered a beer, and concentrated on trying not to think about the man who had been tortured. He finished the beer, ordered another. It wasn't helping. He needed hard liquor, he needed to get drunk, but he knew he did not dare.

Beer had spilled down the side of his glass and he traced patterns on the table-top. Crazy, he told himself. Crazy. He had set off to find his father and had ended up probably killing him. Correction, probably killing both of them – because that was a real prospect if he went in. It was a funny feeling. It didn't seem like this when you were genuinely on a story – being a journalist let you convince yourself you were somehow shielded from reality and danger, allowed you to see yourself not as a participant but as an observer. If someone was firing at you, he wouldn't know that, of course. But you did, and it was that which made the difference. Not this time. He could not be any more deeply involved.

He'd been keeping watch on the other occupants of the bar out of the corner of his eye. They'd been nervous when he had first arrived, but looked as though they had relaxed now. A man in a long black leather coat entered with a woman a pace behind. He looked like a pimp. He ordered a drink for himself, looked around, whispered to the woman, and she walked over to Stephen's table. She held out a cigarette without speaking. When he did not react, she began to say something, but then she saw his eyes and she returned to the bar. Stephen tensed himself. He couldn't afford trouble, but nor did he want to leave before Benson returned. He waited to see what the pimp would do. The man listened to the woman, threw back his drink, said something that made her laugh, and led her back into the street.

Benson rejoined him two hours later. He brought a beer from the bar, sat and slid Stephen's passport under the table.

'Thank God for contacts,' he said. He looked drained.

Benson carried a small, canvas haversack. 'For you,' he said. He explained that it contained brandy, fruit, cheese and bread. 'You'll probably need them,' he said.

There were also two cartons of Kent cigarettes which he had bought on the black market. 'Use them carefully,' Benson said. 'They're the real currency of Romania. Not just American cigarettes. *Kent* cigarettes. God knows why. Someone once told

372

me that a relief mission flew in crates of them years ago and they've been special ever since. Sounds a load of cock to me but, whatever the reason, they're like gold nuggets.' There was also a pack of printing samples which Benson had collected from another contact. No wonder he looked drained, thought Stephen.

Benson had also checked trains. The night train was still running. The journey was scheduled to take fifteen hours. If all went well, Stephen would arrive in Bucharest late morning. God knew what he would find – or what he would do. He would have to hit the ball the way it landed.

Benson gave him two telephone numbers and a password to memorise. 'If they're still there, they'll help you.' An earlier suspicion hardened in Stephen's mind. Benson's contact with the Romanian dissidents on previous visits had gone far beyond simply reporting their activities. Once, that realisation would have angered Stephen, would have diminished Benson in his eyes – he had always believed a reporter's job was to *report*, not to get involved however good the cause. But now he was simply grateful that it increased the help that Benson could give.

They said goodbye outside the bar, shaking hands formally. Benson did not say 'good luck'. He just said, 'You've come a long way from sorting through your mother's bits and pieces in a house in an English village.'

'Even further from a gambling club a quarter century ago,' said Stephen.

'Just don't die on me,' said Benson. 'That girl's too young for you – but she wants you.'

CHAPTER TWENTY-SEVEN

The metal plate on the train said it had been made in East Germany. There were three other men in Stephen's compartment. Two Russians going to Moscow and a Hungarian who said he was a glass importer. Stephen, rehearsing his story for the border guards, explained that he was a publishing consultant who had been visiting Budapest to explore printing facilities; while there he had decided to investigate opportunities in Romania.

All found his words amusing. Didn't he know how backward Romanians were? The Hungarian asked him a riddle. What was a Romanian sandwich? He waited until Stephen shook his head, and then produced the answer: 'A meat coupon inside two bread coupons.'

The laughter was too loud, too forced: they were all thinking of the massacre they knew had taken place at Timisoara. With the Romanian dictator facing his first serious threat in twenty-five years, there was no knowing whether the train would be allowed through.

They reached the border at midnight. Stephen, nerves taut, watched Hungarian soldiers leave the train and Romanian troops in Russian-style caps with ear flaps replace them. Fog swirled over the platform, forming ghostly patterns.

The checks and formalities lasted over two hours. Stephen's passport with its new visa – he did not know whether it was genuine or forged – was scrutinised carefully, passed around, discussed. He was questioned about the reasons for his visit. He carried one case, a travel grip, together with the haversack that Benson had given him. Contents were poured out unceremoniously; fingers probed for hidden compartments. The brandy bottle was held up to the light, opened, sniffed. The printing samples were taken away and returned by a civilian in a leather coat who listened to Stephen's story with expressionless face before slapping them on the table without speaking. Another guard asked him whether he 'had Bibles'.

Stephen concentrated on remaining courteous without showing fear. With men like these you had no rights. The wrong expression or an unguarded word were all it took to provoke them into detaining you or turning you back. Normally, visas were dispensed at the border. Not this time. Those without were shunted to one side. A German, who protested angrily, was led away.

Stephen waited, remembering other times, other borders, some more dangerous than this but not as nerve-racking because this time he *had* to get through. His passport had been taken away again. Yet another man appeared, this time in a grey suit. He held out the passport. 'This is not you,' he said.

'The photo was taken four years ago,' said Stephen.

The man disregarded the answer. 'You are a journalist.'

Stephen forced himself to be calm. He knew the man was only probing. Obviously, journalists were trying to get into the country. It was a stock accusation.

'I'm a printing consultant. Nothing to do with journalism.'

A pause while the man stared at him, eyes seeking reaction. Then the passport was thrust back at him. Stephen took it, stood uncertain, and then a guard gestured for him to move. He was cleared.

Back in the compartment, as the train pulled out, the Hungarian said, 'They're edgy. Must be wondering how long they'll survive. They say the revolutionaries have been poisoning the water.' It was the first reference to what had happened in the country. The banter earlier in the journey had been a group pretence at normality. The two Russians, burrowing themselves down on the top couchettes, pretended not to hear. Stephen muttered noncommittal words. He had no wish to get involved in a discussion about Romanian politics. Years of being a reporter had taught him the importance of fading into the background. Besides, he had only the man's word that he was a glass importer. If informers were everywhere in Romania, why not here? Why not this man?

'It's said there was firing at the train earlier this week,' the man continued. But Stephen, like the Russians, had made himself deaf.

He woke several times during the night. His head rested near the window, and in the moonlight he watched woods give way to villages with wooden houses, gentle streams through pastoral fields yield to sheer rock. Frequently he saw soldiers beside the track, giving strength to the Hungarian's words.

He kept thinking of his father's change of heart, his decision to risk himself by entering this country instead of making a run for it. He was convinced that it was seeing him that had brought Kenyon's second thoughts. For all his words about bending with the wind, about hating ideals, his father did have lines he would not cross – the way he would only deal in drugs that, though illicit, were safe and effective showed that. Over the years, there must have been many pressures to handle more profitable but contaminated medicines. This decision to take medical supplies into Romania, though, went further than that: it was a positive, deliberate act, one tempting enormous dangers, carrying massive risks. And the reason? Stephen could see only one: his father was emulating the idealism he saw in the son he had abandoned.

Just as the search had changed Stephen, so too had it altered his father.

And, out of those thoughts, another returned – one full of a terrible irony. In his dogged search for his father, Stephen had put him more in hazard. First, physically, by helping Miller find him. And then, by bringing about the emotions that could easily lead to his death.

As Bucharest neared, the train became a local stopping service for peasants on the way to market. Outside, horse-drawn carts outnumbered cars. At a petrol station, an enormous queue had formed. 'Waiting for their monthly ration,' explained the Hungarian.

The Gara de Nord was packed. Soldiers and groups of tough-looking men in bomber jackets strode through the crowds. Many incoming passengers were taken aside to be searched; passers-by averted their eyes with years of practice.

The cab-driver who took him to the Intercontinental wanted paying in cigarettes, but Stephen pretended not to understand: by now he had learned their value, and would keep them in reserve.

The hammering he had taken in the previous days had produced in him a numbed, almost robotic, feeling. He was like a long-distance runner: he could not go any faster but he felt he could keep on going for ever. What was happening around him barely registered. The early mist had gone and the late morning was dry, sunny and bright. The wide, tree-lined avenues and the cafés were a reminder of why Bucharest had once been known as the Paris of the East. That should have lifted him – but it did not. But then neither did the constant sight of Securitate fill him with menace and fear.

His hotel room was on the eleventh floor and he stared down at the city below. Cranes cut across the skyline. He knew they marked the passage that had been ripped through the old city for the Boulevard of the Victory of Socialism. It – and the cranes – led to the building that dominated his view. The still uncompleted one thousand-room House of the Republic, the Ceauşescus' gold and marble palace on which tens of thousands of near-starving workers had literally slaved for a decade.

Something got through then. He unstoppered the brandy he had brought with him and drank deep. Benson had supplied a slim guide to the city which the border guards had failed to find. It had a fold-out map. It was not very detailed but it was adequate for his purpose. With Benson's help, he had already studied and memorised the route to his father's rendezvous point, a carpet warehouse in the old district.

The big question, of course, was whether his father would keep the rendezvous. He might have been arrested already. He could have had another change of heart – decided that, after all, it was too dangerous and turned back.

Stephen dismissed the thoughts. He *had* to assume it was all going ahead. He ate lunch in the hotel, walked in the afternoon, trying to check whether he was under surveillance. He could see no one. His cover, he knew, was flimsy, and would not survive even slight scrutiny. To add some credibility, he had telephoned the Ministry of Commerce to ask for an appointment regarding printing facilities. He had been cut off almost immediately. But, at least, the attempt would have been logged at the hotel's switchboard.

Now, as he walked, he waited until he was certain that he was not being followed before using a public box to call the numbers Benson had given him.

The first rang and rang. He tried the second. It was answered almost immediately.

'Is that the Tourist Office?' he asked as directed by Benson. 'I would like to speak with Mr Pascu.'

'Mr Pascu is out. This is Mr Popa.'

The right answer.

'I have a pocket calculator that was promised for your son. I wonder if I could give it to you some time.'

The man should have answered with another memorised phrase. But he disregarded it to ask anxiously, 'Is it urgent? It is a difficult time.'

'Very urgent.'

There was a pause, and Stephen feared the other had broken the connection.

'Hello!'

'I am thinking. Please be patient.'

Then. 'There is a café.' He named it. 'Be outside at six o'clock. A car will pass, flash its lights and turn the corner and stop. You will get in.'

The car was a black Dacia, the kind used by officialdom. The driver wore the uniform of a militiaman. Stephen had no time to weigh up the situation, just long enough to clamber into the opened door before the vehicle pulled away.

They drove for a few minutes, turned into an empty side street and stopped. Much of the city was in darkness. Electricity was in short supply: at ten o'clock it was turned off completely.

'This is a dangerous time,' said the man. He spoke in English.

'I know. I am sorry, but Benson said you would help me.'

'You are a journalist too?'

'Yes, but it is not that.'

He explained. He had no time for caution. If he were to achieve anything, he had to make use of the little contact he had – and hope to God there had been no infiltration by the secret police.

The man thought long. 'There have been more outbreaks of unrest in the country. You know that our wonderful president has been abroad in Tehran? He arrived back today. He is to speak on television tonight.'

He paused to light a cigarette. He smoked like a soldier, sucking through cupped hand to hide the glow. 'It is difficult,' he repeated.

He was struggling. There was nothing Stephen could do or say, only wait. Again he got the impression that the dissidents owed

378

Benson for more than his journalism. If he received co-operation, it would be because another reporter had done things he would never have allowed himself to do, got involved in a way normally he would have hated and condemned. Another irony!

At last the man made his decision.

'I will do what I can. Benson has been a good friend. You too will take out information, publish it? I will give you facts.'

The man dropped him back at the café. Stephen was to be at the same spot the following morning at 9 a.m.

The warehouse was on a corner with entrances to two streets. Once more, Stephen had to force back doubts about whether his father would ever make the rendezvous. All that he could do was believe that he would and be ready to warn him.

It had been tempting to approach the warehouse head-on. But Kenyon's contact could be anyone there and, anyway, even if he found the right man, how could Stephen be certain he could convince him he was genuine?

The militiaman was on time. His name, he volunteered, was Dumitru. From the cut of his uniform and his self-assurance he ranked high. He had brought a black bomber jacket and a beret for Stephen to wear.

As Stephen slipped them on, he explained that he had commandeered a room overlooking the warehouse.

'I have warned them to say nothing to anyone,' he told Stephen. He laughed sadly. 'Fortunately, it is easy to persuade people there are spies everywhere.'

He swept through a shop with Stephen at his heels. Nodding officiously to the shopkeeper he led the way to the first floor.

A colleague, a much older man, was waiting. Dumitru introduced him as Petre.

'He will stay with you,' he told Stephen. 'I regret I must go. Our leader was on television last night – you may have seen. He is blaming the Fascists and the hooligans and the foreign spies. Today he is to address his people from the Central Committee Building. I must be there.'

'That's why there are so many police and troops on the streets?'

'They are demonstrating that everything is under control – and they are also reminding people it is their duty to go to the square to listen. It would never do if our glorious leader did not get a suitably large and adoring audience.'

Once he had left, Stephen and Petre settled down to watch the street. They had only a few words of Italian between them; it was soon exhausted.

After about forty-five minutes Petre nudged him and gestured in the direction of a van that had stopped close to one of the warehouse's entrances. They tensed and then relaxed as it became obvious that it was a false alarm – the vehicle had broken down. One wheel was at a strange angle. The two watchers saw the driver kick at it angrily and then walk away, no doubt to find help.

Kenyon arrived soon afterwards – but Stephen almost missed him.

His attention was fixed on a minibus that had stopped minutes before about one hundred metres away. What held him was the fact that it was occupied by men in uniform. He was worrying what, if anything, it meant when he became aware of the closed truck that had already come to a halt outside one of the warehouse's entrances.

He switched his attention to it. As he watched, the driver's door opened, and an unmistakable figure dropped down on to the pavement.

His father.

Stephen's eyes swivelled back to the minibus. He had a nervous gut-feeling. It had begun to move – slowly, in the direction of the warehouse.

There were three vehicles in Stephen's vision now. His father's truck, from which another man was just emerging, distinctive yellow-and-black-check scarf flapping. The minibus with its uniformed men. And the broken-down van.

An inner voice screamed that he was witnessing a set-up.

He rose to make for the street, but new movement below held him – men had begun to clamber from the back of the broken-down van. They must have been waiting for Kenyon's arrival.

Neither they nor Kenyon had noticed the uniformed men in the bus.

Stephen thought, it's like the Keystone Cops – except it's for real. Transfixed, unable to do anything, he saw the men from the van begin moving in on Kenyon and his companion.

And then the militia bus arrived.

Moments later, Kenyon and his companion and their pursuers were being rounded up by three armed soldiers and shoved on to the bus.

Stephen's head reeled: how could the militia have known? Had Dumitru betrayed them? Then he realised what was happening – they were among the people being 'persuaded' to swell the crowds in the square for the president's speech!

Petre tugged his arm. They reached the street as the bus was pulling out of sight. A battered delivery van was near and Petre commandeered it, flashing his ID card. The driver, terrified, drove in the direction of the Central Committee Building as ordered.

They had to abandon the vehicle well short of their destination. The bus had vanished from sight, and all they could do was head for the square on foot.

It was a mild, sunny day and the square was crowded with people waiting for Ceauşescu to appear. At the front of the crowd, the faithful held aloft banners and flags. Hopeless to think of finding anyone here! Stephen cursed his bad luck as he concentrated on staying close to Petre.

Suddenly, a murmur swept through the crowd, and above in the distance Stephen saw figures appear on the balcony of the Central Committee Building. The President stood out in his black astrakhan hat and coat with matching astrakhan collar. The dumpy figure of his wife was beside him. On either side stood aides and security men.

The crowd hushed and then a surprisingly old and weary voice echoed over the loudspeakers. Gradually it began to hammer home points, pausing only for the orchestrated clapping.

Stephen's eyes were never still, one moment on the president, the next scanning the crowd. And then – incredibly – he saw them. Or at least he saw the distinctive bright check scarf of his father's companion.

Tugging at Petre's sleeve to alert him, Stephen began to edge his way through the crowd in the man's direction. As he did, he heard the mood of the crowd change. Booing broke out, hesitantly at first, and then louder and more widespread. Ceauşescu's voice faltered. And then came whistles of derision.

Stephen sensed the enormity of what was taking place. He

stopped and stared about, noting the complete bafflement imprinted on the faces of Securitate men. Nothing like this could ever have happened before.

The journalist in him acknowledged the importance of the moment, instinctively recording the image of the huge square packed with the resentful press-ganged throng, the puppet dictator on the distant flag-draped balcony.

Then his professionalism evaporated as he saw what was happening under his nose. His mouth dried with horror as he realised how the men immediately around his father's companion were using the confusion and anonymity of the mob. While the rest of the crowd were concentrating on the distant balcony, they were directing their whole being to murder. They had joined hands in a tight circle around their victim and were squeezing their own bodies closer and closer together. The man was being crushed in a human vice. Briefly, through a gap, Stephen saw the man's head thrashing in agony as the air was forced from his body. He was trying to scream, but the pressure on his chest and diaphragm prevented any sound emerging. Except that he could see what was happening to him, it must have been like being buried alive under tons of earth.

From less than nine feet away, Stephen and Petre saw all this. They fought to break through. Petre shouted that he was Securitate, a mistake because, in its new mood, people turned on him.

Stephen, shouting in English to pacify the crowd, helped tug Petre clear. Arms linked, they finally broke through, but it was too late. The men were melting away and their victim had already sunk to the ground. Petre fell down, tried to help, but was swept on by the crowd. The last Stephen saw of the man was a white face vanishing under a stampede of crushing feet, a thin line of blood slowly running from the corner of his mouth like the trail of a snail.

The crowd was swaying now, locked together, scuffling and yelling. More screams broke out, in front of him a woman stumbled and shrieked. Securitate men were moving in every-where. Many of the people around Stephen were instinctively pulling coat lapels up over their faces to hide their identity from the secret-police cameras they knew must be photographing the scene.

A burst of gunfire echoed. Petre began to pull at him. He was yelling urgently in Romanian, but the message was obvious: this was no place to be caught. And then Stephen saw his father. He was elbowing his way through the outer ring of the crowd with two of his pursuers closing on him.

Stephen and Petre emerged from the crowd a few yards behind them. Kenyon's pursuers were grappling with him. Stephen dived for one man, Petre for the other. Stephen's target, caught unawares and off balance, crashed to the ground, face first, taking the whole weight of Stephen on top of him. He did not move when Stephen hauled himself back to his feet. He turned to help Petre, but he was not needed. The man he had tackled was running away.

Kenyon tried to break away, but Stephen grabbed him.

'It's me,' he yelled. 'For God's sake, it's me.'

Behind them there was fresh gunfire, more persistent now. From the corner of his eye, Stephen could see Securitate men swinging clubs.

Petre was already moving and they ran to follow. Away from the square. Across a wide avenue into a series of narrow streets, until finally they reached a shabby courtyard. It was empty but for a parked flatbed truck. Petre gestured they were to climb into the back. Before yanking a grubby tarpaulin over them, he pressed a warning finger to his lips, and then he held up both hands, spread his fingers twice – twenty. They heard him walk away. They waited in sweaty silence, trying to stifle their harsh breathing, listening to muffled firing, to sudden shouts. Later, there were footsteps, Petre's low voice, the truck rocking as two people climbed in. It drove off even before the doors had slammed.

It stopped perhaps fifty minutes later. The cover was pulled back and they were rushed into a side entrance of an anonymous-looking factory building. Steps led down to a basement, and they took a succession of passageways into a windowless room.

The inside of the door was padded to keep in sound. The walls were whitewashed. There was a bare hanging bulb and two oil-lamps, unlit. The room was dominated by a printing press so old that Stephen suspected Caxton could actually have used it. There was also a motley collection of chairs and a camp bed.

Dumitru joined them there an hour later. He was no longer in uniform. Kenyon had collapsed into one chair. His eyes were closed and he was breathing heavily but evenly. Stephen was sitting next to him, his hand rested gently on his father's shoulder.

'Is he all right?' asked Dumitru.

'Just winded, he says.'

Dumitru talked quickly, anxious to be away. Outside, he said, unrest was growing. There had been clashes in several parts of the city. Stephen and Kenyon were to stay until they were told they could leave. Later, someone would bring food and water.

'What is this place?' asked Stephen, though it was obvious.

'An underground printing press.'

'What if someone needs to use it?' asked Stephen.

Dumitru shrugged. 'They won't. There has been no paper for weeks.'

They sat silent with each other. Later that day, much later, another man brought a parcel of food and drink. They should eat sparingly, he warned. He did not know when he could return. The troops were shooting on the crowds. People were burning cars and fighting back. Who knew what would happen?

When he left, their silence continued. They were both too drained emotionally to talk. At last they slept.

When Stephen woke the darkness was total. He had made an uncomfortable bed from chairs. He heard a scuffling, like a rat, and struck a match. His father was sitting on the end of the camp bed. He was bent forward, his head in his hands.

Stephen lit a lamp. They would have to be careful; there was little oil. The electricity – or the bulb – had failed soon after they arrived. He hugged his jacket round him against the freezing cold.

'Are you OK?' he asked.

'I never thought I'd see you again,' said Kenyon. His voice was so low that Stephen had to strain to understand it.

'Nor me you.'

'How did you find me? If you hadn't, I guess I'd be a piece of cold meat now. One of the corpses piling up on the street.'

Stephen hesitated, not knowing whether to answer. It could be partly the light, but his father looked ninety years old.

'Aren't you going to tell me?' The voice had found some strength; its tone was more insistent.

'I found the hut by the lake.' Stephen paused. 'You left just before some friends arrived.' He told the rest, trying to keep it emotionless like a piece of testimony in court. It still sounded bad.

His father did not speak for a while. Then, he asked, 'Will he be all right? We didn't want him to come, thought it would be too dangerous – he'd got a family.'

He looked straight at Stephen. The lamp threw shadows across his face.

Stephen said, 'I don't know. I hope so. Benson said it was a good hospital.' Then he asked, 'Why did you come? Why didn't you make a break for it as you planned? Was it me?' A million-dollar question!

Kenyon appeared not to hear. 'I've fucked up a few things in my life,' he said. His tone was sad, matter-of-fact, not maudlin.

'We all have.'

Kenyon continued, again as though he had not heard.

'You,' he said. 'You're one – I'd have liked to have known you, watched you grow up. By the time I realised that, it was too late. Some things, you can't go back on. Saddest thing you learn as you get older – you can't go back. Over means over.'

Stephen began to speak, but Kenyon was already continuing. 'I've admired you – I told you that, didn't I? You've got ideals. I never had them, not real ones.'

A long silence followed. This time Stephen made no attempt to disturb it. He suspected his father had something else he wanted to say.

He was right. At last Kenyon spoke again. This time he acknowledged Stephen's question.

'Why did I come?' he repeated. His voice had dropped even more, so low that Stephen had to lean forward. 'I saw a chance to do something positive for once, not just go with the tide. That's why. That's all.'

Without thinking, Stephen reached out, found his father's hand.

'You belittle yourself,' he said. 'You did a fucking courageous thing. Braver than anything I've ever done. My ideals are the kind that don't cost anything.'

They fell silent. Both men embarrassed, unaccustomed to giving or receiving such intimate admissions.

Stephen spoke first, needing to lighten the moment.

'Well,' he said, 'you know me now. *And* I'm only forty. Not old to have a father.'

'Good headline for your paper,' said Kenyon. 'Sixty-Three-Year-Old Man Has Forty-Year-Old Son – Sensation.'

They began to laugh, and the laughter swept away any remaining barrier.

Kenyon placed his other hand on top of Stephen's.

A few seconds' silence – and then the dam burst.

They both began to speak at the same time. And it all came out. No real order.

Often not important, just recollections of everyday things:

High school in St. Louis after an English school: 'You can't imagine how exciting and frightening. I asked someone, "What are the rules," and he said, "What rules. . . ?" '

Going home to England: 'The first time, I just couldn't believe . . .'

'Me too. It was like that after Germany. Maybe I shouldn't tell you this, but hell . . .'

Sometimes catching up:

'You saw the Count? He's still alive? Wow!'

'Pamela. Tell me about her. She's still a looker, you say. Is she married?'

Occasionally serious:

'I can't tell you. Truly, I just can't . . . what I felt, what she meant . . . Sometimes it comes back, fleeting, like the feeling you get from a chance whiff of perfume. You know?'

Straight questions:

'So why journalism? Katharine encourage you? Her husband? Never met him – a nice guy?'

'You drink a lot? I understand all journalists drink a lot? No! You telling the truth? Good. Look what it did to me.'

And, on the second day, a deeper layer:

'So the phone went, and this voice said, "Stephen Kenyon? I think maybe you'd best come down here," and I said, "What is it?" and the voice said, "Look, I think it'd be better if you took a cab" . . . and I said, "Look, what the hell is it?" because I couldn't think and they hadn't given a name or anything, and the voice said, "It's Ms Tarlach O'Brien." And I said – I must have been mad but I didn't see; I'd just left her – and I said, "What about her?" and the caller got resigned and must have thought she'd never get me down there unless she said something, so she went on, "I'm sorry, Mr Kenyon, I've got to tell you she's dead." Those exact words. Just like that.'

'I lie awake a lot and sometimes I think, I should have stayed. I could have licked the drink. Got out, found something new. I was still in my thirties, goddammit. But,' voice falling, 'it wasn't like that. It was like . . . sliding down a long dark chute, not knowing what's ahead, but not able to turn around and go back . . .' A shrug. 'That make sense?' A self-conscious laugh. 'To me, neither. What the hell! Hindsight. It's all easy with fuckin' hindsight.'

For two days and two nights they talked like this, interrupting conversation only to eat and to sleep fitfully and for a single visit from Dumitru. He told them that the Army were refusing to obey the president and were engaged in heavy fighting with the Securitate.

At times, the feeling that he should be outside, witnessing, reporting, disturbed Stephen. But it was not as strong as the need to talk and to listen – to catch up on a missing quarter century, to capture in a few hours a relationship neither had ever really known.

'You've changed me,' Stephen admitted.

'We've changed each other.'

They were in a period of silence, moments of shared thoughts not words, when, late on Saturday, 23 December, Dumitru returned.

His elation burst through the room. Nicolae and Elena Ceauşescu were captured; the Army claimed to be in control of most of the country.

'We can leave?' Stephen asked.

'Maybe. That was the good news. Now the not so good.'

There were two 'not so good' pieces of information. The first was that there was still fierce street fighting in Bucharest itself. The second concerned them specifically.

'There have been people making enquiries about you both – even in the midst of this,' Dumitru said. 'I think you are right – you should leave. It is best we get you out of the country as soon as we can. Much interest is not good.'

He left soon afterwards and they expected him back any hour. It was two days later, though, before he returned. They had not eaten for twenty-four hours, and they grabbed the chicken legs he brought.

They were still eating, sucking on the bones, as he led them out into the light.

'Do you know what day it is?' he asked.

Stephen and Kenyon stood blinking in the unaccustomed brightness. They had their arms around each other's shoulders.

In the distance, gunfire sounded. A few yards away stood an armoured car; its aerials were festooned with tinsel.

'Happy Christmas,' Dumitru said.

The revolution was over.

Two days later, on Wednesday, 27 December, they flew out in a transport plane that was returning to Budapest after delivering relief supplies.

Both carried forged Canadian passports – among the documents found in plenty at Securitate headquarters – which they used in Budapest. Stephen still had his own passport; Kenyon's Irish passport, torn and bloodstained, had been left behind with Dumitru with one final request for help. That the passport be 'found' in a shelled-out building, as though the occupant had died there. In due course, word would get back to Miller and everyone else that Kenyon was dead.

Silence had returned to them both.

Stephen had bought tickets at Budapest airport with his credit card, and they sat waiting for their flights.

Kenyon's, to Zurich, was due to leave first. He had papers and funds there, he said.

'Where will you go then?'

This was one area they had not discussed, not once in the thousands and thousands of words.

'Brazil's a nice place, I'm told.'

'You can't keep running,' said Stephen, but he did not believe that.

In any event, reason told him that his father could not return with him to England. Even though, hopefully, enquiries would convince any searchers that Kenyon had finally died in Bucharest, it clearly was not safe for him to fly to London. Nevertheless, Stephen could not completely stifle an irrational hope . . .

Nothing was said, and Stephen choked back his thoughts. They had talked all they could. There were no more words left. Now, all was feeling.

After the Zurich flight was called and after they had held each other in a long, close embrace and long after he had watched

Kenyon walk out of sight on his way to the aircraft, Stephen waited.

Just in case.

But Kenyon did not turn back.

It was cold and clear in London. At the airport, Stephen made straight for a telephone. He felt incomplete. Something had been given and taken away. Now that it was over, now that he was safe, he felt lost, empty. Only Jessica could help, but there was no reply from the number in the country. Nor from her parents' London apartment. Maybe that too was over. Maybe that too had been no more than an emotion-filled interlude. How long had it all lasted? It was an effort to think back. Five months – *less* than five months – since the first hint that his father might still be alive. Even less than that since Jessica had turned up at his flat. He closed his eyes, and he could see her legs disappearing up the steps outside of his window – the pelmet skirt, the Doc Martens boots – and he could taste again that first guilty, wanting feeling. And then, another sight, unbidden – his father walking slowly out of view, not turning.

He shook himself back into the present.

He tried Jessica's numbers once more before taking a cab. As it pulled out of the airport, he concluded wearily that Jessica's family probably spent this time of year abroad. Had she gone with them? Reluctantly? Resignedly? Willingly?

At the door of his flat he fumbled for his keys.

Paying off the cab, he had transferred them from his trousers to his overcoat pocket. Now, in his tiredness, he made them snag the lining. He tugged impatiently, not caring whether he tore the pocket, and they came free. Something fell to the floor. His change from the cab? He stooped to look.

The door opened from inside.

'You're back,' Jessica said, as though it was the most natural thing in the world for her to be there saying it.

He hauled himself up, the object he had dropped in his palm. He looked at her, then at it, too overwhelmed by emotions to move or to speak. He wanted to embrace her, but the piece of rough dull metal held him.

A spent bullet. *The* spent bullet. Cut out of his father's head after missing his brain by a quarter of an inch. The talisman he carried everywhere. The one he had once left in a hotel in Milan and had made an eight-hundred-mile round trip to retrieve, even though it meant him losing a deal. His father must have slid it into his overcoat pocket at Budapest airport, knowing that, for now, it was not safe for them to be together. What had he said? 'It goes wherever I do. Wherever it is, I am.'

He realised Jessica's voice had risen in alarm.

'What is it?' she asked, puzzled, worried.

He tucked the bullet back into his pocket. He realised he was smiling. The message was obvious to him: his father was saying, I can't come now, but the bullet is my vow to return.

The explanation could wait. For now, he said, 'A promise. Just a promise. I'll tell you later.'

He reached out for her then, and he saw she was crying.

'Are you sure?' he said, new thoughts filling his mind. 'You know I'm too old for you.'

'Not any more,' she said. 'That was a long, long time ago.'

And she took his hand and they went inside.